ECHOES IN THE SQUARE

The Marchants lived in the Big House in Linden Square, a strong family held together by the ties of convention, custom, and wealth. If the marriage between William and Agnes Marchant was an unhappy one, they managed to conceal it from the society world in which they lived. Their twins, Duncan and Cecily, were handsome and doing everything that was expected of them, and if James, their youngest, was slightly unconventional, they managed not to let it inconvenience the rest of the family.

The Rowlands lived in the mews flat over the garage. Jos, a simple man, drove the Marchants' family car and tried not to notice the unhappiness and discontent of his wife, who was emotionally tied to the Marchants. The light of Jos's life was Janey, his daughter. Everything that was good in Jos's life centred on Janey. She was the best of them all in Linden Square.

D1323057

ECHOES IN THE SQUARE

Sally Stewart

CORGI BOOKS

TRANSWORLD PUBLISHERS
61-63 Uxbridge Road, London W5 5SA
a division of The Random House Group Ltd
www.rbooks.co.uk

**ECHOES IN THE SQUARE
A CORGI BOOK : 9780552134675**

First publication in Great Britain
Corgi edition published 1989

Copyright © Sally Stewart 1989

Sally Stewart has asserted her right under the Copyright,
Designs and Patents Act 1988 to be identified as the author
of this work.

This book is a work of fiction and, except in the case of
historical fact, any resemblance to actual persons, living or dead,
is purely coincidental.

A CIP catalogue record for this book
is available from the British Library.

This book is sold subject to the condition that it shall not,
by way of trade or otherwise, be lent, resold, hired out,
or otherwise circulated without the publisher's prior
consent in any form of binding or cover other than that
in which it is published and without a similar condition,
including this condition, being imposed on the
subsequent purchaser.

Addresses for Random House Group Ltd companies outside
the UK can be found at: www.randomhouse.co.uk
The Random House Group Ltd Reg. No. 954009

The Random House Group Limited supports The Forest Stewardship
Council (FSC), the leading international forest certification organisation.
All our titles that are printed on Greenpeace approved FSC certified paper
carry the FSC logo. Our paper procurement policy can be found at:
www.rbooks.co.uk/environment.

Typeset in 10/11½pt Cheltenham by
Colset Private Limited, Singapore.
Printed in the UK by CPI Cox & Wyman, Reading, RG1 8EX.

2 4 6 8 10 9 7 5 3

Chapter 1

By midway through the afternoon of a cool June day it was becoming clear to Jane that she hadn't set out very well equipped for life on her own. There was the matter of a complete lack of money for one thing, which would have troubled her less if she'd thought to provide herself with some iron rations. Tragedy, the first real one of her life, apparently wasn't a bar to getting hungry. There'd been no conscious choice about where to go – in times of trouble her refuge had always been the same spreading elm tree beside the Broad Walk in Kensington Gardens. Big and nicely climbable, it safely hefted her above the eye-level glance of passing park-keepers, but she could see that it was less than ideal for a long-term stay. One of the keepers did come to stand almost directly beneath her branch, still not seeing her tucked into its crutch against the trunk of the tree. She watched him slowly wander about beneath her, prodding his nailed stick into bits of litter lying on the ground. If she'd had a penny to spare she could have dropped it in the brim of his buckled hat. Then he moved away and she wished she'd spoken to him . . . it would have been a bit of company, someone to talk to. As well as hungry, she was beginning to feel very much alone.

That could be admitted to, but there was something she wasn't prepared to face . . . the moment when the keepers closed the gates for the night, shutting her inside. The daytime spaces of the Gardens were known to her, but she wasn't sure that she'd be able to bear them in the dark. The night-time still held shameful terrors for Janey Rowland aged eleven and a bit.

No question now that she badly wanted to go home, but it would have taken more courage than staying where she was. She couldn't go at all unless Jos came looking for her. She needed him to smile at her and take her hand as he always did when they went out together, before she could be certain that the ground was firm again beneath her feet. Come soon, Jos . . . come smiling, please. She knew *he'd* have forgiven her for the disgrace she was in, but Mam was a different matter. Jane had a vivid picture of her mother's face in her mind's eye – deathly white against the darkness of her hair. Likely as not she'd have told Jos that a daughter who'd shamed her in front of the Marchant family wasn't to be searched for.

Hard to believe, now, that this dreadful day had started normally. If disaster was always going to come so suddenly, life looked like being a dangerous business. A Saturday and no school to go to had meant time to help Jos replant his precious window-boxes before she was needed to go to the Marchants' house – No. 2 Linden Square, just round the corner from the mews. Mam had been the children's nurse a long time ago when the Marchant twins were small; now she was called Cook-General there. Jane usually did no more than help her mother in the kitchen, but today she'd been sent upstairs with a cream-jug left off the coffee tray in the drawing-room. Mam's instructions had been clear: knock on the door, then walk in; but before she was halfway across the hall Cecily Marchant's voice had come floating towards her. It was a clear, imperious sort of voice that would thank you to listen carefully to what it had to say. Jane listened, because suddenly her own name was mentioned.

'It's tiresome of Charlotte, and entirely typical. She *would* have to get the measles now. Having Jane would be better than an odd bridesmaid walking by herself when all the others are in pairs, I suppose, but she'll look ridiculous. A funny little shrimp swathed in pink tulle, with a wreath of rosebuds on her errand-boy's haircut. It's enough to reduce the rest of them to giggles before they're halfway up the aisle.'

Ridiculous? It was cruel, but Jane knew that it was true. She couldn't walk into the drawing-room after all. When she reappeared in the kitchen with the cream jug still in her hand Ano Rowland opened her mouth to order her upstairs again, changed her mind and took the jug herself without a word. She didn't usually permit her daughter any whims, but just occasionally Jane dug her toes into a position from which no amount of punishment could shift her. It looked like being one of those days, and meanwhile the Marchant coffee was cooling, creamless, upstairs. As soon as her mother disappeared Jane walked over to the mirror hanging on the back of the kitchen door . . . dark hair cropped so short that it had an undeniable tendency to stand on end, and a face in which none of the features seemed to fit. Ridiculous was the word for it. She accepted the fact, but hated Cecily. Then Ano came back and said briefly that they were both to go upstairs, being asked for in Mrs Marchant's bedroom.

It was a room in the house that Jane had never before entered and for a moment curiosity overcame all the other emotions she struggled with. It was the largest bedroom she'd ever seen, a softly scented place of silken hangings and shaded lamps. Lovely, she thought, but surely it was marred by having far too many mirrors? No less than three of them were clustered on the dressing-table, and she couldn't get away from herself whichever way she looked. Mrs Marchant smiled kindly as usual, but Ano instructed her to remove her pinafore and cotton dress. Jane would have disliked that even without the knowledge that Cecily was staring at her – beautiful unridiculous Cecily, whose

7

cool blue eyes assessed without much hope the possibilities of a makeshift bridesmaid. Then a cloud of rose-coloured tulle was thrown over Jane's head and allowed to settle around her. She was entranced by the sight of it. It even smelled different from the clothes she normally wore, and must look beautiful. But something was wrong, and the women who stared at her were beginning to smile. She couldn't move a step for the pink drift all round her feet, and the bodice began to slide off her narrow shoulders.

'It will need taking in . . . just a trifle?' Mrs Marchant's suggestion toppled Cecily into a helpless gust of laughter. Even Ano sat on the dressing-table stool smiling at the joke. Jane looked at their staring laughing faces, hated them, hated the pink dress even more. It wasn't hers; let measly Charlotte take it back again. She was having nothing to do with it. She dragged it off, kicking her feet free of the trailing mass of material.

'I won't wear it,' she shouted suddenly, scarlet with rage. 'I won't . . . I won't!'

A hot mist of tears blurred her eyes, but she could still see the scandalized expression on her mother's face.

'Of course you'll wear it if you're told to . . . Jane . . . come back here at *once!*'

Ano Rowland was accustomed to being obeyed by her family, but for once the habit of obedience was lost in the sheer need to escape any more humiliation. Jane fled down the stairs and out into the street, blind to the fact that she'd forgotten to put her own dress on again. Ano caught up with her on the doorstep of the cottage. She was pushed inside, and then her mother's wrath poured over her in a scalding waterfall of words.

'Look at you . . . running through the street in your petticoat like some little slut. Everyone in the mews staring at you, I don't doubt. You'll put your dress on and go back this minute to say you're sorry to Mrs Marchant.'

'No, I can't . . . please, Mam . . .' The thought of Mrs

8

Marchant was bad enough, Cecily even worse; but to run the gamut of a row of watching eyes in the mews simply couldn't be done.

'You'll do as you're told – now!' The dress was rammed over her head, and Ano's hands bit into her shoulders, shaking her to and fro.

'Let her alone, Ano ... don't ever lay hands on her again.' Jos had come up the stairs from the garage below; stood in the doorway watching them. He was a quiet and gentle man, only rarely moved to anger by other people's cruelty to each other. Jane had never known him even speak roughly to his wife, much less menace her as he seemed to be doing now.

Ano's hands fell away from her daughter as if she'd been stung. 'Why shouldn't I lay hands on her, pray? She's just made a complete fool of me in front of the Marchants.'

'I don't care what she's done ... she's not to be hurt.'

'You don't care! Of course not, Jos Rowland. When did you ever care about anything except a nice quiet life? Driving someone else's car for the rest of your days ... that's about the limit of your ambition.'

'What I choose to do with my life is my affair.'

'It's mine too, unfortunately,' she spat at him. 'I'm your wife, remember?'

The bitter fight went on, but looking from white face to flushed one, Jane knew that she was no longer what her parents were quarrelling about. Her mother's fury of five minutes ago was forgotten in the need to vent a lifetime's frustration, and Jos was fighting a battle of his own. If Jane could have prevented the world falling apart by offering to wear a dress ten sizes too large, she would have done so. But there seemed no stopping now the terrible thing she'd started. She couldn't breathe for the electricity in the air ... couldn't listen another minute to the sound of her parents hating each other.

All that had happened she didn't know how long ago,

but when she peered out through the leaves of the tree she could see the gardens were emptying. Uniformed nannies had wheeled their prams towards home and the shouts of older children there on their own gradually dwindled and died. Their dogs went with them, and only the sense of her own loneliness grew and grew. She told herself that she wasn't frightened, but she *was* lonely, no question. Perhaps if she shut her eyes and said her prayers . . .?

'Janey . . . you thinking of staying up there?'

The quiet voice didn't belong to Jos, but if God had seen fit to send her James Marchant instead, she was beyond wanting to quarrel with Him. By now almost anyone would have done, but James would do better than most. When she opened her eyes he was standing within the leafy shadow of her tree, a tall thin boy whose face looked older for the moment than his gangling body. He was sixteen to her eleven, four years younger than the Marchant twins. Duncan and Cecily had grown up ignoring him, and it had made a bond between him and the chauffeur's daughter. He knew about the friends she wasn't allowed to make in the mews. She was aware that the anxiety she sometimes felt about the grown-ups who controlled their lives was shared by him. Nothing was for certain what it seemed . . . like the beautiful shining floor of ice that had once given way beneath her feet. She could still remember the shock of icy water, and her brother Brian dragging her out. He'd stood her in front of a night watchman's brazier afterwards so that Mam shouldn't know her clothes had got wet.

She stared down at James from her perch above his head, thankful to see him but afraid to depend too much on the idea of having been looked for. It would be no surprise if he were sick of Duncan and Cecily and simply looking for a tree-house of his own.

'Have you left home too?' she enquired doubtfully. Her

tear-streaked face swam greenly among the leaves. Dark tragic eyes defied him to laugh at her, or even smile.

'Not today, at least,' James said after a moment in which he seemed to consider the matter. 'I only came because your father was getting anxious. He called at the house to see if you were still there. He said something about going out to look for you, but I explained that I thought I knew where you'd be.'

Only James, of all the Marchants, gave her the feeling that the Rowlands existed in their own right. Mrs Marchant smiled kindly, it was true, but always across some invisible gulf, and the rest of the family didn't see them at all. Old Lady Carterton, the Marchant children's grandmother who lived much too near for comfort, was the worst of all. She never called Jos anything but 'Rowland', and tapped her umbrella on the ground when she wanted him to do something. Brian swore she was a witch. How else could she know when he made faces at her behind her back? They'd amused themselves drawing pictures of her sitting on a broomstick made out of her long-handled umbrella until Ano had caught them at it and put a stop to the game.

Jane dragged her mind away from the memory to concentrate on the grievous matter in hand. 'I can't go home never . . . ever.'

The careful correction remembered even in the midst of so much woe was a tribute to Ano's insistence that her daughter should speak properly, but it made James angry. He didn't much like Joseph Rowland's wife for reasons that he couldn't quite pin down; but he was certain that he disapproved of the way she discounted her daughter. Only Brian mattered in her scheme of things.

'Never's a long time,' he suggested gently. 'Is it really as bad as all that? I gather there was a bit of a fuss this afternoon, but I'd forget about it if I were you. Cecily's got far too many bridesmaids already.'

Impossible to say, even to James, why she'd really run

11

away. 'I was supposed to wear someone else's dress,' she explained with dignity instead. 'The other children in the street laugh at me as it is because they know I'm always got up in Cecily's cast-offs. Mam saves them up for me until they fit, but it takes so long that no one's been wearing things like that for years by the time I come to them.'

James saw the humiliation of it but finally allowed himself to smile.

'You look a proper caution, Janey. Your face is striped like a kitten's, what with dirt and tears. Let's go home now. You need cleaning up, and I'm getting hungry.'

She was hungry herself. There'd been more than enough time to realize that life in a tree in Kensington Gardens had very little future in it. Her feet dangled in space while she found the branch below the one she'd been sitting on, and from there she could jump the rest of the way to the ground. She went with him across the deserted grass, but James had the feeling that whatever troubled her could suddenly send her flying away from him. He took the precaution after a moment or two of hanging on to her hand.

'Did Jos . . . did he seem very cross when you saw him?' she asked out of a long silence.

He was used to her habit of calling her father Jos and now saw nothing odd in it. More often than not, in fact, she seemed to be taking care of *him*, as if some element of danger in their lives drew out of her an instinctive wish to protect the one who was most vulnerable.

'Jos wasn't cross,' James decided slowly. 'Worried, though.' Whatever had happened that afternoon had been enough to shake Joseph Rowland out of his usual serenity. James thought he'd have been more likely to laugh at Jane's refusal to wear the bridesmaid's dress. If he'd been made angry, there'd been some other reason, and his daughter had taken flight because of it. She'd have been astonished by the amount James understood about the

12

Rowland family, wouldn't have believed him if he'd said he found it more interesting than his own. He knew about the games she wasn't allowed to share in the mews because Ano thought her children were a cut above the others in the street. The restriction left her not only lonely but uncertain as to where she belonged – not in Linden Mews, apparently, but certainly not in Linden Square. Even that wouldn't have mattered so much, but for the knowledge that she didn't count in Ano Rowland's eyes. Love and fierce ambition could only be spared for Brian. James didn't like him either, but he couldn't help feeling sorry for a boy two years older than himself who was going to have to 'make something of himself' whether he liked it or not. It was his mother's phrase, used when she wanted them to understand that Jos's supine acceptance of the way things were was by no means good enough for her. Her son was going to be different. He'd inherited her dark Welsh looks and her intelligence, and his success was going to make up for everything life had denied *her*.

James glanced down at Jane and saw her lost in some unhappy reflection of her own. It was time to give her a bit of warning, maybe. 'Don't be surprised if Jos and Ano *are* cross when you get back. They'll have been anxious, you see, and people are inclined to get tetchy when there's no longer any need to feel worried. You'd think it'd be the opposite, but that's not how it works.'

'They were . . . tetchy . . . before,' Jane said sadly. 'Do . . . do your parents ever row?'

'Can't remember it happening, but it's not the end of the world if they do. Grown-ups can't help getting a bit het up at times.'

Her upturned glance looked unconvinced by this attempt at comfort, but she made no comment on it. They left the Gardens and crossed the Bayswater Road in silence. At the corner of Linden Square she expected him to say goodbye, but he walked with her past the Marchants' large double-fronted house and round the corner into the mews that ran along the bottom of its garden. James was a friend, she thought gratefully. Without him she'd probably have been tempted to turn tail and run away again. Jos might be himself again, but there was no telling what Mam's attitude might be. They were so often in doubt about this, she and Jos, that they'd agreed it must have to do with Ano's being Welsh . . . something she couldn't help, like freckles or feeling sick on trams.

Mrs Marsden, French despite her name and Mam's only crony in the mews, waved as she and James walked by; then a curtain twitched in Mrs Cooper's sitting-room. Mam was right – she *was* the talk of the street and the shame of the Rowland family. She swallowed a sob and took the flight of stairs up to the flat above the garage at a run; anything to get it over with. The door opened before she got to the top; Jos must have been watching for her.

'Janey, love . . .' It was all he managed to say, but his arms hugging her said more, and nothing else mattered much if Jos had forgiven her.

'I'm obliged to you, James,' she heard him say.

'Pleasure, Joseph.' Her friend had turned and run down the stairs before she could say goodbye. Nemesis, in the shape of Mam, awaited her in the hall. Ano looked pale and taut still, but then she always did and her dark eyes always seemed to burn like that in the whiteness of her face. She stared at Jane's grimy face and hands, then pointed in the direction of the bathroom at the end of the passage.

'Go and wash . . . you're not sitting down to your tea like that.' No welcome home, but at least the events of the afternoon weren't going to be referred to.

Clean again and slightly comforted by Jos's little smile across the table, she doggedly swallowed the bread and butter that now stuck in her throat. Anchovy paste, one of her favourites normally, would remind her from now on of today. Ano's face relaxed halfway through the uncomfortable meal because the door burst open and Brian walked in. He was in Saturday-afternoon rig – flannels and a blazer that had belonged to Duncan Marchant. Ano thought he looked better in it than any Marchant, and when he smiled at her she couldn't help smiling back.

'Up the Welsh! They made mincemeat of Middlesex . . . skittled them out for less than a hundred runs,' he said cheerfully.

'Good match was it, boy?' Jos enquired.

'He's just told you . . . Glamorgan won,' Ano said irritably.

Brian looked from her to his father's face, to Janey helping herself to another slice of bread and butter with a hand that trembled slightly. He accepted the helping of pork pie his mother passed him and remembered that he had news for her that might lessen the thunder and lightning in the atmosphere.

'Saw Mrs Marsden on my way in, Mam . . . she said to tell you the dress is ready for a . . . a something or other . . . a fitting, would it be?'

'It would, but Louise Marsden's wasting her time, by the look of things. I doubt if we'll be going to the wedding,' Ano said grimly.

Jane's face across the table implored him to leave the subject of Cecily's wedding alone. Brian gave her an encouraging wink and tried again. 'Got some good news. Mr Sykes gave me a ten-bob rise this morning . . . said I'm the best apprentice he's had at the garage.'

'Of course you are. No credit to him for working that out. Still, I suppose it's something that he realises it.' Her voice was sharp, but she put an extra spoonful of sugar in her son's tea. He had a long way to go still, but she could be sure that he was going upwards; it made up for a husband like Jos and a daughter whose eyes sometimes reproached her for despising him.

15

Ano's only Sunday duty at the Marchant house was to prepare lunch for the family. Mrs Bloggs who did the 'rough' was absent at weekends, and Jane usually went with her mother to make herself useful about the kitchen. She was getting out cloths and silver polish when Ano nodded in the direction of the drawing-room, a flight of stairs up from the kitchen.

'You know what you've got to do first . . . go and do it, without any argument this time.'

She didn't intend to be defied by her daughter again, but in any case Jane recognized where right lay. Rudeness had always to be apologized for, and even Jos had suggested mildly the evening before that rude was what she'd been. She climbed the stairs bravely enough, but resolution wavered in the lonely spaces of the hall. She wasn't in the habit of walking uninvited into Mrs Marchant's drawing-room, and it was likely that the rest of the family might be there . . . even Cecily's grand fiancé, the Honourable Charles Willoughby. They'd stare at her, smile probably while she stumbled through the apology she'd rehearsed but now forgotten. She was still examining the dreadful idea when Duncan Marchant came running down the stairs.

'Hello, young Jane . . . what's up?'

Misery was briefly swamped in the kindness of his smile. He was godlike in her eyes, no matter what Brian said about him; a blond and beautiful inhabitant of another world, hung about with the glamour of being 'up' at Oxford. His jacket was flung like a cloak about his shoulders . . . other people wore them without that dashing air. Ano observed darkly from time to time that he wouldn't amount to much, but Jane was of the opinion that for once her mother was wrong. A young man as handsome and bright as Duncan Marchant couldn't help but achieve whatever he set his heart upon. She was about to confide her present dreadful errand to him, but it was too late. He was already at the front door, en route for Hurlingham and a Sunday morning game of tennis with friends. She was grateful for the smile, hadn't really expected more. He'd have been kind if he'd had time.

She continued to waver there, wondering whether it would be possible to get into the drawing-room if she took it at a run. The matter hadn't been decided when James came ambling down the stairs.

'Hi, Janey . . . everything all right at home?'

His dark face grinned at her, but she knew that the question wasn't as casual as it sounded. 'I didn't say thank you for coming to find me,' she remembered.

'All part of the service! I thought you might like a little memento, by the way.' He'd hoped it would take the sting out of that desperate hour or two hiding in a tree. She stared at the sheet of paper torn out of his sketch-pad . . . the drawing had been done hastily in charcoal, but it was recognisably herself peering out from a nest of leaves, enormous eyes and ruffled hair making her look like an abandoned baby owl that wasn't sure it knew how to fly.

He watched her strained face break into a grin at the sight of it. 'Can I have it, please . . . to show Jos?'

He nodded, then thought to ask why she was standing in the hall. 'Ano send you up with a message for my mother? She's in the drawing-room, if so.'

'Not a message, exactly,' Jane admitted reluctantly. 'I'm to apologise for all the fuss yesterday . . . but perhaps Mrs Marchant won't want to be bothered.'

'Get it over with, Janey. It's like a visit to the dentist, worse the longer you think about it.'

She wasn't convinced, but he settled the matter by towing her by the hand across the hall.

Mrs Marchant was indeed in the drawing-room, sitting with her back to them at the grand piano that almost filled the window recess of the big room. Unaware that anyone had come into the room, she stared at the music propped up in front of her and then began to play. A silver thread of notes came trembling on the air. Jane smiled at James . . . pretty it sounded, and she hoped he would let his mother go on. Pretty? The thread grew stronger, darker, swelled into a tormented cascade of sound that throbbed with more sadness than she knew existed in the world. She stood rooted to the ground, apology forgotten, even unaware of the astonishing fact that it should be gentle, ghostly Mrs Marchant creating this avalanche of sound. She felt bereft when the storm subsided and slowly died into stillness again. James glanced from her wrapt face to the woman still seated at the piano; it was time to take both of them in hand.

'Mama, you've got a visitor,' he said firmly. 'Turn round, please, and pay the poor girl some attention.'

Agnes Marchant did as she was told, surprised to find that she'd had an audience but not put out as far as Jane could see.

'Take no notice of James,' she suggested in her soft voice that, unlike Cecily's, never insisted that it should be listened to. 'I don't know why it is, but all my children like to make me sound half-witted at times.'

She was a tall, slender woman, with delicately cut features and fair colouring that the twins had inherited. James took after his father in looks, which she often thought perverse of nature when it was Duncan and Cecily who constantly reminded her of William. James teased her, but with loving kindness; her daughter's blue eyes, on the other hand, said clearly that she was of no account . . . feeble, and irretrievably passée. Agnes accepted humbly that her only real talent was disregarded by everyone but James. Though not, perhaps, by little Janey Rowland who still stared at the piano as if she could wish it into bursting into galvanic life on its own.

'Did you like the prelude?' she asked gently. 'It was written by a Pole, a man called Frédéric Chopin. I'll play you some more if you like.'

'Dear Mama, another time?' James suggested, seeing that the interview had gone off the rails again. His mother was capable of sitting at the piano for the rest of the morning, and Jane had clearly forgotten what she'd come for. He gave her an encouraging pat on the shoulder and thoughtfully removed himself from the room so that the apology could finally get itself said.

'I was to . . . to say I'm sorry for all the fuss yesterday,' Jane launched out bravely. The woman in front of her merely looked bewildered; if there'd been a fuss, she couldn't even remember what it was about. 'The fuss about the bridesmaid's dress,' Jane explained with a touch of disappointment that Mrs Marchant hadn't found it important enough to recall without prompting.

'Oh, that!' Amusement glimmered in a shy smile. 'The dress *was* a trifle on the large side, don't you think?'

Jane thought of the yards of pink stuff flowing all round her on the carpet and grinned. 'A trifle,' she agreed, liking the word and the woman who had offered it. The grin grew wider, escaped in a chuckle that occasionally took charge and pitchforked her into a fit of helpless laughter. Agnes Marchant caught the infection and the pair of them abandoned themselves to the joyous business of laughing. They finally sobered up and wiped their eyes, and an air of constraint destroyed Jane's feeling of confidence. For a moment Mrs Marchant had been her friend, now she looked distant again. She'd seemed to be enjoying herself too, but you could never tell with grown-ups; the knife-edge between what was right one moment and wrong the next was one she was constantly falling off with Mam. Perhaps the fit of laughing was something else that now needed apologising for? But Agnes Marchant was merely following a surprising train of thought of her own. It hadn't occurred to her before to question Cecily's opinion. Ano Rowland's daughter *was* a plain shrimp of a child with an air of watchfulness about her. But twice this morning

Agnes had seen her released from the straitjacket of her mother's idea of how she should behave; music and laughter had briefly entranced her into beauty. It seemed a pity to let all that luminous joy be hidden again inside a child who'd already reverted to her usual tense watchfulness.

'Shall we forget all about the fuss?' she suggested gently.

Jane nodded, happy to agree and pleased to find this unexpectedly different lady in front of her so much more sensible than Mam ever seemed to give her credit for. She sent a last lingering glance at the piano, but knew that it was more than time to leave. Time enough to make a dozen apologies, her mother would say when she got back to the kitchen. Mrs Marchant's voice halted her on the way to the door.

'Jane, I'm quite often here by myself, playing. Come in and listen if you'd like to.'

In return for the suggestion she got not the radiant smile she'd been hoping for but a nod of the head that hinted at some understanding arrived at between them. The matter was great and solemn and Agnes was sufficiently aware of the fact even if she didn't perceive that her conventionally elegant drawing-room now gleamed and glimmered in Jane's mind as enticingly as Aladdin's cave.

'You took long enough,' Ano said in the kitchen.

'I had to wait . . . Mrs Marchant was playing the piano.'

Ano Rowland didn't doubt it. When did the poor creature upstairs ever do anything else? Jane was tempted to say nothing about Mrs Marchant's invitation, but what had James advised? 'Get it over with, Janey.'

'Mam, I can . . . can go again if I like . . . to listen, Mrs Marchant said.' She hated herself for pretending that it didn't matter . . . felt sly, and somehow traitorous towards her new friend upstairs; but there was always Mam's 'welshness' to contend with. Brian could twist her round his little finger, but Jane was sadly aware of not having the same knack.

20

Ano stared at her daughter, aware of suspense held painfully in check. Just for a moment the fact that she was Jos's girl as completely as Brian was her own son was a matter for sharp regret. The feeling didn't last very long, but it was what Jane had to thank for not being forbidden to go again to Mrs Marchant's drawing-room.

'You might as well do that, I suppose, as pine to go and play in the street with those hooligan children next door.'

It was permission of a kind. The key to Aladdin's cave was in her hand.

Chapter 2

Cecily's wedding took place a week later. It was the beginning of July 1938, and she wasn't at all surprised to see the day dawn with the opalescent London haze that promised heat to come. If asked beforehand she'd have been certain that fine weather would be forthcoming, since it was what she required. Over breakfast in Linden Mews Ano made a last attempt to get Brian to attend the wedding with the rest of them.

'Change your mind and come,' she suggested hopefully.

'Not me . . . I've got better ways of spending a fine Saturday afternoon than staring at a bunch of stuck-up women, and twerps in top hats and fancy suits.'

At eighteen, he was opinionated, determined to see slights everywhere, and stridently in favour of doing away with the ruling classes. The food Ano lavished on him still left him thin, and zest for the fascinating business of living crackled around him like an electric charge. He left Jos bemused, but Jane felt proud of a brother who told her confidently that he was going to change the world. She believed him. Cecily Marchant might sneer at a mere garage-hand whose mop of dark springy hair looked as if it was permanently in contact with engine grease, but people like her were the ones he was going to sweep away first. Jane thought Mam might have known that wild horses wouldn't drag him to a wedding that involved Cecily.

Jos put down his newspaper, wondering for the

umpteenth time how such a firebrand came to be his son. International Socialism was plain daft in Jos's view; things were as they were, and there were going to be people on top of the heap however the world was organized. 'Someone has to rule,' he remarked mildly. 'If you get rid of the present lot, happen you won't like any better what you get in their place.'

Brian sighed and closed his eyes. The sheer frustration of talking to the old, who couldn't or wouldn't understand. 'I keep telling you . . . *we're* going to take their place, people like us. People like me,' he amended with a glance at Jos's unenthusiastic face.

'And you're going to solve all our problems, I suppose, by chopping the heads off the nobs and singing the Red Flag. There's a bit more to ruling than that.'

Brian took a deep breath, always ready to try again, but even Ano was getting bored with an argument she'd heard many times before.

'You've both got more to do than sit there needling one another. Jos, there's the car to clean . . . hadn't you better get on with it?'

He was required to drive Cecily and William Marchant to the church. It should have been the Guards Chapel, with Charles Willoughby in the Grenadier Guards, but the date clashed with another ceremony there and Cecily had opted for St James's, Piccadilly, instead. She'd been surprised by her mother's suggestion that Ano and Jane should be invited to drive with her to the church.

'In *your* car, you mean?'

'Why not? They'll be without Joseph to take them.' Agnes had sounded sharp for once. 'Ano was your own nurse long before she came back here to work for us, and Joseph's been with your father for twenty years. I don't see anything odd about inviting them to be guests at your wedding. They're not onlookers, allowed to straggle along if they feel inclined.'

'Ma, I'm sorry!' Cecily had held up her hands in mock

23

surrender. 'Let them be guests by all means if you think they'll enjoy it . . . dear Brian as well if he isn't otherwise engaged, blowing up the House of Lords or some such trifling thing!'

It had made her mother smile with a slightly shame-faced air. She was aware of secretly hoping Brian wouldn't want to come. It was hard to feel comfortable with a young man who was clearly wondering how best to dispose of her when the new age dawned.

When it was time to leave Ano cast a critical eye over Jos, resplendent in a new pearl-grey uniform.

'Well, I can't *see* anything wrong, and the car's a master-piece,' she admitted finally. 'But if you're thinking of coming into the church for the service, you're not to sing out loud.'

Jos was a cheerful singer in church, but as nearly tone-deaf as made no odds. Ano took little interest in music, but even so her Welsh soul revolted at the noise he made.

She and Jane had only to walk round the corner of the mews to the Marchant house where Mrs Marchant's car awaited them. Jane was white-faced with excitement and the fear that she might suddenly feel sick. Her new patent-leather shoes were beautiful beyond belief but they squeaked with every step she took . . . was life always going to be like that . . . flawed?

Mam was excited too, she knew. Because Jos had said she was looking beautiful? She was, no question, and walked along the street like a queen, aware of twitching curtains as she went by. Apart from Louise Marsden, she kept away from the other women in the mews, despising them for their gossip over endless cups of tea. But she didn't mind them staring at her, especially today. Louise had been a seamstress in Paris before she married an English soldier at the end of the war. Nowadays she worked for a select dressmaker in Grosvenor Street, but she'd made Ano's wedding outfit in her own home. The lime-green dress and wide-brimmed matching hat made her the Ano she knew she ought to have been, not Mrs Rowland, Cook-General. It didn't surprise her that Agnes Marchant almost mistook her for a guest she didn't recognize, but the tribute she needed came from the startled expression in William Marchant's eyes. It acknowledged her elegance, but instead of the woman in front of him he was seeing again the white-skinned black-haired girl who'd taken charge of the nursery when the twins were born.

Memory held him paralysed, while the rest of them felt uncomfortable in a silence no one knew what to do with. Agnes stared at her own fussily expensive dress, wondering where it had gone wrong. James saw the stricken expression on her face and moved across to lay a friendly arm around her shoulders. 'Time you were leaving, Mum.'

She managed to smile at him, then looked at William. Her eyes wrenched him out of silence to take charge of them all again.

'It's *more* than time, my dear. We'll see you in church as soon as I can get Cecily and that flock of little pink lambs in there to the point of admitting that they're ready!' He tried to sound brisk when he spoke to Jos's wife. 'All well at your end, Ano?'

She smiled composedly at him. 'Jos will be here with the car in fifteen minutes' time.'

William opened the car door and shepherded his wife in. Then he put a hand briefly on Ano's bare arm to steady her as she got in. James saw the faint tinge of colour that rose in her normally pale face, and took his own seat beside the chauffeur, wishing Janey was a prattler; they badly needed someone to chatter as if the undercurrents dragging at them all didn't exist. She did save the situation in the end, enchanted by the discovery that she was to sit on a little chair that cunningly pulled out from the back of the partition behind the driver. Facing backwards, she could see the road being unrolled majestically behind them –

much better than having it gobbled up in front before she had time to notice anything. She explained this to Mrs Marchant, who kindly agreed it might be so now that she thought about it. She smiled at the sight of Jane enthroned on her seat like a very small duchess, and the tension in the car eased. Jane smiled back, liking Mrs Marchant. She'd thought something was wrong a moment ago, but perhaps it was only her own excitement.

In Piccadilly guests were already gathering outside the church, and passers-by were clustered round the wrought-iron gates that separated the pavement from the church-yard. Londoners never minded a free show put on for their Saturday afternoon entertainment, and the signs were unmistakable that a big fashionable wedding was in the offing. Jane felt pleased with herself for not being one of Cecily's pink lambs. She had no taste for being stared at, and in any case there was a great deal too much to be looked at on her own account. James, subjected to a wedding rehearsal in the church beforehand, had reported that there were worse ways of spending an afternoon than inside St James's.

'Look at it properly, Janey . . . it's one of Christopher Wren's most beautiful churches,' he'd told her.

She'd nodded, trying to look knowledgeable. It wouldn't have been hard to confess to James that she wasn't acquainted with Mr Wren, because he liked telling her things, but the pre-wedding bustle had left him short of time.

'No one else in the congregation will care, or look at any-thing except their neighbours' hats, but I expect you to do better than that, Janey. There's a pelican carved out of wood by a wizard called Grinling Gibbons . . . look for it just above the altar.'

'Funny place to find a pelican.'

'True, but that's where it is, and if the music isn't up to much you can listen to his flock of angels – they're playing trumpets on the organ case!'

She'd promised to do her best, glad to be sharing plea-
sures with him that he didn't offer his own brother and
sister. James didn't air opinions much, only facts, but she
suspected that he shared Brian's view of the toppered
twerps and twittering debutantes who made up Cecily's
friends.

Inside the church she was sidetracked by the sight of
the awe-inspiring toque that rested on the top of Lady
Carterton's head, then remembered what James had said
– 'no hats, Janey.' Her eyes went in search of the pelican.
Yes, there he was, looking so alive that he might have only
just perched there that moment. She'd have liked to offer
him the bird of paradise on her ladyship's hat as a tasty
mouthful. Then Jos slipped into the pew beside her, and
agitation in the porch behind them suggested that Cecily
and her retinue were about to launch themselves up the
aisle.

A few minutes later she floated past on her father's arm,
mysteriously unfamiliar, transformed by the occasion, the
gleaming white dress, and a mist of Brussels lace, into a
fairytale creature Jane no longer recognized. Wedding
magic had been at work on a girl she normally found cool
and unkind. Even Brian might have been impressed in
spite of himself, she thought. James needn't have worried
about the music. It hung in the high echoing spaces of the
church, airborne, floating down to her along the bars of
light that slanted through the tall windows. Happiness
washed over her, drowning even the memories produced
by the sight of pink bridesmaids' dresses. There wasn't an
ugly thing in sight, Jos's hand held on to hers, and for once
at least her stormy mother seemed at peace.

William Marchant's state of mind she didn't know about.
He was a man who did nothing slowly from choice. It was a
penance to walk at the agonisingly slow crawl the organist
confined them to, but it gave him something else to think
about than the sight of Ano Rowland in her green dress.

27

This was his daughter's wedding, for God's sake; not the moment to have his thoughts invaded by memories of another woman. A flash of scarlet was something else to concentrate on – Charles, waiting for them at the end of this interminable aisle. In full-dress regimentals he looked everybody's idea of a toy soldier, forever changing guard at Buckingham Palace 'when Christopher Robin went down with Alice'. They weren't going to be toy soldiers much longer. William felt certain that another war was coming . . . not the mindless slaughter his own generation had been lost in, but something just as destructive and bitter. The thought of it made him finally part company with the organist and lose his step.

'I'm the one who's supposed to be nervous,' Cecily whispered beside him.

'Sorry, darling . . . it's the pace of this funeral march . . . can't seem to get the hang of it.'

Agnes, standing in the front pew flanked by Duncan and James, saw them exchange smiles. They understood each other very well; better than *she* understood them. The procession came to a halt a little way ahead of her, Cecily beautiful and confident . . . not a bit like an earlier bride at a simple wartime ceremony. Beside her, unfamiliar in his morning dress but with one empty sleeve tucked into a pocket as usual, William looked very little older than the man she'd married. Twenty-one years ago he'd been still in uniform, just released from the hospital where she'd worked as a VAD and his damaged left hand had finally been amputated. He was tired and sickened by a trench war, thankful to be alive but frightened by the fact of being maimed. Jangled nerves and a mutilated body craved someone he might not have noticed in different circumstances . . . Agnes Carterton, pretty enough but nothing special, too diffident to push herself, but propelled by a forceful mother into agreeing to marry him. It was too late to realize they were as suited to be yoked together as a tiger and a lamb.

Even elementary VAD nursing had seen to it that she knew what were called the facts of life. She submitted to them dutifully, but with so little relish that William's love-making had diminished and finally died. The twins, born a year after their marriage, were a face-saving excuse; she was weak and tired and must be left to regain her health. It would have been easier to stay an invalid for the rest of her life but her forthright mother had finally reminded her that she was supposed to be William's wife. He'd regained all his old health and vigour and expected more of the woman he'd married than a pleasant hostess who played the piano better than most professional musicians. She accepted the warning and three years later James was conceived. But he was born with so much difficulty that William went back to sleeping alone.

Agnes had lived ever since with the knowledge that she was a failure. The failure was well-concealed, but in her view that made things worse, not better. The world took them for a model couple – more prosperous than most, living a life that other people envied. The tea and rubber-broking business in the City inherited from William's father went from strength to strength, because the frustrated vitality he needed to find an outlet for was poured into Marchant & Ferguson. Lady Carterton tried to convince herself that she'd been right to push her gentle daughter into marriage, and had never faced the fact that it might have been the wrong marriage. Agnes continued to love her husband and children and despaired of finding a way of telling them so. The feeling William poured into Marchant's *she* poured into music, and she was passionately grateful to him for seeming content with a woman whose only real and remarkable talent was for playing the piano. Not even their children had been permitted to guess that he couldn't tell Bach from Beethoven.

Cecily and Charles set off on a long continental honeymoon

and life in Linden Square without her settled down again after the wedding frenzy – settled down too much for William, who missed his daughter. They were two of a kind, he and Cecily, and Agnes thought the restlessness she detected in him was because he found the house too tame without her. She wasn't surprised when he suggested one morning an immediate trip abroad.

'You know I was planning to go to Ceylon in the autumn,' he said suddenly. 'Let's go now, all of us, while the boys are still on holiday. We'll make a real visit of it.'

She'd been with him to the tea plantations in the past, still vividly remembered the heat and dust and alien strangeness of it all. 'I'd rather you took Duncan and James and left me behind, please, William. I should only be a nuisance to you, wilting in the heat all the time.' It sounded feeble ... Cecily was right, she *was* feeble, but it was better to admit it than find herself a millstone round William's neck. He looked so unsurprised that she knew he'd expected her to refuse.

'Well, if I can't persuade you to come, James must stay here and take care of you. I'll take Duncan, because it's high time he began to get a grasp of things. Shall I have an hotel booked for you somewhere ... Scotland maybe?'

Agnes considered the idea, then shook her head. 'I think we'll stay here. James would prefer it, because he's happiest left to roam about London, sketching things. Anyway, it's rather nice and peaceful when everyone else has gone away. We'll potter happily on our own.'

She saw the faint ironical lift of William's eyebrow. She'd been less than tactful; but if he thought she was supposed to be happy in the company of her husband rather than pottering with her son, he didn't say so.

A week later he and Duncan daringly flew to Ceylon, instead of making the long sea voyage. Friends and acquaintances drifted away from London for the summer but she and James weren't the only people left behind in the dusty city. What seemed empty to Agnes Marchant looked much the same as always to people who had no choice about going away. Holidays were picnics on Hampstead Heath, or the excitement of a day-trip on a steamer down the Thames. Jane saw nothing wrong with either of these treats, but she had no wish to leave London while Mrs Marchant remained behind. That invitation still glimmered in her mind, and with the man Jos called the Guvnor safely out of the way she thought she might find the courage to creep into the drawing room.

Once the long summer holiday from school had started she went most days with Ano to Linden Square. Her appointed task one morning was in the kitchen as usual, but the sound of the piano being played began to seep down the back stairs. Mam was at the top of the house somewhere and it seemed safe to sit on the stairs for a bit and listen. One stair led to another, led her finally to the door of the drawing room. Mrs Marchant's back was towards her, an armchair was close by. She was still curled up in it half an hour later, entranced by a recital that had spanned, without her knowing it, the great sonorities of a Beethoven sonata and the rainbow harmonies of Claude Debussy.

When the sounds finally died away she wriggled out of the chair, but tumbled on to the floor with a small thud because her foot had gone to sleep. Mrs Marchant looked round to find her sprawled on the carpet.

'Jane dear . . . have you been there all the time? You were as quiet as a mouse. I'd have played something different . . . I don't suppose you liked everything I chose.'

'I did,' she said truthfully, 'but the last bit best. It sounded like raindrops with the sun sparkling on them.'

Agnes made a mental note to revise her next programme. 'Same time tomorrow?' she suggested with a smile.

'Yes, please.' The conversation was over and it was time

to go back to the kitchen. On the way downstairs she considered the idea that had just occurred to her. Mrs Marchant had *liked* her being there . . . perhaps she was lonely too, poor soul? It was a phrase borrowed from Edie Bloggs, who liked to regale Jane with the misfortunes of all her neighbours while she scrubbed the kitchen floor. The theory that Mrs Marchant might be lonely was offered to Jos later in the day but he brushed it aside.

'Daft idea, Janey. Leddies like Mrs Marchant don't get lonely. Stands to reason . . . how could they when they're always on the go? It's hairdressers and dressmakers, morning calls and afternoon tea . . . never a moment to themselves if you ask me.'

She had to accept that he knew about such things, being always on the go himself. At the moment he wasn't needed to drive the Guvnor to the City every morning, but his time was spent ferrying Mrs Marchant and Lady Carterton to all the appointments that seemed to fill their days.

'I think she's lonely inside,' she insisted, disappointed that for once he'd failed to understand something she couldn't explain but perceived to be true.

The following afternoon she was in the Marchant garden, dispatched there by Ano with a colander and a bagful of peas to shell. She disliked the job because more pods than not seemed to have a wriggling maggot inside and Mam always insisted that the good peas had to be salvaged before she abandoned them. James caught sight of her from his bedroom window, sketched her for the fun of putting her disgusted expression on paper, and finally wandered out into the garden himself.

'Hello, Janey. Like the poor old policeman, you look as if your lot was not a happy one!'

She grinned at him. He wasn't beautiful and dashing like Duncan, but it was easy to talk to him. 'It's all these fat sluggy things inside . . . I hate them.'

'Leave the squelchy-looking ones to me.'

32

Duncan, if he'd helped at all, would probably have left the squelchy-looking ones to *her*, she realized. She hovered over the heap looking for a trouble-free pod, unaware that James studied her. It had become second nature to him to look carefully enough at people to see them. He found himself hoping very much that Janey Rowland wouldn't grow up without his knowing what became of her. She was adult already, in a way; seemed older than Cecily, and aware like himself of the stresses around them. The relationship between the Marchants and Rowlands was uncomplicated on the surface. James thought that one day he might discover why it filled him with such a sense of unease.

'I tackled my father before he went away,' he said suddenly. 'It seemed time to break the news to him that I want to be an artist, not a tea and rubber broker.'

Jane knew all about the Firm in Mincing Lane, and about its importance in their lives. She thought she wouldn't have wanted to tackle the Guvnor about that, or anything else . . . he wasn't a gentle man, like Jos. 'What did he say?' she asked sympathetically. 'Was he cross?'

'Not cross . . . puzzled more than anything. We're supposed to come into the world wanting to join Marchant's! He said there hadn't been an artist in the family before – made it sound as if the idea was faintly disreputable!'

It was her turn to stare, realizing suddenly that he didn't seem to be a schoolboy any longer. He had Mr Marchant's black hair, not springy like Brian's, but clean-looking and always slightly untidy. He had his father's long straight nose as well, but the shy rare smile had been taken from Mrs Marchant. Jane knew about his dream of becoming an artist, and had been allowed to look at his drawings for years. He was clever, no question, but did he really not want to do what Duncan was doing . . . go riding about tea plantations on real elephants – not like the ones in the zoo? If the pictures in her geography book at school didn't lie there would be beautiful dark-skinned women in saris coloured like rainbows, with baskets of tea-pods on their backs. 'James, don't you want to see *everything* there is to see?' she asked wistfully.

He helped himself to a handful of shelled peas and nibbled them while he thought about the question. 'Of course I do, Janey, but I can't afford to waste time. There's too much to learn. Sitting in an office in Mincing Lane *would* be a waste of time.'

She didn't smile at the idea that, at sixteen, he must waste no time. Brian had much the same point of view and was constantly telling her so. But a Marchant hadn't so much catching-up to do. James stared at her puzzled face, aware that she was trying to understand what made him behave so differently from the rest of his family.

'I'll show you,' he said suddenly. 'We'll go to the National Gallery and you can start looking at some real paintings . . . then you'll know what I'm talking about.'

He was careful to ask Ano's permission for the outing, and Jane awaited him next morning in all the splendour of her new squeaky shoes and a cotton dress so starched that she could scarcely sit down in it in the bus. James asked for 2d tickets from the bus conductor with an aplomb she greatly admired. He even handed her on and off the bus as if she'd been a grown-up lady. Jos treated Mam like that, of course, but she was aware that Mam was lucky. They got off the bus at Trafalgar Square and she'd have been happy to stay there visiting each of the lions in turn. James said sternly that they'd come to look at paintings. If she wanted to see lions he'd take her to the zoo another day! Chastened, she followed him up the steps of the National Gallery.

Inside the most imposing building she'd ever visited she stared with passionate concentration at everything she was told to stare at. By the time they walked along the Mall to St James's Park to eat the sandwiches Ano had provided she emerged from the morning onslaught with a single picture glowing in her mind.

'What did you like best, Janey?'

She'd been afraid he'd ask, aware that she couldn't disentangle a name from the welter of information he'd poured over her. All she could do was describe the radiance of a small painting of the Virgin Mary and her Child . . . like a hundred others she'd seen except for the tenderness and simplicity of the two figures against a star-inlaid sky of heavenly blue.

'Duccio,' James said quietly. 'Good for you!'

She didn't know why and he didn't explain because he was already laying aside his sandwich to pull the ever-present sketch block out of his pocket. What she watched him draw was an old tramp stretched out on the grass nearby, shoes neatly placed beside him and a battered hat tilted over his face to keep the sun out of his eyes. She sat quiet while the sketch grew under James's hand, but when he put his pencil down she asked the question that bothered her.

'Why draw that old man? Why not beautiful things, like we saw this morning?'

'I suppose because he's part of our lives, Janey. Everyone's worth noticing.'

'You mean *he's* more worth noticing than some of Cecily's friends?'

'I think I do,' James agreed solemnly. 'I'm not sure he *isn't* even rather beautiful in his own way.'

She was aware of his trick of teasing with a perfectly straight face. She stared again at the sleeper on the grass, then at James.

'Well, he still looks like an old tramp to me, with a dirty face and a hole in his sock.'

She thought this candid opinion might disappoint her artist friend but he leaned over to give her a sudden surprising hug.

35

'What was that for?' she wanted to know. It was easy to know why you displeased people; almost impossible to be sure about the reverse.

'Because you didn't pretend . . . most people do!'

She went home hoping that James would suggest taking her somewhere else, but by the end of another week William and Duncan had returned to London. The drawing room at Linden Square seemed out of bounds again, and even the gaudily beautiful handkerchiefs Duncan had brought back for her as a present didn't quite make up for the loss of her visits to Mrs Marchant.

'Doubt if you can actually use them, Janey,' Duncan said with a grin. 'I think they're probably intended for show!'

'For best,' she agreed quickly. She wouldn't have used them anyway. They were part of her little store of treasures, to be taken out and fingered occasionally. She glanced at his face, thinking that foreign travel had agreed with him. He'd soon be going back to Oxford, but to an admirer of not quite twelve he was already moving about in a world she couldn't even imagine, much less inhabit herself. Unlike Cecily, he was kind enough to notice that she existed . . . but only because she was Jos's daughter. It wasn't any good pretending that he'd bother to notice the daughter of the chauffeur next door. Daydreams were all very well, but she was never going to grow up fast enough for Duncan, and even if she did she'd still be Jos-the-chauffeur's daughter.

The truth of it was rammed home a day or two later. The Rowlands' only home was in London; the Marchants suddenly acquired a weekend cottage in the country. William Marchant had decided that London was unbearable from Saturday morning to Monday. 'The house seems too quiet,' he said ruefully, when Agnes stared at him. He was a Londoner through and through, and she would have imagined that a cottage in the country was the last thing that would have appealed to him.

'You still miss Cecily,' she said, selecting from what she thought troubled him the item that could most safely be mentioned.

'Yes ... there was always something happening when she was around! We'll try the Thames Valley ... near enough to London to tempt friends to visit us.'

A thatched cottage at Long Wittenham was found, and the weekend routine abruptly changed. Jos drove them down on Friday afternoons, collected them again on Monday mornings, and Jane mourned the new development. It wasn't only that she missed her friend James, and the music recitals, but the sight of the house on the corner of the square standing empty at weekends was a straw in the wind, slight but worrying, to warn her that nothing stayed the same. Brian didn't want things to stay the same but amid all the uncertainties that made her anxious she clung to the familiar pattern of days shared between the mews and Linden Square. What would become of them if the Marchants disappeared entirely from their lives? Ano snapped at her when she asked the question.

'Why should they disappear? What rubbish you talk at times. In any case, it's not for *you* to worry about.'

Did Mam worry about it, all the same? Jane had expected that free weekends would make her happier, but the truth was that her mother was more sharp-tempered than before. She didn't even look at the drawing of the cottage-in-the-country that James brought back to London for her.

Much to *his* surprise the weekend exodus became enjoyable. His mother discovered a passion for gardening, Duncan overflowed the house with his friends, and more often than not Cecily and Charles dropped in from some other weekend visit nearby. The only one of them he suspected of finding village life a bore was the person who'd originally suggested it. William read the Lessons in church on Sundays in a beautifully resonant voice, but

James doubted whether he remembered afterwards which verses had been read. With the house full of guests his father seemed cheerfully content, but still the feeling persisted that he stifled some underlying frustration. James wished he knew what it was . . . wished William wasn't such a private man that they didn't even know what he felt about the constant restrictions of a one-handed life. Did he yearn to do something as simple as drive his own car, loathe the daily grind of going to the City?

William was aware of his son's observant eye upon him and found it both irritating and touching. 'Like it here, James?' he asked one late summer afternoon when they were supposed to be keeping the score for the final cricket match of the season.

'Very much, although I didn't expect to. After London I thought it would be a bit slow, but now that's what I like about it.'

'Slow it certainly is,' William agreed as the village hero at the wicket turned his back on a ball for the fourth time. 'You'd think we'd got all night to finish this match.'

He smiled at his son, grateful that he'd been able to explain away a restlessness that had been noticed. Country life was too slow for him; that much James could be allowed to know. What else it lacked no one could be allowed to know.

Chapter 3

Regular visits to the cottage ceased at the end of the summer, when it was time for Duncan to return to Oxford and James to go back to school in Dorset. The fact that she would see nothing of either of them until Christmas didn't worry Jane ... that was normal, and what was normal she could put up with more easily. She might have noticed that her mother's frame of mind had improved as well but for the fact that she was much taken up with the upheaval about to start in her own life. The almost unbelievable had happened ... she'd won a scholarship to St Olave's. It was a day school, but famous in its way, and just about as remote from the children in the mews as the regions of the moon. Now *she* was to wear the beautiful blue and scarlet uniform, take her place in a roll-call of pupils that spanned centuries of London history. Jos was so proud that she couldn't explain to him that she felt sick with fear, but she had to confess to someone and finally chose James before he left for his own school.

'What shall I do if I can't ... manage?' she asked desperately.

'Of course you'll manage ... find your feet in no time. You'll feel a bit lost to begin with, but everybody does.' He stared at her tense face, wondering whether an ancient grammar-school was the happiest place for her. The other girls were unlikely to be the daughters of cooks and chauffeurs. He didn't know much about schoolgirls, but what he remembered of Cessy's friends wasn't encouraging . . . a bunch of cruel little snobs he'd thought them. A misfit from Linden Mews would have been tortured by them, thoughtlessly.

'Janey . . . just be yourself. Do you remember what Will Shakespeare said? ". . . To thine own self be true; thou canst not then be false to any man." Take his advice if you can. He knew a thing or two!'

She grinned at him, as he'd meant her to. James made it sound almost easy. What else could she be, if not herself? She was ready to change the subject, and pointed to the sketchbook under his arm. 'May I look, please?'

'I'm going to call it "Lost London",' he explained solemnly. 'The drawings may not be up to much, but at least they're a record of some of the things that are going to disappear.'

She flicked over some pages, then stared at him, mystified. 'How *can* they disappear? We need them. Look, there's the coalman . . . he was delivering this morning. I went down to the cellar to watch the coal come shooting through the hole in the pavement.' On the next page the unmistakable face of Mrs Bloggs smiled at her. Edie had been caught mop in hand and dressed in working rig – plum-coloured felt hat and a flowered overall decorated with a glittering brooch. She admitted to liking a 'bit of sparkle', and made the most of Mr Bloggs' job of foreman dustman, which allowed him to have first pickings from the 'dust'. Jane regretfully turned the page and saw the knife-grinder working at his strange contraption of pedals and wheels. Opposite him a line of nannies sailed by behind their prams, on their way to their daily rendezvous in the park.

'The larger the pram, the bigger the air of consequence, you notice,' James explained.

She grinned but pointed at a picture of the muffin-man,

tray on his head and bell in hand. Around him wheeled a flock of errand-boys delivering parcels. Each and every one of them was part of London life, as necessary as the policeman on his beat and the lamplighter making his evening rounds. James was usually reliable, but not in this matter of wholesale change. He smiled at the expression on her face which said clearly what she was thinking.

'You may not like the idea, Janey, but things aren't going to stay the same. The coalman will disappear because our houses will be heated in a way that doesn't involve people like Mrs Bloggs humping scuttles full of coal up endless flights of stairs ... and quite right, too! The horse-drawn carts will go because it's quicker and cheaper to make deliveries by van.'

'But the horses ... they know the way,' she insisted desperately. 'They don't even have to be told which houses to call at.' Whatever else got swept away, she couldn't do without the milkman's horse or the ice-cream man who sold her penny water-ices tasting mostly of the cardboard they were wrapped in. What would be left if life was stripped of everything that made it familiar? She bent down suddenly and sniffed the page in front of her.

'Why did you do that?' James wanted to know.

'I was smelling the coke before the nightwatchman disappeared!' She stared at the drawing of his little canvas hut in the road, remembering the day Brian had dried her off in front of his glowing brazier. They'd been offered tea too, she remembered, so strong that she hadn't been able to finish it. 'Brian talks a lot about things changing, too, but he *wants* them to change.'

'I know – go to Speakers' Corner any Sunday morning and you'll hear them all promising that the day of the proletariat's about to dawn.'

James wasn't given to sounding contemptuous about other people, but she could tell he didn't think much of the proletariat, whoever they might be ... people like her and Brian, presumably. She didn't like being lumped with people he despised and it made her retaliate. 'Brian says society's rotten ... the way it's organised.'

'He's right,' James agreed, taking the wind out of her sails. 'But when he and his friends start tearing down what's wrong with it they'll take apart more than they can put together again.'

He spoke so seriously that her own face immediately mirrored the coming holocaust and he had to remind himself that she wasn't yet twelve ... nowhere near old enough to be troubled by the problems of the world. 'No need to look so anxious,' he said quickly. 'Revolutions aren't much liked in this country ... we'll probably muddle through without a catastrophe!'

It was her last conversation with him before he went back to school and she set off for her first day at St Olave's. Watching her go, arrayed in her beautiful new uniform, Jos was suddenly shaken by a strong desire to call her back. Her face under the blue velour hat already looked different before she'd set foot in the place; he didn't know how he'd be able to bear it if they made a stranger of Janey. He told himself he was the fool Ano sometimes called him, and went back to polishing the car. There were real worries enough in the world without inventing them. Mr Neville Chamberlain had come back from Munich telling everyone there'd be no war in Europe, but Jos had his doubts all the same.

William Marchant was even more convinced that all Chamberlain had done was buy them a little time. He'd have liked to talk to Charles Willoughby about it, but his son-in-law was mostly out of London, with his regiment doing a spell of duty at Windsor Castle. When he and Cecily did come to Linden Square, she didn't allow the conversation to get bogged down in a subject she considered boring. She was greatly enjoying married life, and nowadays only flitted in and out of her parents' house like a brightly coloured butterfly on the way to its next port of call. William was finally driven to consulting Jos one morning as they crawled towards the City through a series of traffic jams.

'What's your opinion, Joseph? No more territorial claims, says Hitler. Do you believe him?'

'No, sir, I can't say I do,' Jos answered heavily. 'He got Austria without a struggle, and we've just let him carve up Czechoslovakia as the price of keeping him quiet. Why should he stop now? I reckon Poland will go next, and his friend Mussolini will help himself to whatever *he* wants to pinch. They're a bloody good pair if you ask me, beggin' your pardon, Mr Marchant.'

It was a long speech for Jos to have made, and he normally never swore. William appreciated the anxiety that had prompted it.

'Don't beg my pardon . . . it just about sums them up,' he agreed morosely. 'They're running rings round us, as usual. Look at Spain! While we piously fold our hands and look the other way those two swine make that war ten times worse than it need have been. International agreements are no longer worth the paper they're written on, but our gentlemanly prime minister doesn't seem to have woken up to the fact.'

They were held up again at Cambridge Circus and there was plenty of time to watch the crowds hurrying past. William shut his eyes against a vision of civilians and buildings blasted into dust. Guernica's agony inflicted on London? It was a real and dreadful possibility. He forced himself to make the effort of changing the conversation.

'Haven't seen young Jane lately . . . how's she settling down at St Olave's?'

'Fancies herself in the uniform no end,' Jos confessed with a slow smile. 'I'm not so sure about the settling-down.'

'Why not? No problem with the work, I should have thought . . . not with her school record.'

'It's not that, sir . . . she laps up the work like a kitten at a saucer of cream. I think she finds the other girls a bit of a problem.'

'Bullying at a girls' school? Surely not.' Jos had noticed before that clever men like Mr Marchant often needed simple things spelled out to them; it was odd when they understood everything else.

'She's a scholarship girl, you see . . . not there because she's being paid for, like the rest. Janey says they swank . . . talk about their brothers in smart regiments, and splash a lot of pocket money around. She doesn't talk about it, but I think she wishes she had something to swank about.'

William considered the glib and obvious answer. It ought to be enough to boast about that she'd got to St Olave's on her own merits, but he was too honest not to accept that it begged the question. Society was unevenly organised and basically unfair. The result was that a small girl probably found herself despised by others who hadn't the shadow of a right to despise her. It seemed difficult to say so and he asked instead a question it hadn't occurred to him to ask before in all the twenty years Joseph Rowland had worked for him.

'Do *you* mind not having the things to swank about that the world at large seems to consider so important?'

Another traffic jam enabled Jos to glance at him for a moment. 'You being the guvnor and me the chauffeur, you mean? I can't say it worries me. I reckon we all have a place in the scheme of things. It worries Brian, though! He can't wait to turn the world upside down.'

'Then it's "throw the middle classes to the wolves", I suppose?'

'Well, the aristocracy has to go first, he tells me,' Jos pointed out consolingly. 'But I wouldn't give much for the

44

chances of the middle class after that. Funny thing is that with all his high-sounding talk about equality, it seems to me that he only wants what everybody else wants . . . to scrabble to the top of the heap himself.'

'Everybody except you, apparently!'

'No ambition,' Jos admitted with a rueful smile. 'At least that's what Ano tells me. She's got enough for both of us, though, and she'll see to it that Brian doesn't finish up a chauffeur.'

William nodded, but seemed suddenly to have lost interest in the conversation. He only roused himself to talk again when they were drawing up outside the doors of Marchant & Ferguson.

'Did Mrs Marchant mention this evening, Joseph? A theatre visit . . . we'll need you, I'm afraid.'

'She told me, sir . . . Mr Rattigan's new play, I understand.'

A rare note of dryness in Joseph's voice made his employer smile again. 'Not your idea of a well-spent evening?'

It was a rum conversation they were having this morning, Jos thought . . . not like the usual casual chat about the weather or the state of England's cricket team. 'I suppose my idea's a comfortable chair and the newspaper to read,' he admitted cautiously, 'but your life and mine, they're a bit different, sir. All I have to do is drive this car as well as I can. I don't have responsibility for a lot of other people's lives hung round my neck, and I wouldn't like it if I did.'

William halted on the point of climbing out of the car. 'Oddly enough, that's what I *do* like about it! I'll see you this evening, Joseph.'

Jos touched his cap and got back inside again to start the slow journey back to Bayswater. It occurred to him to wonder if the Guvnor had believed him when he said he didn't envy a man who had a richer, freer life than his own. But it was all a matter of the way you looked at things. Jos felt inclined to pity someone who couldn't even eat his dinner without climbing into a dress suit! The truth was that wealth and privilege had drawbacks attached to them; as long as men like Mr Marchant accepted both sides of the coin Jos didn't want to take it away from them.

That didn't take much thinking out, but Jos had something more worrying on his mind. Young Janey, pride of his life and joy of his heart, had made him anxious yesterday. He'd driven the mistress out to tea but wasn't required to bring her home and had no duty to perform until it was time to set out for the evening run to Mincing Lane. He had to drive past the school on the way home, and thought of his daughter soon to be trudging back across Holland Park on an afternoon of pouring rain. The Guvnor would certainly say that he might wait and bring her home.

He waited at the kerb, heard a bell ringing somewhere inside the building, and a moment later the doors burst open. A trickle of girls emerging became a flood . . . all of them wearing the dark-blue tunics and blazers, and hats with the band of scarlet silk that filled Janey with such pride. Peas in a pod . . . he'd never spot her in that chattering giggling mass. He'd forgotten for the moment that she would spot *him*.

Jane saw him standing patiently in the rain, the glossy Marchant car parked behind him. She was about to smile and wave, but the voice of Angela Hope-Smythe checked her.

'I say . . . look at the super car . . . who do you suppose the chauffeur's come for? Lucky cat, whoever she is.'

'He's come for *me*,' said Jane.

Angela's self-confidence, never in doubt before, suddenly deserted her. Had they all been wrong about little Jane Rowland? It was hard to believe, but even harder to disbelieve the existence of the chauffeur.

'You didn't say,' she muttered, aware that her own stock would have gone down for being so certain Rowland didn't need to be accepted on terms of friendship.

'I don't *have* to say,' Jane pointed out coolly. She walked away from the others, towards Jos, allowed him to open the car door for her, and climbed in. The taste of sickness was in her throat. It would be no more than she deserved if she had to get out again to be sick in the gutter while Angela still watched.

'Rotten old afternoon, love,' said Jos beside her. 'I thought you'd be glad of a ride home.'

She forced herself to smile at him, but her face was sheet-white under the beautiful hat Ano had insisted on buying too large so that it would last longer.

'Everything go all right today?'

She heard the anxious note in her father's voice but could do no more than nod at him. Something *was* wrong, Jos knew, but for the first time in her life Janey wasn't going to share it with him.

He cast around for comfort to offer her. 'Kippers for tea . . . your favourites!'

She swallowed convulsively but managed to agree. 'Lovely!'

Jos didn't make a habit of airing his worries to Ano but late that night he found himself confessing that Janey bothered him.

'There's something she doesn't like about the place. For two pins she'd have burst into tears on the way home.'

'I dare say she would, with you standing outside the school in your chauffeur's uniform.'

He was, he realized, the fool his wife so often called him not to see in time that Janey would probably rather have got soaked to the skin. There was such terrible pain in the thought that she might have felt ashamed of him that he forced himself to think only of her.

47

'We shouldn't have let her go to St Olave's . . . making her choose between them and us.'

For once the misery in his face moved Ano to kindness. 'You're afraid she'll choose them. She won't, in the long run.'

'A child like that shouldn't have to decide,' Jos suddenly shouted, 'It's all wrong. I agree with Brian. The sooner this rotten society's swept away, the better.'

'You were pleased enough to have her go, and don't forget she's getting something else – chances *we* never had. That's worth a few battles along the way.'

It was how Ano saw life, he thought, in terms of battles lost or won. She would never forgive life, or him, for the chances she hadn't had. He felt defeated, aware that though she'd been as good and hard-working a wife as any man could have wished for, she'd never allowed him to think he'd been able to make her happy. On her way out of the room Ano fired a parting shot at him.

'Just because she's small you think Jane's soft, like you. Don't forget she's my daughter too.'

Funny how easy it *was* to forget. Jos sometimes had the feeling that they were two families, him and Janey, Ano and Brian. Ano had been his wife for nearly twenty years, but he didn't know her any better now than the day she'd arrived in Linden Square at the age of nineteen, to be interviewed for the job of nursemaid to the Marchant twins. Jos could see her now in his mind's eye . . . white skin, black hair and luscious mouth, totally at odds with a suitable dark-grey costume and unbecoming hat. She didn't care much for babies but she'd been glad to get the job, she told him afterwards.

'Why, if you don't like looking after children?'

'It's much better living here than working in a munitions factory, and even that was better than existing in a mining village in Wales. Back-to-back slums and coal dust everywhere. I'd do anything rather than go back to that.'

It was understandable, even though Jos still hankered after the place *he'd* sprung from ... the Norfolk estate that had been Lady Carterton's home. His father had been head-groom there and Jos still privately held the view that motor-cars should never have been allowed to replace horses. He'd fallen fatally, shyly, in love with Ano but never really expected her to decide that she could do worse than marry him. The astonishing day came when she did, and he was the one to feel uncertain.

'I'm not much of a catch.' He could still hear himself saying it, remember the smile that took the sting out of her answer. 'I know, but what else have I got to look forward to? Years of being handed on from one family to another until I get too old to work!'

Jos had been reassured. There was a streak of recklessness in her that worried him, but now he'd be able to take care of her. That he had done, even if he hadn't been able to make her happy. She left the Marchant household to marry him, and Brian was born. By the time Jane was five and starting school, Ano had gone back to Linden Square as Cook-General – bored in the mews, she'd said, with only those stupid women to talk to. There'd been plenty of time to accept the fact that she regarded him as a failure, but the idea that Janey might come to share the view was going to take some getting used to.

She never referred to that afternoon again and Jos never repeated the mistake of going to collect her from St Olave's. Whatever had ailed her seemed to disappear, and she only looked upset again when he once asked why she never brought school-friends home to tea.

'They're silly cats ... I'd rather have tea with you.' That much was true, but the extent of the lie she was committed to made her feel sick. Casual references to the house in Linden Square had been left vague, but she'd known perfectly well what they concealed. With a mixture of dread and relief from self-disgust, she waited for the inevitable day when Angela Home-Smythe walked along Linden Mews and saw her helping Jos polish the Marchant car.

Chapter 4

The Christmas holiday came and went with her seeing almost nothing of the family in Linden Square. Without knowing it, she had Cecily to thank for this. A London Christmas was a bore, said Mrs Willoughby, and persuaded William Marchant that they must take part in the village festivities at Long Wittenham – midnight carol service, and the pantomime in the church hall on Boxing Day and all. Jane no longer minded it when the house on the corner of the square was empty – in fact she now preferred the Marchants to be away, finding it impossible to go on with her friendship with Mrs Marchant or meet James on their old friendly footing. She was sunk deep in deception; if they ever knew, they would despise her even more than she despised herself. These days she was quieter than usual at home, but Brian was too busy following the course of the Civil War in Spain to pay her much attention, and Jos reluctantly followed Ano's advice and left her alone. He was willing to accept that women were strange creatures . . . look at Ano herself, not at all pleased to find that they'd have Christmas on their own. She had bitten his head off when he'd supposed she'd be glad not to have to cook the Marchants' Christmas dinner.

One way and another life was full of problems, but as winter gave way to spring Jos knew that full-scale disaster was looming. Forgetting the promise given to Mr Chamberlain that he would leave the map of Europe alone,

Hitler invaded Czechoslovakia, and the shadow of war moved closer. But whatever might be happening in Prague, the ritual pattern of life in London went on for a little while undisturbed. At the end of March Boat Race Day arrived as usual, made more exciting this year because Duncan had finally achieved the glory of rowing for the Oxford boat. All the Marchants and most of the Rowlands sported dark-blue favours the size of cabbage-roses, and peaceable Jos was provoked into a row with Ron Cooper in the mews.

'Daft idiot,' said Jos, explaining this lapse to Jane. 'He *would* have it that Oxford are going to lose.'

Brian pretended to take no notice of a stupid pastime indulged in by the stupid upper classes, but returned at tea-time from an afternoon spent on the towpath at Putney with the news that Ron Cooper had been proved right.

'Poor old Oxford . . . "all rowed slowly, but none more slowly than Duncan"' The chant struck him as so irresistibly funny that he went on repeating it until Jane had finally been goaded into heaving a book at him. Since he was unsporting enough to duck, it missed its target and smashed Ano's cherished cut-glass vase instead. For once she frowned at Brian.

'Your fault,' she said sharply. 'You were being aggravating. I expect *you* to replace the vase.'

'We'll share, half and half,' Jane suggested, silently saying goodbye to weeks of pocket money.

'You'll do no such thing . . . I said Brian.' Mam had spoken, and even he didn't waste time arguing with her.

Jane nowadays avoided going to Linden Square whenever she could, but there was no getting out of helping her mother there the night of Cecily and Duncan's twenty-first birthday party. He was just down from Oxford for good, delighted with himself for getting a barely passable degree. She hadn't seen him for months, felt suddenly heartsick at a glimpse of him in the hall, talking to the guests who were beginning to arrive. In formal evening dress he looked so beautiful that she wanted to weep for the gap that separated them. He didn't even notice her . . . like the rest of the help hired for the evening, she'd become part of the wallpaper.

It was better to stay in the kitchen, where she didn't have to watch what was going on without being part of it. But Ano dispatched her upstairs again to show the waitress how the food lift descended from the dining room to the kitchen. They had almost got safely out of the room again when the door opened and Cecily and James walked in. Jane waited in the expectation that Cecily would smile and say hello. There was even a moment in which she couldn't help looking, without envy, on such perfectly finished beauty. But pleasure died out of her face as Cecily swept around the dinner-table, ignoring her completely. Resentment took its place, and the bitter taste of hatred was on her tongue. She loathed this spoilt doll in her sparkling silver dress. Cecily Willoughby, tall and slender as a wand, all golden hair and white translucent skin, was everything Jane Rowland would never be. She was scarcely aware of James, unfamiliar in any case in his first evening clothes. He was another Marchant, even though they had once been friends.

He hesitated too long about saying 'Good evening, Janey', tongue-tied by tensions in the room he didn't know how to deal with. She stared at him so blankly that he thought for a moment she didn't even recognize him.

'I know we've hardly seen each other for months and I look different in this ridiculous get-up, but it's me . . . James!'

She nodded, about to confess that she liked the way he looked, but Cecily spoke across them with a long-suffering air.

'The cards, James . . . ?'

It was Jane who answered. 'They're on the sideboard . . . madam!'

She got it wickedly right, James thought; just on the hither side of parody. It would have been lovely if Cecily had been prepared to share the joke, but a glance at his sister's face slew the faint possibility. Perhaps the memory of the bridesmaid's dress still rankled.

'James, dear, the hired help have work to do, and so do we. Shall we get on with the job of putting out these place cards?'

The battle was unequal; how could Janey win in the end? He saw her face go white, but she was smiling when she turned to the waitress who'd been watching the little scene.

'Time for the hired help to make themselves scarce. If you've got the hang of the lift, shall we go?'

On the way out of the room she had, in a sense, the last word – a respectful bob in Cecily's direction that James, at least, enjoyed. She was more like Ano than he'd realized.

'Young Jane's getting cheeky – Ma's fault for spoiling her.' Cecily was examining her perfect face in the mirror over the fireplace, saw in the glass that James had come to stand behind her, dark eyebrows drawn together in a frown exactly like William Marchant's.

'Finish the damned cards yourself, Cessy. I've lost whatever appetite I had for this dinner-party. If Charles doesn't beat you every Friday evening, he should do . . . you need it.'

She looked startled for a moment, then smiled at him with acid sweetness. 'My mistake . . . I should have said she's been spoiled by Ma and you. Let it be a lesson to you to make friends with your own class in future.'

He stood staring at her, hands dragging down the pockets of his despised dinner-jacket in a way that would have broken the tailor's heart.

'You're almost too good to be true, sister dear. Has no one told you that the world is changing? The person who needs to learn some lessons is you.'

'Remind me to apply to Jane's delightful brother. He'd be only too happy to oblige!'

She flashed him a dazzling smile and walked out of the room. He decided that, as family evenings went, this one was being remarkably unpleasant. His parents spoke to each other like courteous strangers, Duncan was unbearably full of himself, and he'd been landed with his holy terror of a grandmother at the dinner-table. What was wrong with them all? There was no time now to think about it; he was supposed to be putting place cards round the dinner-table, and there was the rest of the evening to get through.

William Marchant's birthday present to Duncan was three months' freedom on the Continent before he was required to buckle down to the stern realities of City life. Jane knew that he was going away and regretted it, even if he never had time to notice her. The house always seemed more noisily cheerful and alive when he was there. James she was careful to avoid for several days after the birthday party, but he caught her one Saturday morning when she was in the scullery polishing a pair of brown and white brogues.

'Duncan's,' he said unerringly. 'Why doesn't the lazy swine clean his own shoes? You're not his servant.'

Coming on top of the scene in the dining room, it wasn't what he might have said if he'd had time to think about it. The words came tumbling out before he could stop them, born of some sudden anger at the sight of her cleaning his brother's shoes. It occurred only dimly to James, and it didn't occur to Jane at all, that he was jealous of a flashily charming brother who'd always dazzled her.

'I'm not Duncan's servant, specially,' she agreed. Then fierceness broke through, reminding him again of Ano Rowland. 'We *are* servants, though. Does it matter what we do?'

'Of course it matters,' he shouted, hoping she wouldn't

ask him why. 'And while we're on the subject, I've got a bone to pick with you. What the devil did you mean by all that madam and curtseying nonsense the other evening?'

It *had* been nonsense, she realized, her own hurt dignity just as much as Cecily's high and mighty tone. The thought made her grin at him reluctantly. 'Showing proper respect,' she explained. 'I thought Cecily would like it!'

'You thought nothing of the kind, and she didn't like it at all.' Jane looked pleased. 'I think you're right,' she said happily. James didn't smile back at her and her mood changed abruptly. 'I'm all betwixt and between . . . don't know who I am or where I belong. What can I do about that, James?'

Her eyes were full of despair, not devilment. She wore the blue and red St Olave's uniform, played lacrosse, learned French . . . but she was still Jos-the-chauffeur's daughter. How the devil *should* she know who she was? He stared at her, taking account of changes. The features that had seemed too big for her face a year or two ago were settling into harmony with each other, her eyes were set under beautifully marked dark brows, and her mouth was lovely. She was still small, but her body was beginning to take shape, and the games she played at school were giving it strength and balance. He wished the outward changes were all there were, wished he knew what comfort to offer her.

'It's more difficult for you, Janey,' he agreed at last, 'but the truth is that we all have to flounder around a bit, before we can be certain who we are. Look at me . . . trying to break out of the Marchant mould and turn myself into something the rest of the family feels slightly ashamed of! In my own way I'm as mixed up as you are.'

She smiled sadly, aware that it wasn't really true. It would have been a relief to confess the muddle she'd got into at school. Time was when James would probably have roared with laughter at the idea of her using Linden Square and the Marchants to pad out her own standing a bit among a pack of impressionable snobs; but she no longer felt sure of him. The gulf that hadn't troubled them as children now seemed less easy to jump over. He might despise her ... worse, share the knowledge with Mrs Marchant and Duncan. She stifled the longing to confide in him and asked a question instead.

'Shall you learn to be an artist at Oxford? Duncan had a lovely time there.'

'He'd have a lovely time anywhere,' James pointed out acidly. 'But Oxford's not my cup of tea at all. Good Lord, can you see me cutting a dash in a punt on the river, or tripping the light fantastic at college balls?'

'With difficulty,' she agreed. 'So what *are* you going to do?'

'Three years at the St Martin's School of Art, I hope. Father's slowly getting used to the idea that Marchant & Ferguson can do without me. He's got Duncan lined up, and Tom Ferguson's nephew is being groomed as well.' To a more familiar Janey he might have made a confession of his own – that his father hadn't got used to the idea enough to conceal his fear that his younger son was unacceptably soft; a painter seemed such an unmanly thing to want to be. But Jane was growing up hero-worshipping his brother; he couldn't be certain that she didn't share the Marchant view.

'I shall go to St Martin's and unlearn all the bad habits I've been teaching myself for years,' he said abruptly.

'I used to like what the bad habits produced.'

'Kids' stuff! I hope I'll be ashamed of it in a year or two.'

She thought of the tramp in the park the day they'd gone to the National Gallery, and James's insistence that he was worth capturing on paper. Kids' stuff ... like taking young Janey Rowland to the zoo? She had been back since to the National Gallery with her class at school, expended all her pocket money on a reproduction of the little Duccio painting that Jos had helped her mount on a piece of card. It held pride of place in her bedroom. James saw sadness in her face and knew that he'd gone wrong again. She was unpredictable nowadays, and he was a tactless fool – it made a combination difficult to overcome.

With spring days lengthening into summer, the week-end visits to Long Wittenham began again. The Marchants' absence from London gave Jos a little more free time to tend his window-boxes and roam through the parks with Jane. She enjoyed the walks with her father, but they didn't entirely make up for the feeling that without the family in Linden Square something went out of life in the mews as well. Jane wasn't sure why this should be so, except that it had something to do with Mam, who always seemed more Welshly unpredictable when she wasn't required to be working at the Marchants' house. It was odd when she didn't seem to have a very high opinion of the family. Jane had once tried to get Brian to explain it, but he'd been unusually sharp with her and told her not to meddle in things that didn't concern her. She couldn't help feeling that anything she could fathom out about her stormy mother *did* concern her, but she let the matter rest, more convinced than ever that what she didn't understand was important. Apparently unlike everybody else, she found herself missing the gentle presence at weekends of Mrs Marchant. She'd have liked to talk to her about singing in the school choir, and taking part in a performance of the St Matthew Passion in the Albert Hall on Easter Sunday. As it was she had to be content with Jos, who smiled to himself every time he thought about his daughter singing in the Albert Hall. He went to the Hall for the first time in his life, and insisted to Ano sitting next to him that he could pick out Jane from a tier of other schoolgirls high up beside the organ pipes behind the orchestra.

She was glad he found something to smile about because his nightly reading of the newspaper left him very depressed. Brian made matters worse by worrying Ano with hints of volunteering for the International Brigade still fighting Franco's Nationalists in Spain.

'Leave them to fight their own battles. It's not our quarrel,' she'd say whenever he trailed the subject in front them.

'It *is* our quarrel . . . Fascist swine bombing women and children, and the rotten government of this country doesn't even care.'

'Of course it cares; don't talk rubbish,' Jos said fiercely for once. 'We signed an agreement not to interfere and abided by it. Hitler and Mussolini haven't, but that's not the Government's fault.'

'Everything's the Government's fault,' his son said bitterly. Even to his ears it wasn't much of an argument, but he was feeling too sick to care. Where did high principles get you in a world where nobody could be trusted? Even his heroes in Russia had just signed a pact with the Nazi fascists he hated so fiercely. It was a betrayal so dreadful that he couldn't bear to think about it.

William Marchant had the subject on his mind as well, but when he raised it with Jos one morning on the way to the City, it was from a different angle.

'Things look bad, Joseph . . . Hitler making sure Russia won't stab him in the back when he makes his next move. He's quite sure already that France and Britain won't do anything to stop him. Poor little Poland doesn't stand a chance now.'

'It brings us in, though, sir. We're pledged to help Poland.'

'So we are . . . I'd forgotten the pledge,' William said with savage irony. 'Pledge or not, does our worthy prime minister strike you as a man resolute in the defence of right against might?'

Jos blinked; the Guvnor was properly on edge, no question. But the truth was that everybody, himself included,

59

was torn in half, not sure what they dreaded most – having the country go to war, or the unthinkable disgrace if even now it refused to do so.

Two days later William Marchant was proved to have been unfair. Hitler's armies invaded Poland at dawn on the first day of September 1939 and a few hours later they listened to Neville Chamberlain announce over the wireless that Great Britain was now at war.

That resolute leap into action was followed almost immediately by the wail of the first air-raid sirens over London. The warning turned out to be a false alarm, and that was typical of what rapidly came to be called the phoney war. Restrictions multiplied, breeding still more regulations that seemed downright ridiculous. Benighted travellers raged at the unnecessary disappearance of any sign that told them where they were, and neighbours looked at one another with feverish suspicion when hastily installed black-out blinds fell down, exposing beams of light to non-existent German raiders.

Ano smarted under a reprimand from their self-appointed Air-Raid Precaution expert in the mews. 'I suppose that fool Edmunds thinks I'm a spy,' she said furiously. 'He walks about the street as if he owned it, puffed-up little popinjay!'

Jane grinned at a description she recognized as being merited; there was an undeniable resemblance to a pouter pigeon about Mr Edmunds these days. But Jos was more tolerant. 'We might be glad of him one day. It's his job to catch people like you who go switching on lights without a thought.'

'Nobody asked him to take the job. Now that he can strut about with his tin hat, he thinks he's somebody at last.'

Ano hated the black-out above all else. For years she'd had to make do without electricity in the mews, and had still hardly got used to the pleasure of walking into a room and simply flicking a switch. Jane still missed what she'd always known – the exciting plop and hiss when the fragile gas mantles were lit, and the uncertainty of knowing when the incandescent shells would burn into holes, leaving the room to sink into darkness until a new mantle had been installed. Compared with the soft light of the gas lamps, electricity seemed cold and harsh, but it had one undeniable advantage: she no longer went upstairs to her attic bedroom at night carrying a candle that either threw monstrous jumping shadows on the wall or blew out altogether, leaving her frightened in the dark.

She helped Jos criss-cross the windows with the strips of sticky tape decreed by Authority, but couldn't rid herself of the feeling that they were playing some kind of game. She didn't believe in the reality of bombs that would flay them with fragments of flying glass, any more than she believed in the need to go to school accompanied by a gasmask. She hated it as Ano hated the black-out, dreaded the class-time practice of fighting her way into its evil-smelling rubbery isolation, and rejected the idea that she might one day have to put it on in earnest. Duncan seemed to share her point of view that the war was something separate from real life. Brought back early from his continental holiday, he was now part of Jos's morning delivery to Mincing Lane. He was outside the house one morning when Jane came round the corner of the square. There were changes to be observed in little Jane – little no longer, in fact. His practised eye noted that she was getting quite leggy, attractive in that blue and red rig.

'How's life, Jane?'

For once she thought he sounded as though he had time to wait for her to answer. 'It feels unreal,' she said truthfully, conscious of the gasmask slung round her neck.

His bright smile lit the morning for her. 'Nothing to worry about . . . it's a bit of a lark, but it will all fizzle out before long.'

It wasn't Jos's view, but Ano certainly convinced herself that they'd never have to sink to using the communal air-raid shelter. She hadn't spent years of her life trying to make it clear that the Rowlands were different from everybody else in the mews only to be lumped in now with Jack Edmonds' chattering wife and the Coopers' hooligan children. But it was another silent reproach to offer Jos. If he'd bestirred himself a bit more they'd have had a house of their own and a garden with an Anderson shelter outside the kitchen door.

The possibility of flying glass and floating gas might be distantly vague, but there was an immediate threat which led to Jane's first-ever battle with Jos. Evacuation was so urgently in the air that she thought it time to make things clear: she didn't intend to be one of the schoolchildren being hustled out of London.

'Don't be daft,' said Jos with unusual firmness. 'Of course you'll go with the rest of them. You've always wanted to see the country . . . now's your chance.'

'Not without you and Mam, and Brian. If you're not coming as well, I'll see the country another time.'

'You'll do as you're told and see it now,' roared poor Jos, with a bang on the table that was meant to convince her that the subject was now closed. She merely smiled at him with devastating sweetness.

'What's the good? I'd be like those poor cats that can't settle in a new home. You know what they do . . . keep walking back to the old one again.'

She would too, he thought helplessly; it wouldn't do a particle of good for Ano to lay down the law and say she'd go wherever she was sent. Even if they got her to leave at all, one rumour of an air-raid on London and she'd be back somehow, even if she had to walk, to make sure they were all right. Uncommon cussed his daughter was when she got the bit between her teeth. He'd been inclined to disbelieve Ano when she'd said Janey was like her, but he could see the truth of it now.

The first and youngest contingent duly left St Olave's, hung about with label, gasmask, and the packet of digestive biscuits recommended as unsickly travelling rations. But reception at the other end was muddled, and the local school so overcrowded that the dispatch of the next wave of pupils was temporarily halted. No air-raids came after all to make evacuation seem necessary, and the rest of the school remained in London. The danger seemed to be over and Jane decided it was safe to return to Brian the five shillings borrowed in case a train-fare back to London might be needed.

But after weeks when nothing seemed to happen, the war finally took a small lurch towards reality. Cecily called in at Linden Square one morning, sounding bright as usual, but Agnes felt sure that the brightness was requiring effort.

'Charles is off to France with the British Expeditionary Force,' she announced gaily. She saw her mother's face change. 'Nothing to get het up about, Ma. Charlie says it's a training exercise to stop the men getting bored. They'll be home again in no time.'

'Of course, dear,' Agnes agreed at once. 'Nothing like those terrible trenches in the last war. All the same, one can't help wishing dear Charles didn't have to go.' She had become unexpectedly fond of a nice conventional son-in-law who treated her with the same mixture of gentle teasing and kindness that she'd got used to from James; had even begun to suspect that there was more to Charles Willoughby than simple niceness. He was certainly coping with a headstrong wife with much more firmness and finesse than she'd expected.

'He thinks it's time we did something . . . trust a professional soldier!'

Cessy's blue eyes suddenly met her mother's anxious gaze and brightness deserted her.

'I'll miss him, rather,' she confessed abruptly. 'I married him because he was suitable and nice and would let me do whatever I pleased. It was going to be fun being Mrs Charles Willoughby. It *has* been fun, but I'm beginning to like doing what *he* pleases. It's a fine time to discover the fact!'

'I'm glad you've made the discovery, all the same,' Agnes said gently. 'We'll help, darling, as much as we can.'

When Charles came to say goodbye to them William manoeuvred him into his study.

'Is it true what you told Cessy . . . a training exercise? A bit of flag-waving for the sake of Anglo-French relations?'

'Let's say I hope so,' Captain Willoughby admitted with a smile. 'It will be a bit of real bad luck if we actually meet some Germans! We shall be fighting them with weapons left over from the last war. That's not what the Germans will be fighting with.'

'But the Maginot Line, dear boy . . . the French say it's invincible.'

'They do, don't they?' he agreed politely. 'I'd believe them if the damn thing were complete . . . it isn't, by a long way! All the Germans have to do is go round it, and I can't help feeling their generals are bright enough to work that out.'

William Marchant's troubled face made him add quickly, 'I probably shouldn't have said that. It's not our job to go spreading gloom and despondency. Needless to say, I don't talk to Cessy like that.'

His regiment embarked for France a few days later, but despite press photographs of smiling troops waving from train windows, a deadening sense of stagnation still hung in the air. Opinion was gradually hardening that the non-war would eventually peter out into an uneasy peace. Poland – 'poor little Poland' – had been shared out between Germany and Russia, but no one seriously believed that an Allied army could be expected to march half-way across Europe to set it free again. No one except Brian Rowland, at least, who thought just that. Jane felt like weeping for his added misery when Russia suddenly invaded Finland. It was a brutality to beat that of any Fascist dictator, but practised by the Bolsheviks he longed to call his brothers.

'It stinks, Janey,' he said fiercely. 'The whole bloody world stinks!'

'If it didn't, we wouldn't be fighting to make it better,' she suggested by way of comfort. At nearly thirteen she was at the age when it was necessary to fall in love with the poems of Rupert Brooke. Twenty-five years earlier he'd felt just as Brian was feeling now, and rejoiced in the chance to 'turn as swimmers into cleanness leaping, glad from a world grown old and cold and weary'. That was what her brother wanted to do, and it didn't surprise her in the least when he came home later than usual one evening and announced that he'd given in his notice at the garage.

'What a time to do it, just before Christmas,' Ano said sharply. 'Have you got somewhere else to go ... there's your apprenticeship to think of.'

The grin on his face warned her what was coming. 'Yes, I've got somewhere else to go. I volunteered for the Navy this afternoon. Thought I'd rather choose where I went than be drafted into the Army. Found I couldn't face the thought of bumping into the Honourable Charles!'

He'd hoped to make Ano smile but she was much too upset.

'You should have waited at least till they made you go. And why the Navy, may I ask? You've never been further than a day-trip to Margate on the Golden Eagle ... you'll be sea-sick before you get outside the Thames.'

She deeply distrusted the sound of the Navy. The hazards of war were bad enough, but there was all that water to contend with as well.

'Thought I'd see more of the world afloat. You must admit it's time I got further than Margate!'

She wasn't ready to admit anything at all. For once near

tears, she wasn't even comforted by the knowledge that Edna Cooper's slob of a son further along the mews would certainly wait to be conscripted. But it made no difference; Brian left at the end of the week for Pwhelli. A commandeered Butlin's holiday camp there had been renamed HMS Glendower, but even that touch of Welshness didn't comfort Ano. Christmas seemed unreal without him, and in January the announcement that food rationing was to start set her fretting again.

'There you are,' she said to Jos. 'Rationing! That means ships are being sunk. I *knew* Brian should have chosen the Army.'

Jos wanted to put an arm round her, but she wasn't a woman who accepted small tendernesses. He could only try to reason away fear. 'It only means the Government want fair shares for all this time,' he said gently. 'You can remember well enough how it was in the last war – the rich bought up all the food on the black market and the poor went hungry. Don't worry so about the boy, my dear. It stands to reason he won't be sent to sea for a long time yet . . . he doesn't know enough.'

Ano had no confidence in reason when applied to Sea Lords at the Admiralty; she was ready to believe them capable of anything. Still, what Jos said made a sort of sense. She nodded and set off as usual for the house in Linden Square. Mrs Bloggs was already there when she let herself in by the kitchen door, and jerked an expressive thumb in the direction of the upper regions.

'The Missus is in a taking upstairs,' said Edie with relish.

It was odd to feel a sudden constriction of the heart . . . ridiculous, after all these years, to imagine that Mrs Marchant's 'taking' could have anything to do with her. She made herself put on her morning overall as usual, and walk calmly up the stairs. Her employer waited for her in the dining-room, white-faced certainly, but not in the state Mrs Bloggs had suggested.

'Bad news, Ano,' she said immediately. 'Duncan's papers have come.' Her eyes did fill with tears at the thought of it. 'They . . . they recommend the RAF because he spent a few hours flying with the University Air Squadron.'

In spite of herself Ano felt a twinge of pity for a woman she normally despised. Lady Carterton she resented for making her feel that a Rowland's only reason for being alive was to wait on her betters. But at least in her ladyship Ano recognised a fellow-fighter. If times got hard old Lady Carterton would survive. If times got desperate she wouldn't baulk at impaling on the lethal point of her umbrella any German stupid enough to let himself get within range of her. But her daughter was a different kettle of fish, helpless in the face of life's problems to do anything but fly to her piano. It didn't seem to have given her much comfort today.

Ano remembered what Jos had just told *her*. 'Nothing's going to happen for a long time yet. Mr Duncan's like Brian . . . got months of training ahead. By the time either of them are ready, we'll find the war is over.'

Agnes forced herself to smile and agree with comfort kindly meant even though she didn't believe a word of it. Her Cook-General had a son who was just as vulnerable as hers. 'Mrs Bloggs has just been saying much the same thing – "look on the bright side, ma'am!" '.

Bright or dark, there was still the ritual pattern of the day to be followed as usual, and they settled down to the business of planning meals. But ever afterwards the moment of Duncan's summons remained for Agnes the point at which the world began slowly but surely to slide towards chaos.

Chapter 5

It wasn't to be much longer before the stalemate everyone had complained about exploded in the flash and roar of gunfire. Almost overnight life changed; from *nothing* happening, suddenly everything happened at once. Hitler lifted his little finger and sent the grey-green river of the Wehrmacht flooding through Europe. Denmark was the first to be taken by surprise, then Norway was overrun with the same unbelievable speed. The Navy managed to rescue King Haakon VII and bring him to London, but a British force sent to land on the Norwegian coast at Namsos had to be humiliatingly withdrawn.

William Marchant still went through the motions of taking an interest in tea and rubber, but three-quarters of his mind refused to concentrate on anything except what was happening on the Continent. The grim accounts that he read began to fill him with despair. Bungling incompetence and amateurish muddle were all that England had, apparently, to set against the streamlined efficiency of the Nazi war machine. The First World War all over again, but much worse; because in place of Kaiser William was a power-drunk fanatic convinced of his destiny to rule the world. Against such a man England could only offer Neville Chamberlain!

But not for much longer. William was as flabbergasted as everyone else by the events of 8 May. The Government called for a vote of confidence in the House, which astonishingly it lost. The Government fell, and Winston Churchill was appointed to lead a national coalition.

Brian's letters home said nothing about the new prime minister, of whom he couldn't be expected to approve, but he informed his family that they could take heart from the rest of the news. Clement Attlee was a quiet man, but uncommonly canny. His great hero, Ernest Bevin, would work miracles at the Ministry of Labour, and Herbert Morrison was the only man alive who could handle the tricky business of supplies. Jos shared his son's optimism with William Marchant one morning. They were still driving to Mincing Lane each day, but each day it seemed to Jos the Guvnor got more disheartened.

'Seems we're on the right road at last,' he said cheerfully. 'Socialists in the Government! Brian thinks we haven't got a thing to worry about. The war's as good as won.'

William tried to drag his mind away from nightmare worries about the Maginot Line. If all the Germans had to do was go round it, it didn't matter how many Socialists sat on the Front Bench at Westminster.

'Where *is* Brian at the moment? Duncan's somewhere in Scotland, being taught to fly a Spitfire . . . he says it's better than anything the Germans have got; thank God, if so.'

'Brian's at Devonport now, waiting to be drafted. He's been selected as a CW candidate – which he says means commission warrant. Ano's not sure how she feels about that. No question that he ought to be an officer, of course, but she has the idea there might be more safety in numbers on the lower deck!'

William doubted privately whether safety and Brian Rowland would ever have much in common. He was born to trouble as sparks flew upward. Cecily would certainly say that if he wasn't torpedoed by the Germans he stood every chance of getting himself court-martialled for organising a mutiny among his crew. Still, William shared his relief at the shake-up in the Government, and went further in thanking Heaven for the new prime minister. No one but Churchill could bulldoze the country through the mess it was in now.

Two days later there was even more reason to think so. The German armies poured into Holland, Belgium, and Luxembourg – unstoppable, apparently, even when anyone showed the slightest sign of trying to stop them. But William turned off the wireless communiqué with the sick feeling that Europe was like a mesmerized rabbit in the path of a stoat. Anxiety *had* to be shared, but with whom? His wife seemed to have retreated into some private sanctuary of her own. He didn't know whether he wanted to leave her there or drag her out to face reality, but in the end she spoke before he did.

'William . . . what about the Maginot Line?' The quiet question fell into the silence in the room.

What indeed, and what if Charles was right and it simply wasn't long enough? 'It's still there,' he said briefly.

'I know . . . but Cessy was here this morning. She'd seen some maps . . . read something about the Line petering out at a place called the Ardennes.'

'Dense forest,' William said gruffly. 'Impenetrable for tanks, and that's what the Germans are using to advance with.' He marvelled again at a talent in women that never ceased to surprise him. They could be counted on to alight instinctively on the one thing a man wished them to avoid noticing. Agnes looked at his drawn face and allowed herself to be silenced, saying merely that she would tell darling Cessy about the forest.

But, as he feared, it turned out not to be dense enough. Little more than two weeks later the unthinkable had happened. The Line and the French armies had been outflanked, the Dutch had surrendered, and the King of the Belgians was asking for a separate armistice – this despite the fact that British troops were still fighting on his soil at his request.

All but cut off, their destruction or capture seemed inevitable. The retreat ordered by Lord Gort began, and for the men still fighting their way to the coast down an ever-shrinking corridor, Dunkirk shone at the end of it like some unattainable Shangri-La. The troops who had already managed to get there knew it for what it was – an inferno of burning fuel tanks, ruined quays, and bomb-blasted beaches.

Cecily took to haunting the house in Linden Square, imploring William to explain to her exactly what was happening.

'I need to know,' she kept explaining feverishly. 'Tell me, Pa . . . I can't bear not knowing what's happening to Charlie.'

'The Navy's there, darling. They'll evacuate our men somehow . . . trust them.'

But the Navy's task was almost hopeless. The shoal-ridden shallow waters off the coast marooned the ships too far off-shore. With the quays already destroyed, troops could only be ferried out to them. It was agonizingly slow, and under murderous bombardment the losses in men and ships were terribly high. There *had* to be little craft, with shallow enough draught to be able to drive almost on to the beaches.

Within a day or two that was what arrived: a ramshackle rescue fleet of pleasure-boats, trawlers, motor cruisers – anything that would stay more or less afloat, manned by crews whose only hope of navigating themselves across the unknown waters of the Channel simply lay in staying close to the one in front. The extent of the makeshift armada was scarcely known except to people at the Channel ports and at London railway stations where trainloads of wartorn exhausted troops kept arriving. But the word got known that somehow the Army was being brought home.

Cecily lived almost permanently attached to the telephone, terrified of straying away from it in case Charles should phone. William gave up the pretence of working and stayed at home. It was he who answered a ring at the telephone, and put the receiver back on its hook just as Agnes walked into the room. The expression on his face drove the blood from her heart.

'Duncan . . . Charles . . .?' she whispered. 'Which . . .?'

William stared blankly at her, trying to relate the question to the conversation he'd just been having with the headmaster of James's school.

'It's James . . . he went missing last night, but they didn't realise it until he didn't show up for breakfast this morning. It seems that he and another boy cycled to Poole and didn't come back.'

Agnes looked bewildered. 'It sounds unlike James. He's not normally a nuisance. What does he think he's doing, do you suppose?'

William was briefly tempted to evade the question, but she would have to know in the end. 'He thinks he's helping . . . the boys were seen on a launch about to sail out of the harbour. It was on its way to Dunkirk.'

Such silence filled the room that he wondered whether she had even understood what he'd just said. She should have fainted or wept, not stared at him in this strange still fashion. He struggled with a terrible desire to shout at her, 'Dunkirk, for God's sake, Agnes . . . I suppose you've heard of that?'

'I'll tell you what James was doing,' she said at last . . . 'proving himself to *you*. He knows you despise him because he wants to paint instead of kick balls about and make a lot of noise. *You've* sent him to Dunkirk.'

Her blue eyes were full of hate, and her accusation was terrible in its quietness and its certainty. William thought it might even be true.

For the first time in his life the world had gone out of control . . . all known landmarks blotted out; even fear for James was momentarily drowned by the discovery that his

72

wife felt passionate enough to hate him. His right arm sketched a small imploring gesture in the air towards her, fell again because she didn't even notice it.

'My dear . . . I'm very sorry,' he said at long last. 'There is nothing we can do except wait for news.'

William defeated? It was like seeing one of the eternal verities disproved before her eyes. Even in his worst moments at the troop hospital she had never seen him look stricken as he did now, and nothing since had been too much for his confidence and strength.

'It was an unforgivable thing to say . . . I'm sorry,' she whispered.

'You said what you thought was true!' She hadn't retracted the words, he noticed, only apologized for them.

'Yes, but I wanted to hurt you as well.' The enormity of *that* made her stare at him with eyes full of horror. 'Just for a moment I could ease the nightmare about James by hurting you. That's what war does to people . . . distorts them into all sorts of hateful shapes they didn't know they were capable of.'

'Yes, but it sometimes makes them perform tremendous things they didn't know they were capable of, as well,' he reminded her.

'Like Jamey . . . oh, dear God take care of him.' Tears began to trickle down her white face, and this time when William's arm went out to enfold her she didn't reject the comfort he offered. After a moment or two she raised her head and said again, 'I'm sorry.' His mouth brushed her cheek. 'Don't be,' he said gently.

She walked out of the room, but he didn't move for a long time after she left him. For more than twenty years he'd imagined that he was the sufferer from a marriage that had coupled the wrong two people together; liked to believe that, in the circumstances, he'd behaved better than many men would have done. His wife had had a more than averagely comfortable life, and the frustrations that had driven him almost to bursting point had somehow been kept away from her. Agnes had never seemed anything but content, aware of her good fortune and grateful for it. Wrong . . . all wrong! She was anything but content, and the long charade had been pointless after all. If James didn't come back from his great adventure their marriage wouldn't survive, even as a charade.

When Ano went home after lunch she needed Jos's advice for once.

'She's attached to James . . . I don't know whether to tell her or not about him.'

Jos gave the matter thought. 'Don't see any point,' he decided at last. 'Time enough for her to know if she has to. The lad may come back safe and sound.'

'Well, you'll have to do something about the expression on your face: Otherwise she'll know there's trouble the moment she claps eyes on you.'

Jos did his best and smiled determinedly when Jane came in from school. She kissed him as usual, but her eyes stayed fixed on his face.

'You're upset about something . . . tell me what's wrong.' She felt sickly that it must to do with Brian but couldn't force his name past her tongue.

'Your mother heard some news at the house this morning,' he confessed miserably. 'Seems young James has gone over to Dunkirk . . . to help, like!'

'*James* has? How could he do that? He's at school.' She was inclined not to believe something so far-fetched.

'Cadged a ride on a boat, with another boy. The school rang Mr Marchant.'

It was true after all. Her friend, James, who ought to have been safe at school. 'Now perhaps they'll value him,' she said finally.

Jos thought it an odd thing for her to say. He'd expected her to be upset. Women never did what you thought they were going to do.

'The Marchants? Don't be daft, love . . . of course they value him.'

Jane shook her head. 'Mrs Marchant maybe . . . not the others,' she said definitely and walked out of the room.

'Janey got it out of me,' he murmured helplessly when Ano came back. 'She's walked off somewhere, but she seemed a bit odd . . . I think perhaps I'll go after her.'

'You'll do nothing of the sort. Let her alone.'

Ano sounded sharp as usual, but Jos was aware in her of concern for her daughter and allowed to himself that she probably knew best. But it was a terrible world, no question, when schoolboys went into hell and small girls had to come to terms with adult pain.

Force of habit when seclusion was required led Jane across the Bayswater Road into the green emptiness of Kensington Gardens, but it was a mistake to walk past the tree from which James had rescued her. 'The war's a lark, Janey,' Duncan had said. He'd have changed his mind by now. She'd been excited, to begin with . . . felt self-important to have a brother in the Navy, thought Duncan looked more beautiful than ever in his blue RAF uniform. Even the news of terrible happenings on the Continent hadn't seemed real enough to hurt. But now desolation washed over her like a drowning wave. The sunlit gardens around her went dark, and she crouched with her head on her knees, fighting off faintness. Two small boys squatting by the edge of the Round Pond took it for granted that she was watching what they did, and went back to the task of launching their little boat with immense concentration. She was alone in the darkness that had always terrified her. James had known about that and told her not to be ashamed of being frightened.

'We all have something we're scared of . . . it just happens to be the dark for you,' he'd explained one day.

'Not grown-ups, they're not scared, surely?' She'd been

75

hoping fear was something you grew out of, like a band round your teeth.

'I think so . . . with Mama, it's spiders! She still hates them. But the dark won't hurt you, Janey. There's a poem about it, only I can't remember more than the first line . . . "Fear not the dark, the little tree grows taller in the wood". Think of the tree quietly getting bigger every night.'

She'd thought of it often since, and now the words 'fear not' came back to her with the comfort of a strengthening candle flame. The children's toy boat bobbed towards her and got trapped by a piece of wood floating on the water. She leaned out to free it and send it dancing on its way back to them. It was time to wipe away her tears and go home to Jos.

James arrived back at Poole two days later – tired and hungry, according to his house-master who reported the news to William, but otherwise not much the worse for wear. A gash across his forehead and a damaged wrist could, though, justify his being allowed to come home immediately instead of waiting a few more days for the end of term.

William and Jos found him on the platform at Waterloo, surrounded by all the luggage and bits of equipment that had had to be brought home now that he'd left school for good. William wanted to hug him, told himself that it would be an embarrassment to his son, and frowned instead.

'Convalescence or disgrace?' he asked severely.

James's face split in a sudden grin that made him look eighteen again, rather than an adult stranger whose inward eye was still focused on terrible visions. Proving himself, if Agnes was right, had been an unforgettable business.

'They didn't quite know what to do with us at school. We broke the rules, so punishment seemed to be required. On

76

the other hand, it wasn't exactly joy-riding. In the end the solution seemed to be to pack us off home early.'

He spoke cheerfully but William wondered how long it would take for his eyes to lose that haunted look. Far from despising his younger son, he felt painfully proud of him, but he found himself regretting more than ever the fact that James should want to become an artist. It seemed a waste of such excellent material!

'Was it very bad over there?' he asked after a moment.

'Shambles,' his son said simply. 'But I can't describe how well the men behaved. I was perfectly all right at the time because there was so much to do, but the funny thing is that I kept on being sick when we got back to Poole.' An afterthought apparently occurred to him. 'Any news of Charles?'

'Not yet . . . early days,' said William. 'Everything's in such an appalling muddle, of course.'

James agreed, and turned to smile at Jos, busy stacking luggage on a trolley.

'Morning, Jos . . . how's the Rowland family?'

'Pretty well, thank you, James, and very glad to see you home again in one piece. Janey's been keeping pretty quiet but I think she's been doing a powerful lot of praying.'

His eyes still crinkled in the smile that James had known since childhood, but when he bent down there was a change that hadn't been noticed before. Jos's grizzled hair was beginning to get thin on top. It was a shock to realize that he was growing old, even though it was common knowledge that he was a good deal older than Ano. James's glance shifted to his father's face. New-found clarity showed him differences there as well – skin drawn more tightly over the bones of William's face, accentuating the jut of his beaky nose, eyes sunk more deeply into their sockets. Then a transforming smile softened the hard features.

'Prepare yourself for a hero's welcome, James. The reception committee was gathering already when we left home. Even your grandmother had just arrived!'

'Help! I've never outgrown the effect she has on me. One glare and I'm ten years old again . . . on my way to church and I've lost my money for the collection!'

'If it's any comfort, she has much the same effect on me,' William said frankly.

They arrived in Linden Square just as the wail of an air-raid siren sounded and the reception committee had to disperse hastily. There was time to receive a desperate hug from his mother before Lady Carterton instructed them to make for the shelter in the garden. Family reunions could take place there, she observed firmly, as well as anywhere else. James was grateful for an interruption that staved off the moment when Cecily asked him about Charles. In the end she didn't do so. Another change to be noted – his usually tiresome sister was behaving with a self-restraint that must have been costing her a great deal.

Agnes contented herself with saying very little except 'dear James', but there was no need to fear a lull in the conversation; Lady Carterton had plenty of opinions to air, ranging from the fact that he'd been thoughtless to cause his parents such anxiety to the equal certainty that the French were an undependable nation and the Belgians even worse. Nobody felt inclined to challenge any of these statements, but it was a relief when they heard the blare of the all-clear.

By the middle of June 330,000 troops had been brought back from Dunkirk, but Charles Willoughby was not among them. For as long as possible Cecily clung to the hope that he might have been taken prisoner, but on the day the Germans finally entered Paris she was informed by the War Office that he'd been killed in the retreat. 'The Grenadiers had played a crucial part in holding the perimeter. Without their extraordinary gallantry, in the highest tradition of the regiment, many thousands of men would have been lost, but it was deeply regretted that Captain Charles Willoughby . . .'

It was part of the new strangeness of their lives that the person she shared the news with first was the brother she'd mostly ignored in the past. James had taken himself round to her flat, aware that she was nearly desperate with uncertainty. The War Office letter was still in her lap when he arrived.

'I'm sorry, Cessy,' he said awkwardly. 'Didn't like to mention it before, but I heard some talk about the Guards and the Black Watch and the job they were doing. If it's any comfort at all, the others wouldn't have stood a chance without them.'

She smiled at him with strange brilliance. ' "For the sake of the many a few were lost." A neat little epitaph, wouldn't you say?'

James was only painfully aware of not knowing what to say. She was encased in self-control so fragile, but he thought she would never forgive him or herself if it shattered in front of him.

'Shall I . . . I break the news?' he muttered at last.

'I'll come round soon, but get the worst over for me, please.'

'What about the Willoughbys?'

'I shall have to have an interview with the General, but he'll be easier to cope with than Ma and Pa. The Willoughbys have been professional soldiers for ever . . . how should a son of theirs die except in battle! Oh, God! Go away Jamey, but tell Ma I *won't* be wept over.'

He did as he was told, and even managed to persuade his mother that the best thing she could do was leave Cecily alone. When she arrived in Linden Square the following day she brought the additional news that she had joined the WRNS. She was taut as a bow-string, unbearably calm. Agnes agonized over her secretly, wishing they knew each other better and that she herself didn't always feel inadequate when it came to helping the people she loved so dearly. Cessy might have wept for Charles, but it would have been done in the privacy of her own home. She was as cool and brittle as a piece of glass; love and sympathy could find no grip on such a surface.

William was so like her that he was almost silent about Charles's death, but Agnes was aware of the tormented man beneath the calm facade. His patriotism was real and far from passive. He hated England's enemies and was galled unbearably by his inability nowadays to gird himself and go forth to battle with them. The loss of Charles fanned smouldering rage into flame. It was like living with a volcano on the verge of eruption, until he came in one evening and she detected a change in him.

'You're different,' she said immediately, 'what's happened?'

His smile was slightly shame-faced for once. 'That means I've been like a bear with a sore head recently. Sorry, my dear! What's happened is that I thought I'd try pulling a few strings. Hadn't much hope but I found one or two old friends still at the War House and they've agreed to find a use for me. So I'm rejoining the army. A one-handed man's better than none at all, and it means another able-bodied chap set free to fight.'

'What about Marchant's?'

'Dear old Tom will carry on.'

She gave a little grimace. 'Old Tom Ferguson isn't much older than you are – three years, if I remember correctly.'

William smiled at the unaccustomed dryness. 'True, but admit that he's a very elderly forty-eight! I haven't seen him break into a run for twenty years. I've talked to him, of course; he's quite willing to hold the fort alone.'

Agnes nodded. Willing partner or not, nothing would have stopped William doing what he believed ought to be done. She still looked thoughtful, but Marchant's had disappeared from her mind.

'Do you remember how we used to smile when Joseph explained Brian's extraordinary views? It was true that things weren't very equally organized and we paid lip service to the idea that for some people life needed to be improved. But it didn't enter our heads that it mean *our* comfortable life would have to change.'

She hesitated and William prompted her curiously. 'Yes, I remember, but what's made you think of that now?'

'The fact that I realize Brian was right. Even if . . . when . . . we win this terrible war, nothing is going to be the same. It's true, isn't it, William?'

Every so often she surprised him, making him wonder how much else about Agnes Marchant he didn't know at all.

'It's true up to a point,' he answered slowly. 'But I don't believe for a moment in the wholesale revolution that Brian Rowland used to predict so joyfully. That's not how this country prefers to do things. Changes will come gradually, peacefully.'

He didn't know whether she was convinced because abruptly she asked another question. 'What about Joseph? Can he still drive you to Horse Guards, or wherever it is you'll have to go?'

'It won't be long before there's no petrol for private motoring, so I shall learn to take the twopenny tube like everybody else. In any case, Joseph's got a scheme of his own. He told me about it this morning. He's too old to enlist, but he's going to offer his services as an ambulance-driver. Who better? He must know London like the palm of his hand.'

'What about the rest of us?'

'Ano will go on helping you here, and the Rowlands will continue to live in the cottage in the mews. You'll go on as before.'

'*Nothing* is "as before".' The exclamation was torn out of her with such passionate weariness that William felt ashamed of his own excitement. He was actually looking forward to getting back into uniform again. It was surely the truth that wars were harder on women.

'There's still something else to face,' she went on after a moment. 'The moment when James comes in and tells us that he's not going to St Martin's after all, because the war can't get along without *him* either.'

'My dear, he's eighteen,' William said gently. 'Certain to be called up even if he doesn't volunteer.'

He did volunteer, choosing the Navy as Brian Rowland had done. Agnes suspected that they had the memory of Dunkirk to thank for that. Before James went away he walked round to the mews one morning, determined to visit Jane since she came so seldom now to Linden Square. It was a Saturday, and she was outside, busy polishing the car for Jos. She was unprepared for the sound of his voice behind her, seeming deep and grown-up. At fourteen, she was old enough to wish her hair was tidy, that she wasn't engulfed in one of Brian's old sweaters. A quick glance showed her the healing scar across James's forehead, and the new sternness about his face. Then she looked away again, apparently more interested in the window she was polishing than in talking to him. James remembered Jos saying she'd done some praying for him, but it was hard to believe. It was strange to feel awkward with her, but she was giving him no help. With Duncan it would have been a different matter; one easy smile from his dashing brother and Janey would have been herself again.

'Everything all right at school?'

She merely nodded. 'You've finished for good, Mam says. Lucky you!' End of that subject, apparently, and she stared at the bit of wash-leather in her hand as if it contained the secrets of the universe.

'I'm just off to the place Brian went to in Wales. I only

hope I can understand the language they speak up there.'

'I expect you'll do.' It was one of the expressions she occasionally borrowed from Jos. 'Brian's at sea now ... convoy duty in a destroyer. Mam worries like anything ... we all do.'

'Yes, I dare say.'

Why was it so hard to talk to him? Time was when any thought that came into her head could have been poured out to him. Now all she wanted to do was burst into tears, and what a disgrace *that* would be. James looked away from her strained face and found himself staring at a small clump of children playing ball against the wall of the street air-raid shelter.

'Don't little girls skip any more?' he asked suddenly. 'I remember it was the skipping you always longed to join in.'

'Skipping comes earlier in the year,' she explained with gravity. 'But hopscotch first. *That's* the first thing they play when they come out in the street again after the winter.'

'Shakespeare got it wrong in that case – "daffodils that come before the swallow dares ...". I wonder why he never mentioned hopscotch as a sign of spring?'

'He wasn't a child in London,' she said, suddenly smiling at him. 'How should he have known?' Constraint vanished and she recognised her friend James again.

He held out the package he'd been clutching. 'I came to bring you these. Don't know whether you really want them, but I liked the idea of making you a present of them.'

Her face went white with the pleasure of it. 'Your sketch-books! Of *course* I want them. Oh, James ... I'll take such care of them.'

'If I can, I'll send you some drawings to add to them ... glimpses of Service life!'

She stood with the books cradled in her arms, dark hair blowing about her face – a child known to him all her life, a girl he no longer knew at all.

'Time I was off. I still have to say goodbye to her ladyship.

She's probably getting a little homily ready for me about being bloody, bold and resolute, not being quite sure yet that I've got enough moral fibre!'

'I don't know why she isn't sure . . . you're a bit like her at times.'

The extraordinary idea made him smile and she stared at him, committing his face to memory. With her face lifted he was suddenly moved to duck his head and brush her cheek with his mouth in a kiss that was awkward and sweet. Then he walked away, kicking back to the children a ball that had rolled in front of him.

Jane stood holding the sketchbooks, watching him out of sight even though she knew he wouldn't turn round. Brian, Duncan, and now James . . . all gone away from her into a world that made strangers of them. She often felt quite old, but knew even so that growing-up wasn't done with yet. But if it was going to be more painful than this, she didn't know how she was going to manage it.

Chapter 6

James's departure was one sign of change; William Marchant's appearance in the uniform of an Army major another. It coincided with Jos's life being stood on its head. He became one of a growing army of shift-workers, sleeping during the day and driving his ambulance at night through the darkened streets, and Jane was much too proud of him to conceal the nature of his 'war work'. If driving an ambulance was something the other girls' fathers didn't do, so much the worse for them. She still didn't talk openly about Linden Mews, but no longer mentioned the family in Linden Square either. There were more things to worry about now than Angela Hope-Smythe's opinion of her, and in any case she'd achieved a certain footing of her own. It was accepted that Jane Rowland was a cat who walked by herself; she was friendly and helpful if left in peace, fierce when provoked. Jane had grown used to the idea of being excluded from a charmed circle, even took a certain pride in being slightly different from the rest of them. She was beginning to know who she was at last, and was dimly aware that growing up in the turmoil of war would probably make the painful process easier.

Ano still spent her mornings in Linden Square but always left after lunch to serve meals in a forces' canteen. Jane had the feeling that Mam, like Mr Marchant and Brian, actually relished the strange new life that had been grafted on to their previous one. Brian came home on leave almost unrecognizably changed . . . grubby talkative garage-hand no more. He was now commissioned – a very new sub-lieutenant, it was true, but the dangers of service life suited him, and even discipline was swallowed like a dose that he realized would be good for him. Ano was proud of him, but pride didn't entirely explain the change in *her*. Jane noticed the same change in Major Marchant. Military uniform suited him better than a dark suit and bowler hat, and she sensed in him the spark of excitement that burned in Mam. She'd never realized it before but they were two of a kind, positively enjoying what people like Mrs Marchant and her dear Jos came to terms with because they had to. Jos at least had the satisfaction of doing work that was essential, but for Mrs Marchant there was nothing but anxiety about Duncan and James, and the struggle to cope with domestic tasks taken over from Ano.

'Poor soul . . . you can't 'elp feelin' sorry for 'er,' Edie Bloggs confided to Jane. 'Yorkshire puddin' made out of dried egg and milk powder ain't that easy for *me*, so what chance 'as she got?' Not a lot, Jane feared.

Duncan came home on leave soon after the Germans began bombing raids on the RAF airfields like his own along the south coast. She met him on the corner of the square, paying off his taxi. He was in uniform, but a silk scarf knotted carelessly round his neck reminded her of a pre-war Duncan. She felt sick with the longing to meet him on equal terms for once, to be rid of eternal school blazer and panama hat, to be beautifully grown up.

'Hi, Janey . . . you're looking blooming.'

It sounded bucolic when she'd have preferred to be pale and interesting, but she couldn't help smiling at him all the same. 'You look splendid; I boast about you all the time at school!'

'Quite right too.' She would have lingered but Mrs

Bloggs appeared, bucket in hand, to scrub the front steps and share if she could in the conversation. Duncan was sorry to see Jane go. She was progressing nicely in all sorts of way, but in one way he was glad to see she hadn't changed and hero-worship was as warming as red flannel.

His mother was ready to hero-worship too, and he enjoyed sounding casual about what it was like to be in action for the first time. But when she'd gone to bed William offered him a glass of carefully hoarded whisky and put a question which shattered devil-may-care confidence.

'What's it like up there?'

Duncan took a sip of Perth Royal. 'A hell of a muddle ... a few minutes' screaming confusion and at the end of it you're either dead or alive.' The hand that held his glass trembled slightly. He frowned at it, putting the glass back on the table. 'What are the brass-hats saying? A German invasion before the end of the summer?'

'It looks almost inevitable,' William said slowly. 'Hitler will never have another chance as good as this. Sooner or later America *must* come into the war, and then the odds will change completely. God knows we need them to.'

'He can't invade without being in control of the air. He *has* been up to now, which is why he's been so successful. That means wiping the RAF out first.' It was said calmly enough, but his blue eyes were fixed unseeingly on the cut-glass tumbler under his hand. William wondered what terrible visions he saw instead.

'What about the others ... where are they all?,' Duncan presently roused himself to ask.

'Cessy's commissioned ... at Dover at the moment, where life is unpleasantly noisy!'

'I can believe it.'

'James is still doing initial training at Chatham, but he'll be posted soon.'

'And I suppose young "Red" Rowland is reorganizing some poor sod of a captain's lower deck for him?'

William smiled at the thought, but shook his head. 'By no means! He's been commissioned too, after a nasty spell in the North Atlantic. I don't think he's actually red these days, although nothing will change him from being an out-and-out socialist. Red or blue, the Rowlands are immensely proud of him.'

'Nothing new ... Ano always was. Poor little Jane never got a look in.'

Before William could point out that she didn't now strike him as being either of those things, Duncan reverted to the subject of his twin again. 'Cessy all right? I wrote to her after Charles was killed, but she never answered.'

'I'm not surprised. She doesn't mention his name. Your mother thinks it's a bad way to handle grief, and so do I, but she has to be allowed to cope with it in whatever way she can. Bloody bloody war!'

Next morning, still in his dressing-gown, Duncan wandered downstairs in search of breakfast, and found Jane letting herself into the kitchen by the garden door.

'I'd have brushed my hair if I'd known I was going to have company!' Something different about his smile ... not careless as it used to be, but caressing almost ... made her heart flutter in her breast.

'You're not getting company, exactly,' she managed to explain. 'I'm only passing through with a message for Mrs Marchant. Mam will be here in a moment or two to take care of you.'

She had never seen eyes so blue and bold; it was hard to look away from them.

'You might at least stay until Ano comes. You're supposed to make a fuss of one of England's heroes!'

It was said with an extravagant enough air for her to be able to grin at him again. 'I'm also supposed to go to school!'

An airy wave and she was gone, taking with her the delightful feeling that he'd have liked her to stay. Duncan wanting Janey Rowland to stay – it was the stuff that dreams had been made of.

Within a day or two he was back with his squadron, and almost immediately his prediction to William began to come true. The prelude to an invasion was to be the destruction of the RAF. Waves of German bombers crossed the Channel every day, with London as their target. In order to protect the capital the Spitfires and Hurricanes must go up to meet them, to be overwhelmed by flocks of Messerschmitts hanging like hungry hawks in the sky above the bombers. The Battle of Britain was well and truly joined, and it was a battle unlike any other – a screaming tangled mass of aeroplanes, tracer bullets, and smoke painted on the blue of heaven. People watched it from the ground, too hypnotized to think of taking cover.

'Hitler's got to wipe out the RAF,' Duncan had said, but the summer days of 1940 went by and still the little aeroplanes with their roundels of red, white and blue outflew and outfought the odds massed against them. Invasion fever lay over the land, coupled with a strange sense of elation. Those summer days were terrible ones in which to be alive, but no one from Churchill downwards doubted that they were splendid as well.

The invasion didn't come, but more and more bombers came instead. Ano knew the moment had come to swallow pride and take herself and Jane to the communal shelter in the street. It was irritating, and late in the day, to find that she'd been wrong about her neighbours; even silly Edna Cooper stayed calm, and turned out to be unexpectedly likeable. In the racket going on around them they learned to distinguish between the rain-shower sound of a flock of descending incendiaries and the whistle that heralded a high-explosive bomb. Land-mines were bigger, and therefore nastier, and there was the hazard of bombs that didn't explode on landing. They grew accustomed to the din of an anti-aircraft battery in the park, and stumbled out of the shelter at the sound of the all-clear into the familiar reek of cordite in the air.

Sometimes the interval between the wail of the siren and the throb of the first bomber overhead was very short – so short one morning that by mutual consent Ano and Mrs Bloggs made for the kitchen table against the inside wall of the house. For once armed neutrality was forgotten. They'd been awe-inspiringly formal with one another since the day Edie arrived and made the mistake of referring to Ano by her Christian name.

'The name is *Mrs* Rowland,' Ano had pointed out coldly.

'Sorry, I'm sure.' Offended, Mrs Bloggs had been on the point of walking out, but she'd remembered Bert laid up at home – no time to be proud, it wasn't. That had been five years ago. She was still there, liking Mrs Marchant, loving Jane, and relishing her daily skirmishes with Ano. Her figure had thickened considerably and the kitchen table was barely adequate. Thinking of Jane, she pushed Ano under the table first. There wasn't much room left and her backside would have to take its chance. A deafening explosion and the usual sickening sensation of the house around them being lifted on its foundations before settling down again ... it had been close, that one. Ano heard the crash of glass breaking, then nothing except a groan behind her.

'Edie—' there was a war on and protocol was forgotten '—you all right?'

She turned round and saw Mrs Bloggs' face behind her screwed up in agony. 'You're not all right ... you've been hurt.'

Edie backed out slowly, hand pressed to her bosom. 'Nothin to worry about, ducks. Times like these I keep my best brooch on, but the pin come undone and jabbed me!

Bert always says vanity'll be the death of me!' The sound of another approaching whine sent them back under the table again.

'Where's Janey?' Edie wanted to know when the next explosion had rocked the house but left it still standing.

'Back at school. They'll be in the shelter till the all-clear goes.'

'Soddin Germans, makin' little kids grow up in this. As for bein' invaded, let one of 'em land in me back yard and I'll be out there with a kitchen knife an' no mistake.'

Ano didn't doubt it, looking at the heavy stubborn face beside her. It hadn't occurred to her before, but Lady Carterton and Edie Bloggs had a lot in common; if they didn't have a knife handy, a rolling-pin would do. The all-clear sounded and they crawled out, swept up the glass littering the kitchen floor, and made themselves a reviving pot of tea – friends at last, smiling at one another.

The raid was almost the last of the regular day-time ones. In the hope of reducing losses of planes and air-crew, German tactics switched to night bombing. Londoners adapted themselves to a new existence, sleeping in their own Anderson shelters, or communally underground in the deep-level tube stations. Jane sat with Ano, knitting with difficulty in the dim light, thinking of Jos steering his ambulance through the darkness and dreadfulness outside. The nights were long, a mixture of boredom, discomfort and sudden flurries of fear, and there seemed no reason why they should ever change. She had the feeling that they would live like this for ever more – go to bed in a bunk in the shelter and walk home in the morning scuffing through spent bits of shrapnel.

One night there *was* a change: St Olave's was hit and had to be closed for repair. With nothing to hurry for she took her time about helping to tidy the shelter, walked slowly home to find Mam talking to the Major.

'Morning, Jane . . . noisy night again!'

'Yes, but Mr Edmunds says it'll be quiet tonight. Should be a full moon.' Her pale face grinned at the prospect but Ano set no store by Jack Edmunds. 'It'll be bedlam in that case. Have you ever known him right yet?'

The Major was looking at Jane. Agnes was right – it was time she had a break from air-raids, and a little duplicity could be excused to ensure that she got it.

'I've got a favour to ask, Jane. I want Mrs Marchant to go down to the country for a little while – she badly needs a rest. But she won't go on her own. Would you keep her company at River Cottage, just while St Olave's is being repaired?'

'You mean . . . leave Jos and Mam behind?'

He nodded, aware that the idea was finding no favour. 'Just for a little while. I wanted your mother to go too, but she insists on staying behind.'

Jane badly wanted to insist as well, but Mrs Marchant was her friend and friends had to be helped on occasion.

'I'll go for a day or two,' she agreed finally. 'After that I'm coming home.'

They all left London on a fine still Sunday morning – Jos driving the car, the Major going to make sure they were safely installed at the cottage, and Ano invited along for the rare pleasure of a ride. Golden September light lay over the battered city, and the barrage balloons hung motionless in the sky – silver fish put under a spell of stillness. The journey had to take account of hazards along the way – a broken water-main here, an unexploded bomb there – but Jos wove his way calmly round the obstacles, chatting to the Guvnor beside him. Jane sat in the back with Mrs Marchant and her mother, torn as usual by too many emotions. She couldn't help being excited at the prospect of going to River Cottage but it fought with the misery of knowing that Jos would drive back to London without her at the end of the afternoon.

She wouldn't cry – she'd made up her mind to that – or disgrace Mam by sticking her toes in at the last minute and refusing to be left behind. She was too old now to be making scenes. It would have helped, though, if conversation in the back of the car had been as easy as it seemed to be in the front; for some reason she didn't understand, it wasn't. James's sketch-books on her knees were her only comfort. Mam had been sharp about lumbering up the car with them, but she'd had no intention of leaving them behind. She sat quiet, not knowing what to say, but soon another anxiety began to plague her – the shaming fear that she might need to be sick long before they got to Long Wittenham. She hiccupped, swallowed hard, knew that she was fighting a losing battle with nausea. William Marchant turned round and saw her face, clammy and deathly white. He murmured something to Jos, and the car was pulled into the side of the road.

'Plenty of room in front, Jane, and you'll see more,' he said casually. 'Why not come in here with us?'

The breath of fresh air achieved in making the exchange saved her, and sitting in the front afterwards seemed to make all the difference. She glanced gratefully at the man beside her, now chatting to Jos again. He looked her way unexpectedly, caught her staring at him and solemnly winked – no doubt about it, it was definitely a wink. Funny, in all the years she'd been scuttling in and out of the house in Linden Square she'd never got to know the man Jos called the Guvnor. A bit alarming, she'd always thought him, and he hadn't understood about James wanting to be an artist. But he did understand about people who felt sick in cars. Now that she was able to take an interest in the journey he talked to her as well as Jos. Finally they crossed a placid stream flowing gently between fields greener than any green of a London park, even in springtime. The Major smiled when she mentioned this.

'They're water-meadows, Janey, and therefore some-times completely submerged, thanks to the River Thames.'

The Thames ... this rivulet? She was tempted not to believe him; couldn't, at least, hide the disappointment in her face.

'Old Father Thames is only a youngster here,' her guide explained. 'You're used to seeing him at Westminster Bridge when he's in his prime!'

The road ran beside the river for a mile or two, twisted about with it in sympathy, then veered absent-mindedly away, forgetting that it had intended to keep the water company.

'Long Wittenham High Street,' announced the Major. She thought of the High Street, Kensington, familiar to her since childhood, then stared at a row of cottages sleeping peacefully in the sun. Could this really be a high street, or was he making fun of her? It hadn't occurred to her before that he would have James's trick of laughing with a straight face, but it must be so, because she was suddenly sure that she was being invited to share the joke with him. In the same moment she noticed that his face looked very tired ... she was glad she hadn't made a fuss about coming after all.

When Jos stopped the car in front of River Cottage, it was like no house she'd ever seen before. Whitewashed and thickly thatched, its small dormer windows in the roof were almost lost in a bristling fringe of thatch. More hedgehog than house, and only half-awake at that. You couldn't look at it without smiling, she thought. Inside, there were odd small flights of stairs and unexpected cor-ners where light fell on polished wood and the scent of lavender and beeswax lingered. Once seen, it wasn't a house to be forgotten, but there was a bad moment, all the same, when she watched Jos settle Ano and the Major in the car and drive away.

'Come and look at James's tree,' Agnes Marchant suggested gently, after a glance at her desolate face. 'He planted it the first day we arrived here and already it's taller than he is.'

Jane followed her blindly across a terrace and out into the garden. The grass was shaggy and needed mowing, and the borders were untidy as well, but beautifully aflame with the colours of autumn – bronze, crimson and gold chrysanthemums, lanced here and there with the mauve spires of Michaelmas daisies. Where the ground began to shelve towards the river stood a willow tree, small as yet but fully aware that one day soon it was going to be a very fine tree indeed. Jane stared at its trailing stems, already beginning to drip tiny yellow leaves on the grass; it would be nice if James were here. Her glance shifted to the river quietly ambling past, and the birch trees on the far bank, being turned to gold by the last of the evening sunlight.

'It's very peaceful,' she said at last, 'not much like London.'

'No, but I dare say London is where you'd rather be. It's kind of you to keep me company.'

Jane was accustomed to Mrs Marchant's soft voice, that never gave the impression of saying anything important enough to be listened to. Now, though, she caught an echo of something that *was* important, suddenly struck by the idea that made her stare at the woman who'd so unexpectedly become a friend.

'The Major said come to stop you being lonely, but I don't think that's it at all; are we here because of me?'

Agnes Marchant's faded blue eyes stopped looking at the river and focused instead on the face in front of her. She was reminded of the fact that Jane noticed things – not only noticed but thought about them, pondering the strange ways in which grown-ups behaved. It made her a more interesting companion than children of her age usually were, but there were matters now that Agnes hoped she wouldn't notice.

'Let's say we're here for the general good,' she suggested oddly, then smiled at Jane. 'There's no reason why we shouldn't enjoy it as well!'

Chapter 7

Jos's state of misery when he drove away roughly equalled Jane's and it was a relief when the Guvnor settled himself courteously in the back of the car with Ano. Neither of *them* seemed talkative either, which didn't surprise Jos; one of the nastiest things about a war was that you were always saying goodbye to people.

Finally William roused himself to murmur to the woman by his side, 'Mrs Marchant seems to think I'm not capable of getting myself something to eat . . . she insists that you'll be kind enough to keep an eye on me.'

He hadn't meant to look at Ano, didn't know how it came about that he watched a slow smile touch her mouth.

'Of course . . . it's my job to . . . keep an eye on you.'

He looked away again, but the memory of her mouth stayed in his mind's eye – short curving upper lip, full lower one with the hint of a dimple in it; not easy to forget, Ano Rowland's mouth.

The following evening he was firm with himself; stayed so late working at his desk that he could be certain she'd have left by the time he got home. Resolution held the next evening, too. He forced himself to pay a duty visit to his mother-in-law. They ate some dreadful vegetarian mess, and then played interminable games of whist. Hilda Carterton made it clear that she disapproved of her daughter being in the country.

'I can't think what Agnes is doing at the cottage. She ought to be with you here in London.'

'She wanted to give young Jane Rowland a rest from nights spent in air-raid shelters; they're by way of being great friends. Apart from that, Agnes herself needs a rest. That continual Ack-Ack racket gets her down.'

Lady Carterton looked as if nothing got her down. Offered relief in the country too, she'd flatly refused to leave London.

'*You* look a bit frayed, William,' said the Job's comforter opposite him. 'You're not as young as you were, despite that smart uniform!'

It was maddening but true! He smiled at her with an effort that made his jaws ache, and pointed out that it was her turn to lead.

Afterwards, walking home through the dark streets, her remark came back to him. It was cruelly true that youth had been spent in an earlier war, and his prime in all the frustrating years since, but dear God, surely he wasn't beyond being pleased or giving pleasure?

It wasn't conscious thought but instinct that drove him into clearing his desk as quickly as possible the following afternoon. On the way back from the underground station at Notting Hill Gate he almost broke into a run. Perhaps he still hadn't come early enough? But when he burst into the house she was there, laying a solitary place for him in the dining room.

She smiled at the sight of him, as though she couldn't help herself, but said what any privileged servant might have been expected to say.

'Fish-pie this evening! It's a red-letter day when the fish-monger has cod on offer.'

William waited for his heart to stop thumping, then walked to the decanter on the sideboard and poured sherry into two glasses. 'If it's a red-letter day, we ought to drink to it.' He handed a glass to her, and stood watching her over the rim of his own. Was he wrong, after all? She sounded so matter-of-fact and calm.

'It's not much of a day for Jos, I'm afraid,' she remarked, after a slow sip of wine. 'Someone's away sick . . . he's had to go on duty early.'

Still nothing in her voice helped him but he could wait no longer.

'Ano, will you . . . please . . . forget the fish-pie and come to bed with me?'

He could hear his own heart beating, but no other sound in the room. Ano was so still, he could scarcely believe she was breathing. Oh, Christ, he *had* been wrong!

'Shall I take back an insulting suggestion . . . apologise for raking up a past we ought to have forgotten?'

At last she looked at him. 'Don't apologise. It's just that it's been such a long time . . . I'd come to believe it would never happen. I can't believe it now.'

The yearning in her voice halted him in the act of walking towards her. At this moment in time he wanted above everything else in life to make love to her, but what Ano wanted from him was a great deal more than that; he felt shamed by the difference in their amounts of need.

'Ano, my dear . . . don't expect too much. There's an opportunity in front of us for a little happiness that it seems madness to waste. But if I'm being intolerably selfish, say so and I'll leave you alone.'

'I want you to be as selfish as you like . . . I don't care about anything as long as you'll love me.' The tears that had remained unshed for twenty years ran down her face but she didn't even notice them. It was William who wiped them away, and then led her upstairs. He couldn't think of Agnes or Jos. There was nothing in the world but this need between them that must at last be satisfied.

Two evenings later James turned the corner of Linden Square with a forty-eight-hour pass in his pocket and good news he was bursting to share. Midshipman Marchant, in a brand-new reefer jacket white-tabbed on the lapels, had done well enough in preliminary training to be selected for a navigation course at Greenwich. From there to the job he wanted – deck officer on a destroyer – was only a stretch of hard work away in James's present mood of citadel-storming self-confidence. Pity that Mama and Janey were both away . . . he'd have liked most of all to talk to them; but he liked the idea of them being together at River Cottage. It was tempting to go down, but time was too short.

He let himself into the house and saw an army service cap thrown down on the hall table, but all the ground-floor rooms were empty when he looked in. He climbed the stairs and saw the door of his father's room open. Clothes, shed hastily, were strewn over the bed. His mother's bedroom door was closed. For a moment he thought she'd come back already, but even without putting the idea into words in his mind, there was something that instinct couldn't accept . . . he wasn't sure that his parents ever shared a bed, but if they did do so, it wouldn't be at six o'clock in the evening. In any case there was a certain feel about the house when his mother was in it, and it was absent now. He didn't want to know who was there instead. Then the sound of his father's laugh was answered by a woman's clear voice . . . Ano Rowland's voice.

'Turned to stone' – ridiculous cliché he'd always thought it, used by writers too lazy to think of an original phrase; only it wasn't ridiculous at all. He was incapable of moving in case he blundered into something and made a noise. It needed the worse fear of having one of them suddenly emerge from the bedroom and find him there to finally unlock frozen muscles. He was out of the house before he remembered his bag, then discovered it still clutched in his hand because he hadn't even put it down anywhere. He felt clammy with sweat but cold as well, and utterly confused about what to do next. Go back to the house and bang loudly on the door? His stomach heaved at the thought of his father scrambling into clothes and making conversation with him while Ano dressed and hurried down the back stairs. His grandmother would give him a bed, but what could be the explanation for not going to Linden Square? Almost without conscious thought he flagged a taxi and asked for Paddington Station – it was going to be River Cottage after all.

There was an Oxford train almost pulling out of the station. He even remembered to ask the guard to stop for him at Culham. Then there was nothing to do but sit hunched in his corner seat and think. At a safe distance from the house it was easier to be rational and fair, and James was anxious to be both. The stress of wartime life knocked normal life to hell, but there was something else to be admitted as well; his parents' marriage had been far from normal, and for as long as he'd been able to mull things over to himself he'd accepted the fact that there were tensions he didn't understand below the surface of their family life. His gentle-seeming mother needed those stormy sessions at the piano to relieve some stress that weighed on her, and William's outlet had been in work, but James didn't blame him if it hadn't been enough. He felt less inclination to be fair to Ano; perhaps he'd never liked her because of the fear, dimly recognized, that she was a woman who would enjoy going to extremes. Finally, there was Jos. He was the sticking-point, James decided. He hated his father and Ano equally for betraying Jos.

The journey was slow, but he sat through it unaware of the sympathetic glances of an ATS girl in the seat opposite. Nice-looking, she thought him; striking, really, with that tumbled dark hair and nice straight nose. Pity he didn't seem to notice her, though she probably looked like death in the dreadful blue-painted light in the compartment. Persistence was rewarded at last and he smiled when she caught his eye, but the guard yelled, 'Culham . . . somebody asked for Culham,' and he stood up hurriedly, said good-night and leapt out.

The soft autumn twilight was all about him and he was glad of the prospect of the walk across the meadows to Long Wittenham; time to rehearse why he'd decided not to stay in London. But the vicar got off the train as well.

'Well met, James . . . I can give you a lift, dear boy. I'm allowed a little petrol for my visiting! Come to see your mother, no doubt. She'll be glad. Got a nice child staying with her at the moment, but I expect you knew that.'

There was no need to say anything at all; the vicar's gentle monologues never required answering. His style of driving was all his own too, and James took firm hold of the door handle as they drifted gently from one side of the road to the other. But they finally ambled into the village with the vicar still talking and only a rabbit or two congratulating themselves on running the right way.

River Cottage seemed in darkness, but James's knock on the door was answered immediately by the sound of foot-steps on the stone flags in the hall. His mother stood peering out, stared at his new uniform which she didn't recognize in the dim light, and finally smiled with the warmth that transfigured her face when she was sure love was returned. She was sure about James.

'Darling . . . oh, well done! You've gone up in the world, I see. I didn't dream you'd be able to come.'

'Forty-eight hours of freedom before I start a new course at Greenwich. It seemed worth . . . rushing down.'

With the black-out in place again, she turned up the light to look at him.

'You're fearfully smart! But, dearest, how tired you look. Bed straightaway, I should think, or would you like a cup of cocoa, or something? It disguises powdered milk quite well!'

'Bed, please, Mama. A ride in the vicar's car is enough to shatter anyone; he picked me up at Culham.'

'We can usually think of a pressing reason why we don't need a lift . . . but there's so little traffic on the road that he never seems to do any harm! The water's still fairly hot if you want a bath . . . I can be making up a bed for you.'

When he re-emerged, she was waiting in his bedroom.

'I brought the cocoa anyway . . . you look a bit on the thin side, as well as tired.'

He had his back to her, opening the window, when she asked the inevitable question.

'Was your father all right? I suppose you called in to see him.'

'No, I didn't see him.' It was true, after all. 'It seemed a nice idea to come down here.'

'I'm glad you did, but I hope he's not too lonely.'

Lost in reflections of his own, James missed a note in her voice that he might otherwise have wondered about. 'How's Janey?' he asked by way of changing a subject that looked strewn with difficulties.

'Much better. Not nearly so bomb-haunted, and such marvellous company. It was her idea that we should both learn to ride a bicycle. I don't think she intended that we should keep the rest of the village in a state of helpless mirth, but that seems to have been the result. She's perfectly competent already, but she rides behind me like a collie escorting a particularly stupid sheep!'

'Dear Mum,' said James suddenly, who almost never called her that, 'I'm glad I came.'

She smiled at him and went away leaving him to what he expected would be a sleepless night, but his next conscious thought was the sound of the long-case clock in the hall striking nine the following morning. When he went downstairs the house was empty, but he could see his mother in the garden calling up to someone invisible above her head – Jane, no doubt, remembering her fondness for sitting in trees. He walked out into a typical Thames Valley morning, misty and slightly damp, smelling of cut hay, bonfires, and the dankness of the river twenty yards away.

Agnes smiled as he walked towards her. 'We acquired a kitten yesterday, by courtesy of the farm cat across the road. In the way of kittens, it seems to be able to get up trees but not down them; at the moment Jane is required to help.'

An arm appeared a moment later, offering them a ball of orange-coloured fur. When it was safely transferred, Jane herself slithered down to the ground.

'Just like old times, Janey.'

On the ground she looked taller than he remembered, but there were other changes. Her clear skin was touched by the sun to the colour of honey, and instead of the urchin haircut of the past her dark hair now lay in fronds against her head, like the petals of a chrysanthemum. These were surface changes, but he sensed as well that some watershed separating childhood from adolescence had been passed. For a moment the muddles of Linden Square were pushed out of his mind by the sheer pleasure of seeing her again.

Jane had known since she got up that he'd arrived, but knowing was one thing, seeing him there another when she felt so unsure of him. She was going on fourteen, but he was almost a stranger, a young man who'd now taken a great leap away from her. It was a relief to take Marmaduke back in her arms again, something to hold on to.

'They don't feed you very well in the Navy . . . you're all skin and bones.' Daft thing to have said, she thought. Why not 'Hello, James . . . you're looking very well?' Janey still sometimes got the upper hand of Miss Jane Rowland. She saw his expression change, but didn't know that it was because a note in her voice had suddenly reminded him of Ano. The sudden blankness in his face catapulted her back in time to the evening of Cecily's birthday party, being snubbed because she'd forgotten what her place was in the

104

scheme of things. It was happening again, because she still kept forgetting. She was staying at River Cottage as a guest, but that didn't change anything. Jos's daughter was being given a treat, and James ... James of all people, resented her being there.

Agnes looked from one to the other of them. They'd been such friends, but now something seemed to be wrong. 'Breakfast, James?' she suggested quickly. 'We can manage toast and coffee for you, and some of Mrs Middleton's honey ... I'm almost sure it's illegal, but I'm careful not to enquire!'

Jane watched them go into the house together, aware that his coming had spoiled things. She was homesick suddenly, seized by a wild longing to walk back to Jos. Still clutching Marmaduke, she wandered out of the gate, half-thinking that it might be best just to keep going, but Mrs Middleton was waving to her from across the road. It didn't seem feasible, somehow, to walk to London clutching a kitten and the three new-laid eggs that the farmer's wife had just insisted on giving her because James was home.

She went back into the cottage and put the eggs carefully on the kitchen table.

'What the eye of the Egg Marketing Board doesn't see, its heart won't grieve over, according to Mrs Middleton,' she reported solemnly. 'The nest has been raided for James.'

'It was pitch-dark when I arrived ... how did she know I was here?'

She grinned at the surprise in his face, feeling less strange with him. 'You're forgetting the vicar. He'll have reported by now that you look ... ah, splendid don't you know ... in your new uniform'!

Along with the speed of the village bush telegraph, he'd forgotten her gift for mimicry. He was about to describe the journey back from Culham to her, but she was following a line of thought of her own. 'I'm sure you do look splendid, just as Brian does . . . but I hope you haven't forgotten that you're going to be an artist when the war's over.'

The words were out of her mouth before she remembered that she'd forgotten her place again . . . like as not he'd be asking himself why he'd ever been fool enough to confide in Janey Rowland. But there was no coldness in his face when he smiled at her.

'I hadn't forgotten, as it happens. If I can still remember how to draw I'll go back to trying to be an artist again.'

She nodded and walked out of the room into the garden with the kitten. After a moment or two James asked his mother the question that was weighing on him.

'How much longer are you and Janey staying here?'

'I'm not sure . . . a few more days probably, until we hear that St Olave's is reopening. Does it matter . . . are you likely to get home again soon?'

'I'll be at Greenwich from now on . . . able to nip up now and again for a night in London. But I suppose I was thinking of Pa . . . you said he might be getting lonely.' His voice sounded mildly concerned, any other emotion carefully ironed out of it.

'Yes . . . but we shall go back soon, in any case,' Agnes said vaguely. 'Jane loves it here, but she's beginning to get restive. Much as she likes the idea of becoming a land-girl, there's Jos. She can't see any way of combining the country with keeping her eye on him!'

'You get on very well with her, don't you?' he asked abruptly.

'Better than I ever did with Cecily.' The admission was surprised out of her. 'The odd thing is that it ought to have been *more* difficult, not less; but Jane's a constant joy to me, and I can't get near enough to my own daughter to help her with losing Charles.' In case it had sounded too wistful, she smiled at him and changed the subject. 'Are you feeling deedy? There are some little things that need doing, if so!'

One of them was a broken window catch in Jane's bedroom, which he attended to while she was out collecting bread from the village shop. It was the little room that had once been Cecily's . . . now scrupulously neat, as he would have expected, and almost bare of possessions. But he smiled at the sight of his sketchbooks carefully stacked on the table by the window. Her only other treasures were a handful of books and a set of photographs ranged along the top of the chest of drawers – Jos caught inspecting his precious window-boxes, Ano in her beautiful green hat, presumably taken on the day of Cecily's wedding, and a much more recent picture of Brian, already wearing his sub-lieutenant's uniform. It was a very good photograph and James stared at it for a long time. Then he replaced it carefully where it had been, and applied himself to the problem of the window-catch.

When the time came for him to leave and he'd kissed his mother goodbye, Jane stood stroking Marmaduke. Once upon a time it would have been the most natural thing in the world to announce that she was going to walk with him as far as the Oxford road. Now, nothing seemed to be natural between them.

'Walk a little way with me, Janey?' he suggested gently.

She nodded, and walked ahead of him out of the gate. There were people to wave to in the village street, conversation wasn't needed until they were on the path bordering the river. Then he took hold of her hand . . . she was eleven again, and they were going to the National Gallery to look at paintings so that she would understand. Only his face wasn't the face of the boy who'd taken her to see Duccio's beautiful grave Madonna. He looked stern and sad.

'Don't worry about Mrs Marchant, James . . . I'll take care of her for you.'

'What made you say that?' The question was asked so sharply that she felt snubbed again, and disappointed that *he* no longer understood things.

'Only because . . . because you love her and looked sad when you said goodbye.'

The expression on her face when he glanced at her said clearly that he ought to have been able to work that out for himself. She was right, of course, but just at the moment there was so much that had to be worked out. He might have said so, but a passing van stopped to offer him a lift. There was only time to stoop and leave an apologetic kiss on her cheek before he climbed in.

'Be careful, James . . .' She doubted if he even heard. He was whirled away from her, the sun had gone in, and suddenly she felt cold and sad.

Chapter 8

Sub-Lieutenant Brian Rowland had thought himself lucky to get posted to an MTB flotilla of Coastal Forces, and had no fault to find with the base at Lowestoft, until the night came when he discovered that the past had caught up with him. After a run of nights at sea in thick weather, the skies cleared and a full moon rose in splendour. No German convoy would try to sneak down through the North Sea from Norway to one of the French ports, and no MTBs would be required to go out and try to intercept it. For once it could be a civilized evening in the mess, with people to talk to and, greatest luxury of all, a night's sleep in bed instead of catnaps during the day.

He was standing at the bar, feeling warm and relaxed, when a clear voice behind him cut through the buzz of conversation in the room. The sound of it was enough to make him falter in the story he was telling to the man by his side ... memory showed him a grubby garage-hand; even worse, a grubbier schoolboy scraping up manure after the milkman's horse had trundled round Linden Square. He told himself he was a fool. The voice he'd heard was like a thousand others of its kind, cool and slightly arrogant. It could belong to almost anyone; but it belonged to Cecily Willoughby. He turned round to convince himself that it wasn't her and there she was, staring at him.

'Well, blow me down if it isn't young "Red" Rowland! I don't usually believe all this talk of a small world.'

She was enjoying herself, he thought; aware that he'd been caught on the wrong foot and, true to form, glad of the fact. She was aware of something else as well. A Wren officer's uniform did her white and gold beauty nothing but good, and a confident smile said that its dark severity might have been invented for no other reason than to throw her skin and dazzling hair into perfect relief. It was almost a pleasure to remember how much he'd always hated her.

He put down his glass, pulled a lock of black hair with exaggerated deference, and then deliberately resumed his own conversation again. But he watched her in the mirror behind the bar. She went back to talking to the man she was with, but looked up suddenly and their eyes met in the glass. There was a faint flush in her cheeks and an added sparkle in her blue eyes, put there by anger. Good! It was something to have irritated her. He wasn't going to be upstaged by Cecily Willoughby, née Marchant . . . in fact, he wasn't going to have anything to do with her at all. And that wouldn't be hard to arrange. The other women on the base must loathe her as much as he did, but the men would certainly be queueing up for the pleasure of being trampled on.

He spent the next night at sea, got back to eat a huge breakfast in the mess the following morning in time to see her come in and help herself to toast and coffee. She looked tired after a night on duty, brightness laid aside because she was alone, with no one to impress. The night had been unpleasant, and he supposed that it was gratitude for being safely back again and warm and dry that made him get to his feet and pull out a chair for her at the table. For a moment he thought she was going to snub him by ignoring it, conceded to himself that it would have been no more than he deserved, But she hesitated only briefly, then slid into the chair he held for her.

'Thanks,' she murmured. 'Roughish night it's been . . . no doubt more so for you.'

'The reception on the other side was a trifle warm, let's say.'

110

'I didn't know you were here . . . Mama didn't say. Perhaps she didn't know either.'

It seemed to be all the conversation she felt inclined for but he had the impression that he called to mind memories that defeated her. He pushed his empty plate away, and sat nursing a mug of coffee between his hands.

'I'm sorry about Charles Willoughby . . . Ano told me.' He hadn't known that that was what he was going to say, wished it hadn't sounded so curt and mechanical. Brian Rowland at a loss for words . . . his fellow spouters at pre-war socialist meetings wouldn't have believed that.

'Thanks,' she said with equal briefness. 'My little brother made an unexpected visit to Dunkirk as well . . . did you hear about that?'

'Jane told me.' He was about to say that James had done rather well, but when he glanced at her she was unaware of him. In the grip of some inward vision of desolation that couldn't always be buried under a desperate determination to be the life and soul of every party, he thought she wouldn't have noticed if he'd fallen off the chair at her feet. There was nothing for it but to make her angry again.

'Intrepid of James . . . who'd have thought the artist had so much spirit in him?'

It came out as even more of a sneer than he'd actually intended, but had the desired effect; she rose like a salmon gulping down a fly.

'You think the artist is even more effete than the rest of us, I suppose? Down with the middle classes and up with the Working Man! Like all revolutionaries, you feel obliged to tie labels on people. The Marchant label says "no use to anyone . . . kindly throw away".'

The jibe didn't bother him at all, she noticed; in fact he looked amused and very self-possessed. 'Red' Rowland had come a long way, now that she bothered to think about it. Even after a night without sleep energy seemed coiled inside him like a spring. He was ready for anything and made the other men around him seem only half alive.

'Blame the simple mind of a working-class revolutionary!' he suggested affably. 'Everything has to be labelled black or white because he hasn't got time to stop and sort out shades of grey.'

'He hasn't got time, you mean, for anyone who doesn't bang his own dreary drum. We must all toe the party line . . . life is real and earnest, brother; never mind about love and laughter, and things that have no social message . . . it isn't enough that they should just be beautiful.'

They'd come a long way from Charles Willoughby and Dunkirk, but at least she was herself again, with anger adding the last electrifying touch to her beauty. He was astonished to find that he wanted to tell her so. That would never do at all.

'I've nothing against anything that's "just" beautiful,' he said instead. 'I only want the good things of life shared round a bit, that's all. A bit less for people like the Marchants, a bit more for everybody else.'

'I suspect you mean none for the Marchants . . . your brave new world won't find a place for people like us.'

'Oh, I wouldn't quite say that.' Meeting his bright amused eyes, she thought she knew what the place might be. It was time to deliver some lightly, brightly crushing piece of repartee, but for once nothing came to mind and she was only conscious of feeling sad and tired. She brushed crumbs from her skirt and stared at her watch. 'Bedtime at seven a.m. It's an Alice-in-Wonderland sort of life . . . no wonder we're all in such a muddle.'

'For an effete Marchant it strikes me that you're doing rather well!'

She suspected him of sarcasm, expected to see it in his smile. But his face was grave, and it was almost possible to imagine that he'd meant what he'd just said. She wasn't used to men who moved from laughter to sincerity as easily as this one did; in fact he didn't resemble the men

112

she was used to in any way at all, except that somehow he'd acquired their air of social ease. Linden Mews seemed a very long way away, but if he disowned it she'd still be able to despise him.

'We'll continue the revolutionary argument another day . . . it's time you went to bed.'

She nodded and finally walked away, aware that he still watched her. It was something to remember that she'd inherited her mother's long slender legs. Clad in black silk stockings instead of Service lisle, there was nothing to regret about Marchant legs!

The mess at Lowestoft was small, and shared ground for RNVR and WRNS officers, so that it would have been hard to avoid him if she'd wanted to. She found she didn't particularly want to, but it was irritating that he made no attempt at all to remind her that they knew one another. If he paid her any attention, it was only when she insisted on being noticed, and then he treated her with an air of humble deference that annoyed her and, she suspected, amused him. One evening it even penetrated the slightly gin-hazed attention of the lieutenant she was with.

'Brian treats you like a d – duchess. W – why, Cessy? You're g – gorgeous, but not a d – duchess, as far as I know.'

She was aware of his considering eye, daring her to say that his mother was *her* mother's cook at home. It ought to have been possible to drawl that wars made strange mess-fellows of people, that he was a servant's son who found it amusing to try to embarrass her. For a moment or two during that breakfast-time conversation he'd almost laid hostility aside, but there'd been enough time since to remember that he hated the Marchants and couldn't resist baiting them. All the same, she found she couldn't say what he expected her to say.

"We needs must love the highest when we see it," she quoted after a moment. 'I expect, Rusty dear, that the sub-lieutenant is overcome by admiration.'

Rusty stared from her to Brian, dimly aware that in some way he didn't understand he'd got himself between the points of opposing rapiers.

'You disappoint me, Cessy,' drawled Brian. 'For a moment I thought you were going to have the courage to say that I'm the son of the family chauffeur and cook-general, who's supposed to know his place.'

'It's just what he *doesn't* know,' she flashed. 'Perhaps we could agree to stay out of each other's way in future?'

'Suits me.' He bowed respectfully, then grinned at the sight of her towing the unhappy Rusty away. The poor chap was much too nice for her; now that he thought of it, she needed someone like Red Rowland to keep her under control!

His flotilla was at sea almost every night after that, for a concentrated spell of duty that reduced life to a series of uncomfortable nerve-racking nights, and days spent in catching an hour or two of sleep and getting boats ready for the next order to put to sea. Cecily's own work in the control room left her with too much knowledge of what was going on; she found herself charting with relief the safe return of MTB 399 each morning. She wanted all the boats back undamaged, of course, but for Jos and Ano's sake it would have been unbearable to know that this one had gone missing.

An evening came when the roughness of the weather cancelled the night's operation. Tired bodies and taut nerves could briefly relax. Common sense recommended a quiet dinner and a good night's sleep, but the sound of music and laughter drew a man who'd had his fill of nights spent dodging about the North Sea. An impromptu dance was in progress in the mess, and Brian spotted Cecily immediately in the middle of the floor. She was being held too closely by a Polish member of the flotilla he didn't like. Reason enough to interrupt, but he could have sworn as well that distaste, desperation even, were barely concealed by the smile pinned to her mouth.

114

He found himself tapping Lieut. Wikowsky on the shoulder. A sweet smile countered the other man's glare, and the lieutenant could do nothing but stalk away.

'They don't seem to understand the rules . . . all that hot Slav blood, I suppose,' he murmured.

She remembered that she'd quarreled with him and tried not to look grateful for the change of partner, but the truth was that she hadn't enjoyed dancing with Stefan Wikowsky. It wasn't his fault – she'd encouraged him, desperate as she always now was to escape the cold loneliness inside her. Despite an intensely communal life, it was as all-pervasive as the sea air outside. She was becoming convinced that loneliness would go with her to the grave . . . there wouldn't be another Charlie.

'This isn't what we agreed . . . to stay out of each other's hair,' she pointed out when the music stopped but Brian's arms still enfolded her, waiting for the next record.

'True, but I was hoping you'd forgotten.' He smiled at her, then waltzed her off again. His arms were comforting, but asking nothing in return. The conviction grew in her that Brian Rowland knew her state of mind and, even more strangely, had decided he wanted to help her. They spent the rest of the evening together, occasionally dancing, but more often talking with a concentration that isolated them from the rest of the crowded room. At a certain moment, when she began to speak of Charles Willoughby, he knew that it was the first time she'd been able to do so.

'Agnes and William couldn't understand it . . . thought I was a freak of some kind for not weeping or mentioning his name. I couldn't even explain that it was the only way I had of bearing it . . . pretending that he'd never existed at all. I've noticed the same thing with Duncan – he never talks about the men they've lost in the squadron. But to people outside we seem hard and uncaring.'

'It's protective covering,' Brian said slowly, 'recommended for everyone in hazardous occupations.'

'Yes, but what happens when we have to take the covering off?' Her eyes clung to his, confessing the extent of her fear. 'We shall all be shrivelled up inside . . . quite dead, because warmth and light have been shut out for too long.'

It was a strange conversation to be having in the middle of a mess dance, but no stranger than the fact that he should be having it with Cecily Willoughby.

'We're flippant and cool now because it seems the only possible way to be,' he said eventually, 'but in the end we shall all have to do our remembering. Then there'll be time, and we shall find that we can.'

She hadn't noticed the lilt in his voice, inherited from Ano; when he spoke seriously it gave what he said a kind of poetic authority. 'You didn't know Charles except by sight,' she said after a moment or two. 'I suppose you thought he was a typical Guardee – dashing and rather stupid. He wasn't that at all . . . just simple and very nice, much nicer than I deserved.'

'The "honourable" Charles,' he agreed gently, for once intending no malice.

It was the first of other evenings spent together, any in fact when their off-duty times happened to coincide. There was even a whole day shared, when he borrowed someone's motorbike and they pottered around black-and-white timbered Suffolk villages that seemed scarcely aware of the war. In the course of hours spent together contentment grew, spiced by the awareness that attraction was growing too. It seemed natural to walk hand in hand, better still to be clinging and clung to on the back of the motorbike. Late in the evening he left her reluctantly outside the hotel in Lowestoft which provided the Wrens' sleeping quarters. She put up her face to be kissed but his hands gripped her shoulders, holding her away from him.

'Why not kiss me . . . I want you to,' she said quietly. 'Is it because I have the reputation of being a desperate flirt in the mess?'

'Not that. It's just that what seems to be happening to us is bloody ridiculous. You're Cecily Willoughby . . . I'm still Red Rowland, the chap who wants to upset the Marchant apple-cart. Wanting to make love to you doesn't change that. Oh, God, who cares!' His mouth found hers and after a moment her hands crept up to twine themselves in his thick springy hair.

'Now try telling me again that nothing's changed,' she said unsteadily when he finally let her go.

'Even for wartime, we're going too fast, Cessy. It's a mercy you've got leave due . . . we need a breathing space before we get to the point of no return.'

Her smile glimmered at him in the moonlight, making him regret her leave and, still more, the girl who shared her room in the Wrennery.

'Faint-heart!' Be waiting for me, please, Red Rowland.'

When St Olave's was ready to reopen William Marchant telephoned River Cottage and explained that the time had come for Jane to return to London. 'We've saved a little petrol, my dear, so Jos can drive down on Saturday and collect her.'

'Collect us both, you mean. I shouldn't dream of staying here once she goes home,' Agnes said quickly.

There was a moment's hesitation at the other end of the line. 'Duncan's got leave,' William said finally. 'I was about to suggest that it was his turn to come down and stay with you.'

'But surely he'd prefer leave in London? The village is very quiet these days.'

'I think that's what he needs . . . a little quiet.'

'William . . . is something wrong? He's been hurt?' The questions, just breathed, barely reached him.

'He had to crash-land a few days ago . . . nothing but a scratch or two, I promise you, but he's desperately tired and on edge.'

117

'Well, in that case of course I'll stay.' After a tiny hesitation she spoke again. 'Are . . . are *you* all right, William? I didn't intend to leave you alone for so long.' It wasn't what she'd meant to say, but he was in a hurry to answer.

'I'm quite all right . . . there isn't the slightest need for you to worry about me. Stay there for as long as *Duncan* needs you, my dear.'

Her husband didn't need her . . . had probably never needed her. Pain in her hand was explained by the fact that she was gripping the receiver much too hard. She transferred it to the other hand and calmly asked about Cecily.

'She's almost due for leave,' William explained. 'Her letter this morning mentioned one of those strange wartime coincidences that keep cropping up. Who else do you think is at Lowestoft . . . Brian Rowland!'

'Oh dear . . . how very unfortunate! With the unhappy state that Cessy's in, they're *bound* to quarrel.'

'You'd think so, but she sounds quite cheerful. James rang from Greenwich, sounding not quite so cheerful, despite his promotion. Unpredictable things, children!'

Agnes thought so, too. For no reason she could think of, James obviously hadn't mentioned his visit to the cottage, and it now seemed out of the question for her to mention it either. How one thing led to another! She hated deception, and was appalled by the discovery that she seemed to have an unexpected talent for it. She put the telephone down with relief and went to find Jane. With her, at least, no disguises were necessary. The news that Jos was coming down produced the beautiful smile that Agnes had anticipated.

'It's been lovely,' Jane said truthfully, 'but holidays are for now and then, aren't they . . . not all the time.'

'The holiday lasts a little longer for me . . . Duncan is coming down with your father; he's in need of a rest too, apparently.'

118

'You'll like having him here,' said Jane. It hadn't been lost on her that Mrs Marchant always walked to the window to watch whenever a squadron took off from one of the air-fields that ringed them round. She never said anything; just watched them out of sight, then sat down again.

There was the joy of seeing Jos again on Saturday, but for a moment or two it was quenched by the sight of Duncan Marchant. The bright and brilliantly smiling young man who'd sauntered in and out of her life for years had become this gaunt, tired-faced stranger. When he smiled now his mouth wore the mechanical grin of a ventriloquist's dummy. Even his remembered 'Hi, Janey' rang with such forced gaiety that she was terrified of bursting into tears. After one involuntary glance at Mrs Marchant she didn't look at her again, just hugged her, muttered something about thanks, and fled to the car, clutching Marmaduke. Some time elapsed before she could concentrate on a problem that had more to do with her than Duncan Marchant did.

'Jos . . . the kitten . . . do you think Mam will mind? He's quite house-trained now, and beautiful, don't you think?'

He smiled and agreed that Marmaduke was all that a kitten should be. It was harder to know whether Ano would mind or not. She was . . . chancy these days; sometimes sharp and ill-humoured, sometimes sunk in a quiet apathy so unlike her that he found it more worrying than cross-ness. She worried about Brian, of course. Jos told himself that, and blamed matters otherwise on the fact that she worked too hard and, like most Londoners, hadn't had a good night's sleep for months.

'I'm not sure about the kitten, love . . . we'll have to hope for the best,' he said finally.

She nodded, then aired the other worry that travelled with her.

'How . . . how did you think Duncan looked?'

'Haunted, poor lad; he's seen too many of his friends

119

disappear. Happen the country will give him a bit of peace . . . you look a treat for it, love!'

She smiled at him, thinking that she loved him more than anyone else in the world. 'Have *you* been all right without me?'

'Missed you, Janey. I'm glad you're home.'

For a moment – when he stopped the car at he bottom of the mews – she felt a strange yearning pang for the house they'd left behind. She wouldn't forget River Cottage. Then Ano was there, staring at Marmaduke.

'I couldn't leave him behind,' Jane said breathlessly.

Ano shrugged. '*You'll* have to make sure he doesn't get run over. What have you done to your hair?'

'Mrs Marchant took me into Oxford one day . . . a nice girl chopped it like this. She called it a petal cut, or something.'

'Fancy name, but it looks all right,' her mother said after a considering stare. 'You'd better come inside; tea's ready.'

She was home again; still, there was Jos to set against River Cottage.

Agnes and Duncan were still at Long Wittenham when Cecily came home on leave and asked William if she could stay at the house in Linden Square.

'I could go to the flat, Pa, But I thought we could keep each other company!'

'Of course, my dear. Glad to have you here.'

He sounded unlike himself . . . hearty, she thought, which he normally never was. It wouldn't have occurred to her before, but maybe he was missing Ma. She'd always thought of her mother as being the sort of person no one would ever miss . . . nice, of course, but unnoticeable; but she was having to change her mind about so many things nowadays that she could easily have been wrong about her mother too.

William went off reluctantly to spend an evening with

Tom Ferguson and drag his mind back to the almost forgotten subjects of rubber and tea, with the result that only Cessy was at home when James arrived for a night off in London. She hadn't seen him since their conversation just after the news of Charlie's death; it wasn't all that long ago in time, but both of them seemed to have travelled a long way since then. Uniform made people look older, but even so she was startled by the change in him.

Ano served them with supper and he was relieved to hear himself say 'good evening' to her calmly. A biblical phrase – 'the woman taken in adultery' – leapt into his mind, but he stared at her, surprised that she looked just the same. What had he expected, for God's sake . . . a scarlet brand across her forehead? He tried to concentrate on what Cessy was saying . . . something about Lowestoft . . . wasn't it extraordinary that Brian should be there as well?

'Brian . . . Brian Rowland?'

'James . . . who else? How many Brians do we know?'

He stared at her, wondering why she looked excited when he'd have expected her to be sharply funny about it, or merely cross.

'I . . . I suppose you're icily polite and give him a distant bow occasionally!'

'That's roughly what happened to begin with. No, it wasn't! I was sickeningly condescending, and he handed me the biggest snub I've ever been given.'

She'd changed, James realized, even more than the rest of them. She wouldn't have made *that* confession a year ago, especially about Brian Rowland.

'So, with the score even, you now live and let live?' he suggested quietly.

'It's not quite that either! We snarled a bit at first, but suddenly it seemed bloody stupid, and then I discovered that he wasn't nearly as dreadful as I'd always supposed. That led me on to the next discovery . . . that I had something to answer for as well!'

121

James looked down at his hands, surprised to find that they weren't trembling, then forced himself to smile at her.

'You seem to be having an interesting time at Lowestoft!'

'I am!' A reminiscent smile touched her mouth, making her look beautiful. He'd always thought her face too coolly perfect in the past, never wanted to draw it because it made no appeal to him; it wasn't true now . . . any artist would beg to have her as a model. Something had happened to her, and he prayed to God that it wasn't what he was beginning to fear.

Cessy was talking again, talking because she had to tell someone about the strange new emotions that consumed her, and who easier to talk to than dear James?

'There's been a lot going on recently, and each time the boats have come back into harbour it's been more of a relief to find Brian's safely among them. I don't think I could bear to lose him too.'

It was out before she meant it to be, then decided that she didn't really mind. But James's face across the table had gone so white that she was on the verge of asking him if he felt ill. She'd been too full of herself, as usual, to notice.

'What . . . what does "not bear to lose him" mean, Cessy?'

'That I'm in love with him, of course . . . what else?'

Blank horror stared out of his eyes; then, rather than look at her, he put his head down on the cool polished surface of the table.

Chapter 9

His dark head pushed against the table filled her with a terrible sense of impending calamity. She wanted to demand to know what was the matter, shout at him, but in the end her voice uttered words with desperate calm. 'James . . . tell me what's wrong.'

He lifted his head and jerked it in the direction of the door.

'Ano still here?' he muttered.

'No, she'll have gone home by now.'

He got up to splash brandy into two glasses, then brought them back to the table. 'Listen carefully, Cessy, because I can't bring myself to say all this again. A week or two back I got a 48-hour pass unexpectedly and came home without thinking to advertise the fact. In any case, I knew Mama was at the cottage with Jane. Pa was here, and by the grace of God I didn't shout to him, because he was in bed with Ano!'

Cessy struggled with a wild desire to laugh, born of relief from nameless dread. Dear James . . . he always did take life too seriously. She was about to say that even though they might not care for the idea, things could have been a great deal worse, when he held up his hand to stop her. 'I know what you're going to say . . . the stresses of war, and all that. I thought the same. I crept out of the house like a scalded cat and went down to Long Wittenham, manfully hugging my secret. While I was there I had to go into Jane's room and found myself staring at a recent photograph of Brian.' He stopped suddenly, afraid that if he looked at Cecily he wouldn't be able to say what needed saying.

'Go on . . . Brian, you said,' she whispered.

'It was a chance in a thousand, Cessy . . . the angle of the shot showed me features inherited from Ano, but it was my father looking at me from that damned photograph.'

'You're mad,' she shouted. 'How could we not have known all these years? You were looking for resemblances, imagined them.'

'Not so. I started looking *then* . . . found small details that other people probably wouldn't have noticed, but I've trained myself for years to look at faces carefully. I *know* I'm not wrong, Cessy.'

It had the cold ring of truth about it. She said nothing for a moment, then began to laugh . . . and all the time tears streamed down her ashen face.

'It isn't funny; for God's sake, do anything but laugh,' he shouted.

'It *is* . . . so funny I could die.' The word uttered without thought sobered her. She smeared away tears with her hand and drank the brandy he'd put in front of her.

'There's nothing to be done,' James said wretchedly. 'I suppose we just go on as before.'

'Wrong! I shall ask William about it.'

When he shook his head it was her turn to cry out. 'Why shouldn't I ask him? I've got to know the truth.'

'Because I'd swear he doesn't know himself . . . and nor Mama.'

She threw him a glinting smile that had no trace of amusement in it. 'Then I'll ask Ano Rowland. Perhaps she can remember who gave her a child!'

It would have been a relief to walk round to the mews there and then, but for all she knew Jos would be there; it wasn't going to be a conversation for him to hear. She got through the night somehow, poised between hope and despair, but despair won as the hours crawled by. The truth was that she and Brian were much alike; suppose the attraction of kindred spirits worked for them simply because they *were* kin? It was a terrible theory to try to deny in the loneliest watches of the night.

She was already waiting in the drawing-room next morning when Ano came in and looked round to see if the room was empty before starting work.

'Good morning ... my father's already gone, if that's who you're looking for.' Her voice was cold, but Ano was long accustomed to the fact that she and Cecily Willoughby didn't like each other.

'I don't need Mr Marchant,' she said calmly. 'I know what I have to do.'

Cecily's eyebrow lifted slightly, indicating doubt. 'It seems there are times when you *do* need him.'

She was there for a purpose, it seemed. Ano still wasn't sure what it was, but tension was seeping into the quiet room, and battle lines were being drawn. Her heart was beginning to pound, but it wasn't in her make-up to avoid a fight.

'I don't know that I understand you, Mrs Willoughby.'

'I think you do, but we won't go on fencing, Ano. Just tell me whether or not Brian is my father's son.'

She watched the woman in front of her, aware that she'd been deliberately cruel in not asking her to sit down. Ano stared blindly at her hands for a moment, as if wondering what to do with them, but it was the only sign she gave of whatever turmoil raged inside.

'I don't think I have to tell you anything at all,' she said after apparently giving the matter thought. 'I work here, but the rest of my life is my own affair.'

'Not true, I'm afraid. It might have been so once, and what you and my father did was no concern of ours. Now things are different. Brian and I are together at Lowestoft, and we shall get more together yet. I intend to go back and

125

take the first opportunity I can find of sleeping with him.'

The silence in the room was palpable . . . suffocating. She wanted to scream at the rigid woman in front of her, 'Say something . . . answer me.' But if Ano Rowland could show this stoical self-control, so must she.

'You mustn't let Brian love you,' Ano said at last.

'Because his father's *my* father?'

'Yes.' The word was ground out of her as if it was the only one she would consent to utter.

'Just that?' Cecily flung at her. 'Not, "Sorry, Mrs Willoughby . . . inconvenient for you and Brian . . . a bit upsetting for Mrs Marchant" . . . something on those lines?'

At last Ano was spurred to anger of her own. 'Words! I could say whatever you like, but it wouldn't change anything. If you want the truth, I intended that no one should ever know. They never would have known but for you.'

'Not even my father, or Jos?'

'Them least of all.'

She gave no ground, wouldn't even beg now that they still shouldn't be told. It was Cecily whose voice changed.

'Are you sure, Ano? How *can* you be sure?'

'When Jos and I married I was already pregnant,' she answered steadily. 'That was why I let it happen between your father and me. I was safe . . . on the point of marrying anyway. Your father needed a woman to love, I needed him. It was over soon enough.'

'It *wasn't* over . . . it isn't over yet,' Cecily reminded her bitterly.

'It is for me.' It was said with such desolating finality that Cecily was almost convinced by it, then she remembered what James had said.

'Even that isn't true . . . you're still having an affair with my father.'

Ano didn't even ask how she knew. 'It happened again recently because your mother was away. It won't ever happen again.' The pain of saying it was nothing to the pain of knowing that it was true. For William the hours spent together had completed something left unfinished years ago . . . they'd been too enjoyable to be called a mistake, but she knew as surely as she knew anything that his need of her had been satisfied. It wasn't his fault that she'd need him for as long as either of them lived. Cecily didn't want to feel sorry for Ano Rowland, but she couldn't help wondering what the last twenty years had cost her.

'Why didn't you go away . . . wouldn't that have been easier?'

Ano's mouth twisted. 'Easier! How simple you make it sound. Easier for a Marchant maybe; not for the likes of Jos and me. A man with a job held on to it. Jos would have agreed to go if I'd told him the truth, but I couldn't do that without destroying him. Jane *is* his daughter, but he might have begun to doubt it after a while . . .' She brushed the thought away and looked at Cecily. 'Funny . . . for years I dreaded someone guessing the truth – used to keep staring at Brian to make sure he looked exactly like me. Now, it's almost a relief to have someone else know.'

'I'm not the only one. It was James who told me, because he had to warn me away from Brian.'

'He always *was* the one to notice things,' Ano said slowly. 'I think the secret's safe with him, but I'm not so sure about you.'

'What am I to tell Brian?' The expression on Ano's face made her burst out, 'Oh, God . . . you mean I don't tell him either? Is that what you expect?'

'If he knows, he's bound to change towards us. It's Jos I'm thinking of . . . he mustn't be hurt after all these years.'

It was only to be expected that she didn't propose to think of Cecily Willoughby, but strange that she didn't consider whether Brian himself ought to know the truth. Then Cessy remembered his opinion of the Marchants; to cast his lot in with *them* would be the last thing on earth

127

he'd choose to do, and Ano knew it as well as she did.

After a moment's silence she gave a little shrug. 'End of my second romance! I don't seem to be doing terribly well.'

'I'm grateful,' Ano said in a low voice.

'Tell my father, please, that I've decided to spend the rest of my leave raising hell at Long Wittenham.'

Even in this she was thwarted because her mother and Duncan returned to London themselves in the course of the day. It seemed to Agnes a lifetime since she'd gone away. Things she'd grown accustomed to had to be accepted all over again. It seemed wickedly wrong that the lovely glass awning that had always covered the entrance from the gate to the front door should have been blown to the four winds, wrong that they should have no gate or railings at all. The other houses in the square were in the same battered state as their own, and boarded-up windows where the glass had been blown out gave them a blind dejected air. These things could be repaired eventually, she knew, but what about the hurt being done to people . . . Duncan and Cecily both damaged in ways that even the most loving mother could do nothing about. Better to bewail the loss of railings, because nothing else would bear thinking about. Her own situation least of all.

It had seemed a good idea to take Jane down to Long Wittenham . . . good all round. Jane would benefit from a little rest and country air, and that part of the idea had succeeded perfectly. But the stratagem it was meant to conceal seemed not to have succeeded at all. William was still the courteous self-controlled man who'd outwardly shared her life for more than twenty years; Ano Rowland was a self-contained automaton who did her work about the house as if no joy or sorrow could make any impression on her again. Agnes wasn't sure what she'd hoped to offer them both . . . perhaps nothing more than a chance to take hold of the happiness they'd all missed so far. The one possibility that hadn't occurred to her was that everything would remain the same.

Lady Carterton kept a close eye on the house in Linden Square, and it irritated her a good deal that she couldn't be sure what was going on. She took her daughter to task for abandoning William, but could make nothing of the gentle stone-walling that countered every charge.

'He's looking dreadful,' Hilda Carterton announced as the final shot in her locker. 'It's ridiculous for a man of his age to be in uniform at all.'

'He badgered *them*,' Agnes insisted quietly. 'It's true that he's lost weight and works too hard, but that applies to countless other people as well. It's worse for him, knowing more about the progress of the war than the rest of us. If only America would come in on our side, he'd feel happier.'

'Don't tell me what he feels . . . I know,' Lady Carterton said, with some acidity. 'He came to see me while you were away. I thought we were going to have a nice game of whist, but what I got was a lecture on what Roosevelt and Congress ought to do. The only good news, apparently, was that Italy had just invaded Greece . . . William looked quite cheerful for a moment, because he said it was a mistake they'd live to regret.'

Agnes smiled at the comment, but her mother thought William wasn't the only one to have lost weight. Some scarcely bearable strain was wearing Agnes down.

'Duncan gone back?' she asked abruptly.

'This morning.' It was all she'd meant to say, but vehemence suddenly broke through. 'It's inhuman, this code of behaviour we force on ourselves. Why *should* a young man have to smile and look carefree when he knows what he's going back to? And look at Cessy, with her life in ruins at the age of twenty-two. James won't be at Greenwich much longer, then we shall have him to agonize over too. Lovely Coventry Cathedral almost destroyed last night . . .

there'll be nothing left soon. I don't know how we bear this terrible war.'

'There's a long way to go yet,' Hilda Carterton pointed out grimly. 'We don't yet know what we can bear, but fortunately it's always more than we think.'

Agnes wasn't sure, but she offered the theory to Cessy, who seemed even more brittle now than she'd been just after Charles was killed.

'Gran *would* say that, she's indestructible, like old Queen Mary! The rest of us are like the goods they sell off cheap after an air-raid . . . "war-damaged"! I suppose it's true, after all, that my generation grew up spoiled, but it's properly getting its come-uppance now.'

She tried to smile at her mother, but her eyes had filled with tears.

Agnes cast around for something that would get her thoughts off Charlie. 'Poor darling . . . it must be very trying to find Brian Rowland at Lowestoft, of all people. I expect he irritates you as much as he ever did.'

She heard her daughter's sharp intake of breath and had the strange idea for a moment that it had sounded like a gasp of pain.

'It's . . . yes, I suppose you could call it trying!' Cessy managed to agree.

Brian waited for her to get back to Lowestoft with such impatience that even promotion arrived almost unnoticed. Instead of being something that he'd have felt secretly elated about, it was a piece of news to pass on to Ano and Jos that might have happened to someone else. Heart and mind only wanted to concentrate on Cecily, and trying to jeer himself out of such an extraordinary state of affairs made no difference at all. Getting seriously tangled up with *any* woman hadn't been in his scheme of things, but to have got tangled up with this one was a turn up for the book that left him floundering.

He was already at sea the evening she got back, and she

wasn't in the mess when he searched for her at breakfast the following morning. Then, that night, she was in the bar. He'd forgotten quite how bright her hair was against the dark-blue of her service jacket, how enticing the slow smile with which she greeted a man. The only thing wrong, most terribly wrong, was that she was smiling at another man.

When he went over to her she hesitated for a moment, then offered him the sort of nod that would have done for any casual acquaintance.

'Hi . . .' Her glance flicked over the extra piece of gold braid on his sleeve. 'Congratulations on that – Ano and Joseph must be thrilled.'

He told himself not to be so damned sensitive. She wasn't implying that only the lower orders got excited about a bit of promotion; but she wasn't excited herself, or even pleased, and he'd hoped she would be. He forced himself to smile at her. 'All well with you . . . good leave?'

'Fascinating,' she said with deadly brightness. 'The Rowland family seems to be flourishing. I'm not sure that I can say the same for the poor old Marchants, but we stagger on.'

'Stagger out to dinner with me, please?'

'You're too late, I'm afraid . . . Alec, here, has just asked me.'

If she'd sounded regretful he might have tried to forgive her, but she smiled brilliantly at the other man and allowed him to hustle her towards the door.

He found himself bereft in the crowded room, trembling with something that was either rage or fear. For a week their spells of duty didn't coincide, and if he caught an occasional glimpse of her she was always in the middle of a group of other people . . . deliberately so, he was almost sure. Then a morning came when he was late into the mess; damage to the boat the night before had had to be discussed with the mechanics before he could think of going into breakfast. The room was almost empty, but Cessy was there.

'Don't get up and run away because I shall run after you,' he said baldly, sitting down opposite her. 'Tell me why you've been avoiding me.'

He thought her hand trembled, but she hid it immediately in the pocket of her jacket.

'Imagining things, my dear Brian . . . our shifts haven't coincided, that's all.'

'Well, if that's all the trouble is, when can we get out of this damned place and talk properly?'

'Difficult . . . I'm on odd shifts at the moment, and you know how sticky the Commandant gets if she thinks her girls are burning up the daylight hours. When not working, we're supposed to be in bed.'

'I can't think of a nicer place to talk!'

She couldn't help glancing at him, wished she hadn't. Dear God, when he smiled at her like that! Her hands were now clenched together under the table, she was feverishly hot, icy-cold . . . suffocating in the stranglehold of her own desperate self-control.

'Let's leave it for the moment, shall we?' she managed to mutter. 'There aren't enough Wrens here to keep everybody happy . . .'

His face was grey under the surface brownness of sun and wind. 'Then let's leave it for good . . . I'm not going to stand in a bloody queue, waiting for my turn!'

She could bear it while he stayed angry, but then his voice changed. 'Cessy . . . tell me what's wrong. This isn't how things were when you went on leave.'

One more effort to be made, even if it almost killed her. 'No, it isn't,' she agreed slowly. 'But things change, don't they?'

'I didn't know they changed quite so suddenly. Remember I belong to the working class and the poor bastards need things spelled out for them. Did I only imagine that we were heading towards something important?'

Knowing that his eyes were fixed on her face, she couldn't look at him, only nod.

'In that case I'll shuffle off and let some other poor sod move up a place in the queue.'

She heard the scrape of his chair being pushed back, and the sound of his shoes on the polished linoleum floor. Then the door banged behind him and it was safe to get up and walk back to her own quarters. Tears were raining down her face by the time she arrived, and the storm of weeping that overtook her seemed to be as much for everybody else's grief as her own . . . dead Charles, her parents, Ano, and now Brian.

It was something to be thankful for when Christmas came and his flotilla was shifted to Scapa Flow. He went without saying goodbye, and she became the life and soul of the mess again . . . sparkling fun-loving Cecily, quite dead inside.

Chapter 10

Christmas in London was relatively peaceful, but the lull lasted only until 29 December. Nearly three hundred years after the first Great Fire, the square mile of the City was set alight again, this time in a devastating raid. Jos didn't get home for two days, and when he finally walked in he had the air of a man who was sleepwalking.

'I've never seen anything like it,' he kept muttering, 'fires everywhere you looked.'

'And not a fire-watcher on duty, I suppose, because of the holiday,' Ano remarked bitterly.

Jane remembered James's passion for Wren's City churches. 'What got burned, Jos?'

'Easier to tell you what didn't, love,' he said tiredly. 'But at least they didn't get St Paul's. We hardly had the heart or the time to look, but somehow it was always still there, with its cross on top shining above the smoke.'

By the time the new year dawned the fires were almost out, but the acres of smouldering ruins seemed apt for 1941 – a year of almost unrelenting misery, as it turned out. Shipping losses mounted in a U-boat war the Germans seemed to be winning, and by the middle of the year there was nothing to report but defeat, in a trail that stretched from North Africa to Greece. Agnes couldn't help remembering her mother's prophecy that their troubles had hardly begun. William looked perversely cheerful at the news that Hitler's armies had invaded Russia – a cardinal mistake that would cost him the war, when he should have invaded England instead – but otherwise her husband drove himself doggedly through the long exhausting days, sustained by nothing, as far as she could see, except the refusal to admit that he was almost dead on his feet. Irrationally, William wished that she wouldn't humour him. She was as tired as he was, and just as anxious; it wasn't right that she should manage to be calm and cheerful when she'd always been the weak one. Now and then he fought down a terrible longing to destroy her composure by shouting that he'd slept with her cook-general while she'd been away. The words might have insisted on being said except that he'd done Ano more than enough harm already. The only woman who *could* be used as a safety-valve was his mother-in-law, who still refused to live anywhere but in her own flat.

'She should be here . . . where it's easier to keep an eye on her,' he exploded, after another unsuccessful attempt to get her to change her mind.

'I know,' Agnes agreed, 'but we can't make her come. If she insists on managing on her own still, even now that poor Miss Tibbs is dead, the choice is hers.'

'She *can't* manage – that's the point,' he snapped. 'You have to keep going round there to make sure she's all right, and it's one more person to worry about.'

Agnes waited for him to denounce poor Miss Tibbs for being so inconsiderate as to expire in the middle of a war, but the gleam of humour in her eyes made him suddenly grin himself.

'On balance, I think it's less wearing to keep an eye on her there, than have the high-explosive risk of her sharing a house with you,' Agnes pointed out, as if the matter had been carefully weighed. William let the matter drop, with the uncomfortable feeling that he'd been out-argued.

The problem of a companionless Lady Carterton was unexpectedly solved by Jane, who overtook her one day

135

toiling home with a basket of shopping. After a glance or two at the other arthritic hand clenched round her ladyship's umbrella, she carried the basket the rest of the way and suggested that she could call on Saturday mornings to do any shopping that was necessary.

Jos looked surprised when she got home and reported that the offer had been accepted.

'She didn't exactly jump at it,' Jane said. 'Royalty accepting a favour!'

'I thought you didn't like her.'

'I don't . . . she's probably still the old witch Brian used to call her, unless she's mellowed a bit. But she looked as if she was missing "poor Miss Tibbs"!'

She hadn't mellowed at all, Jane discovered. Indoors, the umbrella gave way to a silver-knobbed stick, but it was banged just as hard, and she had a way of saying 'child' that was fierce and unfriendly.

'I'm fourteen, and my name's Jane.' The information was offered as a kindly hint, to make matters clear.

If Lady Carterton was disconcerted by quite such a frontal attack, she didn't wilt easily. 'Funny sort of name to give you.'

'Jos thought so too,' Jane agreed, 'but I think Mam was right. Plain Jane suits me better than one of the fancy names he wanted . . . like Beatrice, after his favourite Shakespearian heroine!'

She was submitted to a long stare. 'Not as plain as all that,' her ladyship conceded eventually. 'Anyway, there's nothing wrong with Jane – it's a good English name.'

It was truce of a kind, and gradually an unlikely friendship sprang up between them. Jane arrived to shop, but always stayed afterwards to dust and polish in the overcrowded rooms, and listen to Lady Carterton's reminiscences. They were about a way of life lost and gone for ever, and all the more fascinating for that. Jane knew that Grandfather Rowland had been a groom on the Norfolk estate where her ladyship grew up. Jos had grown up there too, but when the estate had been sold and his father died, he'd moved reluctantly to London. She thought he still hankered after country life and would have preferred horses to motor cars any day; he'd said as much one day when she'd asked him about it – 'you can't whisper in the ear of a Daimler, Janey!'

Lady Carterton was curious as well as informative, and interested to know whether inserting Joseph Rowland's daughter into St Olave's had been the mistake she'd predicted. Knowing Jane better now, she was less certain she'd been right. Hilda Carterton didn't greatly mind being proved wrong, but she couldn't bear not to know.

'How are you getting on at that school of yours?' she asked one day. 'Do you like the other girls?'

'I don't like them much, and I expect they think *I'm* a bit rum. But you sort of make friends when you're diving in and out of air-raid shelters together! The work's good . . . I like that.'

It was all she seemed inclined to say on the subject and Lady Carterton knew that she'd been right, at least, to the extent that the subject was a touchy one.

'I gather your brother's doing rather well. Cheeky boy, he was. I didn't always catch him at it, but I knew when he was pulling faces behind my back because *you* couldn't help giggling. Your mother spoiled him, of course.'

Jane grinned at the simple explanation of how her ladyship had known what was going on . . . almost confessed that they'd thought she was a witch and decided not to.

'Brian's been promoted,' she said instead. 'Mam's sure he'll finish up an admiral.'

'Nonsense . . . what about my grandson? They can't all be admirals.'

Admiral James Marchant? Jane didn't think so, but the lady in front of her wouldn't be impressed by the news that he was going to be an artist instead. If he still was. The sketches of naval life he'd promised long ago had never arrived and she didn't expect them to. Aside from the fact that accompanying convoys taking supplies to Russia probably didn't allow much time for drawing, she wouldn't have got the sketches in any case. James had become a stranger when he turned up at Long Wittenham. She still wasn't sure why, but that visit had signalled the end of friendship and the little kiss he'd given her had been a kind of final goodbye. It still hurt when she thought about it, because she'd taken it for granted that he shared her own view of friendship . . . for holding to through thick and thin.

All she could do for him was knit the heavy sweaters and scarves needed by sailors on the bitter voyage to Murmansk. Agnes Marchant tried, and if her son had needed exquisitely fine needlework she could have obliged, but thick oiled wool and wooden knitting needles defeated her. Jane found her one morning reduced to weeping frustration over a garment no amount of wishful thinking could persuade her James would ever be able to wear.

'Look . . . what's gone wrong with it now?' The navy-blue mass she held out could have accommodated a baby elephant with a little stretching here and there.

Jane inspected it but knew better than to smile. 'I think it would be the better for some armholes,' she said truthfully. 'You've gone on knitting a . . . a bit too long.'

Try as she would she couldn't look at it without grinning, and the grin became a chuckle. She caught Agnes's eye, and then they were both off, helpless with the laughter that they often seemed to share together. Agnes wiped her eyes at last, and accepted Jane's offer to see what she could do.

'You play while I unpick,' Jane suggested. She rewound the wool as she went, uncovering knots and blemishes that her friend hadn't even known were there, while Agnes

rewarded her with Debussy's '*Girl with the Flaxen Hair*'.
At the end of the recital Jane put down her needles, convinced of the rightness of the idea that had just occurred to her.

'Knitting isn't how you ought to be spending your time. I've got a much better idea.'

'You're about to suggest that I could do less harm sewing barrage balloons?'

It was probably true, but Jane shook her head. 'It's a still *better* idea! Why don't you play the piano for other people . . . not just me?'

'You're not serious . . . or are you?' Agnes was sufficiently acquainted with Miss Rowland to sound wary. Jane had the tenacity of a bulldog when it came to edging people in the direction she thought they ought to go.

'Of course I'm serious . . . think of Dame Myra Hess. Her lunchtime concerts are packed . . . people long to be taken out of themselves for a little while and think of something other than bombs and battles.'

'Dearest child, that may be, but I'm not Dame Myra.'

'Just about as good, and who's going to measure the difference? They'd be so grateful to listen they wouldn't care if you hit handfuls of wrong notes . . . not that I've ever heard you hit one.'

Made to feel, as she'd known she would, that Jane would be disappointed in her if she didn't make an effort, she diffidently offered her services to the vicar, and found herself giving her first public concert in the church hall. A forces' canteen came next, then hospitals where troops were convalescing. Once convinced that what she offered people was valuable, all nervousness left her. She'd always known that she could play the piano; it was only in other ways that life often defeated her. William protested that she was overdoing things, but she simply smiled and shook her head.

'Yet another sign of the times,' he said, only half-jokingly. 'Husbands were once thought to know best. I'm afraid we shall never go back to that desirable state of affairs!'

'Do you really mind?' she asked after a moment's thought.

'About you being out of the house so much? Selfishly, yes I do! But that doesn't mean that I want to try to stop you.'

The idea that he actually preferred her to be there was no more surprising than the fact that they were discussing it together, but she was nervous suddenly about a subject that seemed to be leading them into dangerous waters.

'I meant, do you mind about things changing,' she said quickly. 'They're bound to . . . with thousands of women doing work as vital as any man's. Look at Cessy . . . I doubt if she'll ever settle down again just to domestic life, although I wish she could find someone to settle down with.'

'I agree with you – about her and about the Victorian male attitude suffering a knock from which it's never going to recover. About time too, but the emancipation of women takes a little getting used to, even so!'

There was more to get used to than she realized. He was alive to changes in himself and in her. The more confident she became about the value of what she was doing, the more serenely she coped with all the anxieties and restrictions of wartime life. He ought to feel proud of her . . . did feel proud, but he was irritated as well. She wasn't supposed to be managing so competently! The strangest thing of all was that while she bloomed, vital Ano faded. Each time he saw her he was aware of the sadness and strain in her face. Some of it was for Brian, of course, and he knew she was hurt that his occasional leaves were never spent in London; but William knew that much of her unhappiness was due to *him*. The fever in his blood for Ano Rowland had gone. He was grateful to her, but he didn't want to make love to her again, and in some instinctive way known only to women she understood what he carefully hadn't said. All he could do was treat her as friend, not servant, but he didn't know whether it made things worse for her or better.

'All well with Brian?' he asked one evening when he got home before Agnes did.

'Of course,' she said proudly. 'Nothing's going to stop *him* doing well.'

'I hope you're proud of Jos and Janey, too. They're worth feeling proud of.'

She didn't answer, and he didn't understand the expression on her face that he glimpsed as she walked out of the room. All he could do was pray for Brian as desperately as he prayed for his own sons. Without Brian she would shrivel and die. He found himself wishing that the link of more than twenty years between Marchants and Rowlands could be broken . . . but where else would Jos and Ano live, if not in the cottage in the mews? It didn't occur to him that she would try to ruin his marriage; he'd have staked his life that she'd do nothing of the kind. All the same, he knew he'd feel less guilty if she would go, and the knowledge was itself an added cause for shame.

Brian never came home on leave, and they saw nothing of James for months on end. Cessy appeared occasionally, looking tired and unhappily ready to quarrel with anyone who got in her way. They walked as delicately as Agag with her, and it was an unacknowledged relief when it was time for her to go back to Lowestoft again. She never asked for news of Brian, and Agnes was careful never to mention the name of someone who'd always managed to irritate her daughter. Compared with global suffering, what was happening to her children probably didn't amount to very much, but looking at Cessy and Duncan, Agnes hated the war with a passion she hadn't known she was capable of before.

On one of his rare leaves from the squadron's present duty of escorting Lancasters to bomb German cities, Duncan rediscovered Jane. She was fifteen now, suddenly grown to slender height, with dark hair still cropped short about a fine-boned face. It had a contained look about it until she smiled. The smile, Duncan realized with surprise, could take your breath away.

She came into the drawing room one day in search of Mrs Marchant and found him there instead, lying back in an armchair, eyes closed against the pain hammering in his head. He was aware only of that until her fingers touched his temples – gentle as a moth's wing at first, then more firmly stroking away the pain.

'It might work,' she murmured behind his head. 'It does when I do it for Jos.'

'Don't stop, Janey. Lucky Jos! How is he, by the way?'

'Tired! But he's off duty at the moment . . . working in your garden. It's called "digging for victory", and the result is that your lawn has disappeared! Jos grows the best vegetables in the neighbourhood, and from time to time he leans on his spade and pretends he's a countryman!'

Duncan turned his head and saw the smile that touched her face when she spoke about Jos.

'Is that what he wants to be? Happy man, to know . . . most of us don't.'

'You know what *you'll* do, surely . . . go back to the Firm?'

'I wonder. I have a sort of feeling it won't happen.'

He spoke seriously for once and saw instantly mirrored in her face the fear that he seemed to think he wouldn't survive the war. 'It's all right . . . I'm not predicting death and glory for myself! But somehow I can't believe in a vision of young Marchant going back to the City in bowler-hat and striped suit.'

'What *can* you believe in?'

'That's the hell of it, Janey . . . I haven't the faintest

idea.' His voice trembled slightly, and she had a glimpse of the fears that laid him waste inside. The dashing young man who'd embodied all her adolescent dreams for years was now this haunted ghost whose hands suddenly clung to hers.

'Something will turn up . . . it always does, according to Mr Micawber,' she reminded him, trying to smile.

Duncan nodded, then surprised her by switching the conversation. 'Do you still hear from Brother James? He used to be your special friend.'

'No, I don't hear,' she said indifferently. 'I think we've outgrown each other.'

'Good, because I can't spare you, Janey. Promise me you won't outgrow me!'

She grinned, relieved that he wasn't too strained to feel like teasing her, after all, and warmed by the knowledge that it wasn't all teasing. He was treating her almost like an equal. It was what she'd always longed for. The only trouble was that she still wasn't quite old enough to help him.

It was Ano who first mentioned that James was expected home on leave, while his ship was being refitted.

'Excitement round at the house,' she said briefly, 'your friend's due home.'

'Mrs Marchant will be pleased.'

'No doubt.'

Jane looked at her mother's taut face, wishing for the umpteenth time that Brian would bother to come home. Scapa Flow was a long way away, but a week's leave wasn't unknown in the Navy. He'd abandoned them for some reason, and she hated him for it on Mam's account. It was Ano, too, who reported James's arrival, but Jane proved to herself that friendship was dead and buried by staying well away from Linden Square. James didn't come near her and she thought he'd have left again without seeing her but for the fact that a duty visit to his grandmother happened to coincide with her return from shopping one morning. He left when she did and couldn't avoid walking

143

home with her, but she made no attempt to start a conversation. For one thing she was too busy thinking about the changes in him. The war that had so weakened Duncan had had the opposite effect on James. He was broad now, instead of slight, confident and aloof where once he'd been glad to talk to her. She'd noticed the same upside-down effects on Mrs Marchant and Mam.

James occasionally shot a sidelong glance at the silent girl by his side. It was damnable not to know whose child she was, and to find himself searching her face for resemblances to his father.

'A lot's happened in the last eighteen months,' he said at last. 'You've grown up while my back's been turned. Pa says you rule them all with a gentle rod of iron, and it's obvious that my dear but doughty grandmother eats out of your hand.'

She listened for a hint of disapproval in his voice and thought she heard it.

'If Mr Marchant said anything of the sort, he's teasing you. But if you've noticed a change in Mrs Marchant, that's real enough. She's becoming quite famous, but it's giving pleasure to people that's made the difference to her.'

'Yes . . . I'd noticed the difference. It doesn't say much for us, I'm afraid. We must have given her the idea in the past that we didn't value her. It wasn't true, but perhaps that's how it seemed.'

Jane wasn't sure about the truth of it, but didn't say so. She didn't say much at all, and the withdrawal he felt so strongly was surely deliberate. His mother might look serene, but he wanted to know why the rest of them did not – his father and Jos seemed tired elderly men, and Ano Rowland was defeated. He was about to ask if Jane knew why, but then she broke the silence first.

'Mrs Marchant worries about you all, but at least your father's cheered up a bit since America came into the war. Hitler made the "cardinal error" of invading Russia instead

144

of us, and Japan has brought in America by attacking Pearl Harbour.'

'I'm sure he's right about them, but there are the Italians as well.'

Her face suddenly lit with the grin he remembered. 'He's like Mr Churchill ... can't bring himself to take *them* seriously!'

James's answering smile made him familiar again and it was easier to talk to him. 'You'll be glad to swap the North Sea for somewhere else.'

'And how! Sometimes I think I'll never feel warm again, and it wasn't only the sub-zero temperatures. The Russians are strange people ... putting up this incredible fight, but you'd think they were the only ones fighting the war. It doesn't hold out much hope for future relations. Is Brian still as communist-minded as ever?'

'I'm not sure *how* he's minded these days, because we never see him. But I don't suppose he's given up wanting the Socialists in power; he thinks it's only way we'll get a just society.'

'I'll make him argue the point one day ... one fine day when we've got nothing more dangerous to do than sit and theorise about life!'

Her smile glimmered again and he thought how lovely she was becoming. Without knowing why, it prompted a question that made her hostile again.

'Seen anything of my dashing brother lately? I suppose dauntless Duncan is still the hero of the family?'

'He's *my* hero,' she said swiftly. 'He gets home occasionally ... not nearly often enough to suit us.'

'Still dazzled by him? You always were, as I remember, although I never could think why.' The snideness of it shocked him, but it was too late to take the words back. Much too late, because Janey was shouting at him.

'You're a pig, James ... I hope you go away soon, because you spoil things when you're here.'

'Sorry I spoke . . . forget it,' he said stiffly.

'No, I won't. Duncan *is* dauntless!' She had to insist on it all the more, for the memory of his hands desperately gripping hers.

'I said forget it,' James roared. They were standing stock-still in the road, unaware that other people walked round them and stared. He grabbed her shoulders and stood holding her so that she couldn't break away, while his eyes searched her face.

'Sorry I spoil things, Janey,' he said, in a quite different tone of voice. He bent down and touched her mouth with his own, then straightened up and walked up the pathway to his own front door.

She didn't see him again, and there was time to get used to the idea that the last hurdle to growing up had finally been stumbled over. He'd occasionally kissed her before and it had been no different from Brian leaving a birthday peck on her cheek. Ano had flatly informed her of the facts of life, and the other girls at school had giggled in corners about encounters with their brothers' friends. Jane had reckoned them hysterical fools or liars. But she could see now that there was more to the business of being a woman than she'd bargained for. She dimly understood that James had kissed her because he was piqued about Duncan. Even that didn't stop her heart thudding when she thought of it. It stopped altogether for a moment when she remembered what she'd said to him. If he did go away and never come back, it would be no more than she deserved.

Chapter 11

The news from the Far East grew steadily worse as the summer wore on ... the Japanese poured over Malaya and Burma in a yellow tide that flowed only in one direction – westwards. But nearer home there were signs of hope. The German advance into Russia was being halted, by the limitless size of the country and the Russians' stoical indifference to their own suffering. In North Africa the month of October saw the battle of El Alamein – the final turning-point in the desert war. Even bolstered by Rommel's Panzer divisions, the Italians were at the beginning of a retreat which would see them pursued back to their own mainland.

William's heart and mind were riveted on such battles: Agnes accepted the fact and left him undisturbed, to fight them in his own imagination. He still found time to visit Tom Ferguson occasionally, and returned one evening to mention that he'd finally met Tom's cousin, Edward, whom he'd heard talk of for years.

'Nice chap,' he said casually. 'He's a Member of Parliament for some far-flung Cornish constituency ... a few years younger than Tom, but he's a civilian because he's extremely short-sighted as well as being in a reserved occupation. He farms a large acreage down there, apparently.'

Agnes listened vaguely, with her attention more given to the programme for her next concert than to a man she

147

was unlikely ever to meet. But when William next met Edward Ferguson he was about to spend an uncomfortable night on a sofa in Tom's bachelor flat, and he took him home to Linden Square instead. She found herself reassuring a quiet fair-haired man who obviously thought she was being given too much trouble. The first visit became a habit whenever he needed to spend a night in London, and Agnes was glad of the friendship for William's sake – he needed a man to talk to. It became another habit for them to sit discussing the progress of the war, while she drifted over to the piano and sat quietly playing for them. To begin with she was intrigued by the liking for each other of two men who seemed to have nothing in common. Edward was sensitive and gentle, not a bit like her barn-storming husband. It took a little while to discover that under his diffident manner lay a toughness and competence equal to William's own.

She was away from the house, visiting a sick friend of her mother's, when a taxi drew up midway through the morning and Cecily climbed out. She'd been dreading her arrival, but it suddenly seemed even more unbearable that there should be no one there at all. Ma *ought* to have been there when she finally needed her. She stumbled down the stairs to the kitchen, and stopped in the doorway, white-faced, sickened by the nausea rising in her throat. Ano did nothing for a moment, taken by surprise, then she reached Cecily and half-carried her to a chair at the table.

'Stay there . . . I shan't be a minute,' she said calmly. Tea was brewed, and she recklessly threw into the cup most of what remained of the week's sugar ration. 'Drink that before you tell me what's wrong . . . if you want to, that is.'

Her voice was impersonal but not unkind. Sipping the hot sweet tea as she'd been told, it occurred to Cecily that it would be easier to talk to this woman than to her own

148

mother. They'd scarcely exchanged a word since the terrible confrontation over Brian, but the shared memory of that had changed once and for all what they knew about each other.

'You look as if you'd been starving yourself. Have you?'

'I think perhaps I did try,' Cecily muttered. 'It seemed one way of solving something.'

'Something like being pregnant?'

Cecily answered with another question. 'What am I going to do, Ano?' Her eyes were sunk in her head, and full of despair. If Cecily Willoughby had once been a girl to envy or hate, she wasn't so any more.

'You'll have to decide first of all whether you want the child or not.'

'It's too late to decide. I wasted too much time hoping I was wrong ... found I wasn't but couldn't make up my mind.'

'What about the father ... does he know? Are you going to marry him?'

Cecily thought of Stefan Wikowsky. God knew she'd thought of him more than enough recently, but she *couldn't* think of him as her husband. 'He doesn't know, although he may guess. I shan't marry him,' she said briefly. 'My Commandant does know, and I shall soon be discharged ... for medical reasons! For the moment I've come home to break the joyful news. A counter-irritant to my parents' other worries – a daughter about to present them with a bastard grandchild!' Her voice rose out of control, hovering on the edge of hysteria.

'There's no need to get melodramatic about it,' Ano said matter-of-factly. 'Yours won't be the only bastard child to come out of the war by a long chalk.'

She went calmly about the business of making toast, and pouring more tea. When it was in front of Cecily she said simply, 'Eat ... you're weak ... not seeing straight at the moment.' It was strange, but she found in herself

149

no desire to gloat over the sight of Cecily Willoughby brought low. Perhaps it wasn't strange at all. She wanted to help William's daughter.

'The hardest thing will be explaining why it happened,' she said slowly. 'If you know the answer, try it out on me.'

Cecily stared at the cup she was holding. 'Yes, I know. I caught sight of myself in a mirror one evening . . . I was looking at a strident hag who smoked and drank too much, wore too much make-up, and was sick to the bottom of her heart of pretending that she hadn't a care in the world. And all the time I was dying of loneliness. I had to attach myself to someone. The only trouble was that I chose the wrong man.'

'In that case you mustn't be talked into marrying him.' Ano spoke with such flat authority that her own life was being offered as proof; she didn't say so, but Cessy knew that her marriage to Jos was in her mind. 'Nothing on earth is worse than marriage to the wrong man.'

It was advice born of experience, and therefore worth listening to, but it only told her what not to do. Perhaps Ano thought so too, because she suddenly spoke again. 'It would be easier to explain to your parents if they knew about Brian, coming on top of Captain Willoughby. Tell them, if you want to.'

It was temptation of the cruellest kind, but after a moment or two Cessy shook her head. 'I won't do that . . . but thanks all the same. And thanks for being kind. I feel better now.'

A rare smile lit Ano's face, which Cessy read correctly. It said that they were both, in different ways, making large concessions and would probably appreciate each other in future.

Her interview later in the day with Agnes and William was even more dreadful than she'd imagined, because they tried so hard to make allowances for a daughter whose life had been shattered by war. Easier by far it would have been to break the news to a mother like Edie Bloggs, who'd have sworn at her for being such a fool and then said 'never mind, ducks; I s'pose we'll 'ave to get over it'. And the expression of shock on her father's face was even worse. The thought of his own bastard son threatened to tip her over into hysterical laughter, until she remembered that he didn't even know about him.

'I'm sorry to be such a disappointment to you,' she said finally. 'Charlie left me money . . . I can go somewhere away from here . . .'

'Dearest, you're talking nonsense,' Agnes said firmly, emerging from silence more quickly than William had done. 'You'll stay here where we can look after you.' She stared at her husband, willing him to say something.

'Yes . . . of course; where else? We'll think about the future when the child is born.'

'Thanks, Pa, but I'll stay in my own flat unless things start to go wrong. Ano knows, by the way. She was here when I arrived home all to pieces this morning.'

She went back to Lowestoft the next day and returned for good a month later. Maternity probably wouldn't have commended itself to her at any time, but she'd have done her best if there'd been someone to do her best for. As it was, she was bored, irritable, and constantly chafed by the knowledge of her own stupidity. Agnes bore the brunt of her changes of mood, and it was Lady Carterton in the end who didn't baulk at pointing out that she was becoming unbearable.

'Looked at your mother lately?' her ladyship enquired mildly. 'If not, I suggest you do. She's worn out with your tantrums, and she's got more than you to worry about.'

'Sorry not to be merry and bright, Gran. But I don't feel very bright . . . In fact, if you want the unvarnished truth, I feel perfectly bloody.'

If she was hoping to shock her grandmother, she was mistaken. The lady watching her didn't turn a hair. 'You feel so sorry for yourself that you can't be bothered to notice how anyone else is feeling. I suppose what's really upsetting you is the knowledge that you've been a fool. We all are from time to time, but we don't expect others to suffer for it. Your mother's too kind to say so, but it's time somebody did.'

Trust Gran not to be overwhelmed by kindness! Cecily looked away from her to her own thickening body ... the daily reminder of just how great a fool she'd been. She was consumed with distaste for herself, frightened of an uncertain future, and infuriated that the old woman watching her should understand her so well. But then Lady Carterton surprised her with a gentle question.

'You miss Charles Willoughby, don't you?'

This grief, at least, she could admit to, but she didn't bargain for the tears that pricked her eyes and began to stream down her face.

'I'm not as good as I thought I was at managing on my own,' she muttered with difficulty. 'Charlie knew how to keep me out of trouble.'

Hilda Carterton hadn't expected to hear her self-sufficient grand-daughter make such a confession. 'This is the worst time to be on your own,' she conceded with more kindness than usual. 'Things won't look quite so bad once the child is born. You need more company ... I know ... I'll ask my friend Jane to keep an eye on you.'

'Jane Rowland? No thanks, Gran.' The rejection was so fierce that she felt obliged to soften it with an explanation. 'She's the irritating child who refused to be a bridesmaid at my wedding, and we haven't hit it off too well since.'

'You don't have to go on holding the bridesmaid thing against her, and she's nearly sixteen – hardly a child any longer.'

Cecily shrugged and imagined that the idea had been abandoned, with the result that she was unprepared for a

knock at the flat door the following Sunday morning . . .
unprepared to the extent that she was only just out of bed
and looking as unkempt as the flat around her. The girl
standing on the doorstep was clean, lithe, and beautifully
unencumbered. Cecily felt sick with disgust of herself and
dislike of the girl who stood watching her.

'My grandmother sent you, I suppose. She's an interfering old cow! Go away, Jane. I don't need help from the
Rowlands.'

It was a strange welcome, but Lady Carterton had
warned her not to expect too much.

'Why turn down a good offer? If you need a little help,
what's wrong with a Rowland?'

The sensible suggestion was delivered in a clear sweet
voice that had no right to belong to a chauffeur's daughter. Worse than that, the daughter's dark eyes said clearly
that she was a resentful self-pitying mess! Cecily
Willoughby was being judged and found wanting. She
turned away from the door and lumbered down the passage, apparently indifferent as to whether Jane walked
inside or not. She heaved her body into the bath, and
reappeared an hour later neatly dressed, with her face
made up and her hair brushed. By then the sitting-room
had been transformed as well, and even the kitchen
looked clean and ordered. Jane, invisible at first, was
found to be still there, on her knees washing the kitchen
floor.

'It's no job for a girl who's heavily pregnant,' she said
cheerfully. 'Leave it to me in future.'

'Nice of you not to mention that I seem to have been
leaving it for some long time past!' Cecily struggled with
herself and finally managed the leap of accepting what
her mother and grandmother seemed to have no difficulty
in accepting. 'Share some coffee with me, Jane?'

'Love to. By the time you've made it I'll have finished
here.'

The leap all but went into immediate reverse, but after a stunned moment or two Cecily heard what the still small voice inside her was saying. The girl still on her knees on the floor had come as a friend; if she was treated as a servant expecting to be paid, she wouldn't come again.

The coffee was made – by Cecily – and drunk in almost total silence. Jane waited to see if things would improve, then took the bull – cow, she told herself – by the horns.

'I'd like to help, but I won't come again if you'd rather I didn't. Dear Lady C. meant well, but she did rather foist me on you.'

Cessy flushed uncomfortably. No wonder Jane and her grandmother got on well together; they both had a talent for coming straight to the point.

'Sorry . . . I've been slinking here in my lair for so long that I've forgotten how to be sociable.'

Jane smiled at her, accepting both the outward apology and the one it concealed. 'It's a lovely day . . . what about a stroll in the park – good for you and young Willoughby!'

Cessy's mouth twisted at the name, but what else could the little bastard be called? 'Mrs Bloggs unnerved me the other day by insisting that I was huge enough to be expecting twins. If she's right I'll probably drown myself and them as well.'

The question of whether or not she should come again hadn't been answered, Jane noticed. It was odd that Cecily should dislike the Rowlands so much, but no worse than Brian's hatred of the Marchants after all. They walked to Kensington Gardens without finding much to say, but when they reached Jane's tree she found herself offering an edited sequel to the trying-on of the bridesmaid's dress.

'Independent little cuss you were,' Cessy said, smiling over the story. 'Something tells me that you still are!'

154

Jane agreed that it might be so. Jos didn't use those words, but he gave her the same impression.

'James was by way of being a friend of yours, apart from the tree rescue. Is he still?'

There was an unexpectedly long silence, and Cessy found herself surprised by the expression on Jane's face. There was sadness and regret in it, and something that looked almost like fear.

'I don't think we're friends now,' she said finally. 'We used to ... to share things, but that was a long time ago.'

'You've outgrown him, you mean?'

Jane shook her head. 'He's outgrown me ... left me behind, somehow. The odd thing is that I've almost caught Duncan up!'

It hadn't occurred to Cessy until then that there were other sufferers from her father's old affair with Ano; but almost certainly Jane's friendship with James was a casualty as well.

Back at the flat, they parted company on the doorstep.

'Next Sunday?' Cessy asked. 'I'll make the coffee!'

'Yes, please,' said Jane.

In the end Edie Bloggs was proved correct, and Cessy's twins were born on a cold night in January 1943.

Agnes supposed that the monotonous diet imposed by food rationing, and the restrictions that hedged every aspect of daily life, made the winter seem longer and harsher than usual. But a morning finally came when the sunshine suddenly flooding through the dining room window spoke of spring. She felt warm and alive and insisted to herself that it was indeed the result of the fine morning ... nothing to do with the fact that Edward Ferguson sat opposite her, sharing a late breakfast after William had left for the War Office. She felt sure of it enough to smile at him, then tried to look severe, afraid that the smile might have been too warm. The gesture was a sop to a

Puritan conscience which told her she enjoyed his visits too much.

Edward noticed the attempt at a frown. It was his habit to notice things in any case, but he found Agnes Marchant of much more interest than most of the people he met.

'Do I impose too often? Just tell me not to come, if so.'

'My dear Edward, what nonsense! You don't impose at all, and you bring us far more food than you consume.'

'I wasn't thinking in terms of rations.'

'Well, then, in whatever terms you like to think.' She felt ashamed of herself for baulking the real issue, but it was impossible to say the truth – that she looked forward to his visits because he was the kindest and most self-effacing of men. When William was in the house nowadays she was always tensely aware of the fact, and aware of the tensions within him. Edward exerted no pressures, and gave her instead a sense of comfort. After years of knowing that she'd failed William, it was as warming as the sun streaming through the window to feel so certain that Edward . . . approved of her! She chose the word carefully in her mind; approved had a harmless ring about it.

She thought he looked bone-tired as usual, but knew him well enough now not to be misled by it. Hidden away beneath the surface gentleness was a core of toughness that would keep him going no matter what, and she suspected that it was more enduring than the nervous energy on which her husband now depended.

'You work too hard,' she said when the silence between them seemed to have gone on for too long.

'Lambing's quite hard work . . . for us as well as the ewes! I shall probably snooze through a very boring session in the House this afternoon.'

'And travel back tonight?'

He nodded, wondering whether he'd imagined a note of disappointment in her voice. She was the strangest mixture he'd ever come across, of blazing talent and insecurity, of serenity of spirit and unsureness of mind. His opinion of William Marchant was very high, but he didn't underestimate the difficulties that a woman might have in living with him. It was the unlikeliest of marriages, and perhaps not the happiest. Agnes was staring out of the window and he could safely stare at her, regretting that he hadn't known her as a young woman. He'd have liked to compare then with now; but his theory was that, in the way of a certain kind of Englishwoman, her beauty was more evident now that it had been pared down by time and experience. He liked the old-fashioned way she had of doing her hair, but at the moment the coil seemed too heavy for her slender neck.

'You're worried about something,' he said suddenly. 'Cessy?'

'I worry about them all, constantly! But perhaps it's her most of all at the moment. She isn't naturally maternal, and even bringing up children with Charlie might have been a strain. As it is, she's bored and lonely to the point of desperation. She does the best she can, but I know how she feels . . . trapped by a mistake of her own making.'

How did Agnes know? The perception of a mother who loved her daughter, or was she conscious of having made a mistake of her own? Edward was quite clear that he would never be able to ask.

'Don't you think Cessy would have done better to put the children out to adoption?' he asked instead.

'I've sometimes thought so, but she's like William, you know. His life's been guided by the belief that you have to be responsible for what you do, with no running away from it. Cessy rather surprisingly shares his point of view.'

'Why surprisingly?'

'Because some people – my dear outspoken mother for one – regard her as typical of an over-indulged generation.

157

Perhaps we did spoil her, but life's got its own back on her now. Her worst problem is boredom. Feeding and cleaning small babies soon palls on a woman with a very good brain, and that's what William says she has.' Agnes remembered belatedly that she was talking to a man who couldn't be expected to have much interest in her problem. 'Sorry . . . boring for you,' she apologized quickly. 'I expect things will get easier. She'll be able to find a nurse for the twins after the war; then she can look for a job that interests her.'

Edward was aware of not much liking Cecily Willoughby; she was too self-assertive for his taste – too modern in fact! – and she undervalued her mother, which said nothing for her judgement. But he needed help himself, and if he could lessen her mother's problems by lessening Cecily's, he was ready to try.

'Could she manage a part-time job now, do you imagine?' he asked finally. 'My secretary at home is married now, with a child of her own. The result is that she can never come to London with me and I'm slowly sinking underneath a sea of undealt-with papers. If Cecily could put in afternoons or evenings at Westminster, it might save us both from going barmy!'

'Edward, I'm almost sure she'd jump at it. If so, we'd arrange things somehow so that she could manage it.'

Cecily grabbed at the offer with the instinct of a drowning woman reaching for a lifeline, but her face darkened again almost at once. 'Pa will never agree,' she said with certainty. 'He only brings himself to accept them at all with an effort that I can't bear to watch, and if it means lumbering *you* with the twins, he'll tell me to look after them myself.'

Agnes knew that he'd still not got to the point of feeling that the children had anything to do with the Marchants, but she couldn't cast Cessy down by saying so. 'Men are not interested in small babies,' she said instead, 'even the kindest of them.'

'It's not quite what I meant, but you don't have to sound apologetic. My esteemed father-in-law won't acknowledge them at all, and there's no reason why he should.' She hadn't discussed with her parents the only interview she'd had with General Willoughby since the twins were born. If he could have stopped her giving them his name, he'd have done so; as it was, her brief connection with Charlie's family was over and done with.

Grudgingly or not, William accepted the new arrangement, and while Cecily rushed to Westminster to work for Edward each afternoon the twins were left in Linden Square. Agnes adored them, and so did Jane, but Ano found a quite unexpected pleasure in looking after them.

Their christening was timed for one of Duncan's leaves because he and Jane were godparents. James, a godfather by proxy, was somewhere in the Mediterranean and his only contribution was a sketch of his brother with a yowling infant on each arm. which turned out to predict the event quite accurately. Daniel bellowed all through the service and Daphne matched sob for bellow in a combination that Duncan pointed out afterwards was especially unnerving.

'Enough to put us off parenthood for good, Janey,' he said when the ordeal was over and they were safely home again.

She stared at him for a moment. 'Us' sounded almost as if he were talking about the two of them combined, but she turned the odd idea aside. 'The vicar's beard upset the twins,' she explained instead. 'I knew we were in for trouble the moment he walked in!'

'Poor little bastards.' Duncan looked at the two of them now happily gurgling at anyone who cared to pay them some attention. 'Pity Cessy's such a rotten mother! Still, they've got us, so it doesn't really matter.'

It was the same note sounding again, but she decided after a moment that he'd taken more seriously than she expected the promises he'd just made for the children at the christening. It was only gradually borne in on her that he meant what he'd said. Whenever he was at home, he behaved as if the twins belonged to him, which meant that they belonged to Jane and, therefore, that she belonged to him as well. It seemed to make up a unit he found satisfying. It was odd that he shouldn't want more exciting leaves than she and the children provided, but he was tired and nerve-ridden; things would change when the war ended and his life went back to normal again.

By the time their fifth wartime Christmas arrived the tide of battle in Europe, at least, was beginning to set the right way. The Italians were out of the war, if they could ever have been said to be seriously in it, and Allied armies were slowly pushing the Germans up the mainland of Italy. William knew that huge concentrations of men and materials were being assembled along the southern coast of England, representing an invasion force which would soon be landing across the Channel. The end of the war was still distant, but there was no doubt that it was in sight.

When the invasion finally began on 6 June 1944 – D-Day – Jane's schooldays at St Olave's were nearly over, but they were to end as they'd begun, diving in and out of air-raid shelters. The Allied landings on the coast of Normandy prompted a German counter-weapon in the shape of the 'flying bomb'. They came to be called doodle-bugs, but the familiar name didn't make their death-rattle sound any the less horrible to a civilian population reaccustomed to safe and friendly skies. Lady Carterton called them the devil's invention and Jane agreed with her. There was something obscene about the fear they instilled. When the motors cut out, there was a heartstopping wait while the bombs appeared out of the cloud and completed their dive to the ground.

Still, they were a short-term menace. It was possible to put up with them, knowing that it was only a matter of time now before the war was over, and in any case she had other things weighing on her mind. She was certain that she wanted to become a nurse. The idea of helping to mend people seemed, in the summer of 1944, the most appealing one she could think of. She longed to enrol as a student and get started, but implicit in the excitement of the thought was the usual drawback. Living in a teaching hospital would mean separating herself from Jos. One Sunday morning, wanting to talk to him, she tracked him down to the Marchant garden . . . *his* garden, it had almost become. He was engrossed in the delicate job of transplanting lettuce seedlings and unaware of her watching him. He handled the tiny green shoots as if he loved them. He *did* love them, she realized. He ought to have been a countryman, living his days according to the natural rhythm of sunrise and sunset, summer and winter.

'Jos . . . have you got time to talk?' she asked when he caught sight of her.

He straightened his aching back and gave the smile that was kept only for her. 'It's another way of describing what I need . . . a breather! What shall we talk about, Janey?'

'Big subject,' she said solemnly, 'the future! I can't help wondering what's going to happen to you when I go off to St Thomas's. Do you suppose you'll go back to working for the Major? Brian always used to insist that everything would be different after the war. It won't be long before we discover whether he was right. But it's very unsettling, not knowing.'

'Yes, but worrying won't make it any better, love. I don't know what will happen, any more than you do. It depends on the Guvnor. He may not want a chauffeur any more; he's managed pretty well without one these past years. And who's to say what *he'll* have to go back to? The Firm's still there, and Ceylon's all right, I suppose, but Marchant's rubber plantations have been in Japanese hands for years. The more I think about it the more I think Brian probably *is* right. Nothing's going to be the same again.'

He sounded unperturbed, sure that whatever life held in store could be accepted one way or another, simply because it had to be. Looking at him, Jane thought how much she loved him. There was nothing smart or showy about Jos, nothing to impress. In his old gardening clothes he could have been taken for any tired ordinary working man who asked nothing more of life than to be left in peace, to dig his garden and chat over the fence occasionally with his neighbour next door. But there was much more to him than that, and it grieved her deeply that Ano had never wanted to discover what it was.

'It will be strange not to be living in the mews myself,' she said after a moment, 'But I can't imagine you and Mum not being there, whatever happens.'

Jos brushed earth from his hands and rubbed them on the seat of his trousers. 'Shall I tell you what I'd really like, Janey? A little house in the country with a bit of land round it for growing things . . . not just vegetables, but as many flowers as I could cram in . . . everything I could think of! Funny thing is, I got talking to her ladyship one day about the past and what do you think she said . . .? "Joseph . . . I think a little house could be arranged!" Seems she still owns one or two. It sounded like paradise to me; the only trouble is I can't see your mother wanting to bury herself in the country, can you?'

She'd have given her own hope of paradise to deny what he'd said, but Mam needed London. 'Jos, don't you think Brian's a toad not to come home sometimes . . . she misses him so.'

'It might help, but it wouldn't be enough to make her happy,' he said slowly. 'She never has been what you'd call happy, but it's worse now.'

162

She tucked her hand inside his. 'Not your fault ... the unhappiness is inside Mam. *We* haven't been quite enough for her, somehow.'

'No, and for the life of me I don't know why.' Leaving himself aside, which Jos found it easy enough to do, he reckoned that a daughter like this one would have been enough to make most women happy, let alone the fact that there was also Brian. Jane's worried face made him shrug the problem aside. 'What shall we take her home ... peas, or some of my beautiful new carrots?'

'Both,' said Jane. 'For once we'll overwhelm her with riches!'

Chapter 12

Ano's wishes in the matter of where to live mattered as little in the end as Jos's dreams. On a fine morning of summer Jane was summoned to the headmistress's study. It was almost her last day at school, and she was to remember it for the rest of her life. Miss Haslip smiled at her with terrible kindness, gestured at Agnes Marchant standing by the window, and walked out of the room without saying more than a quiet 'Come in, Jane'.

Silence hung heavy in the room until she found enough voice to murmur, 'Something must be wrong, I think.'

Agnes nodded, aware that for once evasions and stratagems could do nothing to release her from the moment of horror she was trapped in. For years she'd dodged other people's emotions and kept her own more or less succesfully out of sight. Now, the debt she owed life was about to be paid in full.

'Another flying bomb fell this morning ... you probably heard it here. It destroyed two houses in the mews.'

'One of them was ... was our house?'

Tears were beginning to run down the face of the woman opposite her. Jane thought she hardly needed to be told the rest of what Mrs Marchant was trying to bring herself to say.

'Ano and your father were there. Ano was killed immediately. Joseph was brought out alive, but he ... died on the way to hospital. Cessy wanted to come instead of me, but I couldn't allow anyone else to tell you.'

The effort of saying it left her trembling with weakness, as if she were recovering from some almost mortal illness. She couldn't look at Jane's face, and stared instead at a bar of sunlight lying across the complicated reds and blues of Miss Haslip's Turkey rug. She would hate Turkey rugs for as long as she lived. The room was completely quiet except for the far-off sound of a piano being played and girls' voices practising 'Jerusalem'. She'd always remember that, too.

Jane stared at a spot on the ground, trying to believe what Mrs Marchant had just said, decided she wouldn't believe it because Jos couldn't possibly be dead. Then she made the mistake of looking at Agnes Marchant's face and knew that it was true after all. Jos *was* dead, and it was the punishment she'd always known she'd have to bear one day. The taste of sickness was in her throat, but she swallowed hard and heard a voice she didn't recognize as hers ask, 'Who . . . found them?'

'Jack Edmunds risked his life to crawl into the wreckage. *He* didn't tell me that, of course; one of the other men did. I spoke to him afterwards . . . Jos managed a word or two . . . his love to Jancy.'

She pulled her feet away from the ground where they seemed to have taken root, and wandered over to the window. 'Mam never thought much of Mr Edmunds, but Jos always insisted we might be glad of him one day.' Numbness was splintered by the sound of his name and she turned to Agnes a face disintegrating with despair. 'How am I going to manage without Jos?'

Mrs Marchant moved towards her, reaching out her arms. 'Dearest . . . he'll have known that *we* would do our best,' she said brokenly. She held Jane in her arms until the racking storm of weeping was over. Miss Haslip came back into the room, and finally the two of them went home together. William Marchant was already there, summoned by Agnes's telephone call, and it was he who prevented Jane from going into the mews. He'd been himself and knew the little house had crumpled completely under a direct hit. There was nothing to be salvaged from it that could safely be retrieved, and the only thing Jack Edmunds had found was the marmalade cat, Marmaduke, mewing on a pile of rubble. It was like being born again into the world, owning nothing. Even James's sketchbooks lay somewhere under the wreckage. It was a loss hardly worth noticing now, but a loss all the same. She remembered him insisting that the London they knew was going to vanish. That, at least, had been true.

Brian was out of reach when William tried to telephone, but it hardly seemed to matter to Jane. She hadn't seen him for eighteen months, and hated him for the fact that Ano had died without a visit from him for so long. He was less familiar to her now than Duncan . . . a stranger with whom she had childhood memories in common and some vague sense of being linked. But he walked in unexpectedly one day and she burst into tears at the sight of him.

'Sorry, brat,' he said, wrapping his arms hard about her. 'I've been neglecting you all, and now it's too late. Sins of omission, doesn't the Bible call them? It has a nasty habit of being right.'

'I always hoped you'd come for Mam's sake, but she didn't complain . . . said that you had your own life to live.'

'Yes, my own important life! What about you, Janey?'

'I manage, because the Major and Mrs Marchant and Cessy are so kind,' she said simply. 'I shall never stop missing Jos, but in a strange way it's almost a relief to know they're beyond the reach of any more harm. Mam didn't seem to look forward to anything, and Jos knew he couldn't have the thing he wanted most. He'd have turned

166

down a lovely life in the country for her sake, but all the time he knew that nothing he could do would make her happy. I don't know why. But sometimes I thought it was what the poet said . . . she was "desolate and sick of an old passion".'

She broke off suddenly to stare at her brother. 'You're very like her, you know. Promise me you won't make the same mistake – refuse to enjoy what you're given because you reckon it should have been something better.'

He wrenched his mind away from the memory of Cecily, who'd obviously been too like Ano as well. 'I'll do my best, brat. You've got Mam's eyes and hair, but you're just like Jos, if it's any comfort to you. While we're on the subject of promises, make one to me. Don't get so swallowed up by the Marchant tribe that you forget you're a Rowland.'

She stared at him, then began to laugh, but her thin arms hugged her body as if she was in acute pain.

'Was it so funny . . . what I just said?'

'Funnier than you know, anyway. At St Olave's I used to pretend that I *was* a Marchant, or at least a Rowland who belonged in Linden Square. I was ashamed of the mews . . . even disowned Jos one day when he called to collect me in his chauffeur's uniform. I deserved to lose him.'

The flat conviction in her voice said that she wasn't to be argued with on the subject, but he tried all the same. 'You're talking rubbish, brat. You did what any other child would have done in the same bloody class-ridden circumstances. Jos would have laughed if he'd known.'

'I don't think so. He did know I was upset . . . offered kippers for tea to comfort me!' With an immense effort she dragged herself back from memories and smiled at Brian.

'Now, when it no longers matters, I live in Linden Square! The Major insists this is my home, but I'm just

167

having a little holiday at the moment. At the end of September I shall start my student training at St Thomas's . . . won't really need a home then.'

'Yes you will, and we'll make one together as soon as I get out of the Navy.'

It was more kindness than she'd expected from him, and she didn't say that it would now be hard *not* to imagine herself as part of the Marchant tribe. She didn't want to go on talking about a family that had always irritated him, or mention Cecily and the twins. He wouldn't be shocked by the thought of illegitimate children, but she didn't want to hear him gloat over what had happened to a girl he'd always particularly disliked.

'What about you?' she asked instead. 'When the Major tried to telephone, they said you were away. I suppose you can't talk about it?'

'Just to you. We were getting bored with crossing the North Sea, and had the better idea of holing up in some small Norwegian fjord. We camouflage the boats during the day, and operate from there at night – very successfully! The local people are indispensable to the scheme, and quite extraordinarily brave. That's why we shall win this war, Janey, because of ordinary people like them . . . and Londoners, and the Russian farmers who burn their own land rather than leave it for the Germans. It's them we'll have to thank, not the admirals and generals strutting about in medals and gold braid.'

She grinned at him suddenly. 'Proletarian principles alive and well, I see!'

'I should think so.' He bent to give her a rare kiss. 'I must go and catch that blasted train again, Janey. We'll think of a plan, though, when this party's over. Agreed?'

'Yes, but you don't have to worry about me . . . I'm a big girl now.'

It was his turn to smile. 'What I had in mind was that you could take care of me!'

When he'd gone she realized how much she missed him, after all. The Marchants, dearly as she loved them, were not her own kith and kin. In the middle of telling Agnes about Brian's visit, it struck her for the first time that her friend was looking unwell. Twenty-four hours later she admitted to feeling as ill as she looked and retired to bed with what developed into a severe attack of bronchitis. Even when the worst of it was over, she recovered only very slowly, and Jane often found her staring listlessly into space, apparently too tired to struggle with whatever problems oppressed her. She couldn't seem to recover from the death of Ano and Jos, but Jane felt sure that it wasn't only grief that left her sitting at the piano but forgetting to play because her mind was elsewhere.

With Agnes ill, the running of the house fell to Jane, helped by Edie Bloggs, who missed her old sparring partner so much that for weeks she couldn't walk into the kitchen without weeping. In order not to upset Jane, she thought up a stream of excuses for her tears, that ranged from grit in her eye to the skinning of onions, but when Jane kissed her damp face one morning she relieved her feelings by breaking into a tirade against the Germans who, singly and collectively, she consigned to a slow and painful rotting in hell. For Jane herself, nursing Mrs Marchant, looking after the twins when Cessy was working, and running the house, were enough to send her to bed at night too tired to lie awake and weep for her own loneliness. But during odd moments of the day she did wonder how they were going to manage when she went to St Thomas's. If only Agnes would begin to look less frail, they could talk about things. But in the end it was Cessy who forced them to consider the future.

She arrived back at Linden Square later than expected one evening, with an expression on her face that said the afternoon hadn't been quite as usual.

'If the brats and Ma are all right for the moment, can we talk, Janey?'

'They're all right ... keeping each other company upstairs. What do you want to talk about?'

'The future. It would have needed talking about anyway, but Edward offered me a full-time job this evening.'

Jane blinked, but said calmly, 'You'd better tell me the rest of it first.'

'I was rehearsing it on the way back and it didn't sound quite so unbearably selfish and unreasonable as it does now. Edward's secretary down at St Margaret's is expecting another child, so she's resigning completely. He *must* have help there, and although the present arrangement has worked in a fashion, what he really needs is someone free to commute with him between Cornwall and Westminster. There's a big house to keep going there, as well as the estate and farm to run. If I don't take the job on, he must find someone else. In which case I shall go back to being a woman whose only function in life is to push food into a couple of infants and keep them clean.'

'They need more than that. If you don't think so, you're what Duncan called you once – a rotten mother.'

'I realize that, but I can't help it, Janey, and I can't pretend that taking care of them seems enough to justify my existence.'

'I'm surprised Edward made you the offer ... he knows the situation here.'

'He expects me to turn it down, but knew I'd have been bitterly hurt if he hadn't given me the chance. I've slaved over the job, and loved doing it. What matters most is the fact that he's come to trust me. Six months ago he reluctantly took me on to stop Ma quietly agonizing over me.'

Diverted from the matter at hand, Jane stared at her. 'Are you sure about that? How do you know?'

'It's one of my few accomplishments – measuring my effect on men! Edward likes my mother very much

170

indeed, but he didn't like me at all. Now I'm rather proud to say he's changed his mind ... about me, not about her.'

Jane smiled in spite of herself, aware that in such matters Cessy was infallible. In other ways it was time to take note of how greatly she'd changed. The strangest change of all was that it should concern her whether a farmer MP verging on middle age liked her or not.

'What happens to the twins if you take the job ... do they live down there.'

'That's the rub ... it simply isn't possible. Edward wouldn't mind, he's rather taken with them. But I couldn't cope with the job and them as well, and we'd be constantly chasing up and down between St Margaret's and the House of Commons.'

'If you've got your eye on me, there are all sorts of problems,' Jane said slowly. 'I love the children, but I don't know that I want to put them before my training ... and that's due to start in another week or two. Apart from that, what about Agnes and William ... this is their house, after all.'

'I know the problems, and there's one you haven't touched on. You can't afford to work for no pay. If you did take the twins on, you'd have to take a salary as well, and not go all high-minded on me.'

'I'm not in a position to be high-minded but, Cessy dear, it's a bit of a facer. How long would this go on for?'

'For the remaining life of this Parliament. After that everything might change and Edward might not even be re-elected. Could you hold off starting your own career for that long ... say, another year? Is it too much to ask, Janey?'

Her beautiful face looked strained and the expression on it convinced Jane of something that had frequently occurred to her during the past few months. Cecily loved working for Edward Ferguson because she loved Edward Ferguson.

Suddenly it was Cessy who spoke again. 'It's blackmail
. . . I'm a sod to have mentioned it. I'll ask Edward if we
can try it with the twins down at St Margaret's.'

'You'll do no such thing. They're a bit insecure as it is.
Leave them here, if your parents agree, and I'll take on
the job of looking after them for a year.'

Cecily stared at her, on the verge of tears which she
normally never shed. 'Charlie's highest form of praise . . .
you're a brick, Jane Rowland!'

Jane emerged from a hug, grinning at her. 'It's better
than "independent little cuss", I suppose.'

Cessy was prepared for her father to dislike the idea,
but when she aired the suggestion cautiously she was
shaken by the extent of his disapproval.

'The twins don't have to come here,' she pointed out
uncertainly. 'I could ask Jane to move into my flat.'

'She's not a pawn to be moved about a chessboard.
This is her home, and the question of where the children
are is immaterial,' he said brusquely. 'The point is that
they're *your* responsibility. I object strongly to Jane's
being made to feel that she must take them off your
hands because she has the mistaken idea that she owes us
something. If she insists on helping you, then they must
be here where I can keep an eye on them. But I don't
approve at all.'

Cecily went away to confess to her mother that she
now knew what it felt like to be run over by a very large
steamroller. 'Shall I give up the idea?' she asked eventually, too uncertain to realize that she was consulting her
mother seriously for the first time in her life. 'Pa's right in
a way, but he doesn't understand what the job means to
me. He's got a strong Victorian streak still . . . a woman's
place is in the home, rocking the cradle and fidgeting
with the tea cups. Not so long ago I'd have said it was
your idea too, but you've got very modern, Ma dear!'

Agnes looked away from her, wondering whether it

was modern for a middle-aged woman to feel painfully jealous of her own daughter. Probably not and history was littered with poor creatures like herself, who didn't even recognize the trap they'd fallen into until it was too late to get out. She wanted to weep with the hurt of it . . . deny Cessy the chance, if she could, of spending all her days with Edward Ferguson. But it was no more possible than deciding that she would suddenly stop breathing. When she turned to face Cessy her face was more or less under control again.

'There's still nothing wrong with the idea of a woman staying in her own home . . . it doesn't happen to fit *you*, that's all. Leave it to me for a while . . . let me see what I can do.'

Ma had sounded strange, Cessy thought, as she went away. But the strangest thing of all was that she felt confident enough of herself to intervene.

Agnes didn't feel confident at all, but her daughter couldn't be allowed to miss this chance of happiness, and the fact that, in helping Cessy, she would be expiating some feeling of personal shame, made her resolute in tackling William. He wasn't easily tackled these days . . . wrapped up in an almost obsessive concentration on the battles taking place in Normandy. They'd begun by not referring to Ano's death . . . now, it seemed even more impossible to talk about it . . . but the subject lay between them, unacknowledged and unhealed.

'William . . . Cessy's plan . . . may we talk about it, please? Something has to be decided for Edward's sake.'

'Let us decide by all means – for Edward's sake!' Before she could ask herself why he should sound so inimically polite, he spoke again. 'Cessy's plan, as you call it, is outrageous, my dear. I can't help thinking we've brought her up very badly; nothing matters except what *she* happens to want.'

Agnes's face whitened at the condemnation in his voice.

'Aren't you being a little harsh? She's done her best since the twins were born, but this job with Edward isn't the passing whim you make it sound. It's very important to her, and if she can't do it full-time she must give it up altogether.'

'Some people might say that her children should be important as well, especially since they have no father.'

'I realize that, and I suppose we agree that she should never have had them at all; but it happened because she was lonely and unhappy. Not only because of losing Charlie. I think something else went wrong at Lowestoft that she's never been able to talk about. Blame her upbringing if you like, but blame the war as well.'

'Yes, let's blame the bloody war by all means,' he agreed slowly. 'I don't mind the children coming here, but I do mind Jane being expected to put her own life aside. She's prepared to do it, but that's because her own upbringing has been different.'

Agnes turned away so that he shouldn't see her eyes fill with tears she couldn't wipe away. It was unlike him to be deliberately cruel, but she was being told that Ano Rowland had succeeded where she had failed.

'Jane knows that nothing is "expected" of her,' she insisted steadily. 'She's kind, but not stupidly kind, and she knows that doing it out of a mistaken sense of obligation would never work. If she does it, it's because she loves the twins, and loves Cessy enough to want to help her.'

'There are other jobs . . . does it have to be this one, now, with Edward?'

In some strange way she knew that they'd reached the heart of the matter. It required all her strength to smile at him. 'It matters to Cessy, because she works very well with him. Jane agrees . . . says it's wasteful to have Cessy coping with the twins rather badly when she could be coping rather well with Edward!'

It sounded so indisputably like Jane that a reluctant smile

touched William's mouth. 'I'm afraid I can hear her saying it,' he conceded.

'There's another thing . . . she's only eighteen, and her life's been torn up by the roots. I'd be happy to keep her here for another year.'

'You win, my dear! Let Cessy take the job with Edward, and I shall learn to come to terms with my grandchildren.' It was so generously said that Agnes suddenly unburdened herself of an anxiety that had begun to trouble her.

'Does it strike you that we aren't the only ones who don't seem able to manage without Janey? Duncan devotes himself to the twins whenever he's here, but it's only because where they are, Jane's likely to be also.'

It clearly hadn't struck William, because he stared at her in amazement. 'Do you mean he can't manage without her to the extent of wanting to marry her?'

Agnes nodded without saying anything.

'Well, it hadn't occurred to me – I suppose because he doesn't behave like a young man in love. But if it happened, I imagine you'd be delighted.'

'I think I should be heartbroken,' she said astonishingly. For a moment he thought it was all she was going to say, but the surprise in his face forced her to go on. 'Jane deserves a complete marriage, not a travesty of the real thing.'

William's eyes searched her face. It gave no hint that she was thinking of anyone but Duncan and Jane, but he wasn't tempted nowadays to make the mistakes about his wife that he'd made in earlier years. Nor could he ask if their own incomplete marriage was in her mind.

'Why should it be a travesty . . . it's obvious that they're very fond of one another?'

'At the moment Duncan simply wants to be taken care of . . . it may be all he'll ever want. That wouldn't be enough for Jane in the long run.'

She spoke quietly as usual, but with the certainty of a

woman who knew that she was right. The certainty said again that she knew about marriage when it was inadequate. William fought to keep his mind on the people they were supposed to be discussing. 'You said yourself Jane isn't *stupidly* kind, so why worry unnecessarily?'

'Because she can't bear to see Duncan diminished from the dashing young hero she always saw him as. If he needs her help now, she won't abandon him.'

'Aren't *you* being harsh now . . . on Duncan?' he asked sharply. 'You make him sound like a man who's always going to need a prop.'

She didn't reply and, after a long glance at him, walked out of the room, leaving him with the knowledge that there was no answer she could bring herself to give.

Chapter 13

It was the beginning of the 'cruellest month of the year': April at its most unpredictable. This morning, after weeks of cold depressing rain, there were so many dancing motes of sunlight filling the shabby room that Jane forgot the serious business in hand and reverted to a game not played since childhood. If she almost closed her eyes and squinted along a ray of sunshine she could make it shatter and reform into constantly changing patterns of coloured light. For a moment she was ten years old again, entranced by its magic. Then a tug at her hand reminded her that she was supposed to be sitting on the floor for the purpose of helping to build the Eiffel Tower in wooden blocks. She went back to the task, and Daniel hoisted himself to his feet to plant a damp kiss on her cheek, forgiving her for the brief lack of attention. Daffy, younger by three-quarters of an hour and always trying to make up for it, took advantage of a moment when his tower was unprotected. When it lay in ruins on the floor she smiled sweetly at her brother. Jane hoped that at the age of two and a bit Daffy was as beautiful and destructive as she would ever be. But confidence was not great in the matter, and her growing-up looked interesting – full of possibilities for disaster.

It was Daffy, facing the door, who gave warning that someone else had arrived. 'Man,' she announced briefly. It wasn't her usual intense interest in a stranger, but Daniel had to be watched in case he made a revenge attack on her

177

own beautiful tower. Jane twisted round, then scrambled to her feet, smiling with pleasure.

'Brian . . . what a lovely surprise! I didn't dream of seeing you.'

'Hello, brat.' He came forward to kiss her, grinning at the astonishment in her face.

She hadn't seen him since his lightning visit just after Jos and Ano were killed. His flotilla had been posted to Mediterranean duty almost immediately afterwards, and in the course of nine months she'd received a couple of scrawled letters from him. It was necessary to take stock, coming to terms with a weathered self-confident man of twenty-five who could have passed for thirty-five. Hard, now, to see in *this* Brian Rowland the awkward argumentative boy for ever lecturing them on how to set the world to rights. There was nothing of the greasy mechanic about him and, along with smartness, he'd acquired poise as well. It wasn't anything to weep about, but tears pricked her eyelids all the same . . . if only Mam could have seen him now! There'd been some talk of their making a home together after the war, but Jane had set no store by it; her life and Brian's had gone in different directions, and he particularly disliked the direction that hers had taken. Still, he *had* taken the trouble at last to come and see her.

'It's lovely to see you,' she said again.

'And you, Janey.' His eyes took in the thinness of her face and body, and the neat darns in the sleeves of her jersey. 'You're looking a bit war-weary, though.'

His gaze descended to the twins, both now on their feet and staring at him curiously.

'I'm sure your letters haven't mentioned *them*, so presumably they aren't yours. What are you doing here, anyway? When I last saw you you were just about to become a student nurse.'

'It's a long story, but my training got a bit delayed, on account of these two. Meet Daniel Willoughby, and his

178

sister Daphne . . . known more often than not as Daffy.'

'Willoughby? How can they be? He was killed five years ago. I don't much know about children but these are . . . how old?'

'Just over two,' she answered tranquilly, apparently unconcerned about all that she left unexplained. He wanted to ask, but was certain that the small bright-eyed creatures examining him knew they were being talked about. Jane suddenly scooped one of them up from the floor . . . the girl? He wasn't sure, but it, him, she was suddenly deposited in his arms. Jane merely grinned at the expression of horror on his face and hoisted Daniel over her own shoulder.

'She won't bite! She likes men as a rule.'

Just like her mother, he might have pointed out, if Miss Willoughby hadn't required his full attention. She was small but solid, and he could vouch from now on for the fact that the youngest generation was coming to no harm from the general shortage of food.

'Time for their morning milk,' Jane explained. 'Come down to the kitchen with us, and I'll make coffee as well.'

He followed her down the stairs to a large semi-basement room he hadn't been in for years. The house was shabbier than he remembered, and pushchairs had left dusty wheelmarks on the black and white tiled geometry of the hall floor. Pre-war elegance had seeped away, and so had pre-war atmosphere. He missed the remembered smell of furniture polish, cigars and perfume, faintly laced with the acrid tang of soot from the open fires. There were no longer coloured panes of glass in the front door to send shafts of crimson and violet light along the floor, and the gaps where they'd been were still filled in with bits of plywood.

In the kitchen Jane inserted the twins into their high-chairs, put beakers of milk out of reach, and brought mugs of coffee to the table. She saw Brian's glance round the room and knew what he was thinking . . . it still seemed unbelievable not to see Ano there. She dealt expertly with the beakers, one in each hand, then smiled at her brother.

'I don't know where to start, there's so much catching up to do. Are you in London on leave?'

'Yes . . . thought it was time I checked up on you, but I've got some people to see as well. I want to start thinking about the future. I had half a mind to stay in the Navy, but my long-term ambition is to get into politics, and the two don't seem to combine! So I'm working on another job, ready for when the Navy pays me off . . . equal partnership in a garage. I shall be the brains of the outfit and another chap in the flotilla's putting up the money – or, rather, his father is.' He took a gulp from the mug in front of him and grimaced at the taste. 'God, Jane . . . is this the stuff you've been drinking? There isn't even any sugar in it.'

'Coffee and chicory, and as much sugar as we can spare,' she said calmly. 'You've probably done better than civilians in the matter of food. Unlike most of Europe, we're a long way from starving, but we have to pinch and scrape.'

She was busy with the children and he could take his time about looking at her. Like the house, she was shabby and tired, but these were surface changes; there were much more fundamental alterations which he needed time to understand.

'You've grown up while my back was turned,' he said abruptly. 'Little Janey Rowland . . . gone for ever. Another casualty of this bloody war.'

'She'd have gone anyway,' she reminded him. 'Time has a habit of moving on!'

But for a moment she was little Janey again, washed over by memories of a child who'd had to watch the other children playing in the mews, and been taunted by them because she wasn't allowed to join in. They'd mimicked Mam too, but only when it was safe to do so behind her back. Her Welsh temper had been fierce, and her hand never known to miss its target.

'What's been happening here?' Brian's voice dragged her back to the present again. 'Mrs Bloggs let me in . . . for a terrible moment I thought she was going to kiss me! The family are obviously in residence, but you still haven't told me what you're doing here.'

Jane settled a small skirmish between the twins, and mopped up some spilled milk. Then she gave him a rueful smile. 'You can't help talking about them as though they set your teeth on edge, but it makes me angry when they've been so kind. William's just been invalided out of the Army early, much to his disgust. So, for the second time in his life, he's back in the City, picking up the pieces of Marchant & Ferguson. Quite a task, I think, although Tom Ferguson has done his best to keep things going. Agnes has survived the war better than you might suppose. In fact, she's found herself, rather unexpectedly. She still tends to drift about like a gentle ghost, but now we know that for the fraud it is! She still gives concerts, and they've become rather famous.'

'Of course! She sits strumming the piano all day while you cope with this barn of a house single-handed. No wonder you look worn to skin and bone.'

'Not single-handed. Agnes helps, when she remembers! And don't forget dear Edie Bloggs. Fortunately she dotes on the twins.'

Brian knew he'd been right about fundamental changes in Jane. It wasn't just the business of growing-up; as a child she'd been confused about where she belonged. Now, she belonged to herself . . . Jane Rowland, at home inside herself, at ease in Linden Square or anywhere else.

'What about the rest of them?' he asked. 'Dashing Duncan's still the hero of the family, I suppose, if you'll forgive my teeth being on edge again!'

'I shall take no notice! His squadron's in France at the

moment, but William's hoping he'll rejoin the firm, of course, when the war's over. How many times a day do we say that, I wonder? It's become a magic incantation . . . everything will go back to normal when the war's over. But I doubt if Duncan will be dashing again – a fighter-pilot's war has taken terrible toll of him.'

Her brother shrugged. 'He's survived, hasn't he? Lucky, if you ask me.'

She might have known that he wouldn't be generous to Duncan. He'd grown up hating a privileged boy two years older than himself who'd seemed to patronize him. It would have been a relief to share her anxiety with someone outside the family, but it obviously couldn't be Brian. Duncan's occasional visits had now become a strain, although he still managed to preserve the façade of idolised elder son in front of Agnes. He was less careful with William, but it was Jane who bore the brunt of his presence in the house – helped conceal the drunken 'sorties' with surviving friends, or listened to the painful bouts of self-examination that always followed. She knew how little was left inside his bright shell; not enough to cope with conventional City life and its time-honoured rules and rituals.

The room had gone quiet and Daffy was bored. She considered the possibilities for a moment, then swiped her brother's beaker clean off the table. Her dazzling smile at Brian invited him to agree that she'd been very clever, and reminded him painfully of Cecily. Jane intercepted Daniel's natural attempt to clout his sister with her own empty mug, and announced that it was time they got some fresh air. They were bundled up in woolly coats, then she hoisted a wriggling body under each arm with the smoothness born of much practice, and carried them outside to a play-pen rigged up on a small patch of grass outside the kitchen window. Brian stood looking out at a garden not much like the one he remembered; most of it seemed to be given over to the growing of vegetables, and something he vaguely thought might be marrow plants even swarmed over the mound of the air-raid shelter.

Jane gave the children a selection of toys, and then stood laughing with them. Her short dark hair was ruffled by the breeze, making her look younger than she'd seemed indoors. She was like Ano to look at, but only in that, he thought. At eighteen she was completely her own woman . . . competent because necessity had made her so, and serene in a way that their stormy mother never had been. Jos, though, now that he came to think about it, had had just that same quiet certainty about him.

She was still smiling when she came back into the room. 'Sorry about that. They're normally letting off steam by now in Kensington Gardens.'

'When does their mother remember to relieve you of them?'

'She doesn't . . . relieve, I mean, not remember. The twins live here.' Jane said it calmly, but steeled herself for the firework display that was almost bound to come. When it did, it started quietly.

'Willoughby, you said,' Brian commented. 'Why that? They must belong to someone else besides dear Cecily . . . or should I guess from that that she can't remember who it is?'

His sister's dark eyes, that *were* inherited from Ano, surveyed him across the table. 'You don't have to guess anything of the kind. Of course, Cessy remembers . . . but she chose not to marry the father, that's all; things didn't . . . didn't quite work out.'

'You mean she changed her mind about the poor sod of a victim she'd marked out? It seems to be a habit of hers.'

Jane frowned at a bitterness that seemed to go far beyond childhood dislike. He'd always liked Cessy less even than the rest of the Marchants, but she couldn't account for the real venom in his voice.

183

'Do you want to hear the rest of the story, or not?' she enquired.

'Apologies, brat . . . on you go.'

'Well, she had to leave the WRNS, of course, before the twins were born. She got a part-time job afterwards, working for Tom Ferguson's cousin, Edward. He's an MP who also farms a lot of land in Cornwall. Eventually Cessy had to take the job on full-time or lose it altogether. We agreed that she should do it, and I'd postpone my nurse's training for a while.'

'So she gets off scot-free while you prop up her parents for her and keep her misbegotten children out of the way! You're a mug, Jane. Do you realize that?' His beautiful Welsh voice was still soft, but she was aware of the anger leaping inside him. It was odd that he should get so worked up, even if Cecily, of all the Marchants, had had the greatest ability to rile him.

'What do you expect me to do?' she asked reasonably. 'Walk out and leave Agnes to cope with the twins?'

'Why not try leading your own life for a change? Kiss this bloody family of leeches goodbye . . . they're doomed anyway.' He was well and truly launched, but had to halt abruptly in mid-flight because another voice was beginning to make itself heard just outside the kitchen door. Agnes Marchant, who often started a conversation before she actually arrived, came into the room.

'Jane dearest, it was *my* turn to give the children their milk . . . you should have called me . . .', she hesitated, confused by the sight of a man in naval uniform getting to his feet. A flash of hope that James had walked in unexpectedly died as her eyes focused on the man's face.

'Brian? . . . yes, it's Brian Rowland,' she decided with a faint air of surprise. 'How . . . how well you look.'

He bowed, thinking she would tell him any moment that he'd grown! Like Jane, she had the look of a woman who didn't eat quite enough – both of them probably denying

184

themselves food to keep Cecily's bastards as plump as partridges. Her too-long narrow skirt spoke of pre-war fashions, and a cardigan that might once have matched it had now faded to a different colour from too many washings. Only her hair reminded him of a younger Agnes Marchant. It was still beautiful, still wound in the elaborate coil she'd never had cut when every other woman had gone bobbed or shingled.

She stood in front of him now, thin and rather dowdy; but, damn it to hell, she was still Mrs Marchant, who could make him feel young and awkward again without even trying. Articulate amusing Lieut. Rowland, shrewd man to watch because he was undoubtedly going to go places, was only a larger version after all of the urchin who'd had to earn his pocket money cleaning shoes at the Marchant house or scraping up bucketfuls of horse manure in the road under Duncan's pitying stare. He was so afraid the old habit of deference would assert itself again that he stood hands in pockets, looking insolently at ease, but cursing inwardly because he still couldn't quite bring himself to sit down at Agnes Marchant's table until she invited him to.

'Are you staying?' she asked, suddenly remembering that he had no cottage in the mews to go home to.

'Some friends in London are giving me a berth,' he replied. 'I just dropped in to see Jane.'

'Oh . . . well, stay to lunch, at least, won't you?'

It sounded fatally hesitant to his ears, and he wasn't familiar enough with civilian rations to know that she'd only faltered at the thought that there mightn't be enough food to share with unexpected visitors. Jane correctly read the expression on his face and hastily joined the conversation.

'It's not an offer we can make every day . . . but you're in luck! Curried vegetable pie, thanks to what we grow in the garden and a delicious recipe from Lord Woolton. I made lots.' She turned to smile at Agnes. 'Red-letter day! Not only a visit from Brian, but Cecily's calling in as well.'

Brian hadn't thought his lordship's pie sounded much of an inducement, but he'd have eaten whatever Jane put in front of him for the sake of not missing Cecily's visit. He was intensely curious to see her again.

'Lunch sounds quite a treat,' he said untruthfully to Mrs Marchant. 'It's kind of you to let me stay.' Smoothness had returned. Childhood had briefly betrayed him, but now he was himself again, and it wasn't a moment too soon if Mrs Willoughby was about to walk into the house.

Agnes smiled and drifted vaguely towards the door, promising to come back in time to do something to help.

'Which means,' Jane explained when the door had closed behind her, 'that she'll go upstairs and pore over a piano score until I go and drag her back to earth again. Now do you understand why I don't walk out and leave them?'

'I understand all right, and I'll repeat what I said before. Get out while you still can. Tell Marchant to find a keeper for his wife, and hand Cecily back her brats again; otherwise you'll be trapped here for ever.'

She was silent for a moment, torn between surprise at his concern for her and the need to make him understand. 'I'm trapped already,' she said finally.

'Because they took you in a year ago, and you've still nowhere else to go? Rubbish, Jane. You've paid them back ten times over already, I don't doubt. In any case, I shall soon be able to provide you with a home.'

She thought he meant it, and that the offer wasn't only prompted by a desire to wipe the Marchants' eye. Beneath his surface hardness was more affection for her than she'd realized. She didn't want to hurt him, but how to explain what it was that *did* hold her there? It *wasn't* gratitude, which William had always insisted she didn't owe them. It wasn't even habit, although her life had been linked with the lives of the Marchants for as long as she could remember. It was simply a matter of need. Without them, she would be unbearably lonely, and in their different ways they needed her ... William and Agnes, Duncan, Cecily and the twins. Brian did *not* need her. The remaining Marchant, James, didn't need her either, but that was a grief that concerned no one but herself.

'It's a big subject ... what we do with the future,' she said finally. 'Too big to tackle now, and I ought to be feeding the children if we're to have our own lunch in peace. You can make yourself useful and help!'

She smiled at the startling afterthought, but he discovered that she meant it. Something was concocted in a saucepan on the stove, and ten minutes later she brought the children in, and handed him a twin, a spoon, and a bowl of something that looked like porridge.

'Daffy's greedy . . . all you have to do is keep shovelling!'

He was doing just that when the kitchen door opened and Cecily Willoughby walked in.

Chapter 14

He was caught with a spoonful of gruel on its way to Daffy's mouth, and felt a fool through no fault of his own. Damn Jane for putting him in this ridiculous position, and for smiling at him when she read exactly what was going through his mind. But irritation didn't stop him registering the impact that Cecily Willoughby still made. His first impression was that she was unchanged after four momentous years; his second that there *were* changes, but they were all to her benefit.

He had slightly the advantage of her for once, having been forewarned. 'Greetings, Cecily ... as beautiful as ever; perhaps even a little more so!'

It took a moment or two for her to recover from the shock of seeing him, but the mockery in his voice brought colour back into her face again.

'Greetings to you, my dear Brian, and what a surprise! We imagined we'd lost you permanently to Hibernia ... or the fleshpots of the Mediterranean.'

The amused drawl was in place again, and she seemed unconcerned as she wandered over to drop a kiss on Jane's dark hair. He could remember every word of their last conversation, but what would she do if he mentioned Lowestoft ... make a great effort to remember that they'd both been stationed there?

'Excuse me for not leaping to my feet in the prescribed manner,' he said smoothly. 'As you see, I'm rather encumbered at the moment.'

'But doing it as to the manner born! Who'd have thought to see the Navy's Lothario tamed into such charming domesticity!'

His moment of advantage hadn't lasted long; he wanted to strike back at her, wipe that smile off her beautiful face.

'Perhaps you'd like to take over? She's yours, after all, so I'm told.'

Cecily shook her head and, in spite of himself, he watched the movement set a fan of golden hair dancing; then it fell into gleaming order again. She didn't even look shabby, like Jane. What did clothing coupons matter to someone who could spend the next few years still working her way through a huge pre-war wardrobe? She was dressed now in a suit of pale-blue tweed . . . just the thing, he supposed savagely, for mingling with the landed gentry in her boss's country constituency!

Jane looked from one to the other of them, feeling as if she might be needed to rush in with a blanket to smother dangerous sparks. She pointed at Cecily's rig, and said wistfully, 'Every time you arrive I realize what a slut I look! If only I were six inches taller. To think I used to resent wearing your cast-offs . . . I must have been mad!'

'Find something you can chop the bottom off and help yourself, Janey. All well here? Ma looks blooming, and so do these two.'

'Bless them, they're in the pink. I'll give you the treat of lending a hand with Daniel while I see to our own lunch.'

Brian cheered inwardly at the firm friendly instruction. He might still think the Marchants battened on his sister, but it was impossible to pretend she stood on anything but equal terms with them. Daniel was dumped in a pale-blue lap and Jane disappeared. He didn't seem enchanted with the change. Brian was happy to see that his own spoonfuls were going into Daffy much more smoothly. Sensible chap, Daniel . . . he liked him!

'You don't seem to have got the knack,' he commented

as Daniel baulked at accepting what remained in his bowl. 'No good trying to rush it. But patience was never your long suit.'

Cecily smiled at her son, willing him to agree to the final mouthful.

'Nor yours either, as I recall.'

'True! Birds of a feather we were . . . meant for each other entirely.'

His Welsh lilt had now become a stage-Irish brogue, but the softness of it wasn't meant to disguise the hidden barb. He saw her hand tremble as she replaced the spoon in Daniel's bowl, but she looked across at him steadily.

'You're curious about the twins, no doubt . . . wondering how I fell so completely from grace?'

He smiled lazily at her. 'Nothing to do with me . . . not a thing to do with me,' he said very deliberately.

Just for a moment she was tempted to tell him the truth about themselves. Ano and Jos Rowland were dead. The words were on her lips, almost tumbling out, when she remembered that Agnes and William were very much alive. The truth must wait so much longer that in the end it wouldn't matter whether it was ever told or not. She said nothing at all, and a moment later Jane came back into the room, followed by Agnes proudly announcing that she'd remembered to lay the table in the dining room upstairs.

The vegetable pie was unexpectedly delicious and, as Cessy said, hunting for the precious bits of bacon Jane had hidden inside was more exciting than looking for pieces of silver in pre-war Christmas puddings. The meal became positively cheerful, and it was only when she asked Brian what he intended to do when the Navy no longer needed him that any strain crept back into the conversation.

'A business partnership to begin with,' he said, 'but that's a beginning. My long-term plan is to get into politics.'

Cecily's carefully darkened eyebrow rose a fraction.

'Not a pillar of the Tory Party for sure. Perhaps a Liberal, or are you still bent on reforming the world?'

His smile glinted at her across the table. 'Bent on reforming this country, certainly. I remain what I always was . . . a Socialist.'

He was only half-serious, Jane thought, amused to see how far he could provoke them. She hoped Agnes wasn't paying attention to the conversation, but for once Mrs Marchant had not only listened to what was being said, but had taken it in as well. She looked horrified.

'A Socialist, Brian . . . but what about dear Mr Churchill?' Jane held her breath, but the question only made him grin; she supposed he'd expected Tory idiocy from Mrs Marchant.

Cessy, less sure of him, stepped in to draw his fire away from her mother. 'You're anticipating an election?'

'Of course . . . there must be one the moment the war's over. This Parliament's ten years old – practically dead on its feet.'

'And then you expect a change of government?' she enquired silkily. 'Shall you be out canvassing for the so-polished Ernest Bevin, or that odd-looking man whose hair stands up like a fox's brush?'

'I shall certainly try my hand at canvassing, but there'll be a change of government in any case, without any help from me.'

He spoke with such conviction that Jane stared at him, belatedly aware that he was wholly serious after all.

'You mean Mr Churchill won't be re-elected?' she asked quietly. 'It would seem like treachery after all he's done for us.'

Her brother shook his head. 'You mustn't confuse politics with sentiment. He's had his moment of glory. Now it's time for someone else to have a turn.'

Cecily inspected her polished fingernails, then smiled at Agnes across the table, who was looking worried. 'It's all right, Ma dear; no need to get worked up. Brian's crystal ball has got a crack in it. *He's* madly keen on change, but nobody else is. All they think about is getting back to life as it was before the war.'

'Wrong, my dear Cecily. *You* may want that, but almost no one else does. Why should they? What most of them had before was poverty, unemployment, and slums that haven't improved since Dickens' day ... is that what they're supposed to be yearning to go back to? They haven't been fighting this war for the sake of poor little Poland, or beautiful big abstractions like freedom from tyranny; this time they've been after a decent life for themselves and their children. They'll vote for the politicians who share their views, not a bunch of diehards trying to restore the status quo.'

Agnes blinked at this new Brian Rowland. The sentiments hadn't changed much from five years ago, but he hadn't expressed them then with this self-confident fluency. But she was uncomfortable as well as impressed, having been reared in the belief that politics was no subject for a lady's lunch-table. How right the precept had been! People could never help getting intense about politics, and turning the conversation into a harangue. She stood up, smiling apologetically.

'Excuse me, please. It's time for the children's recital.' She drifted through the doorway leading to the drawing-room next door, and a moment later the silvery beauty of a Chopin nocturne came floating on the air.

'Do I gather that's really for the children's benefit?' Cecily murmured.

'We find it sends them to sleep beautifully,' Jane said cheerfully. 'They used to be very resistant to the idea of an afternoon nap, but we had the brainwave of putting cots in there. Now they curl up like angels as soon as Agnes starts to play.'

192

'Cots in the drawing-room. My God, Pa must wonder what we've sunk to!'

'Gracious living still what it was in your neck of the woods?' Brian's savage question finally wrecked the surface friendliness. 'Liveried retainers pulling their forelocks, while nanny keeps the children out of the way?'

A flush of anger intensified the delicate colour in her cheeks. 'The gibes fall thick and fast, but they're not very well directed. Let me straighten you out, dear Brian. Edward drags up and down, representing a straggling isolated constituency in Parliament. He also runs a thousand acre farm and grows essential food more efficiently than most with the help of an elderly shepherd, a boy, and a couple of land-girls. Two-thirds of his house is given over to convalescent airmen, we live in the other third with the land-girls. Normally we work there most of the day, commute back from Westminster late at night. I wouldn't call it gracious living myself.'

Brian stared at her face, aware that when he wasn't hating her he still liked her more than any woman he'd ever met, apart from Jane.

It was his sister who broke a silence that struck her as being uncomfortably tense. 'Honours just about even, I'd say,' she murmured.

He shook his head at her. 'You mustn't be blinded by family feeling, Janey. I've just been trounced!' His smile begged Cessy's pardon, and Jane looked away from a glance that spoke of something shared between them. Then he stood up to go. 'I'll see you again before I leave London, brat. Don't forget to think about the advice I gave you.'

There was silence in the room when he'd gone, each of them busy with their own thoughts. Jane considered the fact that he was probably right – there was nothing to be done about the future yet, but she must know what she intended to do when the arrangement with Cessy came to an end. Cecily's thoughts had gone back to the past, and she was conscious of a great regret that she still couldn't help Brian by telling him the truth. She was grateful on her own account to have got through a meeting she'd always dreaded. The past was exorcised, and so was passion; he was simply a man she could have liked very well in different circumstances. Odd, now, that she could see so many small resemblances to her father in him when they'd never crossed her mind before.

After a while she roused herself to ask a question. 'May I know what Brian's advice was?'

'A well-intentioned brotherly suggestion that it was time I gave some thought to the future ... when the Marchants don't need me here any more!' She smiled as she said it and wasn't prepared to have Cessy take the matter seriously.

'I expect what he really said was why do you allow us to make use of you. We all do, me especially, I suppose. But Duncan fastens on you like a leech every time he comes home, and even Ma seems to have taken you over in her own gentle way.'

'We hang together for mutual comfort, let's say. Imagine how empty my life would be without you all.'

'Let's say whatever you like, but it doesn't alter the truth: the Marchants would be sunk without you. We *shall* have to think about the future, Janey.'

'I know ... but not until after this election we hear so much about. Our lives seem to hinge on the way a bunch of Cornish citizens vote for Edward!'

It was her turn to hesitate before asking a question. 'Speaking of Edward ... am I right in thinking he's come to mean rather a lot to you?' The expression on Cecily's face made her regret asking. 'Sorry ... I didn't mean to pry; forget I said anything.'

194

'I think it would be a relief to tell you,' Cessy said slowly. 'Do you remember the song about the man who meets his last love and "loves her as he's never loved before"? That's roughly how I feel about Edward, but with my usual flair I have, of course, picked the wrong man entirely. He finds me useful, and a poor substitute for the woman he really wants in his life.'

She made an attempt to smile, but Jane saw that her eyes looked stricken. Time was when Cecily Marchant would have demanded to be given what she wanted ... that was what life was for. Only, in the end, life hadn't seen it that way.

'It's hard to see you as anybody's "poor substitute",' Jane suggested. 'Sure you're not mistaken?'

'Quite sure,' was the bleak answer. 'Edward puts up with me, and he worships the ground my mother walks on.'

She normally never called Agnes anything but Ma. 'My mother' in this context seemed both terrible and touching.

'Poor you, if you're right. And poor Edward.'

Cecily stared at her. 'I think you may be pitying the wrong man. Spare a thought for my father. It seems to me that he's holding his breath at the moment, hardly daring to breathe.' She'd managed to shock Jane into complete silence for once, but when she spoke again it wasn't about her parents.

'How long is it since you heard from James?'

'I *never* hear from James. I'm an afterthought kindly tacked on to the bottom of his letters to Agnes.' It still hurt, even though she spoke as if she found it amusing. Cessy thought her eyes didn't look amused at all. 'There's usually a PS which says, "How's young Jane?" He probably doesn't even remember that I no longer wear a gym-slip and panama hat!'

'Pity to have lost touch,' Cessy said casually. 'There

'seemed to be such a bond between you at one time.'

'He resents the fact that I'm here.' Jane hadn't meant to confess that to anyone, but suddenly the words were in her mouth, insisting on being said. 'He wrote when Ano and Jos were killed, but even then it felt as though he'd had to force himself. Even before I came to live in Linden Square he'd . . . abandoned me. Funny to think of it being James who couldn't accept me when you and Duncan didn't mind at all. It's life catching you "on the 'op", as dear Mrs Bloggs would say!'

They were still entangled in the net Ano and William had made for them. Cessy all but blurted out the reason for James's withdrawal . . . remembered just in time that there was nothing she could safely say to explain why he'd been so uncharacteristically unkind. In different ways they were all still affected by what had happened a quarter of a century ago. But it was strange that James should have let it spoil his friendship with Janey. Knowing with absolute certainty that she was Jos's daughter, it didn't occur to Cecily that James had abandoned a girl who might easily turn out to be his half-sister.

The flurry of excitement caused by Brian's visit died down, but the normal quiet routine was marked by indications growing stronger day by day that the war in Europe was almost over. Agnes was thankful for that much grace, but inclined to be pessimistic all the same.

'The Japanese still have to be beaten,' she pointed out when Jane remonstrated with her for looking sad. 'I suppose the boys will be sent to the Far East, and that seems to be a worse war even than the one in Europe.'

'James, at least, is long overdue for leave. Their Lordships at the Admiralty will have to give him a breathing-space.'

Agnes didn't look as if she had any confidence in their Lordships doing anything so reasonable. She was composed

as always, but these days Jane sensed in her a different
kind of tension from the anxieties that had been part of
her life since the beginning of the war. She was still the
kind and gentle woman who hid daily fear about her sons,
gave public concerts, and liked to think that she was helping Jane. But something else occupied the centre of her
attention as well. Cessy hadn't said that her mother
returned Edward's affection . . . but surely it had been
implied? Jane found herself noticing in Agnes small signs
of inner excitement that were like bubbles rising to the
surface of an otherwise still lake.

They were agreeably surprised, after all, about the
reasonableness of the gentlemen at the Admiralty. Edie
Bloggs, left alone in the house one morning, greeted them
with the breathless announcement that James had
telephoned.

'Give me quite a turn to 'ear 'im,' she said breathlessly.
'Portsmouth, 'e is . . . likely to be 'ere any time.'

It was easy to smile and agree that it would be lovely to
see James again, but Jane remembered asking him to go
away once before because he spoiled things. It would be
harder to avoid him this time, because she lived in the
house that was his home, but somehow she must be able
to get through a few days without irritating him too much,
or being enraged with him if he sneered at Duncan again.

He was due to arrive the following afternoon, but she
took no notice of Agnes's suggestion that she should be at
home to welcome him.

'You and Lady C. are all the reception committee he
needs,' she said smilingly. 'We'll let his godchildren sneak
up on him gradually.'

She found herself ridiculously plagued by nerves, and
kept the twins out so long that Daffy finally complained
with bitterness that it was long past teatime. There was
nothing for it but to go home and get the meeting over

with. The sight of a naval cap lying on the hall table almost paralysed her with shyness, but the twins headed for the kitchen with the certainty of homing pigeons and she forced herself to follow them down the stairs.

She was cutting up banana sandwiches when the door opened and James walked in – so tall and brown-faced and unfamiliar that for a moment she thought it couldn't be him. But the dark unruly hair was just the same, and the deep-set eyes examining her steadily.

'Meet your godchildren,' she suggested unsteadily. 'Daniel's the one with the curls, much to Daffy's grief.'

He squatted down to receive a dutiful peck from Daniel, and a more enthusiastic one from Daffy, who did indeed like men. Then he stared at her again.

'When I last saw you, you were going to become a nurse, not a children's nanny.'

Had he meant to underline her real place in the household? She supposed so, and wondered how she could have expected anything else. James had been kind a long time ago to a child in Linden Mews; in his own home she was an interloper. She'd have hated him if she could, but Jane Austen had been right about women's hearts . . . stupidly, they were so much stauncher than men's.

James stared at her shuttered face, and thought it had become beautiful in its fine-boned thinness. He'd kissed her goodbye a lifetime ago, but he knew that if he moved towards her now, she'd simply walk away from him. It was intolerable not to know where she stood in their muddled relationships. Damn Ano and his father to hell and back again.

'I'm still going to be a nurse,' she said out of a long silence. 'It just got postponed a little, that's all.'

He looked at the twins again, and found them watching him with the inquisitiveness of a couple of baby robins. 'They're the spitting image of Cessy . . . true-blue

198

Marchants, the pair of them. I recognize that familiar expression which says the world's their exclusive oyster!'

'It's the expression all two-year-olds ought to have,' Jane said lightly. 'Time enough for them to discover that the world occasionally has to be shared with other people.'

'True, oh wise one!' It sounded so like the old James for a moment that she glanced at him and found him smiling.

'I lost your sketchbooks,' she said suddenly. 'I meant to take such good care of them, but they . . . they went with everything else.'

'My dear girl . . . as if they mattered. I wrote you a very inadequate letter afterwards, but to say anything at all about losing Jos seemed such an impertinence that I almost didn't write at all.'

She nodded because it still wasn't possible to talk about Jos. 'Your parents have been marvellously kind, and Cessy too. She might have produced these two for no other reason than to keep me busy! Duncan adores them as well, and takes his duties as godfather very seriously.'

She was babbling, she thought, talking too much because she was stupidly ill-at-ease with him. If only he would go away, so that she could bath the children and put them to bed. Supper still had to be cooked, but she could plead a headache to account for her own absence from the dining-room. James must be allowed to have his first meal with his parents in three years without feeling that the servants' daughter, promoted to the dubious status of family friend, expected to be present as well.

With a perfect sense of timing Daffy rescued them from a silence that was becoming painful. She wasn't used to being ignored and saw no reason to let the situation continue. Her plate was sent sliding off the table, while she smiled enchantingly at James.

'Nice man,' she suggested hopefully.

He did what was expected of him and picked it up, but was quick enough to intercept its immediate flight downwards again.

'Harden your heart,' Jane advised. 'She'll have you doing it for hours otherwise.'

She moved about the kitchen tidying things, while he talked to the children, and his strong impression was that she didn't want him there. Perhaps he'd become shockingly vain and self-important, but why couldn't she look as if she was pleased to see him?

'I get the feeling of being slightly in the way,' he said when she re-emerged from a visit to the larder.

'Of course you're not . . . it just happens to be a busy time of the day.' For the first time since he'd come into the room he saw the ghost of her old grin touch Jane's mouth. 'There'll be plenty of time to get acquainted with your godchildren, if that's what's worrying you. Daniel, especially, likes paying morning calls. He does a circuit of the bedrooms every morning, just to make sure we've all survived the night. You can expect him tomorrow any time after 6am!'

'Just like being at sea,' James observed thoughtfully. 'I wonder why I thought I was coming home to be cossetted!'

He smiled impartially at the three of them and finally went away. She let out a sigh of relief, and told herself that the worst was over. They weren't going to become friends again . . . she felt sure of that, because something she couldn't identify stood firmly in the way . . . but they could manage well enough to conceal the lack of friendship.

He'd been home two days when peace in Europe was officially declared – VE Day, 8 May, 1945 . . . five and a half terrible years after Neville Chamberlain had declared war on Germany. Hitler was dead, the Third Reich in ruins, and the continent of Europe could begin to lick its wounds and put itself together again. Agnes still seemed

200

so strangely oppressed that William was provoked into being rough with her.

'Remembering that we've lost Charles, Ano and Jos, unbridled rejoicing would be out of place, but we *have* just won a war at unparalleled cost and effort,' he pointed out sharply. 'You're expected to look pleased about it.'

'I *am* pleased, of course I am,' she protested quietly. 'I'm sorry if I sounded dismal, but we talk so glibly of putting the world together again and I wonder if we can. Things can be mended, but what about the damaged people?'

William shrugged the question aside. 'Some, of course, can't be repaired . . . it's the cost I mentioned.' The truth was that so many lives had been shattered beyond hope of repair that his own troubled life mattered very little in the scheme of things. But at the moment it was his own life that seemed to matter most of all. He'd had to accept small glimpses of a woman not as content as he'd always blindly supposed, but they hadn't prepared him for what was happening now. It was hard to believe that Agnes, of all women, could not only inspire love in a sophisticated man several years younger than herself, but seem inclined to love him back. Nothing had changed on the surface of life in Linden Square, but William was certain that it was direly threatened. He wanted to feel angry and ill-used, and only succeeded in feeling frightened. But if it led him to sound ill-tempered and uncaring about whether the rest of the world lived or died, her choice between him and Edward Ferguson would be easy.

He was about to apologize when she smiled brilliantly at him. 'The war's over, James is home, and Cessy and Edward are coming to dinner. We'll put a ring round worries for this evening. Cornish chicken is on the menu as a special treat. Edward swears that it's died of old age, but it looks to me as if it might have been enjoying the prime of life!'

It was murderously hard to look cheerful when he was

convinced that, between one moment and the next, some great decision had been reached.

'If it's to be an occasion, I'll see if I can blow the dust off some wine in the cellar . . . it might still be drinkable.'

It was the last refinement of torture that he'd be eating the man's damned chicken, and have to smile and look pleasant while every mouthful stuck in his throat.

Chapter 15

They were there to celebrate the outbreak of peace, and a
little pre-war elegance had been salvaged for the occasion
. . . for the first time in years the table was formally laid
with gleaming silver, and William's hoarded wine glowed
golden in their glasses. He hoped it was doing more to lift
the spirits of his guests than it was doing for him, but even
that was doubtful: Jane and James seemed quiet, Edward
thoughtful, and Cessy strangely subdued. Only one of
them, Agnes, was celebrating something. Dressed in old
black lace, with her hair shining like silver-gilt in the
candlelight, she'd mysteriously moved into the centre of
the stage. Delicate colour touched her cheekbones, making
her youthful again as well as beautiful.

William found himself looking at her too much, and
usually found her smiling at Edward. It wasn't even a relief
to concentrate on Cessy who was deliberately, he could
swear, refusing to compete with her mother. She had
decided that it should be Agnes's evening. But sadness
drained the life from her face, and when her eyes glanced
in Edward's direction they were full of despair. William
thought it would be easy enough to hate Ferguson on his
own account, but a positive pleasure to do it on behalf of
Cessy.

They should have asked Gran, James realized, when yet
another awkward silence threatened to take hold of them.
She was proof against any embarrassment, and the task of

keeping a conversation going had never defeated her yet. As it was there was something wrong with the rest of them, and only his dear Mama was in sparkling form. When the next pause came he was ready for it.

'All this talk of an Election . . . when do you suppose it's going to be? Edward, you must be in the know – can't you drop a hint?'

Their visitor gave a little shrug. 'Very soon, is all I can say. Churchill would have preferred the Coalition to see out the rest of the war in the Far East, but the Labour people in the Cabinet are determined to press for a firm date – so he'll want to outmanoeuvre them by calling it before they're ready. Six weeks is my guess . . . while everyone still feels grateful to him!'

Agnes hurried into the conversation, certain that William would resent what had just been said. 'Jane's brother, Brian, was here a little while ago. He seemed convinced that there would be a Socialist victory.'

'Rubbish, my dear. Churchill's got all the cards in his hand.' William sounded more contemptuous than he meant to, and more confident than he actually felt. But he hoped Edward would feel obliged to argue with him – it was becoming necessary to get to grips with the man.

'If it were to be just a civilian vote I'd probably agree with you,' Edward said calmly. 'There's a factor that can't be predicted, though – the way that thousands of service men and women will vote. They don't necessarily share the public veneration for a man whose record isn't entirely blameless.'

It might be true, but it was also certain to annoy. Agnes looked at William's face, recognizing the storm signals, but she was too late to intervene.

'Which man's record *is* entirely blameless?' he wanted to know. 'What about you, my dear Edward . . . nothing to reproach yourself with?'

It was pointed enough to stab them all into fresh

embarrassment, but after a moment Edward turned the edge aside with a pleasant smile.

'Of course ... a lifetime's trail of sins and errors of omission, like everybody else. But we were talking about Churchill. It's a fact of political life: however hypocritical it may be, the British expect their public men to be even purer than Caesar's wife!'

William snorted. 'Then they'd better choose that anaemic-looking nonentity, Clement Attlee.'

'I share Brian's opinion that it's exactly what they *will* do.'

James decided that he must have been mad or desperate to land on politics as a subject of conversation. He was still casting about in his mind for a less dangerous alternative when Cessy roused herself to come to his rescue.

'Pray, at least, that the good citizens of St Margaret's send Edward back to Westminster when the time comes; otherwise I shall be out of a job! I rather like strolling along the corridors of power as if I belong there. I could probably be just as useful to a bookie or a chimney-sweep, but it wouldn't seem quite the same somehow.'

Edward's sudden grin lightened the atmosphere. 'I'm overwhelmed, my dear Cessy, and not at all sure that you aren't being too generous. Most people would prize the two chaps you've just mentioned far above a plodding MP.'

'It's nothing to do with you personally,' Jane explained kindly. 'She just happens to like the *place*.'

There was more laughter than it deserved, because it was a relief to laugh at something. Then Edward opened the conversation again, talking directly to Cessy as if the others weren't there.

'However the citizens of St Margaret's vote, doesn't make any difference to *us*, I hope. I couldn't manage without you down there ... can't imagine how I managed before.'

'Handsomely said, Mr Ferguson,' she managed, after a

205

fleeting glance at her mother's face. It was no longer delicately flushed, but ashen-pale, and her hand fumbled for the wine-glass beside her plate.

For the rest of the meal she ate very little, and drank as if she was thirsty. The unaccustomed wine made her talkative and her face was a mask of bright despair.

The interminable meal was over at last, and Edward smiled at his hostess. 'You're going to play for us, aren't you, Agnes? It's always the lovely ending to our evenings here.'

Her eyes looked panic-stricken, flew to William, imploring help.

'I'm going to insist that you let her off this evening,' he said firmly. 'Agnes was rehearsing all the morning ... giving a recital this afternoon. If she isn't exhausted, she ought to be.' He rose and walked round to her side of the table, so that his arm could steady her when she stood up. 'In fact, we're a couple of exhausted hosts who are going to totter to the drawing-room and let all you youngsters bring us coffee!'

Agnes achieved a smile of sorts, and the two of them walked together through the doorway into the adjoining room. Behind them four people could pretend that nothing unusual had occurred, unless it was simply that they were out of practice for social evenings.

With the house full, Edward eventually left to spend the night at his reopened Club, and Cecily slept at her own flat. When she got back to Linden Square after breakfast the next morning it was to find James already up and out of the house.

'He's supposed to be idling about on leave,' she said irritably to Jane. 'What possesses my tiresome brother to go rushing off when I particularly want to talk to him?'

'The fact that you probably forgot to mention it,' Jane told her with a tranquil smile. 'He bolted out of the house, late for a rendezvous he suddenly remembered ... the

206

sister of one of his fellow-officers, I gather. I hope she didn't stand him up.'

Cessy hoped she did. 'Janey, put down that blasted iron . . . I want to talk to *you*. I can't do it if you keep waving that thing under my nose.'

Jane gave a long-suffering sigh, unplugged the iron, and from sheer force of habit cast an eye over the twins, happily building sandcastles in the sun outside the kitchen door. At the moment she didn't feel like talking to anybody about anything.

'Tell me what's wrong . . . with you and James . . .' Cecily began.

'Lord love us . . . nothing's wrong! I told you, he remembered . . .'

'. . . the sister of a brother officer. You told me that bit. Now continue.'

'End of story. We were friends years ago; now we aren't. If I'm anything at all to James, it's as a rather boring reminder of the days when I used to tag after him, asking to be shown the things he was drawing, and he tried to make me see things with his eyes. Friendships have a time for blooming, like flowers; ours blossomed early and died.'

Cecily stared at her thoughtfully. 'You hinted once that he resented you being here . . . you're quite wrong about that, Janey. If he knew, he'd be horrified.'

'If you're thinking of telling him, forget it, please.' She saw Cessy open her mouth to argue, and turned on her with a fierceness reminiscent of Ano Rowland. 'I forbid you to talk to James about me. You must promise me, Cessy.'

She had that much right, her friend realized. For all her gentleness you didn't make the mistake of thinking Jane would allow you to run her life. After waiting for an unwilling nod, she deliberately changed the conversation. 'We agreed a little while ago that the future needed thinking about. It certainly does if you're going to stay with Edward whatever happens in the election.'

'I'm *not* going to stay with Edward,' Cessy said bleakly, 'even though it's kind of him to suggest it.'

'I thought it was what you wanted . . . more than anything?'

'It is . . . more than anything on earth. But did you see my mother's face last night? One moment she was floating some way above the ground . . . I'd never seen her look quite like that before. The next, she was destroyed. God dammit, why do we all need men?'

There was a little silence between them, then Jane said quietly, 'Do you help *her* by denying happiness for yourself?'

'Probably not, but the situation's unbearable anyway . . . whether Edward sees me simply as an efficient secretary/housekeeper, or whether he ends up offering to marry me so that some other poor woman isn't tempted to fall in love with him. I think he *does* love my mother, but as some unattainable vision of perfect womanhood . . . not as a woman who shares his bed and scowls at him across the breakfast-table because she's out of sorts. I don't think it crossed his mind that she would ever see herself in such a role.'

'But you think so?'

'I'm afraid she finally made up her mind that she did. That's why Edward's invitation to *me* last night came as such a terrible blow to her.' It wasn't what she'd expected.

'Poor Agnes . . . and poor William, if he realized,' Jane said slowly.

'Oh, he realized . . . that was why he was so kind to her.'

Without knowing that she watched them, Jane's eyes were on the children. As usual, Daniel was patiently trying to teach his sister something she was too impatient to work out for herself – this time it was the problem of making sandcastles that didn't collapse the moment she shook them out of her bucket.

'Does it hurt if I say that Daniel often reminds me of

Charles?' she asked after a moment. 'There are times when I'd swear he *is* Charles's son. I'm a fool to mention it, because it might encourage you to take the twins over again. I love them so much that I shall feel I'm being torn away from my own children when the time comes.'

She spoke cheerfully so that Cessy would know she needn't be taken too seriously, but there was no smile on the face opposite her.

'I didn't think of you growing fond of the twins when I suggested the arrangement. In fact, I didn't think of anything at all except what I wanted to do. The story of my life, Janey! I don't wonder my guardian angel finally got tired of looking out for me, but the result is that I'm knee-deep in mistakes.'

She sounded so genuinely troubled that Jane leaned over to deposit a rare kiss on her cheek. 'There's no need to beat your breast on my account. I've always known I'd have to hand the children over at some point. But I shan't lose them altogether. I'm still their godmother, and I shall insist on interfering until they're at least twenty-one. By then I'll be a crabby old maid of a Matron, putting the fear of God into all the student nurses!'

Cecily smiled at her with great affection. 'You'll make a good nurse . . . it's time you got started. Saying which, it's also time *I* got started. Keep an eye on things here for me, and let me know if . . . if there's anything I can help with.'

James was out all day, from which Jane deduced that his friend's sister *had* waited for him. She was cooking dinner when he wandered into the kitchen, for once not in uniform. In old flannel trousers and a faded shirt he was both more familiar and more obviously *not* the young man who'd gone away with her promise that she would look after Agnes for him. She couldn't blame him if he thought she hadn't made much of a job of that. He was much too good at noticing things to have missed the tensions and undercurrents around last night's dinner-table.

Even less than to Cessy did she want to talk about them to James, and concentrated for dear life on the sauce she was stirring in the hope that he would get irritated with her and go away.

'I get the impression that it's more than my life's worth to interrupt you,' he said gently.

She managed a brief friendly smile, then went back to her saucepan again. 'Not as bad as that, but white sauce has a deplorable habit of going lumpy if you take your eye off it. If you're looking for the twins, they're upstairs, lying in wait for their grandfather. It's the high spot of their day, having him come home and read to them for half an hour before dinner.'

'I wasn't looking for them, as it happens. Much as I adore them, it would be nice to have a conversation with you occasionally without one or other of them chipping in.'

Jane poured the sauce over the remains of the Cornish chicken and put the dish in the oven. 'Now there's only the rice to cook. I can stop looking busy for a moment or two.'

It was a reluctant invitation to him to talk if he insisted on doing so, but he found it hard to begin.

'Last night,' he said abruptly, 'was it as awful as I imagined? My impression was that we could find nothing to say, in case a lot of very thin ice broke beneath our feet. Or have I got so used to the simple wardroom life that I've forgotten how people behave at dinner-parties?'

'As a celebration, it left something to be desired,' Jane admitted slowly. 'Maybe we've got more adjusting to do than we realize. Not having a war on any more is something we have to get used to.'

'Don't dodge the question, Jane. I need to know the score.'

She glanced fleetingly at his brown face, and saw it filled with anxiety. He had a right to the truth, but she wasn't certain that she even *knew* the score.

'Cessy wanted to talk to you this morning, but you'd

gone when she arrived,' she said wretchedly. 'I'd much rather you *did* talk to her. I hate meddling in things that don't really concern me.'

'Meddle away, Janey.'

'Well, perhaps you gathered that the . . . the difficulty centres around Edward. Cessy's grown very fond of him.' She found herself despising the half-truth and tried again. 'She's in love with him, in a way that might have finally given her real happiness, but she imagined he was so attached to your mother that he didn't even notice when she was around.'

'And judging from my father's face last night, he had the same impression?'

Jane nodded, without saying anything.

'Which leaves us wondering about Mama's attitude. She was different last night . . . alight, somehow . . . but do you really see her walking out after twenty-five years of marriage to William?'

'Cessy thought it might happen. I thought not, except that I've always had the feeling that she's been lonely, looking for something she's never quite found. The odd thing is that Edward is your father turned inside-out: outwardly sensitive and gentle, but tough inside, whereas with William things tend to be the other way around.'

James digested this in silence, thinking what an appalling mess they were in. No wonder Cessy had looked defeated last night . . . Fortune's darling must be wondering what she could possibly have done to deserve such continuing punishment. William, too! Whatever his enjoyment of Ano Rowland might have been, he'd lost her in the end to a filthy German bomb, and now it looked as if he was about to lose Agnes as well.

'Does Mama know how Cessy feels about Edward?'

'She knows Cessy loves working for him.' She hesitated, reluctant to go on, but James had told her not to dodge. 'That was how things stood last night . . . only I think we

211

had the feeling that Agnes had made up her mind about Edward, after months of uncertainty. But then, out of the blue, he made it brutally clear that he wanted his life to go on exactly as it is now . . . with no place in it for her.'

'Oh, God . . . so that's why she suddenly looked stricken? Marchant madness seems to be unconfined! Only *you* go serenely on your way, life neatly organized, emotions under control. I can see why Gran approves of you.'

He saw a strange little smile touch her mouth, and remembered Jos too late to stop the unthinking cruelty of what he'd just said. She gave him no time to apologize for it.

'As you say, emotions all under control! It's not quite true . . . I don't know how I shall say goodbye to the twins when the time comes.'

'Will you have to? I should have thought you could keep the job for as long as you wanted it.'

She heard again in what he'd just said a reminder that she was Ano all over again, included in the Marchant household only because she had a job to do there. It had almost ceased to hurt, but not quite.

'Changes are looming. For one reason or another Cessy's work for Edward looks like coming to an end. Then she'll get a job that keeps her in London, and find a full-time nurse for the twins. At which point the most elderly student nurse in captivity will be able to start her training!' Instead of smiling, he was staring at her intently, making her so nervous that she rushed after another topic. 'What about you? I suppose it's too soon to be thinking of the future . . . but after demob, what will you do . . . go back to the Art School idea?'

'I suppose so, although the thought of going back to school seems slightly ridiculous. But I expect they'll have ways of cutting cocky naval officers down to size!'

She smiled involuntarily, and he was startled all over again by the fact that she was beautiful when she smiled.

212

Features not particularly remarkable in themselves, except for her dark eyes, suddenly coalesced into a pattern of vivid loveliness. 'Janey . . . I made it sound just now as if you don't care a damn what happens to the rest of us. You ought to have heaved a saucepan at me. You spend your days taking care of us, from bossy old Gran down to the terrible twins. If you do ever kiss the Marchants goodbye, it'll be the moment when they finally fall to pieces.'

It was so nearly the old James back again . . . the boy who'd fished her out of trees and held her hand when she was in dire trouble . . . that she was tempted to fling herself at him and weep away the years of sadness, effort and grim monotony. But he *wasn't* the old James, and no doubt her tears would be an embarrassment to him. She clung to the kitchen chair in front of her instead, and said with an effort at calmness, 'The Marchants would muddle through perfectly well if I wasn't here. But it will be a relief when we can start to plan our lives again; for such a long time we've just had to let things happen.'

James shook his head with a glimmer of a smile. 'Don't bank on it, Janey. If we get lumbered with Brian's socialist dream, planning our own lives will be the *last* thing we'll do. The State will organize us from the cradle to the grave – paradise or purgatory, depending on your point of view!'

'You know your father's hoping Duncan will rejoin Marchant's,' she said abruptly. 'It worries me, because I don't think he'll be able to.'

She was politely interested in the future of James Marchant, it seemed, but passionately concerned about what happened to Duncan. He should have remembered that was how it had been for years. He couldn't, to save his soul, not sound jealous about it.

'Still carrying a torch for my dear brother, Janey?'

'Wanting to help him, if I can,' she said steadily. 'He's not the self-confident young man you used to know.'

'In that case, City life might be just what he needs . . . calm stability after too many hectic years?'

'Perhaps . . . time will tell, I suppose.' The flatness in her voice said that she was disappointed in him, and disinclined to go on with the conversation. 'Time, too, that I went back to getting dinner ready.'

'And I'm getting in the way! Roughly where we started, I think.'

She busied herself with hunting for the rice-jar, handicapped by the fact that her eyes were full of tears. When she turned round again the room was empty.

Chapter 16

James rejoined his ship, the euphoria of VE Day gave way to the realization that nothing about daily life had greatly changed, and, in the mounting fever of excitement about a General Election called for 5 July, it was possible to forget to refer to the night of the dinner party. Agnes wandered through the days in a state of frozen calm, but she didn't go near the piano. If concerts had been arranged, she found some means of cancelling them. She was a courteous ghost, who smiled and spoke when smiles and talk were needed, because self-control was second nature to her. Jane wondered how long control would last, and how long William could endure a situation he found almost intolerable.

Polling Day was, at least, something to talk about, and the result of it three weeks later, when far-flung service votes had been counted, something to marvel at. Edward was one of comparatively few sitting Members to be returned, in what turned out to be a landslide victory for Labour. Amid the general uproar of shock or jubilation, according to taste, Jane couldn't concentrate on any effect the results might have on their own lives – she was too busy feeling sorry for Mr Churchill. Maybe Brian was right to insist that it was time the old order was swept away. Even so, she couldn't help thinking that a man who'd refused to let them be defeated in the worst days of the war deserved better than this public execution before the war was totally won. She said so over dinner one evening, because impersonal topics of conversation were now the only ones that could be trusted.

'Brian's letter this morning was as joyful as you might imagine . . . true democracy in action – that's what we're going to see now, apparently.'

'It doesn't sound as if you believe him,' William said, smiling at the note of doubt in her voice.

'Well, he also told me that the ordinary people of this country – whoever they may be – would be delighted to see the back of Mr Churchill. But Edie Bloggs, for instance, is horrified, and so is the milkman, and Jack Edmonds. Edie assures me she doesn't want the country run by people who sound just like her! I don't think she knows or cares about "true" democracy.'

'If such a thing has existed since the Greeks coined the word and the idea two thousand years ago! Brian's perfectly sincere in being hopeful . . . a just society at last in an England that has only been green and pleasant for some. But I'm afraid I foresee something quite different – the dead hand of bureaucracy stifling us at every turn, just when there's so much to be done and we need every ounce of vigour and enterprize that we can wring out of tired old bones.'

Agnes roused herself to take part in the conversation. 'But what about the Beveridge Report, William? The Conservatives seemed much too reluctant to accept it. It's time everyone in need had a right to be taken care of.'

'In *need*, of course; but only then. Take away from people the responsibility for their own lives – which is what the Socialist dream *really* means – and the rot sets in. The theory's fine, but I just can't bring myself to believe in it in practice, and God help us all if the Marxist lunatics ever convince the electorate that what they need is a Red Dawn! Russia's wartime performance has been magnificent, but now the problems with her are going to start.'

For once he sounded discouraged, looked too tired, Jane thought sadly, to face the task of rebuilding a shattered business. His thick hair, always untidy like James's, was going grey, and the skin of his face was stretched tightly over too-prominent bones. Even when the Marchant rubber plantations were freed of the Japanese, they would have to be made operative again, and neither William nor Tom Ferguson had a young man's vitality to cope with the task. Jane told herself that she loved Agnes and William equally – wouldn't take sides – but surely her friend could see how much he needed help at the moment, not the racking uncertainty of their present life.

For once, Agnes seemed interested enough not to drift away into some private thought of her own.

'Why should we have problems with Russia? She's been as much part of the Potsdam Conference as America or ourselves.'

'Because, my dear, her troops now plaster Eastern Europe,' William said grimly. 'If you want my view, it's precisely where they'll stay. Elections will be held, because the Russians are committed to allowing them to be held in the countries they occupy, but the result will be puppet governments owing allegiance to Moscow.'

She shrugged and retreated away from him again, just as she'd been doing for weeks. He knew with utter certainty that his only hope lay in doing nothing. For a man not given to being passive or patient, it was the cruellest test of fortitude that Fate could have devised. But he could do nothing but wait for her to decide, and nothing to help her work though her own purgatory.

Ten days after the bombshell of the Election, something much more catastrophic in its implications pushed the novelty of the new Government into the background. President Truman, now in office at the White House after the death of Roosevelt, approved the dropping of an

217

atomic bomb on the Japanese city of Hiroshima. It was followed four days later by another bomb on Nagasaki. The horror of it shattered the brittle numbness in which Agnes had been concealed.

'It's bestial,' she insisted feverishly to William. 'We should never have condoned such an infamous thing.'

He was morbidly sensitive, now, to the idea that he scored or lost points whenever any important issue cropped up between them. It was a terrible temptation to agree with her, if that was what she needed, but if he couldn't keep her by being himself, then he must be prepared to let her go.

'It might have made no difference whether we condoned it or not,' he pointed out at last. 'It's terrible, of course, but so has much else been about the past five years.'

'Yes, but we have to stop *somewhere*.'

'The Japanese were given an ultimatum before the bombs were dropped, and refused it. Think of the alternative – months, perhaps years, of dislodging them inch by bloody inch from every bit of territory they've overrun. That would have been even more terrible.'

'You talk as a soldier, counting heads!' she flashed at him. 'Surely this filthy bomb is more evil than anything else?'

He thought of Ano, stifled to death under the choking, suffocating weight of something that had been her home. How did you measure what was more or less evil? In the end he gave a tired shrug that, in spite of herself, she found saddening. 'Who's to judge?' he asked quietly. 'We have some idea, now, of what happened in places like Belsen and Auschwitz. How do we balance those horrors against any other, or decide which of them damages humanity most in the long run?'

For the first time she realized that he was as muddled and uncertain as she felt herself. In the past he'd leapt

218

from one certainty to another, with not a single one of the doubts and hesitations that had always made her feel stupid by comparison. She stared at him, and made another discovery. His eyes, fixed on her face, confessed that his most painful uncertainty concerned herself. She suddenly remembered the day when they'd heard that James had gone to Dunkirk, and she'd *wanted* to hurt him. Now, for weeks past she'd been guilty of even worse cruelty, allowing him to know that she'd looked elsewhere for some will o'the wisp of happiness they hadn't found together. She hadn't found it after all, and had made him suffer for that as well. So much for prating about other people's inhumanity . . . she felt sickened by self-disgust.

'Belsen and Hiroshima . . . they're only the extreme end of a scale of unkindness we practice all the time. Why do we do such things . . .' tears clogged her throat and blinded her, and she groped for a handkerchief she couldn't find.

He was beside her, mopping at her tears with his own. '*This* is when a man feels the need of two sound arms!'

It was said with a rueful sweetness that made her weep all the more. The regret in his voice was for her, not himself, just as his kindness had always been.

'I'm sorry, William . . . sorry to have been so stupid.'

She meant, he supposed, that she was sorry for the present little scene; didn't dare suppose anything else.

'I've been in a muddle lately. Thank you for being patient with me.'

It wasn't a great deal to go by, but enough to encourage a small shoot of hope for the future. He kissed her tear-stained cheek, and smiled at her.

'Take heart, love. There are horrors in plenty, but you're only looking at one side of the coin. There's a lot written on the other side too . . . kindness and courage, and general goodness.'

She nodded, wishing she could break through the habit

of reticence to say that they were his own virtues. The conviction was growing in her mind that in chasing a chimera that didn't exist, she'd come within an ace of losing the treasure she had. The enormity of her foolishness was unnerving. She must be sure that she wasn't making yet another mistake, but if she could only be still and patient for a little while, perhaps certainty, shining and complete, would lie within her hand.

Whatever people thought about the immorality of dropping atomic bombs, one almost immediate benefit was the one William had predicted; the Japanese accepted the Allied surrender terms. VJ Day came on 15 August and, however tenuously, the world was officially at peace. Cecily celebrated the fact by giving in her resignation to Edward. His face was so expressionless when she'd finished speaking that she wondered if it made the slightest difference to him whether she stayed or went.

'May I know why you want to go?' he asked finally. 'I realise that I work you shamefully hard, but I've always salved my conscience by thinking that you enjoyed the job.'

'No qualms of conscience are needed. I've loved every minute of it.'

'Then why walk out on me now?'

'I must go soon anyway, and it seems better to do it before the work of this session of Parliament becomes too heavy.'

'Begging the question, Cessy?' The question was gentle but hard to evade. 'Why go at all is what I meant.'

She'd been prepared for it and had a cast-iron excuse ready to offer him.

'I agreed with Jane when I took on the job and she took over the twins that it would only be until Parliament was dissolved. If you hadn't been re-elected, the London part of the job would have come to an end anyway. It hasn't, as it happens, but I can't hold her to the bargain any longer. She isn't exactly in her dotage at nineteen, but she's propped us up long enough. It's time for her to live her own life.'

How calm and reasonable it sounded! Cessy felt proud of herself. She felt sick with longing to have him touch her. The sunlight that caught the silver flecks in his fair hair picked out as well the fine hairs on the back of his hands. They never would touch her, and she could bear the fact no longer. But no one in the world, and certainly not a man as diffident about himself as this one, would ever guess that she was riven by the thought of parting company with him.

The silence seemed to have lasted a long time when he put down the paper-knife he was fiddling with. 'I can't possibly dissuade you from doing what you think is right about Jane, but couldn't we work something else out for the children . . . take them down to St Margaret's, for instance?'

'No!' The refusal was so sharp and instinctive that he stared at her, trying to puzzle out the reason. 'I don't think so, Edward,' she said hurriedly. 'You and I would be there so little that it would mean leaving them with a complete stranger. Doing without Jane is going to shatter them, as it is. I can't separate them from everyone else they know.'

'You sound too definite for me to have the right to try to make you change your mind, but I'm more sorry than I can say, Cessy. It's been so easy working together.'

If not very much, it was something to take away with her. She didn't know that long after she'd gone back to her own room he sat staring into space, thinking among other things that life was remarkably and maddeningly perverse. He now hated the thought of her leaving much more than he'd ever disliked the idea of offering her the job in the first place. Cecily Willoughby had turned out to be by no means what she seemed. So much for first impressions! The flippant pleasure-loving doll suggested by her golden beauty had proved at close quarters to be intelligent, hard-working, and possessed of an old-fashioned integrity which he ought to have expected in the Marchants' daughter.

Edward felt uncomfortable about *them*, without quite knowing why. Since the death of his wife only a couple of years after they were married he'd been solitary ... reluctant to pay the cost again that was involved in loving a woman. Agnes Marchant had seemed prepared to be a friend, whose gentleness and warmth weren't to be found in any of his other friends simply because she was a woman and they were men. Now, he had the feeling that friendship had retreated, if not withdrawn altogether, and in William there seemed to be something strangely like hostility only just under control. The only explanation that occurred to him was that they thought he monopolized Cessy's life unfairly. She clearly thought it too. Jane's training was the reason why Cessy said she must leave ... but he was bleakly certain that she was going because she wanted to.

Jane didn't hear about the impending change until William brought down Cessy's letter to her at River Cottage. She and Agnes were there with the twins, taking advantage of several weeks of beautiful Indian summer weather. It now looked exactly as she remembered her very first view of it ... the garden flaring in a last blaze of colour that defied the possibility of winter. James's willow tree was beginning to drip gold on the lawn, and the river lay quietly under the September sunshine. Each time they went to the cottage Jane loved it more and found it harder to leave. It still hurt not to have Jos alive to share it with her. She tried to see it with his eyes, but wanted him there to say, 'Janey love, this is something like!'

The twins ran wild in a garden that offered much more scope than the vegetable patch at Linden Square, and once netting had been stretched across the bottom of the garden, she could let them out of doors without the fear of finding them in the river. Life, like their vocabulary, was wondrously enlarged at River Cottage. What with Mrs Middleton's hen-lens to be visited, Daffy's duck-lucks – they were *hers*, apparently, not Daniel's – to be fed, and, frabjous joy, the moment each day when the beautiful plough horses came ambling back up the village street to the stable-yard opposite the cottage! It had Linden Square beaten hollow.

The twins were at the kitchen door one Friday evening, killing two birds with one stone; keeping one eye on the horses' arrival and the other on Grandpa William's taxi which should be drawing up. He and they had long since forgotten a time when they were wary of each other. But instead of the taxi, the elderly Marchant car stopped at the gate, and Duncan climbed out as well as William.

'Wing-Commander dear, this is a pleasant surprise,' Jane said, smiling at him. She lifted Daffy up for his kiss, but found his mouth on her own instead.

'*Mr* Marchant, as of yesterday,' he corrected her. 'You're supposed to admire this rather loud sports jacket – a present from a grateful country!'

'Demobbed, Duncan? How marvellous ... I didn't imagine they'd let you out so quickly.'

'First in, first out, seems to be the rule, so no doubt Brian will soon be casting his bread upon civilian waters as well.'

He smiled and sounded so cheerful that she told herself she'd been worrying unnecessarily about him. It only needed the knowledge that he was free of war and killing, and the fear of being killed, to let his stretched nerves relax. Adjustment would take a little time, but it didn't look impossible after all. Agnes wept at the unexpected sight of him, announcing at the same time that she was a happy woman who had much to be thankful for.

Jane had no time to read the letter William had brought

down for her until she was getting ready for bed that evening. The news that Cessy was giving up her job with Edward would have to be shared, but she felt nervous about it all the same. Anything involving Edward now seemed hedged about with awkwardness. She went downstairs the next morning, telling herself that it could wait until they got back to London, but it was William himself who brought up the subject as soon as Daniel bustled away from the breakfast-table on his self-appointed task of picking up windfall apples on the lawn. Where Daniel went Daffy followed, and there was peace in the room until William said casually, 'Cessy rang . . . it seems that she's decided to give up her job.'

His eyes flicked to Agnes's face, then looked away again. She'd be upset for Edward's sake, almost certainly; he waited to hear her say that Cessy shouldn't be deserting him. Instead, she sounded puzzled, but not in the least upset.

'I thought Cessy loved working for Edward. What do you suppose has made her change her mind?'

Jane looked across at William, her eyes asking him to let her answer Agnes's question.

'She does love the job,' Jane insisted, 'but we had a sort of agreement that the arrangement wouldn't last for ever. Cessy thinks it's time she took over the twins again and let me get on with my own career.'

'Dearest, that's true, of course,' Agnes agreed, 'but it hardly bears thinking about, all the same. With you gone, and no twins either – no Daniel arriving for his early-morning chat, or Daffy insisting on a "liddle cuggle, gran" – what shall we do? For an hour or two this morning I was feeling cheerful . . . Duncan safely home . . . God's in his heaven, after all. Now everything's going to change again. I know I sound like a selfish old woman, but I don't *want* things to change!'

There was a slight tremor in her voice, even though she tried to smile at them. Then William looked up from the letter he was reading, and stared at her. It was probably the worst time he could have chosen, but it had chosen itself. 'Is that what you *really* want . . . for things to stay unchanged?'

The deliberate question drove the faint colour from her face but she didn't look away from him. Watching them across the table, Jane thought she and Duncan could have left the room without being noticed. She even tried to gesture to him that they *should* get up and walk away, because some moment of truth had been reached for the two people who faced each other across the table.

'Of course I want *some* changes,' Agnes murmured after a long pause. 'I want James home again, and Cessy must find a life that gives her real happiness. But otherwise I'd like God to let us go on as we are, taking care of each other.'

A faint sigh escaped William, and his face was transfigured by a smile of such joy that she put out her hand to cover his lying clenched on the table. She hadn't been expecting that moment of choice, but now that it had come she was thankful for it. All that would ever need to be said *had* been said.

Jane got up after a moment or two, blinked away the tears that threatened her, and addressed herself to Duncan.

'This is where we begin to break the bad habit of years, my dear sir. No doubt you'll soon be wishing you were back in the mess, being waited on by a bevy of dazzled WAAF beauties. Civilian life is grim and earnest, and includes helping with the washing-up!'

He came out of some abstraction of his own to stare at her. 'WAAF beauties? They were good hard-working lasses. Beauties they were *not*, poor souls. If I'm required to help with lowly tasks about the house, I dare say I can manage it.'

Willing he might be, but Jane discovered that it was much quicker to do things herself. She had to tell him three times where to find the dustbin, and reminded herself that it was no wonder if he couldn't concentrate for the moment on anything that didn't have to deal with staying alive in a fighter aeroplane. But when she suggested strolling out into the garden to relieve Daniel of his load of maggotty apples, Duncan suddenly took hold of her shoulders in a grip that hurt.

'What's Cessy going to do ... look after the twins herself, or farm them out while she takes another job?'

'I'm sure she'll want another job,' Jane said slowly. 'She's not very domesticated, you know. But provided she finds a nice kind girl to live in and take—'

'—take over our twins? Certainly not,' Duncan insisted coldly. 'If Cecily doesn't want them, they're ours. *We* must look after them, Jane.'

His blue eyes stared at her, unaware that she winced at the pain of his hands. Fear touched her again, even while she tried to smile at him.

'I know we adore them, but we're only their godparents and Cessy has to decide what becomes of them,' she reminded him. 'And there's another thing, Duncan dear – if I don't have the job of looking after them, I have to find something else to do. I can't afford to loll about doing nothing, even if I wanted to.'

'Don't talk rubbish, Janey. You can't go away to be a nurse, or any other footling thing. Your job's to marry me. Then Daniel and Daffy will be *our* children!'

For a moment the hope remained that he was joking. But when she looked at him his blue eyes were unclouded by the slightest doubt that he'd just said anything funny or unreasonable. She could think of nothing to say in reply, and his rigid expression relaxed into a smile of entrancing sweetness. 'You'll see,' he said simply.

Then he wandered out into the garden, calling to the twins. 'God's in his heaven,' Agnes had said, but Jane shivered in the knowledge that there were some things that were very far from being right with their world.

Chapter 17

For the rest of the weekend Duncan was the charming carefree young man who had gone to war. He teased his mother, talked rationally to William about Marchant's, and spent as much time as possible in the company of the children. They seemed to love him as much as he doted on them, and Jane told herself she was mad to see anything to worry about in that. As well as being irresistible, they were his god-children. The novelty of keeping them amused would probably soon wear off, but for the moment he asked nothing better than to row his deliriously excited cargo up and down the Thames, and reluctantly she had to go with them. He couldn't row and stop them falling out of the boat at the same time, but the more the four of them were together, the more she feared the idea would become fixed in his mind that together was how the four of them should always be.

He didn't revert to the idea of marriage, and she hoped that by pretending to have forgotten it he would more easily be able to forget it too. It would have been a relief to share her anxiety with Agnes, but she could see no way round the awkwardness attached to suggesting to a woman that her son was suffering from mental strain. This weekend, of all weekends, she couldn't bring herself to do it. Agnes and William looked so much happier than for years past that it seemed impossible to dim their pleasure for the sake of airing a problem she ought to be able to cope with

228

herself. All that *must* be done when she got the chance was to warn Cessy that her brother might object if she gave someone else the job of looking after the twins.

By Sunday afternoon Duncan's energy was flagging, and his patience showing signs of wearing thin. Daffy was told not to do something in a tone of voice she hadn't heard from him before, and made the mistake of imagining that he didn't mean what he said. Affronted by an unheard-of slap, she informed him that he was a 'nasty man', before bursting into tears. Order was finally restored, but Jane found herself grateful for the incident. The twins were real children, not angels, and the sooner Duncan realized it, the sooner he'd tire of the idea of playing 'father'.

William got ready to return to London on Sunday evening, but Duncan announced that he intended to stay on at the cottage to look after them. Jane was required to help deliver William to Culham station, but when they'd waved him out of sight she found herself wishing for the first time that she was on her way back to London as well. It had been a mistake to let herself in for the drive back to Long Wittenham alone with Duncan, because he stopped the car and she saw his hands trembling on the steering-wheel.

'Say what you're thinking,' he said jerkily. 'No, don't bother – your face is as transparent as clear water. I'm a selfish swine, and my job is to go back and put my shoulder behind Marchant & Ferguson's wheel.'

She took so long to answer that he swung round to stare at her. 'That *is* what you think, isn't it?'

What she thought was that he'd be better for the discipline that a regular routine of work imposed, but it seemed the wrong moment to say so. 'Tom's done wonders, but there's a lot of ground to make up and it strikes me that your father's very tired,' she said at last. 'But no one could think you don't deserve a rest – William would be the first to insist on it – so don't imagine I'm thinking anything at all.'

The evening silence was complete except for the faint high twittering of swallows still chasing each other about the twilit sky. Not for much longer, she thought sadly. Soon they'd be off on their long flight south and the summer would be over. Her mind went with them for a moment, 'on, on and out of sight' . . . they were free and she was trapped, just as Brian had said she would be.

'I meant what I said about marrying,' Duncan said uncannily, as if she'd said her thought out loud. 'It's the obvious thing to do.'

'Duncan dear, people don't usually marry because it's the obvious thing to do! They marry because it's the only way they want to live.'

'That's why I said it's obvious,' he insisted. 'You mustn't go away, Janey. I can't bear it if you do.'

His voice cracked with the intensity of his need, but she was almost sure it wasn't the sort of need that normally propelled a man into asking a girl to marry him. So much for hoping the problem would go away if she ignored it. It was confronting her now, and she must find some way of dealing with it that would let them both off lightly. Her heart was beginning an agitated thump, but she forced herself to smile at him.

'Let's not rush things. You're only just out of the RAF after five rather terrible years, and ready to think that the devil you know in the shape of Janey Rowland is better than the devil you don't. Everything will look different in a few months' time, and you'll be grateful I didn't take you up on a very rash proposal!'

'Don't laugh at me, I'm serious! Oh God, how do I convince you?'

His hands reached out to pull her towards him and there was no chance to say anything at all because his mouth fastened on hers in a hard hurtful kiss that forced her lips apart. There was feverish strength in it, but so little passion that there'd have been nothing to respond to even if she'd felt the slightest inclination to do so. Frustrated and furious, his hand tore at the front of her shirt and she began at last to feel frightened. Instinct made her fight, although a small cold voice in her brain said it was the wrong tactic. But his arm suddenly connected with the horn of the car and the sound of it blared through the dusk, shocking him into letting go of her. He buried his head in his hands against the steering-wheel; Jane wiped her cut lip where it bled a little, and buttoned up the shirt he'd torn undone. Her fingers shook but she was no longer frightened, only unsure of what to do next and infinitely sad. When her hand reached out and touched his hair, he turned to look at her.

'Pathetic, wasn't it? I doubt if I'm even capable of making love to you, much as I want to. It's what comes of cheating death, Janey. Do it often enough and you're left with the feeling that you've no right to be alive. Why should you be, when so many others are dead?'

She thought, for no apparent reason of his grandmother rigid with anger when she heard that Jos and Ano were dead, of Edie Bloggs insisting with quietly frightening venom, 'soddin' Germans . . . I 'ate every bleedin' one of 'em.' Both of them would have told Duncan to be grateful he was alive, not feel racked with guilt because he hadn't managed to get himself killed. She tucked a cold hand inside his feverish one and felt his fingers lace themselves around hers in a desperate grip.

'I wasn't laughing, Duncan, truly . . . only trying to make you look at life a little less tragically. Things *will* get better gradually, but you have to give them time.'

Her face was only a blur in the dimness of the car now, but he could hear in her voice the longing to help him.

'I need *you* as well as time. Promise me you'll stay, because I can't face Marchant's unless you do. Stay for a little while . . . just till I get used to being "young Mr Duncan" again.'

He reminded her of Daniel, putting off the evil moment

when she turned out the light at night and left him alone with the dark. He couldn't manage the letter J yet and always said, 'Just *one* more story, Chaney'.

She hesitated a fraction too long and Duncan grabbed both her hands and pulled them to his mouth. 'You're going to agree . . . oh God, you are, aren't you, Janey?'

She nodded, helpless to do anything else. 'I'll stay till you get used to being Mr Marchant again.'

'We'll be engaged, just for the comfort of sounding as if we belong . . . I won't hold you to it.'

It wasn't what she thought she'd agreed, and was about to risk another outburst by saying so. Then she closed her lips on the words. If the idea of belonging helped, did it really matter what labels they tied on themselves? It was all very fine to *talk* about wanting to mend people . . . but fine talk buttered no parsnips, Jos always used to say. Dear damaged Duncan needed mending, if anybody did, quite apart from the fact that she owed the Marchants a debt that couldn't ever be repaid. But Cessy would say she'd never make Matron at this rate! She swallowed a laugh that was halfway hysterical, and managed to suggest that it was time they went home.

They stayed another week at River Cottage and an idyllic spell seemed to be cast over the days. The sweet-smelling mist of early morning slowly melted in the warmth of the sun, and by midday a cloudless deep-blue sky vaulted the flatness of the river valley. They spent the days out of doors, in the garden or on the river, and when the feeling of being on the floor of the world palled, they climbed the hill to the Wittenham Clumps, where a breeze always blew. Duncan constructed a kite, and he and the twins flew it with equal delight. So peaceful and happy were the days that Jane felt certain of the rightness of what she had agreed to. Even Agnes was reassured as well. Her face had gone blank when he announced that they were engaged, and Jane almost expected to hear her say the idea was impossible. But finally she had smiled and kissed them both.

'Clever Duncan, to find a way of letting us keep Jane.'

'We're keeping her *and* the twins,' he said proudly.

Doubt only returned at the end of the day, in the safety of the little room under the eaves that had been hers since she first went to River Cottage. Then she faced the fact that for her own heart's peace she should have gone away. Her whole life so far had been lived in the shadow of the Marchants and she would never know what she amounted to without them until she escaped into the world outside. She shivered at the word, hearing the clang of prison bars and Brian saying, 'you're trapped, brat, and it bloody well serves you right!' The dark world outside her little window oppressed her even more, with the memory of James who'd tried to dispel her fear of the night-time. She had the feeling that he would disapprove of her engagement to Duncan . . . say, lucidly as usual, that she'd been misled by the right reason into doing something that was stupidly wrong. Odd how her heart ached still when she thought of James.

But during the daytime the bogeys of the night skulked back into the shadows. The sun shone and Duncan and the children filled the garden with noise and laughter, and she could even feel confident enough to challenge Agnes.

'Duncan looks better already . . . don't you think so?'

'Transformed, dearest. Almost like the boy he used to be.' She hesitated a moment. 'He adores the twins, but is he serious about suggesting that you should keep them? I don't think I agree that you should take on a ready-made family permanently.'

It was a shock to hear the word 'permanently', as if Duncan had given Agnes to understand that the engagement was a normal one that would eventually take them into marriage. 'We shouldn't take them on permanently in any case,' Jane said slowly, 'but he just pretends that they don't belong to Cessy. She gives the impression of not

233

minding what happens to them as long as they're happy and well cared for, but I'm sure she wouldn't be able to part with them for good. What Duncan hates most is the idea of them being farmed out with someone else. When Cessy takes them over again he won't object to parting with them.'

Agnes hoped she was right, and steeled herself to ask another question that troubled her. 'You and Duncan, Janey . . . are you sure it's the right thing?'

It wasn't difficult in the warmth of day, with Duncan waving to them from the top of the plum tree where he was balanced on a ladder picking fruit, to smile and say cheerfully, 'It's the right thing at the moment. It may not need to go on being the right thing!'

'I think you're being used as a crutch . . . it worries me, and it will certainly worry William.'

Jane leaned over and kissed her cheek. 'I'll leave William to you. Don't worry about us . . . things will sort themselves out and, as my dear Jos used to say, "there's no sense to worrying". He was great on sense, was Jos!'

'You're just like him . . . sweetly sane.'

It was a loving vote of confidence that Jane feared she didn't deserve, but there was no chance to say so. Daffy arrived with a present of a ladybird that she'd carefully collected for each of them, and conversation thereafter switched to why a ladybird should be so called when it wasn't a bird and couldn't always be a lady.

Two days later they closed the cottage and Duncan drove them back to London. Jane supposed that Agnes told William of the engagement, and persuaded him into seeming pleased about it.

'You needn't have gone to the length of accepting Duncan, though,' he said gruffly, 'you're part of the family already.'

Cecily looked startled when she heard the news, but said very little, beyond asking whether anyone had thought to tell James.

'Of course, dearest . . . I've written my weekly letter,' Agnes said, looking slightly surprised.

Cecily wrote as well, under a compulsion she didn't quite understand to make clear to him something that she'd intended saying for years.

. . . it's an odd engagement that should never have happened, though not for the reason that may be occurring to *you*. Jane is *not* Pa's daughter, in case it ever crossed your mind that she was. Ano didn't lie about that . . . in fact she didn't lie at all, even about Brian; she just let the assumption stand that Jos had begotten him. Jane's so like her father that you probably can't have been in any doubt. But she has the feeling you abandoned her, and I couldn't think of any other reason why you should. I hope you're sent home soon . . . we could do with you . . .

James put the letter down, stared unseeingly at Valletta's Grand Harbour lying all round him in the sunshine, and felt coldness spread across his skin. He'd abandoned Janey all right, and of course she'd noticed the fact. They'd always known and noticed everything about each other. She'd reminded him of Jos, but she'd *looked* like Ano, and there was a fair chance that the resemblances to Jos arose simply because she wanted to copy him. Even a faint suspicion that she could turn out to be his half-sister had ruined friendship, and now Cessy blithely assumed that he'd 'never been in any doubt'. Dear God . . . no doubt! He picked up her letter again and slowly tore it into shreds. The truth didn't matter anyway, because Jane was engaged to Duncan, and that should have come as no surprise. She'd been dazzled by him from childhood up. All he had to do was learn to smile at the idea by the time he got home.

Brian was demobbed ahead of him, and lost no time in

235

getting his new career started in London. Jane had expected him to disapprove of the fact that she was still entangled with the Marchants, but it was a shock to have him arrive and demand that she should change her mind.

'You don't understand,' she murmured, reluctant to explain what it was he didn't understand.

'Of course I do. Listen to me, brat. Duncan's a broken reed. I know you feel grateful to the Marchants, and have a damnably kind heart as well, but if you think you can do a rescue job, I tell you you're mistaken. I've met plenty of poor sods like Duncan, though the RAF seems to have bred more of them than the Army or the Navy. You're entitled to a real husband, not some pot-valiant hero who wants to play Peter Pan.'

'Don't say that,' she stormed at him, anger lashed to fever-pitch by the fear that he was probably right. 'I won't have you belittle Duncan, or anybody like him.' Her dark eyes burned in the whiteness of her face, reminding him sharply of Ano. 'They're heroes, every one of them, and we're only here because of them . . .'

'All right, Janey . . . calm down. I shouldn't have sneered. But you must face the truth. Like the rest of us, Duncan's got to get on with the business of living in a world that won't remember for very long that he's a hero.'

'He's already beginning to. He didn't have time before the war started to get a grip on things, but William's sure he'll soon be a useful member of the firm.'

She knew she protested much too much, and that William forced himself as well to sound more confident than he felt, but what else was there to do when Duncan tried so hard? His moods, all the same, were a troubling see-saw of highs and lows. There were days when he withdrew into a sullen silence, and nights when he drank himself into an artificial gaiety that was even harder to bear. Her diffident suggestion one day that a psychiatrist might help to control the painful swings from one to the other

236

had sent him out on such a spectacular blind that she'd never repeated it. 'It's only a matter of time' had become a litany she clung to in the absence of any other certainty. Brian stared at her face, tempted to say that he'd *carry* her out of the house if she wouldn't come in any other way. But he remembered Jos trying to persuade her to be evacuated at the beginning of the war. 'Uncommon cussed' he'd called her, and he was right.

'What about the others . . . what are they up to?'

She smiled brilliantly at being given a change of subject. 'Everyone's all right. I expect you know Edward got re-elected? Cessy's on the point of parting company with him, but she'll find herself another job in London. We're hanging on to the twins for as long as possible, but no doubt they'll go back to her when she's settled. James is still at sea, but probably not for much longer.'

'What made Cessy chuck up Edward? My impression was that she doted on him.'

'She doted on the *job*,' Jane said carefully. 'The idea of leaving was to free me from the twins, originally. Now that's . . . shelved for a bit . . . she'll make the break anyway. Edward's job absorbs too much of her life.'

He still looked curious, and she deflected him from probing into Cessy's affairs by suggesting that he should come to supper the following Saturday. 'It's Agnes's fiftieth birthday . . . just the moment to forget a lifelong hostility to my adopted family! If you don't fancy partnering her ladyship, you can look after Tom Ferguson's niece, Clarissa – she's very pretty.'

'Thanks! Sight unseen, I think I'll take Clarissa.' He eyed Jane with a slightly sardonic smile. 'Young Red Rowland rubbing shoulders with the gentry . . . I wonder if my party manners are up to it?'

'Now you're being silly! Come, there's a good lad, and behave yourself.'

His smile changed into a grin of pure amusement. 'Put in

my place, and no mistake! No wonder they all love you . . .
I do myself. I'll prove it by coming and *not* talking politics.
Will that do?'

'Handsomely,' she agreed, reaching up to kiss his cheek.

As once before the menu relied heavily on raw materials
provided by the Ferguson farm in Cornwall. Postwar life
continued miserably austere, but weekly rations could be
laid aside because Edward's hamper included a long-
forgotten substance called cream as well as the butter and
eggs they'd taken for granted in the piping days of peace.
The centrepiece of the buffet was a cold roast goose that
Cessy swore she recognized.

'Feeling bad about it?' Jane enquired.

'Not at all . . . the swine used to try to nip me every time I
went past!'

She was looking so beautiful that Jane, as well as
Edward, concluded she must be feeling happy again; perhaps what she'd needed most was to be able to take the
decision to leave him. It had been done, and she could go
on to the next thing. With their roles reversed this time,
Agnes seemed content to stay in the background. In her
old lace dress again, graceful and slender, she was a lovely
but unemphatic hostess. Edward had the comfortable feeling that whatever had disturbed their friendship for a
while had disappeared again, leaving friendship intact.

Brian agreed with Jane that Clarissa Ferguson was very
pretty, but found Lady Carterton much more entertaining.

'You look prosperous,' she said bluntly to him. 'Your
mother always told us you were going to succeed.'

'I know she did . . . it's quite a lot to live up to, but I'm
doing my best.'

'Still a Socialist, I hear. You won't stick them for long . . .
they're such a dreary lot.'

'Dreary or not, they've got the right ideas.'

Her eyes glinted with amusement. 'Doing away with
people like me, I suppose you mean?'

He pushed away the memory of Cecily saying much the same thing one day, and managed to smile at her. 'No, I don't think I'd want to do away with you.' It sounded like a compliment and she took it as such.

'Very smooth,' she observed approvingly, 'even though I'm not sure that I believe you. You've wasted enough time on an old woman like me . . . go and enjoy yourself with Clarissa over there.'

He was released by Tom Ferguson, coming to take a seat by a lady who secretly terrified him, and decided that he might as well do as he'd been told.

Cessy managed to avoid a private conversation with Edward for most of the evening, but he finally pinned her into a corner.

'Stop hiding behind other people for a moment . . . I want to talk to you,' he suggested quietly. 'Does Jane's engagement make any difference to your leaving me?'

'No . . . why should it?'

'Because Duncan assured me earlier this evening that the twins would be staying with him and Jane.'

'My dear brother has a nerve!' She said the words lightly, but he was aware of anger in her all the same. 'They're *my* children, after all, so I should like to decide what happens to them. Apart from that, why should Janey have a ready-made family foisted on her?'

'No reason at all, of course. It was only that Duncan spoke of it so confidently as a settled thing that I got quite hopeful for a moment. If anything did come of it, Cessy, would you consider staying on with me?'

She couldn't imagine what lay beneath his quiet insistence . . . there was the terrible fear that she might have given herself away and he felt sorry for her, but she'd been so desperately careful not to. On the whole she still thought he looked on her as a useful deterrent, in case some other woman was rash enough to think he wanted his solitariness invaded.

'It's too late, I'm afraid,' she said steadily. 'I've got something else almost lined up.'

'And my impression is that the answer would still be no, even if you hadn't. Am I right?'

She nodded, unable to do more.

A faint rueful smile touched his mouth. 'There's telling you, Edward my boy! I shall accept my congé with a good grace, I hope, but it isn't easy, Cessy.'

She'd have given all she possessed to be able to say she'd changed her mind, but having got this far, she mustn't waver now. Her mother *looked* happy now, but Cessy remembered her face the night of that previous dreadful dinner party. Wishful thinking that Edward might ask her to stay because he loved her always foundered at *this* point – that she'd be getting what Agnes had longed for so desperately.

'Nothing's easy,' she agreed with a brilliant smile. He stared at her for a moment longer, then walked away, and she walked over to her grandmother, who was looking bored with Tom Ferguson.

Chapter 18

As if regretting a glorious finale to the summer, November's weather was wet and sullen, and December's began even worse. It was like the general situation, Jane reckoned – an almost total grey. Socialists might be in power, but in the aftermath of total war a Socialist Utopia was going to be a long time a-coming. Brian explained to her what she knew already – the problems were immense, reconstruction of what had been destroyed was required everywhere, and national wealth had gone in fighting the war. Attlee, Bevin, Cripps and the rest were doing their best, but the fact remained that life in peace-time looked remarkably like life as it had been for the past five years. People were sick of austerity, but food and clothes rationing, shortages, and restrictions were still the order of the day. It should have helped to remember that there were others much worse off than themselves, but it was hard to feel grateful standing in line for something in the pouring rain. She stared at the queue's reflection in the rain-streaked glass of the shop window: a line of women wrapped in head-scarves and shabby macs, wondering whether the cod they were queueing for would last till they got inside the shop. They all looked glum, poor things, and standing there glowering at herself in the glass, she looked as glum as the rest. There *wasn't* any cod left by the time she got to the counter.

'How about some nice roes, dearie,' the fishmonger

suggested hopefully. 'Better than a slap in the face with a wet 'addock, as the sayin' goes!'

' 'Addock, wet or otherwise, would have been a treat, Mr Collie,' said Jane, 'but if roes are the best you can do, yes please.'

She trudged home, wondering how to make roes look like cod but the depression that had settled on her had little to do with the ever-present rain, and nothing at all to do with fish. It was life in general, and her own life in particular that seemed in such a hopeless limbo. Cessy was now in London all the time, working for an eminent barrister, but the twins remained in Linden Square, because Duncan insisted strenuously that it was their home. Jane couldn't make up her mind whether she dreaded or longed for the day when something happened to set their lives moving again; at the moment they were like the actors in a film, frozen into a certain position because the reel had jammed. It was a relief that she didn't have to refuse to get married, but if Duncan had shown any signs of wanting to the situation would have seemed more normal. The present arrangement suited him better than any other, providing as much of a wife as he might ever want, and children he hadn't had the bother of begetting.

The important thing was that Janey was there ... errand-girl, listener to his woes, and bolsterer of his confidence when it showed signs of flagging. If something reminded him that they were supposed to be engaged, he would suddenly engulf her in a boisterish embrace, but it was Duncan convincing himself that he was capable of being an ardent lover. She thought it would have been farcical if it hadn't been so tragic at the same time. In front of Agnes and William she managed to look serene, and only Cessy, less directly involved in the game they were all playing, detected signs of strain.

'Heard from James?' she asked casually when she and

242

Jane were by themselves one evening. 'I wrote to him about you and Duncan.'

'He sent his congratulations – five lines addressed to both of us, or it might even have been six! ... written between coming off duty and umpiring a local cricket match. He sounded mildly interested.'

She was careful to stare at the cardigan she was knitting for Daffy because her eyes were suddenly pricking with tears.

'Agnes had a letter this morning, by the way. James reckons he'll be out of the Navy by the New Year. I hope he won't want to come back here, I don't think he and Duncan would hit it off very well nowadays.' She managed not to say that she couldn't bear to have him living in the same house; Duncan's frail peace of mind wouldn't stand it, and nor would hers. The more remote from them James had become, the more she found his image fixed in her mind, and the more oppressed she was by the knowledge that life had gone irretrievably wrong.

Cessy stared at her downbent head, wishing she could manage to hate both her brothers, for different reasons.

'The times are out of joint,' she announced mournfully, then looked surprised at herself. 'Where in the world did I dredge that up from?'

'Will Shakespeare, I think ... a fragment of your misspent schooldays.'

Cessy looked so pleased with herself that Jane began to grin, they caught each other's eye, and the next moment were both shaking with laughter.

'That's better,' Jane said finally, wiping away the sort of tears she could admit to. 'We were getting unbearably tragic!'

'True, but old William S. can't be gainsaid, Janey. Something's out of joint. There's me slaving for an overweight and extremely pompous luminary of the legal profession (luminary is the sort of word he uses) when I ought to be ministering to emaciated, entrancing Edward; and there's you acting as nanny-cum-mother-confessor to my poor darling twin when you ought to be joyously coupled with James. God may be in His Heaven, as Ma confidently asserts from time to time, but it's time he stopped turning a blind eye to what goes on down here.'

'I expect He thinks we ought to b – be able to m – manage for ourselves,' Jane gasped, striving not to collapse again and hysterically determined not to even comment on what Cessy had just said. Better to pretend that her friend had spoken without thinking, and to slay the smallest hope in her heart whenever it appeared that she and James might one day be friends again.

The following evening she was in the kitchen cooking dinner when Duncan came in, earlier than usual. For once he took it into his head to kiss her, but the smell of whisky that hung about him make her draw back a little. The withdrawal was small but he took exception to it. She was grabbed and kissed again so hurtfully that she fought in earnest to free herself. Duncan sudden got bored with the tussle and let go of her so suddenly that she stumbled and put her hand on the top of the hot stove. He didn't even notice when she winced with pain.

'You don't like my kisses, do you, Janey? I used to think it was *my* fault. Then the penny dropped . . . not my fault at all. You'd be ready enough to co-operate if it was brother James here wanting to make love to you.'

It was a relief to hold her hand under the cold tap . . . something to do besides think what a blessed relief it would be to shout and scream that she couldn't bear a moment longer the life they were leading. When she could trust herself to speak at all, she turned round and looked at him. 'You're talking rubbish, and you know it.'

'I don't think so. Stupid of me to forget that childish attachment to my dear brother.'

'Childish is the word . . . I'm a big girl now.'

He wavered for a moment, uncertain of his line of attack but sure in the dimmest recesses of his brain that he had cause to feel hard done by. Then he remembered another grievance about James. 'Why isn't he here, instead of lolling about in the Mediterranean sunshine? The rest of us have to put up with this bloody climate. Why can't he?'

She'd have thought a moment ago that the last person he wanted to see was James, but he was beyond noticing that his arguments nowadays contradicted one another. 'He'll be back soon,' she reminded him. 'His demob will be through any time now.'

'Then he can bloody well go to Malaya instead of me.'

Duncan made the announcement with such feeling that she realized they had now come to the heart of the outburst. William had suggested Duncan should make the visit, thinking that foreign travel and a complete change of scene would be good for him. He'd seemed enthusiastic about the idea, and it hadn't occurred to any of them that he was whistling in the dark to conceal the dread that lay beneath the surface. '*I'm* not going, to pick up the pieces left behind by the Japs and sort out a lot of disgusting Wogs.'

'Don't call them that,' she shouted, moved suddenly to the kind of rage that couldn't be stifled. 'I don't know about the damage left behind, but there's nothing wrong with the Malays . . . they're charming gentle people.'

'You know, of course – you've been there, I suppose?'

It was so futile, the pair of them shouting at each other about people they didn't know on the other side of the world, that anger drained away even though she wanted to hold on to it.

'You're aware that I haven't been. I only know what William tells me. But if you dislike the idea of going so much, say so – he'll understand.'

His mood underwent one of his disconcerting transformations. From truculence to woebegone pleading took

245

him no more than a moment she could hardly measure.

'You tell him for me, Janey; he'll take it better from you.' His eyes were fixed imploringly on her . . . such blue and empty eyes in a gauntly beautiful face. She reached up to kiss his cheek, and the scene was over. *This* scene was over, but there would be others for as far into the future as she could see.

'All right . . . I'll tell him.'

His face lit with the smile that always reminded her of Agnes; another temporary fear had been removed and he could be happy again. He didn't even mind when she pointed out that dinner would be late unless she could get on with cooking it. In any case, it was time to go and find his friends, the twins. She watched him wander out of the room, hardly conscious of the pain in her hand for the sharpness of other troubles.

She waited until dinner was over, and Agnes was at the piano drifting from one Chopin nocturne to another, before she inveigled William out of the room on the pretext that she required him to look at the kitchen boiler.

'Looks perfectly all right to me!' he said truthfully after peering at it.

'A ploy! I wanted to talk to you. Duncan was upset this evening. He doesn't feel quite . . . quite ready to make the long trip to Malaya on his own. Can it possibly wait a little while?'

'It *can*, but it shouldn't. Our people have done marvels out there, but they need help in getting things going again. If Duncan's not up to going, I'll have to go myself. I suggested it, though, because I thought the trip might help him to find himself.'

He stood still staring at the unoffending boiler for a moment, then shot a glance at her that took in the thinness and pallor of her face. 'It's *not* just a question of time, is it, Janey? We're all trying not to admit the truth to each other, but there's something wrong that we don't seem able to cure . . . not even *your* loving heart knows how to do the trick.'

'What else can we do, except give him time to mend himself?' she asked desperately. 'At the moment his life's like two separate railway lines that need to merge and run on joined up; but they haven't merged yet and his mind's still straddling wartime and peacetime. No wonder he's under such a strain.'

'He's not the only one,' William said gruffly. 'If you get any thinner your brother will rightly say it's time you left the Marchants to work out their own problems.'

'Like the Marchants left me, I suppose, when Jos and Ano died.'

His good arm gave her a rare hug because he wasn't a very demonstrative man, and they went back to the drawing-room together. He was right about Brian, though, who said bluntly when he paid his usual weekly visit that her face looked all eyes and bones.

'It's this dreary winter,' she explained, smiling at him. 'Enough to give anyone the blues.' She couldn't bear another lecture on what she ought to be doing with her life, but there was only one way of deflecting him from it. 'You'll say we're all expecting miracles, but be honest and admit that *you're* feeling let down as well. Didn't you expect that the Government might be able to manage better than this?'

It was like watching a salmon rise to a particularly irresistible fly.

'How *can* it manage better?' he asked fiercely. 'Just look at the problems, brat. Reconstruction needed everywhere, apart from the whole of industry having to be turned back to peacetime production and millions of service people to be resettled as civilians . . . the labours of Hercules were nothing compared to what the Government's got on its plate.'

'We're broke as well. That's what worries William. He

247

says we can't afford to keep patting ourselves on the back and introduce legislation that American loans will have to pay for.'

Brian gave a little shrug. 'What else would he think? He's a dyed-in-the-wool capitalist.'

'He's a businessman. A business pays its way or goes bankrupt. The theory holds good for national economies too, as far as he can see.' Her brother was sufficient of a businessman himself to see the force of the argument, but she reckoned that she'd irritated him enough. 'Talking of businesses, yours must be doing well – you look very prosperous!'

'It's doing well, and it's going to do even better,' he said confidently. 'Mass-motoring is just around the corner, and that's when the garage business really takes off. We've got another prime site already staked out.'

'A successful capitalist in the making!'

'There's nothing wrong with success.'

'Certainly not, and how Ano would have agreed with you,' she said gently.

Brian smiled, thinking that it wasn't so easy nowadays to get the better of little Janey. He didn't like to think anything good of the Marchants, but the truth was that they'd completed what St Olave's had begun. Between them, the school and life in Linden Square had done for her what the Navy had done for him. She looked older than her age, though, and she was far too thin.

'My new flat's ready,' he said suddenly. 'Nice view of the river at Barnes Bridge, and a second bedroom that's amply big enough for a nipper like you. Why don't you think of moving in?'

She wasn't misled by the casualness of it, and got up quickly to drop a grateful kiss on his cheek. 'It's a very kind offer, but I have the feeling that I'm still needed here.'

It jerked such an infuriated snort out of him that she had to smile. 'Needed! I tell you this, brat. If it ever comes to the point where you marry Duncan, you can look for someone else to give you away. I shall refuse to have anything to do with it.'

'I have an odd feeling that you won't have to,' she said carefully.

'You're nearly twenty . . . how much more time do you intend to waste playing nursemaid to Duncan?'

'As much as seems necessary, I suppose.' A note in her voice warned him not to go on with the subject. Jos had been right – 'save your breath, boy, when it comes to arguing with a woman.' Janey looked misleadingly reasonable, but she was as irrational as the rest of them.

'Clarissa Ferguson 'phoned,' she said by way of changing the subject. 'It came out very casually, but I got the impression she'd been expecting to hear from you.'

'I know. I changed my mind.' His sister's raised eyebrow nettled him into explaining himself. 'She's pretty as paint . . . definitely no hardship to run around with if I had the time. I *haven't* got time, and even if I had I should steer clear of girls like Clarissa Ferguson.'

'You make her sound like a threat!'

'She is. I made a mistake once before with someone just like her . . . no, someone who could knock spots off her. But I came to grief over her, and I'm not being had for a mug a second time.'

For no apparent reason Jane thought of Cessy, coming back from a posting at Lowestoft shared with Brian. She'd never referred to what had happened there, but it had been enough to fling her into the hectic affair that had produced the twins. Brian was just as untalkative on the subject of Lowestoft, and he still hated Cessy with the same sort of vehemence that had sounded in his voice a moment ago. Jane remembered the electric current of hostility that had flowed between them the day they'd both walked in and met unexpectedly. It was Lombard Street to a china orange, Jos would have said, that Cessy had been the girl who could knock spots off Clarissa. She couldn't bring herself to ask him, though, and said instead, 'You're not still harping on that old class nonsense! It's as dead as the dodo.'

'Don't you believe it, brat. As long as there's an England there'll be people looking round for others they reckon they can safely despise. The dear old class struggle is alive and well.'

'What about us?' she asked quietly. 'You and I are proof that the compartments aren't nearly as watertight as you pretend, and the war must surely have turned society upside-down.'

'Temporarily,' he agreed. 'You watch it sort itself out again. That's why I don't intend to do anything about Clarissa.'

'I have the feeling *you* don't have to. She's like Tom Ferguson, very dogged!'

He smiled, but shook his head and went away, leaving Jane hoping that Clarissa wouldn't get discouraged in her pursuit of him. He needed something in his life warmer than the Socialist brotherhood, and softer than a chain of successful garages. Miss Ferguson was just the girl to make a contest seem worthwhile, and it would have to be a contest to engage his interest.

The question of Duncan going to Malaya was not raised again, and instead William made a hurried trip himself, getting back just in time to celebrate Christmas with them. He was tired by the long air-journey when he got back, but Agnes sensed that the visit had given him some deep satisfaction that cancelled out surface exhaustion.

'I get the impression that you're glad you went,' she said when they were by themselves, and she'd followed him into his bedroom to unpack his suitcase for him.

'I think thankful is the word. I was tempted to put it off, but thank God I didn't. You can't imagine how well those

250

people have behaved. They simply buried everything they wanted to keep safe from the Japanese ... essential records, money even ... then dug it up again, confident that we should be back to find that they had been trustworthy. Do you remember St Paul's precept, "it is required of a steward that he be found faithful". They aren't Christians, but no one could have been *more* faithful.'

'In that case I think I'm glad you went, and not Duncan. They'll have set more store by a visit from you.'

'Yes, perhaps ...' He fiddled with the hairbrush she'd just unpacked, put it down, picked it up again. 'We can't go on ignoring Duncan's problem, all the same. For one thing it's intolerably unfair to Jane, who ought to be allowed to get out of that engagement if she wants to, and for another we're doing Duncan no service in the long run. It's time to admit that he's damaged to the point of needing help.'

'Let's admit it, by all means; in fact, it's a relief to,' she agreed slowly, 'but I still don't know what we do about it. Duncan can't be made to seek help, and he won't do it voluntarily. Try telling Jane to forget him if you like, but you'll be wasting your time. For as long as he clings to her, she'll make no move away from him or deprive him of the twins.'

'Cessy will do that before long ... and the sooner, the better in my view. Jane should be living her own life, and I'm astonished that Brian doesn't tell her so.'

'He does, loudly and often! She smiles sweetly, thanks him for his advice, and goes on exactly as before. She'll do the same with you.'

'Doesn't it worry you?'

'Of course, but she smiles at me too, and reminds me that Jos didn't hold with worrying! I think more than anyone else I know, she lives by some inner conviction about what is right or wrong for *her*. We complicate things for her by trying to insist that she goes by what *we* want

251

for her. I think she's what Buddhists call an old soul, made wise by the instinctive prompting of her heart. Most of us have to *think* what to do.'

He smiled at the wistful note in his wife's voice. 'I don't know why you should sound regretful . . . it seems to me that you have the same knack yourself. Perhaps it's why you get on so well together.'

'I'm learning, but I think Janey was born knowing how to cope with other people.' It occurred to her that this wasn't the sort of conversation she normally had with William, but he had reached the stage of tiredness where normal reticence was weakened and perception more acute than usual cut through the fog of weariness. 'The journey's catching up with you,' she said after a moment. 'If it will make you sleep more easily I'll promise to talk to Jane again tomorrow.'

She smiled at him with so much affection that he wanted to say he was glad to be back, needed her as much as Duncan needed Jane, loved her more than he'd ever realized. But self-restraint was a habit after twenty years . . . he was paralysed by the fear that she'd be embarrassed if he said what was in his mind.

'I'm glad I went to Malaya, but it's very good to be home.' That much he would allow himself. It was enough to bring a faint colour to her cheeks, and for once her lips touched his mouth when she kissed him goodnight.

'We didn't like you being away. Daffy got fearfully cross, and it did no good to tell her that you'd be back soon, because she wanted you *now*! Just like Cessy all over again which means, I suppose, that she'll have all her mother's painful lessons to learn.'

'Do you do what I do . . . find yourself forgetting Charles wasn't their father?'

'Yes, sometimes. But I'm not going to be tempted into a discussion about it now. It's Daniel's trick – lobbing another question at you just as you're creeping out of the door!'

252

William smiled but his thoughts were elsewhere . . . on something he knew he was going to say after all. 'Agnes . . . I haven't said so for a long while – God knows why not – but I love you very much.'

He felt like a bashful schoolboy once the words were blurted out, and she took a long while to answer him.

'I'm . . . I'm glad you mentioned it.' Ridiculous! She thought she sounded as if she was relieved that he'd found a missing collar-stud. But a smile transfigured her face as she walked out of the room and he knew for certain that she hadn't been embarrassed after all.

They spent Christmas at River Cottage, and the weather co-operated to the extent of producing a picturesque fall of snow. Mrs Middleton at the farm obligingly produced a goose whose reporting to the Ministry of Agriculture had obviously been vague, and Duncan enjoyed himself wandering round the house at midnight filling stockings for the twins. Jane watched him the following morning, helping them toboggan down the hill from the Clumps with an excited posse of village children. New presents were forgotten for the moment in the delirious joy of swooping down the white hillside, cold air rushing past flushed faces, and the runners of the toboggan swishing against the snow. Duncan patiently hauled them up the hill again after each blissful descent, and at such moments Jane loved him for his kindness. It seemed unthinkable that anything could be wrong with him that couldn't be cured.

The vicar delivered the Christmas sermon he'd been offering for the past twenty years, and the congregation roared out familiar carols with the special gusto reserved only for this occasion. Afterwards they gathered round the wireless to hear the King's Christmas message. In this year of 1945 he chose to address himself particularly to the young, who had 'known the world only as a world of

253

s – strife and fear . . . Have faith in life at its best and bring it your courage, your hopes and your sense of humour . . . l – l – let us face the future with hope.'

As usual, some of the words only came out with a struggle and Jane found herself willing the difficult syllables that eluded him to find their way past his tongue.

'Thank God for George VI,' Lady Carterton remarked, as she did at this time every year. 'His brother wouldn't have done at all. Charming, of course, but no amount of charm takes the place of solid worth.'

They greeted this statement with a respectful silence that was eventually broken by Daniel, quietly muttering to himself 'charmin' . . . charmin'.' He collected words that pleased him with the tenacity of a prospector panning for gold, but final 'g's defeated him, making him sound like an elderly gentleman of the Regency.

'What's charmin', Chaney?' he wanted to know.

'It's what *you* are,' she said, smiling at him. 'A good thing, in other words.'

'Is Daffy a good thin' too?,' he enquired anxiously.

'Of course . . . you're both the best things I know.'

The syntax was getting complicated, but 'best' sounded even better than 'good', especially with Chaney smiling at him.

All in all, with Duncan seeming positively cheerful and Cessy managing not to be irritated by her grandmother's well-meant advice, their first peacetime Christmas was unexpectedly enjoyable. If she was missing Edward, Cessy did her best not to show it, and when they drank James's health, as the only member of the family not present, Duncan joined in as readily as anyone else. Jane had inveigled Brian into driving down to dinner on Christmas evening and, shamelessly using the excuse of Mrs Middleton's enormous goose, suggested to Agnes that he should be asked to bring Tom Ferguson and Clarissa as well. If she could have found a reasonable excuse for getting Edward there as well, she'd have done so, because Cessy's gaiety faltered in the small bedroom they were obliged to share.

'For two pins I'd crawl all the way to St Margaret's,' she confessed bleakly, staring at Jane in the mirror as she sat making up a face that looked too pale. 'Sometimes I think I'll explode with the longing to see him smile at me again, even if it's only over a pig return! I hope the girl I found for him is all right. On the other hand, I can't help hoping she's no good at all. Can you tell me why life's so bloody perverse, Janey?'

'No, any more than I can give your daughter an answer to the questions she fires at me all day long. It probably won't help much, but all I can recommend is the advice the King gave us this afternoon . . . "Let us face the future with *hope*!" '

Cessy swung round to examine her friend's face, and suddenly got up to put her arms round Jane in a rare hug. 'Why don't you just tell me to shut up and stop moaning?'

'Because it helps to talk sometimes . . . it's heart-easing, to pinch one of Keats' lovely words.'

' " 'Eart-heasin' " Edie Bloggs would say! Do you suppose Daniel gets his strange brand of conversation from her?'

'Could be – he loves talking to her, and she does her level best to water down a colourful vocabulary. She's obliged to wear all her jewellery at once nowadays, because Daffy has insisted on the maximum amount of sparkle!'

Cessy stared at her thoughtfully. 'No point in mentioning it for the moment, but I'm going to bring our arrangement to an end, Janey. It's time something definite happened. We all know it, but we've been trying not to face the fact. The twins will probably hate the girl I've got lined up, and Ma will miss *them* and so, of course, will you. But it's got to be done . . . don't you agree?' she asked anxiously.

'Yes, I agree . . . oh God, yes I suppose I agree.' She made an attempt at a smile, then went to the window as the sound of car tyres scrunching on gravel outside. 'That's Brian arriving with Tom and Clarissa. Time we went downstairs. I still can't get used to being able to look out of an unblacked-out window again ... there *is* a lot to be thankful for.'

'I know, Chaney. Hope on, hope ever, as His Majesty didn't quite say. We'll start by hoping that Mrs Middleton's goose didn't die of extreme old age!'

Chapter 19

James finally arrived home just in time for the twins' third birthday. Unaware of Cessy's plans for her children, he'd already taken the precaution of explaining to his grandmother that there wouldn't be room for him in Linden Square. She seemed to like the idea of having him as a temporary lodger, but Agnes didn't like it at all.

'Returning hero gets no welcome at family home,' he murmured pensively. 'Leaving aside the hero bit, is that what's bothering you?'

'Something like that, dearest. There *ought* to be room for you here . . . in fact, I'm sure we could manage . . .'

'If we threw the twins out into the street, or told Pa he couldn't have a dressing-room any longer,' he agreed cordially. 'If all else failed we could even turn the butler's pantry into a delightful little bedroom for Chaney. Little would be the word, but she's still quite small, after all.'

Agnes bit her lip, trying not to laugh, but the expression on his brown face of someone anxious to be helpful was too much for her. She began to laugh, and finally mopped her eyes gasping, 'stoopid', just as she had when he was a small boy. 'Dear James, I'm so glad you're home, even if we can't find anywhere for you to sleep.'

'Well, I'd much rather have it that way round. Anyway, I shall enjoy keeping Gran in order. She used to terrify me as a child, but now she seems to like the idea of having an upstanding young chap tell *her* what to do.'

He didn't say that he was grateful the house was already full. Half a dozen empty bedrooms would have made no difference to the fact that he couldn't stay there and watch Jane being monopolized by Duncan. Things were better in Linden Square in one respect; he couldn't miss the change in his parents' relationship, and given what lay in the past for both of them, it seemed a minor miracle to see formal affection warmed by the closeness that was growing between them. At this rate, thought James, they'd end up falling in love with each other! But in other ways he was shocked by the state of his family: Cessy looked sad when she wasn't making an effort to be gay, Duncan was a ghost-ridden wreck of the young man he'd once been, and Jane wore a smile pinned to her mouth as if she didn't dare let him see her without it. Where was the uncomplicated laughing young man who'd been certain that his allotted task in life was to enjoy himself? Now he was anything but uncomplicated; sullen or feverishly gay by turns and always, in front of James, demandingly possessive about Jane. She put up with it and smiled, and it was the smile that hurt James most of all. If she could bear the situation, he could *not*, but it wasn't long before his forthright grandmother wanted to know why he was neglecting his parents.

'I'm not complaining . . . I enjoy your company, James. I suppose you're avoiding Duncan?' Her bright eyes fixed on him defied, even now, the possibility that he might feel inclined to lie to her.

'I suppose I am,' he admitted slowly. 'I get the impression things are difficult enough without me there to make them worse. For some reason I *do* make things worse for Duncan.'

'For Jane, you mean.'

He could think of nothing to do with this remark except ignore it. 'Gran . . . tell me something,' he said instead. 'Why don't they just get married? Duncan's mad about her

. . . in fact he's forever mauling her whenever I'm around. They've been engaged for months. Why not marry and move into a home of their own? Is accommodation so short that they can't find anything?'

'It *is*, but be thankful they aren't married,' Lady Carterton said forcibly. 'My poor grandson's not a fit husband for anyone, and to do him justice, I think he's aware of the fact. But he's terrified you'll take Jane away from him, and he needs her.'

James stared at her in a way that reminded her uncomfortably of her son-in-law in one of his less ingratiating moods. 'Are you saying what I *think* you're saying?' he demanded hoarsely. 'That Duncan's seriously disturbed, and my parents actually connive at this method of keeping him on the rails? Good God, is that really what you mean? Does nobody consider Jane?'

'You're shouting at me, James.' She didn't look away from him, but her swollen arthritic hands had begun to tremble, and he felt ashamed of himself.

'Sorry, Gran. Even if I should be shouting at all, I'm certainly shouting at the wrong person.'

'No one's to blame, my dear,' she said gently. 'The situation just happened. Duncan came home on edge, obviously at odds with the idea of settling down to the different discipline of being a City man. But by then, taking comfort from Jane was no new thing . . . he'd grown used to it long before he left the RAF. The twins were a help too, and somehow he got the feeling that together they made a family. He truly loves them and I think he loves Jane, but the present arrangement is as much as he can cope with.'

'But what about Jane?'

'She sees him as part of the Marchant family, of course. She could no more refuse to help him than she could stop breathing. Don't rush off breathing fire and slaughter on your parents. They aren't any happier about the situation than the rest of us. I suspect Brian Rowland has had quite a lot to say on the subject, because he's *not* disposed to be tender towards the Marchants, but it won't have made a scrap of difference. Jane does what she thinks is right. If staying there, apparently engaged to Duncan, is the only way she can help him, then that's what she'll do, and the rest of us can argue till we're blue in the face.'

'I'll grant you that,' James admitted with a glimmer of a smile on his strained face. 'But letting her be used as a prop . . . is that the best we can do for Duncan?'

'What else do you suggest? That we confront him with an alienist? Tell an apparently normal young man of twenty-eight that he needs psychiatric help? Would you fancy the job of convincing him?'

'No, but I'd be prepared to try, except for one thing: I'm the last person on earth Duncan would listen to. It's sad to say, but my brother can hardly bear to be in the same room with me.'

'He doesn't trust you as far as Jane is concerned.'

'In which he's probably right, but he might at least trust her.'

'He can't help remembering the bond there used to be between you. But that's not all the trouble. He realizes that the war gave you some maturity you didn't have before. What weakened *him* so terribly strengthened *you* and he resents the fact.'

James stared at his grandmother, surprised by her shrewdness and by the sadness in her face.

'You understand him very well, Gran.'

'I love him dearly,' she confessed simply. 'I love you all, although you probably think I'm a bossy tiresome old woman.'

It made him smile at her. 'What we think is that we're rather proud of you. Somewhat in awe still, but definitely proud!'

Lady Carterton did her best not to look pleased. 'Bamboozler! If you're in awe of anybody I'll eat my best hat.'

'Not the one with the bird of paradise sitting on a nest of pink veiling?'

The anxious question made her snort with laughter, and they didn't revert to the subject of Duncan, but it cropped up again with William because James felt obliged to discuss the future with him.

'I can get a place at St Martin's, and an ex-serviceman's grant,' he explained to his father. 'But the world isn't going to lose another Rembrandt or Botticelli if I don't go on with art! I know even less about Marchant's, but if you need more help than Duncan's you must tell me so.'

It left unspoken James's doubt that his brother was providing any help at all.

William's face lightened in a charming smile. 'Nobly said, dear boy! But I have a very clear recollection of the look of horror on your face when I used to set off for Mincing Lane in my black coat and striped trousers. You couldn't have looked more disapproving if I'd been wearing prison uniform, which is roughly, I suppose, how it seemed to you.'

'I think it still strikes me as a kind of prison,' James said truthfully. 'But you didn't answer my question. Nobody has ever thought to ask *you* how you felt about slaving away in the City all these years. Perhaps it's time we did.'

William regarded his son for a moment, suddenly aware that much as Cessy and Duncan appeared changed by the events of the past five years, it was James who'd left behind the unthinkingness of youth more completely than either of them. The idea of an effete and temperamental artist was laughable when applied to this lean fit young man, whose quiet voice and gentle manner must seriously mislead anyone who wasn't allowed to get to know him. William doubted whether even his own family yet knew all there was to know about James.

'There's no need for you to feel sorry for me,' he said at last. 'Odd as it must seem to you, I've always enjoyed my working life. I could wish for fewer problems than there are at the moment, and for a little more conviction about our chances of keeping things as they've always been. That said, I've no complaints. But I know it isn't the kind of life you want to lead. Whatever talents I've had, I've used; you must do the same, James.'

'We come back to Duncan,' his son said quietly. 'Does he help . . . will he ever be able to help fully?'

William gave a helpless little shrug. 'On the good days I feel quite hopeful. But whether we're justified in using Janey as we do, God only knows.' He looked at his son's face and hesitantly risked a question. 'Is she the reason why you don't come to see us very often?'

'Yes, she's the reason . . . I can't bear to see them together.'

'You used to be close, I always thought.'

James's expression was suddenly withdrawn, giving his father no clue to the fact that he was remembering a recent episode. He'd been left alone with Jane for a moment, something Duncan usually saw to it didn't happen. Electricity hummed in the air like a high-tension wire, and because he couldn't help himself he started to close the gap of a few yards between them.

'James . . . friends again?' She threw the desperate question at him and it had the effect she needed of stopping him.

'No . . . *not* friends!' There wasn't time to explain that their relationship had to change because, after a moment of frozen stillness, she turned and walked out of the room.

He stared at his father now and said abruptly, 'Jane knows perfectly well why I avoid her. Duncan knows it too, and sometimes I have the terrible feeling that it's what he enjoys most in life.'

After a long pause William said gently, 'Go to St Martin's, James. Forget about Marchant & Ferguson.'

* * *

Cessy found a new nanny for the twins, introduced her to them gradually during days when Chaney was said to be 'busy', and finally installed them all in her own flat again. They didn't go without protest, but they adapted themselves to the new arrangement less painfully than the adults they left behind. The house seemed much too quiet without them, and even the storm Jane had expected from Duncan didn't come; he retreated instead behind a wall of silent hostility that seemed more ominous than an explosion.

She filled the days with an onslaught on rooms that hadn't been properly spring-cleaned since the beginning of the war, until even good-natured Edie Bloggs called a halt by mentioning sadly that she was 'gettin' on a bit' for so strenuous a programme.

'Sorry, Mrs B, spring-fever!' Jane apologized. 'We'll forget the bedroom and make a cup of tea instead.'

Edie had no fault to find with this, but went home to predict to Albert that the balloon was going to go up at No. 2. 'You mark my words, Bert. I ain't never wrong!'

Things were still the same a week later when Jane sat at home alone nursing a streaming cold. The March afternoon was cold and wet and its misery seemed to have seeped not only into the house but into her bones. Dusk had set in early because of the greyness of the day, but she sat in the shadowy drawing room without bothering to switch on a lamp. It was a relief to be alone, to stop smiling, doing things, pretending. Her face had worn a mask of cheerfulness for so long that it was a miracle features hadn't been worn to a smooth blank underneath. The idea became so dreadful and vivid in her mind that she ran to the huge gilt mirror above the fireplace to stare at her reflection. Someone who still looked like Jane Rowland was dimly pictured there, and she caught her breath in a sob of relief from panic. But she couldn't stop the sobs once they'd started; tears brimmed over her eyelids, flowed down her face, in a torrent of weeping that she was help-less to do anything about.

It was how James found her when he opened the front door and walked into the room. A flick of a lamp-switch in the near-darkness bathed her in a soft pool of light, and there was no hope of concealment. She smeared away tears with the back of her hand, and the gesture transported him back in time to a day when tragedy had sent a small girl to hide in the refuge of an elm tree. He'd wanted to lift her down then and comfort her, but doubt had held him back. No doubt on earth could hold him back now.

'Don't come near me ... I'm full of germs and feeling sorry for myself,' she explained hoarsely.

He went on walking towards her. 'Damn your germs!' She was picked up in his arms and carried to the enormous Chesterfield that flanked the fireplace. All the tears in her heart had been wept, but she could find nothing to say. They'd reached a point of no return, and she knew it as well as he did.

'Why are you alone?'

The quiet question steadied her and seemed to suggest after all that she'd mistaken things as usual; he was being kind because she needed comfort – he'd have done as much for Daffy upset by some small tragedy.

'Your mother's visiting Lady C.,' she muttered. 'That's why I was sitting here in the dark, making a fool of myself and enjoying the luxury of a good howl ... post-'flu depression, they call it. But I'm quite all right again now.'

It didn't have the effect of making him release her, and she forced herself to say with dignity, 'I should like to get up now, James.'

'Would you, Janey? I was hoping you liked it where you were.'

She made the mistake of looking at him. What good was pride, pretence, or the faint sad memory of Duncan when James smiled at her thus? Mouth solemn as usual, but his eyes alight with amusement, and so much love that her heart seemed to stop beating.

'Something has to be done, you know,' he said quietly. 'We can't go on like this. When Cessy wrote to me she described your engagement to Duncan as odd. It's infamous, and I love you too much to allow it to go on.'

Her fingers touched his face in a fleeting caress. 'It's more than I bargained for! Do you remember how Jos used to say that when something so lovely happened that he couldn't quite believe it? You were stiff and unfriendly . . . I even convinced myself you didn't want me here – resented the fact that William and Agnes had taken me in.'

Still he couldn't tell her the truth, but had to say instead, 'I've never in my life done anything but love you. I can't explain the muddle I was in, Janey, but it had nothing to do with you and me. Will you let me tell Duncan?'

He felt her body go rigid in his arms, and hated himself for dragging her back to the thought of that iniquitous engagement. There was silence in the room except for the heavy tick of an ormulu clock on the mantelpiece he'd always hated. It was going to remind him in future of the moment when she told him she couldn't abandon his brother.

'The "odd" engagement was never real,' she said slowly, 'it was just to help Duncan until he felt able to . . . to manage on his own. I don't think he feels able yet.'

'How long are we supposed to wait . . . a year, two . . . half a lifetime? If there was the slightest chance that you could rehabilitate him I suppose I'd have to agree to wait; but there isn't, Janey. Duncan now is the man he's always going to be.'

'He's *better*, James,' she insisted feverishly. 'You weren't here at Christmas-time, but he was normal and happy. He's got to get used to losing the twins at the moment; I can't flaunt *us* in front of him as well.' His face looked so unyielding that her eyes begged him to agree. 'Doesn't it help to . . . to understand one another?'

A faint smile touched his mouth. 'How delightfully prim it sounds! It helps, my dear one, but not very much. I need much more than to be allowed to smile at you occasionally across my mother's dinner table if my brother shouldn't be looking. It's intolerable, Janey.'

'Then you must stay away from your mother's dinner-table,' she said steadily. 'We can't hurt Duncan any more at the moment.'

'We can try not to, if we must. But he knows my secret already, and he'll almost certainly guess that you've got something to hide.'

She was set on her feet, but he still stood holding her within the circle of his arms.

'It's an odd mixture, wanting to weep my heart out again and dance for joy at the same time,' she said unevenly. James stared down at her as if her face, feature by feature, had to be fixed in his memory. He thought she loved him, but she hadn't said so, and what Duncan needed still mattered most. Even now he might lose her. His hands gripped her shoulders, and his mouth fastened on her own. For a moment there was only the sweetness of it, and then need leaping between them, and nothing else that mattered in the whole wide world.

The opening of the front door was lost on them, and the figure of Duncan silently watching them from the doorway of the drawing room. He didn't move until James's arms let go of her and they stood apart, hands still entwined. Then he spoke to Jane, ignoring his brother. 'You mustn't kiss someone else, Janey, you belong to me.'

'She belongs to herself . . . she must be allowed to choose', James said quickly.

He might not have been in the room for all the notice Duncan took of him.

'Tell him to go away . . . we don't want him here.'

'Duncan, it's time you heard the truth.' James spoke quietly but the effect was shocking. His brother spun round, face working with a mixture of rage and fear that distorted his features into a mask of hatred.

'Get out of this house . . . you don't belong here.' This time it was addressed at James, in a scream that rang through the room.

James looked at Jane, eyes asking her to let him complete what had now been begun. Her own, huge and dark with pain, implored him to do nothing of the kind.

'Janey?' he murmured questioningly.

'No . . . not now. Please . . . go.' Just for a moment she thought he was going to refuse, then he walked past her out of the room. The slam of the front door was like the sound of being locked back in her prison again. Duncan moved towards her and clamped her arms in a grip that made her wince.

'Why was James kissing you?'

'For comfort . . . I was feeling sorry for myself, weeping.'

'Well, we don't want him here . . . he mustn't come again.'

'Duncan, this is his home. Of course he will come again.'

It was a mistake to argue with him. His hands bit deeper into her thin shoulders, shaking her until she was forced to cry out at him, 'Stop this . . . I can't bear it.'

The pitch of desperation in her voice cut through the rage that fogged his mind. It sounded as if she were pleading with him . . . he'd won with Janey, and he'd got James out of the house. They must know that he had to win.

'He mustn't kiss you again. You belong to me.'

Had he ever said once upon a time, 'I won't hold you to it, Janey,' and had she believed him? It only added to the sense of being lost for ever in a nightmare that he was now smiling at her, pleased with himself and ready to forgive her for worrying him for a moment. Words that she hadn't known were in her mouth tumbled out, incoherent and

267

desperate. 'Why . . . what's the point . . . you don't want to marry me . . .'

His face darkened again. 'I don't know *what* I want,' he shouted, and flung himself out of the room.

She was trembling from head to foot, but mercifully alone again with time to pull herself together before Agnes came back. Her breathing steadied after a while, and she sat like a small animal in a trap, examining it for a way out and finding none. The clock chimed, reminding her that the day had to seem normal . . . she must instruct her legs to carry her to the kitchen and the dining-room. Agnes came in soaked from walking home in a rain-storm, and soon after her William arrived in much the same condition, since he still used the Tube nowadays, and walked from the station at Notting Hill Gate.

'No Duncan?' William asked when he came into the room, changed into the informal clothes that had taken the place of dressing for dinner since the beginning of the war. 'He was coming home early, I thought. Said he had a bad head.'

'He 'came in,' Jane said mechanically. 'W – went out again, though.'

Half an hour later there was still no sign of him and Agnes announced that their casserole, steadily drying up in the oven, could wait no longer. They sat down to dinner, listening to the rain still hurling itself against the windows and the wind steadily rising in pitch. Agnes got up and pulled back the curtain. 'It's getting very wild,' she said quietly, 'why doesn't he come home?'

At that moment Jane knew the fear within herself had escaped into the room.

'Run into an old friend, I expect,' William suggested. It had happened before. Duncan had bumped into someone from RAF days and eventually brought himself home in a taxi after an evening's steady drinking. Jane knew that she was about to say he'd been upset and would probably come back the worse for wear when the telephone rang in the drawing room. William got up to answer it, there was a low murmur of conversation, and then a pause before he reappeared and went to stand beside his wife's chair.

'Someone was calling from the Radcliffe Infirmary in Oxford,' he said unevenly. 'Duncan's been taken there . . . he's had an accident of some kind.'

'Oxford? He was driving his car . . . he's badly hurt?' The questions barely got themselves through her white lips.

'I don't know, my dearest . . . they just said we should try to get there as quickly as we can. Fetch your coats while I ring James, and pray to God he's in.'

He *was* there, and ten minutes later had his car waiting at the kerb.

'I left Gran with Cessy on the way,' he said briefly. He didn't look at Jane, and she got in the back of the car with Agnes, without the small comfort of a smile that said he hadn't changed his mind about loving her. Agnes spoke only once on the journey down to Oxford. 'What could have brought my darling boy all this way, on a night like this?'

'He must have been coming to River Cottage . . . the place where he remembered being happy.' She held Agnes's cold hand and they said nothing more.

James crossed Magdalen Bridge and drove along the High just as Great Tom on Christ Church tower chimed midnight. Cornmarket was deserted in the wet and windy darkness, and only an occasional cyclist fought against the wind along St Giles. They turned into the forecourt of the Infirmary an hour and a half after they'd pulled away from Linden Square. Even so, they were too late. A tired-faced Sister met them with the news that Duncan had died half an hour before, without regaining consciousness.

'I'm afraid there was never very much hope,' she explained gently. 'He wasn't found for a while . . . but there was almost nothing we could have done . . . I'm so very sorry.'

His face was little marked, because the worst injuries had been to his body, and he looked young and peaceful again. No more fear to be tortured by . . . but no more of anything. 'Nothing will come of nothing,' King Lear had said, and nothing now would come of Duncan. The word beat in Jane's brain until she could bear it no longer, mumbled something to Agnes, and stumbled outside into the cool dampness of the night. The rain had stopped, and even a star or two glimmered through the high ragged clouds still being driven across the sky. Somewhere an Oxford clock chimed one with a faintly cracked note, and then another with a sweeter sound echoed over the silent town.

William sat with Agnes during the journey home, and Jane got into the front seat beside James, aware that they hadn't spoken a single word to each other since they left London. The car wasn't large, and it ought to have been a comfort to feel his sleeve brush against her's occasionally, but there was no comfort to be had because only coldness was seeping towards her, and she knew that if her hand had accidentally touched his, he would have flinched away from her.

Agnes was more fortunate in the back of the car because William held her hand, and the pain they were suffering was shared pain. But when James helped them out of the car, kissed them, and drove away, she saw what the night had done to him. For the first time in her knowledge of him, William looked defeated. Her own grief was over-ridden by the need to help him. She could think of only one way of doing it, and the risk was terrible. But if the ghost of Ano Rowland was ever to be exorcised, now was the moment to try.

Jane hugged them both, and then climbed the stairs to her own room. It took almost more courage than she possessed because she needed the company of other human beings, but Agnes and William must be left alone to help each other.

Agnes shivered in the coldness of dawn, stood with both arms wrapped round herself. 'There's nothing to be done, except go to bed. Would you . . . would you stay with me, please, William? I don't think I could bear to be on my own.'

The silence seemed very long before he said, 'Sit with you, you mean? My dear . . . of course.'

'Try to sleep, too, I meant,' she said steadily, above the thudding of her heart.

Exhaustion had almost wiped his face clear of emotion, but she saw it quiver into life again.

'Are you sure? If it's for my comfort . . .'

'It's for both of us.'

Half an hour later, lying encircled by his arm for the first time in years, she knew that nothing else could have made bearable the memory of Duncan, left lying all alone.

Chapter 20

Duncan's funeral was attended by men and women they hadn't ever known, a few of them still in RAF uniform, who shyly offered sympathy and the opinion that he'd been a good man to fly with. Often enough it was probably a good thing that the dead didn't know what the living thought of them, but Agnes wished passionately that Duncan *had* known that he'd been valued. Stresses had played havoc with peace of mind since, but like the veteran of Agincourt, he hadn't needed to be ashamed of the 'deeds he did that day'.

Edward Ferguson had found excuses to stay away from Linden Square for months past, but there was no possibility of staying away now. Cessy looked composed, but so sad that he was reminded of the closeness of her tie with Duncan; twins were not like other brothers and sisters. On another level, his mind acknowledged that, dressed in black, she looked as beautiful as she would ever look. When he stooped to kiss her cheek she flushed a little, but smiled at him as she hoped an old friend might.

'Kind of you to come, Edward. How is everything at St Margaret's?'

'Muddling along!' Then he corrected himself ruefully. 'How ungenerous of me . . . Ruth does her best. She can't help not being Cessy Willoughby!'

The compliment was acknowledged by a little nod, but all she said was, 'One man's meat! I suspect that a self-

272

opinionated bore called Sir Humphrey Roberts, KC, would rather be rid of me. He looks nervous sometimes, as if he guesses I'm plotting how to murder him without getting hanged for it!'

Edward grinned, and tried not to think of solemn well-meaning Ruth, who needed to have his mildest joke explained to her. Then his face changed as he watched Agnes and William thanking people for coming to say goodbye to Duncan. 'There's something different about them, apart from grief,' he said suddenly. 'Am I right?'

She hesitated, wondering what the discovery meant to him. But now it was time to be truthful.

'We try to pretend we haven't noticed, but yes, you're right. There's something lovely re-established between them. Perhaps it was *never* there before. I can't remember.'

She examined his face, but there wasn't the slightest sign that he was hurt or disappointed by what she'd just confirmed. It was the moment when Cessy decided that somehow, some day, she was going to marry him.

Jane got through the funeral and the days that followed anaesthetised by sadness and guilt, tinged with the ashamed relief of knowing that her prison door was open. She waited for James to work his way through whatever storm of emotions held him isolated from her, and only slowly realized that the isolation was permanent. She'd believed that Duncan alive was a bar to happiness; James seemed convinced that Duncan dead made it impossible. He avoided her when he could, but came to the house one day when only she was there. The memory of an earlier visit couldn't be blanketed by polite enquiries about everybody's health and the weather.

'James, can we talk . . . please . . . if it's only to admit to each other that we feel responsible for killing Duncan,' she said desperately.

'No need for *you* to feel responsible. My brother would

probably have managed to kill himself long before he did, but for you.'

'I'm to be let off, but you *are* responsible. Is that it?'

'Roughly, yes. Technically I know he's dead because he drove a car in appalling conditions when he'd been drinking heavily. Rationally I thank God he didn't kill someone else. Irrationally I *know* that I'm involved. It's a terrible feeling.'

'He said once that *he* felt guilty about being alive when so many of his friends were dead. Then, it seemed an excuse for not being quite brave enough to cope with life. Don't you feel brave enough either, James?'

It took courage to ask *that*, but the question of whether he loved her enough couldn't be asked at all. His face looked stern and remote, and she knew before he spoke that the moment when they might have loved one another had come and gone.

'I don't feel anything at all, Janey. I'm wandering about in some frozen waste-land, aware of the people about me but unable to make contact with them. Have you ever had the sort of nightmare where some infinitely terrible disaster rushes down on you. All you have to do is move out of its way, but you're incapable of doing so. I want to hold out my arms to you, but Duncan stands in the way ... not screaming at me any more, just smiling!'

She couldn't insist, couldn't do anything but accept what he'd just said. If he'd loved her a little more they might have managed it ... but he didn't, and there was nothing to be done. She should have stayed in her prison after all. Pride could keep her from crying out until he'd gone, but she prayed that he wouldn't touch her. A moment or two, or a lifetime, later he made a little helpless gesture and walked out of the room. She clamped a hand over her mouth so as not to call him back, and waited for the slam of the front door.

Agnes, going through her own purgatory of waiting

until the funeral should be over, followed William into his study one day. She felt more sure of him now that they'd rediscovered tenderness, but what she had to say might clamp them back into the separate compartments they'd lived in most of their married life.

He smiled as she sat down opposite him and folded her hands in her lap. She was a restful woman, but he no longer confused that with thinking her to be an emotionless one. 'You look solemn, my love, so this isn't just a friendly visit.'

'No . . . it's to talk about your sons,' she said quietly.

'My son?'

'Sons, William. I know that nothing can make up for losing Duncan, but would it help a little to know that you have another son apart from James?'

'I don't understand you.' He didn't recognize his own voice, and had difficulty in breathing.

'Brian Rowland is not Joseph's son . . . he's yours.'

'Oh God! Oh, God in Heaven . . .' He buried his face in his hands for a moment, but forced himself to look at her. 'You wouldn't say such a thing if you weren't sure. *How* are you sure, when I never knew?'

'I think I always knew. But it seemed so necessary to be sure that I finally asked Ano. I'm thankful I did, because she was killed very soon afterwards. She never told Jos either. Ano was a remarkable woman . . . . I'm rather proud to have known her.'

William's eyes searched his wife's face. 'It must have been an appalling interview.'

'Strangely enough, it wasn't. She'd always despised me until then, afterwards I felt that she didn't!'

'You're right about Ano, but you're just as remarkable,' he said after a moment. 'No other woman on earth could have told me about Brian without wanting to make me feel guilty. At the very beginning I wondered about him, but it seemed so unthinkable of Ano not to tell me that I finally convinced myself he was Jos's son.'

275

'She didn't want Jos hurt . . . she didn't love him, but she was grateful to him. The children know, because James guessed and found himself having to confide in Cessy. She fell in love with Brian at Lowestoft and had to be warned away . . . that's why she was so desperately unhappy that she embarked on the affair that produced the twins.'

'Dear God . . . what are Ano and I *not* responsible for? "The sins of the fathers visited upon the children even unto the third and fourth generation." A snatch or two of pleasure, and the resulting mess looks like going on and on.'

'It wasn't just that for Ano . . . she loved you, and never got over loving you. And *you* wouldn't have snatched at pleasure but for a wife who evaded her responsibilities. You must blame me, too, William.'

His hand reached out to cover hers. 'I'd like you to know the rest. Need reasserted itself because the opportunity was there while you and Jane were at River Cottage. It would have been better if the opportunity hadn't arisen. I found myself relieved when it was over and, try as I would, I'm sure Ano guessed. She looked defeated afterwards.'

Agnes nodded, thinking that if she'd been a vindictive woman she could have reckoned she'd revenged herself on Ano Rowland.

'If Ano had lived I should never have touched her again . . . never even wanted to. There's no reason why you should believe that, but it's true,' he said abruptly.

To his astonishment her eyes were suddenly full of amusement. 'I do believe it! You sounded so cross on the telephone one day that I decided you were finding freedom too much of a good thing!' They sat for a moment without speaking, then Agnes steeled herself to take the last hurdle in front of her. 'I knew for certain that Ano despised me, but I was almost sure you did too. That's why it was such a comfort to persuade myself that I wasn't a failure after all.'

'Edward Ferguson?' he asked quietly.

'Yes. He was too kind to tell me outright that I was a muddled middle-aged woman in pursuit of a chimera. I think he hoped I'd eventually be able to sort things out for myself. In the end I did, but I'm afraid I hurt Cessy in the process. Edward's the man she's fallen in love with, finally and completely.'

'There's no need to worry if Edward sees things as clearly as you think he does.'

'They may both be afraid of hurting my feelings. There's a slight awkwardness about telling him that I want him to love my daughter instead of me!'

William brushed a hand over his eyes. 'God forgive me . . . I used to think *I* was the one who knew what went on, while you—'

'—sat playing the piano!' She smiled back at him, but then became serious again. 'About Brian, dearest . . . what are you going to do?'

'Talk to him, I suppose. But if you think he'll welcome the news that I'm his father, you don't know Brian Rowland. Poor Cessy . . . she must have thought she was caught up in a Greek tragedy. If Janey's the only one who doesn't know, she ought to be told too.'

Agnes nodded. 'I think she's making up her mind to leave us. Duncan's death has made things worse, not better, for her and James, and I have the terrible feeling that there's nothing we can do about it.' The tears that still invaded her when she thought of Duncan began to trickle down her thin cheeks again, and when William's arm gathered her close she turned her face into his shoulder.

With his cheek against her hair, he murmured, 'Is the poor middle-aged lady still searching for her chimera?'

Agnes lifted her head and smiled at him. 'Chimera not needed now. She has the real thing.'

Instead of setting off the following morning for Mincing Lane, William headed in the opposite direction – westwards to Shepherd's Bush, timing his arrival at Brian's garage for a time when he might be beginning to think of going to lunch.

'I was in the area,' William said vaguely, 'thought I'd see if you were free for lunch.'

Brian allowed himself to look surprised, but said cheerfully, 'I'll come provided I'm allowed to do the honours. This is *my* patch, and I've got a favourite riverside pub.'

William knew that it made his own situation more awkward, but he didn't blame Brian for taking charge – how could he? It was exactly the sort of thing he'd have done himself.

'Jane all right?' Brian asked as they walked along.

'Managing, like the rest of us . . . coming to terms with things.'

It wasn't until they were settled in a quiet corner of the bar, with beer and ham sandwiches in front of them, that William started on what he'd come to say. 'I had a reason for seeing you today. You won't be overjoyed by it, and it may even make you exceedingly angry, but you mustn't doubt the truth of it. I learned yesterday for the first time that you are not Joseph's son.'

Brian put down the tankard he was holding, picked it up again and stared at it as if he'd never seen such a thing before. 'Yours and Ano's, by any chance?'

'Yes. Apparently Ano hoped I need never be told, but Agnes has known for some time and Duncan's death, in her view, seemed to change things.'

There was a moment of complete silence, and then Brian put back his black head and roared with laughter. As a reaction it was the very last one William had expected. He was unnerved by it, irritated, and finally angry. His right hand clenched itself round his glass, and Brian, sobered by the sight of it, was moved to apologize. 'I'm sorry . . . you can't feel much like seeing the funny side of things at the moment. It's just that the whole thing's so damned ironic!'

278

'You metaphorically spitting on the Merchants and everybody like them all these years, you mean, and finding you're flesh of their flesh after all?'

'Something like that,' Brian agreed. The recollection of Cessy's face the morning of their last meeting in the Lowestoft mess destroyed the last vestige of amusement. She'd known, somehow, and deliberately forced herself to choke him off. He was lost in memories until William spoke again.

'Ano never gave me the slightest hint that you were my son. But knowing it now, I can see that the relationship is crystal-clear. We don't look alike in the least, but we're alike all the same.'

'I'm sorry, then,' Brian said bluntly. 'I'd rather have been Jos's son.'

'So you don't want to make any change . . . become a Marchant . . . join the firm, even?'

Brian looked at his father, irritated to discover the sort of clear-headed drive and directness that he recognized in himself. 'No thanks. I'm going to stay Brian Rowland, successful garage-proprietor for the moment, and successful Labour MP one of these days. You might find the connection embarrassing.'

'Not at all,' William said blandly. 'I spent six months in the University Communist Club before seeing the error of my ways!'

It made his son grin in spite of himself. 'What about Janey?' he asked suddenly. 'Does she know?'

'Not yet, but I shall tell her. I'm sorry that you and Cessy nearly came to grief, by the way. And perhaps this is the moment to say once and for all that I'm sorry I was never in a position to make Ano happy.'

'I don't suppose you were,' Brian agreed soberly. 'But I wish to God I'd known sooner for Cessy's sake.'

William parted company with him soon afterwards feeling regretful that his son had disowned him so completely.

'New twist to the story,' he said, recounting the interview to Agnes that evening, 'usually it's the other way round!'

'What a pity about Marchant's, though. You and Tom need help so badly—' She broke off abruptly, unable to remind him that they now had to manage without Duncan.

'We'd cope if we had to, but it seems we don't have to. James tells me he's discovered in himself a longing to be a City man!'

Agnes stared at him, transfixed. '*James* has? He'd hate it. What about St Martin's . . . it was all fixed?'

'It's now unfixed, apparently. I did my damnedest to argue with him, but he's the most pigheaded of all our children . . . it must come from *your* side of the family, my darling!'

He believed it, she thought without rancour, absurd as she knew the idea to be. 'Wherever it comes from, James must be made to change his mind. He's never wanted to do anything but paint. It would be the most grievous mistake to allow him to feel that he must try to take Duncan's place.'

'You won't stop him,' William said with absolute certainty. 'James may be the quietest of them, but he's the strongest of the lot. He assures me that he's outgrown the wish to be a student; he'll be a weekend artist, and Monday to Friday apply himself to Trade!' He hesitated a moment, and then added, 'You were quite right about Janey, by the way. James knows already that she's determined to leave. If you can manage without us for a little while, my darling, I shall suggest that we make a quick trip to Ceylon. The Firm needs it and so, it seems to me, does James.'

Before they left, William had his interview with Jane. It wouldn't have occurred to her to burst into laughter, but in its way her own reaction to the news was as unexpected as Brian's had been.

'I wonder if Mam was right to keep Jos in the dark,' she said thoughtfully. 'I think it might have helped him to know.'

'It doesn't usually help a man to know such things.'

William sounded dry, and felt embarrassed to be discussing the matter with his adopted daughter.

'I realize that, but it would have explained why Mam was so unhappy. Jos always knew she was, and imagined it was because of some lack in *him*. If poor Mam loved you, nothing he could have done would have made her happy.'

It explained a great deal . . . all the years of her childhood, in fact, when she'd sensed almost unbearable frustration in her mother, and the sparking tension of a live wire when Ano had been anywhere near William Marchant. Life enjoyed repeating itself, seemingly. Ano's daughter was going to have to find some way of living without William's son. *Ano's* daughter! A thought took possession of her mind, and she stared at him with eyes that insisted on a truthful answer. 'Jos *was* my father?'

'Yes . . . there is no doubt about that.'

She relapsed into silence again, thinking about the complicated Marchant-Rowland relationship. Life not only enjoyed repetition, it was cussedly perverse. A small girl uneasily rigged out in St Olave blue and scarlet had slithered from one pretence to another designed to conceal the fact that she came from Linden Mews. She doubted now whether they'd confused anyone but herself. Brian, always ready to do away with middle-class Linden Square, was the one who'd belonged there after all! The thought of him provoked a grin that William hadn't seen on Jane's face for a long time.

'I doubt if Brian was overjoyed at the news!'

'You doubt correctly, but he managed to remain tolerably polite throughout the interview! Predictably, he insists on going his own way. Wants to have as little to do with the Marchants as possible. I'm rather sorry about that, but he's old enough to know his own mind.'

William hesitated a moment; the ground that he must now venture on was getting dangerous. 'Agnes thinks you're about to go your own way too, Janey. You've the right to run your own life, but you belong to us, as far as heart's affections go, much more than Brian does. You must never forget that, or cease to regard this as your home. Promise me?'

She reached up to kiss his cheek in the loving impromptu gesture once reserved only for Jos. 'I promise, even though I may seem to forget,' she said strangely.

William and James flew to Ceylon three days later, and she managed to be out of the house when their taxi arrived at the door to take them to the airport, taking refuge in Brian's flat overlooking the river until it was safe to go home again.

'Seems I'm the one who ought to be at Linden Square,' he said suddenly, 'not you.'

'I know, but I thought I'd wait and see if you wanted to talk about it.' She stared at a duck standing on its head in the river, and then turned to smile at him.

'I expect it's a silly question, but do you feel any different?'

'Of course not, and I don't remember Ano and Jos any differently, either. But in some way I can't quite put my finger on there *are* things it changes, and I've got to find some way of dealing with William Marchant.'

'Do you blame him?'

'I can't blame him for owning up to what he didn't know, and I refuse to think of Ano as some half-witted innocent seduced by a London villain. I don't see her as a gullible victim, do you?'

'Not gullible,' Jane agreed thoughtfully, 'but she *was* a victim.' Memories were hard to push aside, but after a moment she smiled at Brian. 'I suppose your proletarian comrades will disown you now?'

'No reason why they should ever know. Ano wanted the secret kept. As far as possible I think we should let it stay that way. It can't hurt Ano and Jos now, but there's Agnes Marchant to be considered.'

Jane hadn't expected that, and smiled warmly at him.

Then she went back to staring at the ducks, because they always reminded her of River Cottage.

'Changed your mind about moving in here?' Brian asked suddenly. 'We're still related, so it's perfectly proper for you to be here, if that matters a twopenny damn.'

'It's kind of you, but the answer's still no.'

'Who needs you this time?'

'No one. I'm about to embark on my long-delayed nursing career.'

For a girl who was finally free to start doing what she had always longed to do, she looked remarkably unenthusiastic about it and he was tempted to ask why. But although he was still her brother, give or take a half, kinship didn't give him the right to prod her heart to see what made it tick.

'Well, when you get tired of lugging your lamp about, remember that you belong here.'

Her mouth twisted wryly. 'I seem to belong everywhere – William insists that my home is in Linden Square. I'm not sure that I really belong anywhere – that's how much I still miss Jos, I suppose.'

'You miss Cessy's brats, as well. I wrote to her, by the way. William Marchant told me she'd been in the secret much longer than we have, and that explained what happened to us at Lowestoft. We seemed to have something important going between us, but she came back from leave and gave me a devastating brush-off. I imagined she'd had second thoughts and merely wanted to shove a member of the lower orders back into his proper place again. I reacted accordingly, and the time has come to apologize.'

'Poor Cessy . . . no wonder she was so desperate afterwards. She got into a bad way before the twins were born, and I must have seemed insufferably breezy about helping her. We never know enough about people to avoid making mistakes.'

Brian wondered who else she was thinking about . . .

Duncan, or James? Whoever it was, her face looked sad when she wasn't aware of being watched.

'The Marchant–Rowland relationship has become too complicated,' she said suddenly. 'It will be a relief to get away and start afresh. It's time I stood on my own feet, too; I've been as unconscionable a time about that as Charles II was about dying!'

'Then here's to Miss Jane Rowland, student-nurse . . . sock it to them, Janey!'

Her enquiries at teaching hospitals didn't need to extend very far; the first one she tried, St Thomas's, had a probationer course about to start just after Easter. A scholastic record at St Olave's got her an interview, and record and interview combined got her the offer of a place on the course. It all seemed so simple – and 'meant', she told herself, as she went home to break the news to Agnes, that she felt confident of doing the right thing at last. She'd used up a couple of years listening to what other people wanted her to do; now it was time to work out her own salvation, and 'save her tears in after years' for a life that might have been shared with James.

She made the announcement over supper that she would have to move into St Thomas's in three days' time. The expression on Agnes's face made her add quickly, 'I hate leaving you here alone until the others get back from Ceylon, but if I miss the beginning of the course . . .'

'Dearest, of course you must go, if that's what you want to do. Are you *sure*, Janey? We had the idea that—'

'James might soon be able to make up his mind whether he wanted to marry me? He never will – marry me, I mean. If the idea was in his head for a little while, it was only that he thought he wanted what Duncan seemed to have . . . hardly anything to do with *me* at all!'

She spoke with a fierce brightness that defeated questions or argument. Agnes remembered the look on James's face in the days following Duncan's funeral and knew that it hadn't been put there by a slight attack of jealousy, but instinct told her that the only thing Jane could bear now was simply to get away from them.

'You set off for St Thomas's, then, and I'll take Gran away for a few days. She's so quiet at the moment that I know she's grieving for Duncan.'

There was no one in the world like Agnes Marchant for loving people lightly . . . no rights for her, no obligations exacted from the people she loved. Jane got up from the table suddenly, with her face crumpling into tears. She was gathered into Agnes's arms, and held as she'd been held the day Jos and Ano died.

Cessy insisted on delivering her to the probationers' home when the morning came, but to Jane's astonishment Brian took it into his head to arrive as well. There was a moment of awkwardness when he found his half-sister there, but Cessy cured it by kissing him.

'Hi! I'm glad you're younger than me . . . I shall feel entitled to keep you in order.'

There was to be no agonising post-mortem, her smile made clear, but there *was* a sense of belonging.

'No wonder we liked each other,' he said gently, and it finally laid to rest the unhappy ghost of their love affair.

Agnes wasn't a woman given to feeling resentment, but she did think it hard that she should have to dread her family's return from the Far East when she would otherwise have been longing for it. The waste of Duncan's life and the emptiness of the house without him were enough heartache to struggle with. Without the twins, and Jane gone as well, she wandered about the silent rooms with only memories and ghosts to keep her company. She longed for William and James to come home, but couldn't rid herself of the idea that she'd failed them in some way by letting Jane go.

After the first few moments of confusion when their taxi was being unloaded at the gate, James glanced round looking for someone who wasn't there. Agnes took a deep breath and threw her bombshell.

'Jane's gone. She was offered a vacancy at St Thomas's, and it was necessary not to miss the beginning of a new course.'

She couldn't identify the tremor of emotion that disturbed his tired face . . . shock, anger, grief? The mask was in place again before she'd made up her mind, and he even managed to smile.

'Poor Mama . . . you've been lonely, I expect, and moping rather.'

'I expect I have, but I shall be better now you're home again, and so will Gran.'

'I might as well return to the fold, don't you think? There must be more empty rooms now than you know what to do with.'

Her face lit in a loving smile. 'We could turn the top floor into a self-contained flat. That way, you wouldn't feel too parent-ridden!'

He nodded and walked out of the room, without making any reference to Jane . . . couldn't have mentioned her name if his life had depended on it. He'd spent the long flight home, sitting silent beside William, fighting an inward struggle. Mind insisted that they couldn't be happy at the cost of Duncan's life; heart suggested that to ruin three lives would be three times the waste of one. The struggle that heart had shown signs of winning had been nothing but a waste of time. Life always got its timing wrong. Jane's letter was waiting for him when he got back to his grandmother's flat. It was a masterpiece of breezy careless confidence, and he had no way of knowing how many false starts had been flung in the waste-paper basket before she managed something that sounded convincing. She was 'fascinated by her new life, liked her fellow-students enormously, and happy to be Jane Rowland, student nurse, at last.' She expected Ceylon had been colourful – he wouldn't be able to tell her now that there hadn't been any elephants after all – hoped the City would welcome him with open arms, and sent her love to Lady C. End of message! He tore the note in pieces, then spent ten feverish minutes putting them together again in case he'd missed something. But all he got from a second reading was the conviction that at last Janey was doing what she'd always wanted to do. She'd been tied to the Marchant chariot-wheels in one way or another for nearly twenty years; now she was out in the big brave world, so who the hell did James Marchant think he was to bleat that it was *his* turn to say he couldn't manage without her? If he'd got himself sorted out a little sooner, things might have been different; no, *would* have been. He couldn't have been mistaken about those few minutes before Duncan interrupted them. But he'd let the moment of choice slip out of his hands, and now all he had to do was somehow turn himself into a good City man!

Chapter 21

In the course of her first year at St Thomas's Jane refused to allow herself to go back to Linden Square. She occasionally spoke to Agnes on the telephone, and shared lunch with Cessy or Brian when she had a day off, but venture into Marchant territory she could not. The excuses she found weren't fictitious: she worked awkward shift duties once she'd graduated to the wards, and it was a struggle to keep up with girls younger than herself who hadn't had a gap of two or three years since leaving school. She did her best to mix, but they seemed so *very* much younger; it was rather like being back at St Olave's again – she was still the solitary outsider, even though for different reasons now.

Cessy thought she looked tired and strained whenever they met. She said so bluntly, but Jane explained that there was never enough time for sleep. 'You can't imagine what sociable creatures nurses are! They come off duty half-dead with fatigue, and immediately want to start talking to each other.'

'And I suppose medical students are quite sociable too,' Cessy said pensively.

'There's that as well,' Jane agreed. 'No wonder nurses and doctors always end up marrying . . . they never see anyone else.'

Cessy pictured her in a gingham print dress, with a frilly white cap perched on her dark hair – irresistible to any medical student or doctor in his right mind. James should have chained her to his bed in Linden Square.

'Everything all right with you and yours?' Jane asked casually.

'Much the same as usual, except that Brian has taken to visiting Ma and Pa. He says it's because he's fallen for Agnes. I think he *is* growing fond of her, but he also likes arguing with Pa. They go at it hammer and tongs, Socialist ideology clashing and banging against die-hard Tory self-responsibility. They always end up where they began the argument, but liking each other more and more. One of the happier developments in recent months!'

'What about Edward?'

'Progress is slow, but I detect signs that he's weakening. I imagined that I was up against the memory of a brief but happy marriage. Nothing of the sort . . . apparently it was a disaster. I should have realized that, because men who've been happily married are more ready to try again, having got into good habits! But the Marchant blood is up. Entirely for his own good I shall marry him in the end, even if I have to move into his home before he makes an honest woman of me.'

She succeeded before the end of the year, and stated firmly that if Jane showed signs of not attending the wedding, Brian would be sent to drag her out of the nurses' quarters. The last-minute excuse of an attack of mumps would probably have made no difference to Cessy in one of her true-blue Marchant moods. Jane bowed to the inevitable, and realized that meeting James again in the crowded company of a wedding was the easiest thing she could do. She found herself spending hoarded clothes coupons on a dark-red velvet suit, and set off for Linden Square for the first time in six months. She was outwardly calm because self-discipline had now become a habit, and only when Agnes wept at the sight of her did her own composure crack. Lady Carterton restored them both with the trenchant reminder that they were supposed to be celebrating getting Cessy respectably settled at last, and then Daniel – toothier than she remembered – hurled himself at someone who had been lost to them and was found again. 'Daff . . . it's *Chaney*!'

For the rest of the day she was their exclusive property, and since they were now launched on the fascinating waters of conversing in whole sentences, no one else had the stamina to compete with them. James was burdened with the duties of being Edward's best man, and Jane found it easy to avoid him after a heart-stopping moment when he stared at her without saying anything. When he did speak, it wasn't what she expected. No polite enquiry about her health or happiness, but simply, 'You remind me of someone . . . Lawrence's painting of a boy in a red velvet suit.'

Her dark hair was still short and windblown at a time when young women wore film-star bangs and flowing page-boy hair, and she was anything but voluptuously curved . . . but *boyish*! She'd hoped the beautiful new suit might have had a different effect.

'You look well, James,' she managed to say. 'Working for the Firm obviously agrees with you.'

They were interrupted by Clarissa Ferguson and Jane could let out a sigh of relief. She'd seen him, and the worst was over. Now she could concentrate on Cessy, radiantly beautiful in pale blue, and Edward looking like a man who still couldn't quite believe that the Kingdom of Heaven on earth was in store for him. They were waved off at the end of the afternoon, on a brief honeymoon in Paris, and Jane was thinking she might now decently leave herself when the tall unfamiliar figure of James in morning dress appeared at her side.

'I hope Cessy realizes how honoured she was to get you to come. The rest of us, Agnes included, don't seem to have the same pulling power.'

'You make me sound neglectful,' she said uncomfortably. 'I hate to be, but we don't have much free time, or much energy left after pounding wards all day or night long. I'm three years older than the others in my set, so it's harder for me—'

'—being long past your prime!' His eyes flicked over her thin face and body. She was gauntly beautiful, poised, and apparently perfectly content with the life that left her so little spare time or energy. What else had he expected, for God's sake? It would be a miracle it she was allowed to get to the end of her training, even, before some medical man snapped her up. He suddenly hated the entire profession that had seemed to conspire against them.

'Granted that it's such a terrible struggle that you can't make time for old friends, are you enjoying life, Janey?' The old name hinted at past times and tenderness, but his voice was cool.

'Very much,' she agreed steadily. 'I'm sorry I'd disappeared by the time you and William came back from Ceylon, but it seemed the . . . right thing to do. What about you? Are you content to be a City man?' She thought that if he chose not to answer the question honestly she would have no means of knowing; his face was schooled now, and she'd long since lost the knack of knowing what he was thinking.

'It's not quite what I imagined I'd do. But perhaps I have the makings of a more successful tea-broker than painter. Knowing one's limitations is a painful but useful step towards not coming too much of a cropper in life. If some philosopher hasn't already pontificated on that great thought, I've just given birth to it unaided!'

His mocking brightness defeated her. There was nothing to be said that was worth saying, and his manner suggested that there wasn't much point in them trying to say anything at all.

'I'm late,' she murmured with an effort. 'Time I went . . . goodbye, James.'

She'd half-turned away when his hands clamped themselves on her shoulders, and the touch of them burned her skin through the softness of the velvet jacket. Her beautiful suit that she wouldn't be able to wear again for fear of being reminded of this moment.

'Janey . . . if you did stop enjoying your lovely new life, would you tell me?'

She didn't have to make up her mind how to answer him. Someone tugged at his sleeve, and the best man was required to attend to him. By the time he was free again, Jane had said goodbye to Agnes and William and let herself out of the house.

In retrospect, the winter of 1947 became a nadir of general misery – the yardstick by which all subsequent bad weather and national discomfort could be measured and found easily wanting. The weeks of harsh weather finally ran into months, making shortages of every kind more of a trial than they would otherwise have been. There didn't seem to be enough of anything to go round and, worst of all, there wasn't enough coal or electricity. Supplies were reduced, and finally cut off altogether for hours at a time as one bitterly cold day followed another and people worked, huddled in coats, by candlelight.

In his regular arguments with William Brian admitted that peacetime Britain wasn't the Shangri-La that a war-ridden electorate had voted the Socialists into power for, but he refused to agree that his faith in the Labour Party was misplaced.

'Well, looking in my crystal ball, I predict that Socialism will fail,' said William.

'Because we're broke, and everything, even the bloody elements, conspire against us getting on our feet again?'

'No, simply because of human nature! Let people believe in an idealistic political theory – it's good for them; but don't *ever* let them try to put in into practice. It never works.'

'Because of hidebound reactionary cynics like you!'

Agnes watched William smile, and thought as she so often did how astonishing it was that the relationship between them hadn't shouted itself to the rest of the world years ago.

'I'm hidebound to the extent that I'm never going to accept public ownership as an efficient way of running industry, and I shall die still voting for free enterprise instead of State control!'

'Like I said . . . reactionary!'

James usually absented himself in his own quarters when Brian was expected, but Agnes took him to task for the fact one day.

'Be sociable, dearest, for a change!'

'Not my dish of tea, Mama, political argle-bargle, and I don't know why Pa bothers. He's never going to convince anyone as pig-headed as Brian, who always *did* think he knew the secret of the universe, and certainly hasn't got any less arrogant.'

'He's got more likeable, I think,' Agnes insisted gently. 'I think kindness brings him here, as well as the chance of an argument.' She knew that more than dislike of political discussion lay behind James's avoidance of Brian. Touchingly, there was loyalty to herself and the feeling that he must resent a bastard half-brother on her behalf, but the real trouble was that Brian was a constant reminder of Jane. These days her son looked taut and tired, worked too hard, and got too irritable, but she didn't say so and he rewarded her with a rare sweet smile.

'Winter blues, Mama! Perhaps we'll all feel better if the spring ever comes.'

By the time spring finally arrived, somewhere around the beginning of May, Jane was in the nurses' sick-bay recovering from a severe dose of influenza. After a week of feverishly high temperatures, aching bones and head, she felt weakly optimistic that the worst was over. She was up and about when Sister Tutor called to enquire whether she felt well enough to present herself in Matron's office. The enquiry was polite but only a matter of form; short of a relapse which left her fainting at Sister's feet, it was clear that the rendezvous with Matron would have to be kept.

An hour later she was sitting in another room whose vantage point gave her a view of the Thames quietly ambling past the window. Not ambling, she decided, because Matron fiddled with papers on her desk, and gave time for a nervous mind to wander. The river wasn't aimless; however many twists and turns it took, however many hesitations and second thoughts it had about its route, it knew that it was making eventually for the sea. But where, Oh Lord, was she making for? As of a few minutes ago her own life had become frighteningly objectiveless.

'Matron, are you sure I won't do?'

The question burst from her so desperately the woman sitting opposite felt wrenched with pity. It was ironic in itself, because she'd just been explaining how necessary it was for nurses to distance themselves from the people they were trying to help, if they were to survive in their profession.

'In most ways you'll "do", as you put it, better than any student nurse I've ever met. But there's just one way in which you won't do. You're at least a stone underweight, and you look less fit than some of the people you're supposed to be nursing! I know some of that is the result of influenza, and we've just struggled through one of the worst winters in living memory, but those things aren't at the heart of the matter.'

'I'm not a good enough nurse,' Jane said dully.

'You're too good! My usual task is to suggest to girls that they should work harder, reserve more of their thoughts and their energies for the people they're looking after. It's the other way round with you. Every patient's pain and problems become yours, and no nurse yet born can stand *that* strain for very long.'

The shadowed face in front of her confirmed what she'd just said. She knew something of Jane Rowland's past history, but not enough to understand some obvious contradictions. Young students usually came with too many attachments to their past life; Jane, three years older than most, apparently came with none. Her singleness of purpose stemmed from nothing but a total blank as far as a personal life was concerned. But it was far more likely, Matron thought, that too much had happened to Nurse Rowland, not too little.

'My dear, don't look so sad,' she said gently. 'It may seem like the end of the world to you at this moment, but you're not yet twenty-one. Life won't stay looking hopeless for very long.'

'What ... what happens now?' Jane asked. 'Am I to leave straightaway?'

'You're to go to a convalescent home. By the time you look less like a ghost and feel more normal, you can begin to think about what you want to do next.'

It was the end of an interview which had been much longer and much kinder, Jane realized, than the ones which normally sped failed nurses on their way. She stood up, gave the automatic little bob which accepted dismissal from Matron's presence, and turned to walk out of the room. It was no moment to discover in herself an insane desire to laugh. Get outside the room first, for God's sake, she told the expanse of white starched apron on which her eyes were fixed. A bout of hysteria now would put the crowning touch to an unsuccessful career.

Back in the safety of her own small bedroom, the desire to laugh disappeared as suddenly as it had come. There was nothing funny about the fact that she'd just been judged unsuitable for the only job she'd ever thought of doing. A smile of genuine amusement touched her mouth for a moment at the memory of Jos, snorting with fury because she'd not been given the part she hankered after in a school play. 'They're just daft, Janey . . . don't know what they're missing.' She could hear him saying it still. But experienced matrons *did* know what they were missing, and she told him so in the imaginary conversation she was having with him. 'What's daft about it all, Jos dear, is *me*! Janey Rowland setting out to take the nursing world by storm, ready to show everyone that she could manage on her own . . . no help needed from anyone and nobody's love missed.' Only it wasn't true. Without the people she'd cut herself adrift from, and new friends she hadn't bothered to make, there was only the single-minded pursuit of a career that had finally turned sour on her. It hadn't even succeeded in blotting out her longing for James. Nothing ever would; she was like Ano in that respect too – stubbornly incapable of reclaiming a heart once it had been given away.

She sat by the window for a long time, wishing that understanding of her mother hadn't come so late. All the years of resenting Mam's lack of interest in her and Jos . . . they'd hurt cruelly at the time, but now it was obvious why Brian should have been the only one that mattered. She couldn't have William Marchant, but she'd got something of him in Brian. Jane liked the idea of her brother finally getting to know William; it seemed to make up for some of the waste. She didn't like waste, she realized; it was what hurt most about the last few years. Unaware that her face was wet with tears, she got up at last and began to empty a chest of drawers. Life wasn't hopeless for long, Matron had said. It was to be hoped that she was right, and meanwhile there was nothing to be done except get herself ready for the nurses' convalescent home.

She set off with all her possessions loaded into a taxi, feeling that another small chapter of her life had closed; it seemed to have been a disconnected life so far . . . nothing in it hung together for very long. The only continuing thread was Brian, and she must visit him now on her way to the station.

'Hunger strike?' he asked bluntly at the sight of her, 'or did you get that way without trying?'

'Influenza . . . I'm much better now, and just on my way to recuperate in a plushy rest-home for ageing nurses. I hoped you'd take care of a few of these things for me.'

'Yes . . . if you'll tell me the truth.'

'It *is* the truth, but not quite the whole truth. I'm not going back to St Thomas's. Beware of growing up with an idée fixe, like me . . . you come rather unstuck when it turns out to be the wrong idea.'

'Why was it wrong . . . I thought you loved nursing.'

'I do, but according to Matron, I agonized over patients too much for my own good, not to mention theirs. I wasn't a bad nurse, you understand, just a hopelessly emotional one!'

He thought the smile pinned to her thin face was the saddest thing he'd ever seen. 'Well, if you're not going back, what are you going to do?'

She gave a little shrug. 'I'm not sure yet. First of all I have to go to this convalescent place. I'm still part of Thomas's until I'm signed off from there as being fit and in my right mind. After that I'm free to decide what to do.'

'Do the Marchants know?'

'No, and I don't want them to know. Promise me, please, not to tell them,' she insisted desperately. 'I hope we can pick up threads again one day . . . I hate not seeing Agnes and William, and Cessy and the twins, but I must be managing all right first. I *can't* go crawling back as a failure, asking to be taken in again.'

'Stop talking about failures,' he roared at her. 'It sounds to me as if you were too damned good.'

'In a funny sort of way, I think I was,' she agreed gently.

There was silence for a moment. 'You didn't mention

297

James just now,' Brian said. 'He isn't one of the Marchants you'd like to see again?'

'No . . . No!' she shouted through the quietness of the room.

'I only asked, brat!'

'Sorry,' she mumbled. 'But no one will forget that we were childhood friends . . . I feel like some wretched medieval princess, whom the next brother in line is expected to marry for the sake of the dynasty!'

'My turn to say sorry . . . I didn't realize you felt so strongly about it.'

She felt ashamed of her edginess and so dishonest about the true state of things that it was suddenly a relief to confide in him.

'The lady was protesting too much! I've avoided James ever since Duncan was killed because, in a way, we felt responsible. For the first and only time that James and I admitted that we loved each other Duncan came in and found us. There was a row and he stormed out of the house. We didn't see him alive again. I think his death killed something in James as well.' She stopped talking; the story of her adult life hadn't taken long to tell. After a moment she said briskly, 'My new whereabouts are on this bit of paper. I hope you don't mind that I've asked someone at Thomas's to collect my letters and send them here. Will you forward them to me? Agnes and Cessy write, and the children send me drawings of all the livestock on Edward's farm.'

'They'll have to know in the end.'

'Yes . . . but not till I'm settled in something else.'

Brian stared at the address she'd written down. 'Southwold, Suffolk! Life persists in going round in circles . . . Cessy and I went there once from Lowestoft a long time ago.'

His face looked sad, and Jane deliberately jerked his mind away from memories. 'How's Clarissa?'

'I wouldn't know . . . haven't seen her.' He omitted to say that his only attempt to invite Clarissa Ferguson to dinner had failed. She'd been booked to go to the opera with James Marchant. Move a Rowland toe and it finished up being stubbed against a Marchant!

'Well, I won't nag you about her. You've probably got a lot else to think about. Does the present mess – strikes, shortages, and all the rest – put you off politics?'

'Nothing puts me off politics,' he said truthfully. 'I'm now on the list of prospective candidates. When there's a suitable by-election, I shall fight it for Labour.'

'It's dogged as does it,' she agreed, grinning at him.

'Come back here, Janey, when they shunt you out of Southwold.'

'I may . . . in fact I will, if I haven't had a brainwave before then.' She dropped a grateful kiss on his cheek and stood up to go. 'My train leaves from Liverpool Street in an hour. I must be on my way.'

'You're going by car, and it's outside the door. Don't argue, brat. Just for once oblige me by doing as you're told.'

At Southwold her allegiance to River Cottage and the Thames Valley faltered. Nothing had prepared her for the sense of space and freedom that came from being on the edge of the sea. River Cottage apart, she thought of herself as a Londoner; she would have defended London to the death against anyone stupid enough to attack it in front of her. But here was something she'd never seen before: the great empty Suffolk skies pierced here and there by lonely church towers that rose out of a sea of green, pointing the way to heaven. So early in the year the small town was empty of anyone but the people who lived there; she supposed they were familiar enough with the sight of a gull wheeling against the blue spring sky not to need to walk down to the beach and marvel at it. Blueness of sky, whiteness of scoured sand, and the shifting colours of a sea fretted by the sharp east wind. She was grateful for the wind, because none of her fellow inmates felt inclined to brave it with her.

Muffled up in layers of sweaters, she made for the deserted beach, walked until she was tired, and then hid behind a sheltering breakwater. Although she still tired easily, her mind was working again. It was time to admit that Duncan's death had been a tragedy, but no more of a tragedy than his continued life would have been. She'd been involved in both, but not responsible, and it would be mawkish and unbalanced to go on imagining that she was. She doubted whether James would ever come to see their part in Duncan's death in the same way, but there was nothing she could do to help him. She was still ashamed of what she'd said to Agnes . . . James had *not* pretended to love her as a move in an emotional chess-game against his brother. But in matters that concerned the human heart men were less staunch than women. Give them a cause or an ideology and they'd hold to it come hell or high water, but constancy in love had less appeal for them. She'd been wrong to think he'd go on loving her.

She'd floundered from that mistake into the next one of flinging herself into nursing in such a neck or nothing way. 'Let us face the future with hope,' she'd once quoted to Cessy, another neck or nothing girl; there was nothing wrong with hope, but a dash of moderation wouldn't have come amiss as well, and there'd been nothing moderate about the way she'd set out to shatter her Marchant chrysalis, to prove that she could manage without them. What she'd needed all along was the knowledge that they needed *her*.

She took a deep breath, because the solution to the problem of the future was suddenly in front of her. While her eyes drank in the sight of a skein of wild geese outlined against the sky, her mind went over the idea that she only went off the rails when no one needed her. Matron had

300

judged from vast experience that she couldn't cope with wards crammed full of people who needed help, but what she *could* cope with was a manageable quantity of need . . . a sick or handicapped child, or a family that was struggling against some adversity.

She walked slowly back to the house, wondering how to set about finding a reasonable-sized need. It seemed a problem until she remembered Home Sister . . . a lady who seemed to know almost everything about anything.

She didn't know, as she worked out her future on a wind-scoured Suffolk beach, that one of Agnes's letters to St Thomas's had missed the safety-net so carefully organized for it. Her student friend had gone home for a few days, and a letter with its address thoughtfully written on the back was returned to Linden Square. Agnes had never cured herself of the habit, insisting when laughed at that it sometimes came in useful. Now, she stared at a superscription which assured her that Nurse J. Rowland was no longer at St Thomas's. She showed it to William, who immediately rang the hospital. The ward sister was reticent, but finally confessed that Jane had been ill and had now gone away to convalesce. When pressed to explain why a letter to her had been returned, not forwarded, the sister reluctantly explained that Nurse Rowland would not be returning, and firmly ended the conversation.

Agnes was saying worriedly, 'What can it mean?' when James walked into the room, followed by Brian.

She smiled with relief at the sight of her stepson. 'Brian . . . you probably know! Tell us what's been happening to Jane. The hospital say she's been unwell, but they've returned my letter.'

'She's away at the moment, in what she called a plushy rest-home . . . been working too hard, and got a bad dose of influenza.' Remembering his promise to Jane, he smiled at Agnes. 'Nothing to worry about. She's bound to be in touch with you soon.'

301

His stepmother looked uncertain still, and he firmly changed the subject, but when he left the house half an hour later he found James on his heels, apparently intent on walking with him.

'Going my way?'

'Only while you tell me the truth about Jane. I accept that she's gone away to recuperate, but I think you know where she is and why she's not going back to the hospital.'

His dark eyes held a gaze not unlike his own. They were both aware of the fact, resented it equally.

'She wants to be left alone . . . to think out what she's going to do next.'

James got leaping impatience under control and tried again. 'I need to talk to her. Help me, please, if you can.'

The simplicity of the appeal was disarming; but that was the full-bred Marchant tribe for you, Brian reminded himself, charming when it wanted something. 'Sorry, I *can't* . . . I promised Janey.'

'Why must she be left alone? Because something's gone wrong with a nursing career we were meant to believe was marvellous? What went wrong?'

'She got sick,' Brian explained patiently. 'That was coincidental, not a cause. I gather the trouble was that she insisted on diving in boots and all, as usual – broke her heart and her health, taking everybody else's troubles on board – being herself, in short! She's a sucker for allowing herself to feel responsible for the pain of the whole bloody world.'

Yes, James thought, it sounded just like Janey. 'What happens next?'

'She's not sure yet; that's why she needs time to think things out.'

'I need to see her before she makes up her cussed little mind again. If you won't tell me where she is I'll go to St Thomas's and make such a nuisance of myself that they'll give me the information in the end to get rid of me.'

Brian hesitated, torn between opposing inclinations. There was the promise he'd given, but James Marchant had the look of a man who'd do exactly what he'd threatened. And, although there was no accounting for tastes, he had the feeling that Jane would rather see James than not see him.

'Lawn House, Southwold, Suffolk,' he muttered suddenly, 'and I hope she gives you the air.'

'She well may, and it would be no more than I deserve. But thanks, anyway.' His face lit in a transforming grin, then he turned and walked back to Linden Square. He didn't linger in the house, just smiled at his mother and said, 'Don't wait lunch . . . I may be gone a little while!'

Chapter 22

The drive to Southwold was maddeningly slow. No good fast road offered itself, and James crawled into Suffolk consumed by an irrational but steadily growing anxiety. He tried to tell himself that some aerial spirit wasn't already there ahead of him, warning Jane that he was on his way, but the feeling persisted that if he missed her now, he might miss her for ever. It was something to do with the lonely countryside he was travelling through. The northern fringe of Essex wasn't far from London in distance, but felt as remote as some desolate territory of the moon. Suffolk, when he finally came to it, was even worse; a secretive sort of place that seemed to hug to itself the knowledge that people in general *didn't* come ... they were either born and died there or never found it at all.

But when he did find Southwold late in the afternoon, and the third person he asked managed to direct him to Lawn House, it was only to be told that Miss Rowland was out.

'Try the beach,' a pleasant-faced nurse advised him. 'She spends a lot of time down there.'

He left the car in the drive, and followed the nurse's directions back into the centre of the little town. A green space bordered by ancient cannon was overlooked by a lighthouse that seemed to be keeping an eye on things. Perched on its cliff-top, Southwold was full of a quiet unselfconscious charm that he would have enjoyed at any other time. But the afternoon sunshine was deceptive. He turned into the icy blast coming off the sea and no longer wondered why the beach below him looked deserted. As a place for a convalescent home, Southwold's strength was obvious: it easily sorted out those who were capable of recovery from those who weren't.

He looked down from the top of the cliff on to a long beach of pure white sand, that darkened to the gold of honey where the incoming tide washed over it. To his left it stretched apparently for ever, marked only by the black upright lines of breakwaters getting smaller and smaller as they marched towards infinity. On his right the beach shelved, then climbed to a ridge of sand dunes. Behind them were the sea marches that almost ringed the town. The scene was beautiful in its desolate way, but the pleasant nurse at the home had misled him; the beach was completely deserted. Wherever Janey was, it wasn't here.

She *was* there, but sheltering from the wind in the lee of a small line of beach huts at the foot of the cliff. It was a rare sensation to have the world entirely to oneself; she enjoyed it on the whole, but there was something melancholy about it in the late afternoon . . . some children or a dog playing would have been welcome; she felt very alone with only the wind and the sea for company. Then the westering sun threw a shadow down on the sand in front of her. It was monstrously elongated, but recognizably the shadow of a human being, so she wasn't entirely alone. She disliked the sensation of being overlooked by a giant, and moved out of the shelter of the huts further along the beach. The shadow moved with her, keeping pace, and it was suddenly sinister in the silent deserted place. She and whoever it was up above, watching her, seemed to be the only two people left alive in the world.

The obvious thing to do was to leave . . . climb the slope to the top of the cliff, murmur a polite good afternoon to whoever was there, and walk back into the busy town. But impelled by instinct rather than the rational prompting of her brain, her feet were taking her in the opposite direction, across the beach away from the cause of that looming shadow. It disappeared, but relief was short-lived; she heard the scrape of leather-soled shoes sliding at a run down the steep cliff path, and the afternoon changed from melancholy to fear. She was pitchforked into panic, and began to run, hampered by the soft sand beneath her feet. Fool . . . she was running into a dead-end. There were only two more breakwaters ahead of her; after that the beach swung sharply inland, and the tide was already covering the sand. Soon she'd be stranded, between the sea and the man stalking her from behind. A glance over her shoulder confirmed that he *was* stalking her . . . this was no casual stroller come to look at the sea, but a dark figure with a hand up to his face to shield it from the glare of the sun.

She abandoned the beach and threw herself at the nearest sand-dune. A desperate scramble took her somehow to the top, but she'd gained nothing for her pains. With an agonizing stitch in her side and her heart pounding like a sledge-hammer, it would have been difficult to run another yard, but the truth was that there was nowhere to run to. Below her lay nothing but marshy swamp, broken here and there by a network of tiny creeks and rivulets. There was nothing to do but crouch down behind the top of the bank. Would a sex maniac or psychopathic killer be easily deterred? She thought not, and if he knew the terrain, he'd realize that her hiding-place was inadequate to the point of lunacy; he only had to claw his way to the top of the dune to find her there like a petrified rabbit.

The sound of a voice penetrated above the thudding of her heart.

'Janey . . . you thinking of staying up there?'

The world swung vertiginously around her, and time ran backwards. She was little Janey Rowland again, hiding

in a tree, and her maniac was simply James. She was hallu-
cinating, or going mad. Perhaps, like poor demented
Orphelia, she should simply let herself down into a watery
grave? She hadn't decided when a dark head appeared
over the top of the barricade . . . but surely no figment of
her disordered mind would have wind-ruffled black hair
and flecks of sand on his face that glinted like gold in the
sunlight?

'Not much of a welcome . . . couldn't you even bring
yourself to wait and say hello?'

'I didn't know it was *you*,' she gasped. Indignation got
the upper hand at the memory of so much needless terror.
'I'm supposed to be here for the good of my health, and you
nearly made me die of heart failure a moment ago.'

'Stupid of me . . . I didn't think of that! I did call out, but
the wind's blowing the wrong way. Sorry, Janey.' He
sounded contrite, but couldn't prevent himself from
smiling. 'What would you think about coming down now?'

She stood up, intending to make a dignified descent, but
it was easier said than done. With reaction setting in and
her legs beginning to feel as if they were made of jelly, she
began to slide, cannoned into him, and both of them landed
in a heap on the beach. When she'd been set on her feet
James solemnly brushed sand off the end of her nose.

'Lovely as it is to see you, this must be the coldest trysting
place in Christendom. Can you suggest somewhere a bit
warmer?'

'There's the lounge at Lawn House.'

'Shared with dozens of interested fellow-inmates. No, I
don't think so. We'll have to make do with the local
amenities.' He pointed to a little glassed-in shelter at the
foot of the cliff. 'Made for the job, and we shall even have a
sea view!'

Inside the shelter it was Jane who spoke first. 'How did
you know where to find me?'

'Brian told me – very reluctantly, because I threatened

307

to cause a riot at St Thomas's if he didn't. We've gathered, by the way, that things didn't work out there. I'm sorry about that.'

He sounded sympathetic, but calmly so, as an old friend might sound. Fool, she'd gone wrong again; leapt to the conclusion that he'd come looking for her, when he'd probably just been passing by and dropped in to say hello. Baulked in a kind intention, he'd got stubborn and insisted on finding her. She smothered a laugh that threatened to turn into a sob, but he heard the sound and immediately enfolded her cold hands in his own warm ones.

'Does it hurt to that extent, Janey? I suppose so, since nursing was always the thing you wanted to do.' His eyes were fixed on her face and it was hard to look at him without giving too much away. 'I was inexcusably blind, I'm afraid,' he said ruefully. 'Brian never made any secret of how he felt about the Marchants, but until your letter arrived it didn't occur to me that you were probably sick of us too.'

'I didn't leave because I was sick of the Marchants,' she muttered.

'No? Well, you must have felt suffocated by us all the same. Even before Duncan died, I was waiting in the queue, ready to take you over when my turn came. Your letter from St Thomas's positively sang with the joy of being your own woman at last.'

Never had singing been done with so much effort, she thought. Now, all she had to do was agree that having crawled out from under the Marchant wing she had no intention of crawling back in again; her future had hit a slight snag, but it was temporary, and soon Jane Rowland would be on her independent way again. She was still polishing up some optimistic phrases in her mind when James spoke again.

'Janey . . . when Duncan died I went into a sort of paralysed trance. One thought stuck in my mind, as barbed as a fishbone in my throat: if I hadn't gone to Linden Square that afternoon and used strong-arm tactics on you he'd have still been alive. It seemed impossible to go on with our own lives as if it hadn't happened. Then I found your letter and my own muddle became irrelevant anyway . . . you'd settled on a future that didn't include me. But *that* future hasn't worked out, so it seemed worth finding out whether you can look at me without remembering Duncan.'

'We can't *not* remember him,' she said slowly. 'He's part of the fabric of our lives. But I've had plenty of time to think down here, and I no longer feel guilty about him. Sad that I didn't manage to help him more, but not to blame, any more than you are.'

'Yes, that was roughly how I worked things out in the end. He wasn't destroyed by Cessy taking the twins away, or finding me kissing you . . . those things just tipped the balance, finally made life unendurable. And now we're not going to revert to that subject again because it's time to look forward, not back. Will you marry me, please?'

He was watching her carefully but didn't understand the smile that touched her mouth.

'Marchants to the rescue? Little Janey's come a cropper . . . better go and pick up the pieces again!' Her voice trembled on the edge of tears but she swallowed them with a fierce effort and managed to sound confident. 'There's no need to worry about me at all. I've got the future settled and Home Sister's . . .'

'Home Sister can go to perdition,' he interrupted savagely. 'Listen and listen well! I'm not offering you a hole to crawl into. I want you to love and take care of me as I shall love and take care of you. If there's a little time left over you can minister to the rest of the clan, Gran, Edie Bloggs and Albert as well if you feel inclined. But your main mission in life would be to make up for all the misery you've caused me.'

'Have I caused you misery, James?' she asked gravely.

'Yes, although it wasn't really of your making. Instinct said that you couldn't be anything but Jos's daughter, but we were in such an appalling tangle that I couldn't be sure. The more I needed you *not* to be related to me, the more it seemed probable that you were.'

'*That's* why you abandoned me. I thought it was because you disapproved of having me as one of the family, and it hurt all the more because it was *you*; I'd have expected Cessy or Duncan to resent me, but never you.'

'I'd beat you for that, Miss Rowland, if I weren't feeling so at peace with the world. But I suppose I have something to apologize for, too. Why do you suppose your nursing career didn't prosper? Simply because a respectable tea and rubber broker was crouched over his desk sticking pins into wax effigies of handsome medics!'

'What a pity I didn't know that . . . it would have been something to tell Matron!'

When his face broke into a smile it looked young again, but she thought he'd grown very like William – the same jutting cheekbones and prominent beak of a nose. 'You were rather snubbing when I asked you about the Firm at Cessy's wedding. Do you hate being there, James?'

'Surprisingly, I find I don't hate it at all. When Brian refused to have anything to do with Marchant's, Father did his best to pretend that no help was needed, but he was beginning to look defeated. Someone had to take Duncan's place, and it had to be me. There was so much to learn that I got interested in spite of myself, and I rather like being part of a continuing tradition. In a changing world the tradition is going to have to change too, but I'm damned if I'll throw in the sponge and let your half-brother and mine be proved right about the decadent middle-class!'

'It wasn't only Brian who predicted changes,' she reminded him. 'Don't you remember telling me to look at things before they disappeared?'

'The milkman's horse, for one! You were very incensed about that.'

'He's with us yet, I'm glad to say, but there *are* changes already. I can't see that they're making people much happier, though.'

'People who've just been through a traumatic war and are pitchforked straightaway into a social revolution perhaps shouldn't be expected to look happy. They could have done with a peaceful transition stage which they haven't been granted.'

'I think I've inherited Jos's preference for things to be left as they always have been . . . the countryman's resistance to change. How I wish he was alive, waiting for us in his garden somewhere to arrive and say we'd finally managed to sort ourselves out.'

'You haven't said so in so many words, but I *think* that means you're going to agree to marry me.'

'In so many words, yes please . . . oh James, yes please!'

His arms gathered her against him, telling her there was nothing more to fear. His mouth, at first gentle then insistent on her own, said there was everything to hope for. She was trembling and flushed when he slackened his hold enough to look down at her.

'Marchant's First Law, Janey – the more we've had to say goodbye to, the more we have to cherish what is left.' Then he looked round their shelter. 'I've got attached to this little place, but maybe it's time we dragged ourselves away from it.'

Jane struggled to come back to earth and the mundane consideration of time. The hands of her watch couldn't, unfortunately, be doubted. 'James, I've missed *tea*! Home Sister will be combing the beach for her missing lamb. I shall have to say I was hiding from a sex maniac after all.'

He dropped a swift kiss on her mouth, but then pulled her to her feet. 'Don't tempt me . . . it's hard enough to take you back as it is.' But instead of leading her out of the shelter, he stood staring down at her.

'Sand on my nose still?' she asked, smiling at him.

'A little . . . rather becoming, in fact. I'm still a weekend artist, you know. A sort of young Grandpa Moses! I shall be too late for this year, but I can tell you now what will be the sensation of next year's Summer Exhibition at the Academy – a portrait of my wife. I shall call it "Janey, Laughing"!'

When they got back to Lawn House she apologized for being late, but was taken by surprise when James suggested that she should be allowed to leave immediately. Home Sister began by looking unconvinced, but he was adroit, and his smile was charming. In the end she capitulated without more than a token struggle.

'I wouldn't have believed it,' Jane murmured when they were safely on their way half an hour later. 'Putty in your hands, when everyone here is terrified of her.'

'Nothing surprising about it . . . the poor soul probably hasn't seen anything but sickly nurses for years!'

'You sound remarkably pleased with yourself.'

'I'm light-headed with happiness . . . much inclined to break into song, if only I could sing and drive at the same time.'

'I'll sing, you drive,' she suggested. 'Where are we driving to, by the way?'

'Home, of course. Mama was biting her nails when I left; she'll be in a terrible state of anxiety by now.'

'Home, James! . . . I always wanted to say that. It sounds good as well as comical.'

Good it *was*, with the trees in the middle of Linden Square veiled in a mist of spring green and the battered stucco of No. 2 now gleaming under a coat of fresh cream paint. Other places were beautiful, but this was where she belonged, especially with Agnes opening the front door even before they'd had time to get out of the car, and William running with her down the steps to meet them.

She and James were married six weeks later, and the wedding took place at her request in the village church at Long Wittenham. Being small, it was uncomfortably crowded, but everyone agreed that a crush added to the pleasure of the occasion. The village turned out in force and mistook Edie Bloggs, dressed in full wedding splendour, for a duchess. She was outdone only by Lady Carterton, who sailed into the Marchant pew looking more like Queen Mary than ever. The twins, page and bridesmaid respectively, got carried away with excitement and set off up the aisle without waiting for the bride, but everyone else judged that she was worth waiting for. Jane had asked Ano's old friend in the mews, Louise Marsden, to make a dress for her. The result was a dress of cream silk crêpe, exquisite in its simplicity. She wore no veil, but a cream straw hat which Louise had strewn with poppies and cornflowers. While Cessy went to retrieve her children, Jane stood laughing in the porch, watching them. William watched *her*, wishing with all his heart that Ano and Jos were alive.

'I hope James will insist on painting you,' he said, smiling at her.

'Well, I've asked him to paint my hat! It's Louise's masterpiece.'

'Janey . . . it was good of Brian to let me stand in for Jos today. I expect he'd have liked to give you away himself, but he pretended he didn't want to be done out of the fun of being Best Man.'

'I know, but he likes to do kindness by stealth, and it embarrasses him when people see through him.'

Cessy arrived back breathless, towing a twin by each hand, the organist crashed out a wrong but victorious chord, and it was time for the procession to move off up the aisle.

Nothing marred the rest of the day, the sun shone

throughout, and even Agnes's fear that the strawberries wouldn't go round proved unfounded. It wasn't a day for serious things, but Jane's thoughts kept straying to the past, to the days leading back to another wedding and Cessy's first appearance as a bride at St James's in Piccadilly.

'You wore a pair of very squeaky shoes, I remember,' Cessy said suddenly, while she and Jane were upstairs alone together for a moment.

'Were *you* back in St James's too? I wondered, but you look so happy these days that I'm not afraid to ask.'

'Pa made a better job of marching you up the aisle today than he did me then. Eventful times since then, Janey . . . today's been like one of those rainbow days of spring – a mixture of sunlight and showers.'

Jane had climbed out of her wedding dress, but stood deep in thought, unaware of the fact that in satin slip and bare feet she wasn't quite dressed for going away.

'When I went to see Louise about my dress I made myself walk to the bottom of the mews for the first time since Ano and Jos were killed. There's nothing to see . . . just a neatly fenced-off gap, waiting for the time when a developer arrives to build another house. The thought of it was horrible for a moment – another house, and other people living in it, blotting out the Rowlands once and for all, like a badly taken film running one photograph on top of another. I wanted to beg William to buy the piece of land. But then, what? Just a blank for people like Jim Edmunds and his wife to have to stare at? I could hear Jos saying, "Don't be daft, Janey love," and I knew it *was* daft. It doesn't matter what's built in place of the cottage, any more than it matters that James and I'll be living in the flat you shared with Charles. Layers of experience don't blot one another out. They simply accumulate, adding to the richness of what's left.'

Cessy stared at her, not tempted to smile at a girl who stood there half-dressed while she worked out important things.

'I didn't begin by seeing things that way – in fact I tried to do the blotting out! Thought it was less painful. But it also seemed unfair to Edward to go into marriage with him cluttered up by memories of Charles. I said that to him one day, but he just smiled – said I was stuck with the memories and so was he, because I'm the woman I am now as a result of them. Incidentally, I'm pregnant again.'

She made a slight grimace, but Jane shook her head. 'I won't believe you're not glad this time.'

'Yes, I'm glad, but frightened. It's such a mess of a world for children to grow up in. Not much like the world I remember, and growing less so every day.'

'Let us face the future with hope,' Jane reminded her solemnly.

'There speaks wedding-day euphoria, but it's a good line on which to go away! Should you not put a dress on, Janey love, before going downstairs?'

When they finally went out into the garden again James was prowling anxiously. 'You've been gone so long that I decided you were having second thoughts already.'

'No second thoughts, and no regrets. Cessy and I were upstairs . . . remembering.'

'Without grief, I hope, my love,' he murmured gently. 'Everybody present is happy, and departed spirits are resting in peace.'

Jane nodded at him. 'I think so, too.' Her face broke into a smile at the sight of her brother deep in conversation with Lady Carterton. 'Even Brian's forgotten that he disapproves of the middle classes. He's getting on like a house on fire with your grandmother, and I'm almost sure that he'll feel bound to keep an eye on Agnes and William while we're away. James . . . don't you think we're having a beautiful wedding?'

'Beautiful is the word, my darling.' He tried to look grave about it, failed, and swept her into a hug that made Mrs Bloggs watch them with approval and a slightly misty eye.

'Does yer 'eart good, don't it?' she enquired of the fellow guest standing by her side.

Her Ladyship agreed. It went against the grain, but for once she was going to let someone else have the last word.

THE END

MOVING AWAY
by Louise Brindley

The house stood on a wooded promontory overlooking the bay. It has survived a century of North Sea gales and forty years of neglect and there was something faded and elegant and wistful about it – like Jess herself.

She was bruised and hurt, running from a marriage to a younger man – a man who had deliberately hurt her, then discarded her. The house, the final legacy of a relative she had never met, struck a chord of hope, of safety that made her feel she could face the future again.

Against all advice she decided to keep the crumbling old place, restore it, and let out rooms. And as the house began to take shape, and the strangest assortment of people started to move in, Jess's life began to change – becoming richer and more emotive and passionate than it had ever been.

0 552 13289 6

MOTHS
by Rosalind Ashe

He fell in love with the house the first time he saw it – a Georgian Dower House, overgrown with briars and hidden away in a tangle of old woods and orchard. He had no intention of buying it, but he thought of it as his. When Nemo and James Boyce moved in and began to restore it he felt – at first – a curious sense of intrusion and loss.

But, very quickly, he was possessed by Nemo, by her strangeness, her beauty, and the compulsive spell that the house seemed to weave about them both.

He watched as other men became obsessed by her, drawn like moths towards a candle, to lust, consummation, and death – and as he tried to unravel the eerie mystery of the old house, he found he too was drawn towards the flame that might destroy him.

'A magical novel, passionate, exciting and beautifully written' *Iris Murdoch*

'Technical virtuosity and imaginative power . . . almost as enslaving as its heroine' *Times Literary Supplement*

0 552 13498 8

A WHISPER TO THE LIVING
by Ruth Hamilton

Annie Byrne was born during one of the worst winters Lancashire ever remembered. When the doctor finally got through the nine-foot drifts of snow, mother and daughter were in a pretty bad way, but both the new-born Annie and her exhausted mother – a spinner in the cotton mill – were fighters, tough and determined not to let the world knock them down.

They needed to be tough, for when Annie's father was killed in the war, Nancy married again. And Eddie Higson – once he'd courted and won Nancy Byrne – turned into a nightmare of a man, terrorising the young girl with one secret evil after another.

She had two friends who helped her through these bad years. Martin Cullen, rough, uneducated, loyal, who knew he wasn't good enough for her, and David Pritchard, the doctor who had supported her through the worst times and who had bad problems of his own.

Together they watched her grow into a beautiful young woman, desperately fighting the legacy of her childhood.

0 552 13384 1

A SELECTED LIST OF FINE NOVELS
AVAILABLE FROM CORGI BOOKS

All Corgi/Bantam Books are available at your bookshop or newsagent, or can be ordered from the following address:

Corgi/Bantam Books,
Cash Sales Department,
P.O. Box 11, Falmouth, Cornwall TR10 9EN

Please send a cheque or postal order (no currency) and allow 60p for postage and packing for the first book plus 25p for the second book and 15p for each additional book ordered up to a maximum charge of £1.90 in UK.

B.F.P.O. customers please allow 60p for the first book, 25p for the second book plus 15p per copy for the next 7 books, thereafter 9p per book

Overseas customers, including Eire, please allow £1.25 for postage and packing for the first book, 75p for the second book, and 28p for each subsequent title ordered.